D0294821

COUNTY

# PENDRAGON

*Also by James Wilde*

HEREWARD
HEREWARD: THE DEVIL'S ARMY
HEREWARD: END OF DAYS
HEREWARD: WOLVES OF NEW ROME
HEREWARD: THE IMMORTALS
HEREWARD: THE BLOODY CROWN

For more information on James Wilde and his books,
see his website at www.manofmercia.co.uk

# PENDRAGON

## A NOVEL OF THE DARK AGE

## JAMES WILDE

### BANTAM PRESS

LONDON · NEW YORK · TORONTO · SYDNEY · AUCKLAND

TRANSWORLD PUBLISHERS
61–63 Uxbridge Road, London W5 5SA
www.penguin.co.uk

Transworld is part of the Penguin Random House group of companies
whose addresses can be found at global.penguinrandomhouse.com

First published in Great Britain in 2017 by Bantam Press
an imprint of Transworld Publishers

A CIP catalogue record for this book
is available from the British Library.

ISBNs 9780593076040 (cased)
9780593076057 (tpb)

Typeset in 11/14.25pt Plantin by Falcon Oast Graphic Art Ltd.
Printed and bound by Clays Ltd, Bungay, Suffolk.

Penguin Random House is committed to a sustainable
future for our business, our readers and our planet. This book
is made from Forest Stewardship Council® certified paper.

1 3 5 7 9 10 8 6 4 2

For Elizabeth, Betsy, Joe and Eve, as always.

*Brutus! there lies beyond the Gallic bounds*
*An island which the western sea surrounds,*
*By giants once possessed, now few remain*
*To bar thy entrance, or obstruct thy reign.*
*To reach that happy shore thy sails employ*
*There fate decrees to raise a second Troy*
*And found an empire in thy royal line,*
*Which time shall ne'er destroy, nor bounds confine.*

Geoffrey of Monmouth

*And in a short while the generations of living creatures are changed and like runners relay the torch of life.*

Lucretius

One by one, the torches are extinguished. Shadows drown the great works of man. Stars dim. Candles gutter.

The world is slowly turning from the light.

In Rome, senators and soldiers do not yet see their time is passing. In Gaul, emperors and kings continue to fight their ceaseless battles along the frontier. And in Britannia, fair Albion, cut-throats and courtesans, wise men and warriors, go about their business as if nothing will ever change.

But it will. And soon.

A new age is coming.

The threads are being measured, and cut. In the weft and weave, a pattern emerges. But which thread is spun with gold?

Which one leads to the King Who Will Not Die?

Myrrdin, *A History of the Bloodline of Arthur, the Bear-King*

# ROMAN BRITAIN, AD 367

CALEDONII

VENICONES

*Inchlonaig -
the Isle of Yews*

VOTADINI

*Trimontium*

SELGOVAE

NOVANTAE

Hadrian's Wall

Luguvalium    *Vercovicium*

◦ *The Lake*

*Mare
Germanicum*

MILES    0 ——— 100

KM    0 ——— 100

N

Eboracum

*Kinder Scut*

Mamucium

Lud's Temple

Deva

Lindum

Ratae

Ermine Street

Watling Street

Glevum

Camulodunum

Fosse Way

Verulamium

Londinium

Aquae Sulis    *The Heartstones*

Durovernum    Dubris

Noviomagus

Isca Dumnoniorum    Durnovaria

*Mare Brittanicum*

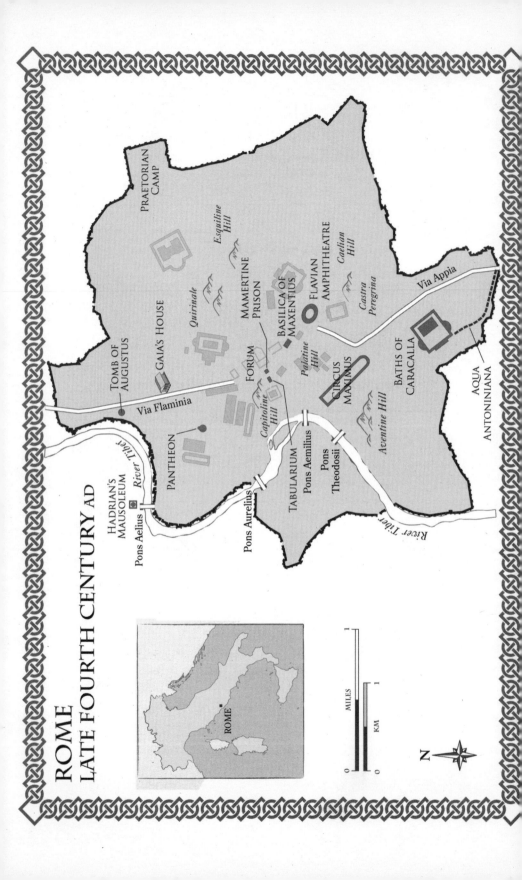

# ROME
## LATE FOURTH CENTURY AD

PRAETORIAN CAMP

*Esquiline Hill*

*Caelian Hill*

MAMERTINE PRISON

FLAVIAN AMPHITHEATRE

BASILICA OF MAXENTIUS

*Castra Peregrina*

*Quirinale*

GAIA'S HOUSE

TOMB OF AUGUSTUS

FORUM

*Palatine Hill*

CIRCUS MAXIMUS

BATHS OF CARACALLA

*Via Flaminia*

*Capitoline Hill*

*Aventine Hill*

*Via Appia*

PANTHEON

TABULARIUM

Pons Aemilius

Pons Theodosii

AQUA ANTONINIANA

HADRIAN'S MAUSOLEUM

Pons Aelius

*River Tiber*

Pons Aurelius

*River Tiber*

ROME

MILES

KM

N

# PART ONE

# The Dragon

*There was a world . . . or was it all a dream?*

Homer, *The Iliad*

# CHAPTER ONE

# *The Arcani*

*AD 367, Late winter, north of Hadrian's Wall, Britannia*

THE SNOWS HAD COME AT THE NIGHT'S DEEPEST, GHOSTING THE black branches. Now, with the thin light of a new day streaking the heavens, the grass glittered and the ground was as hard as iron where it rolled down to the line of trees.

Through those white wastes, the Grim Wolves prowled. Five of them, men as fierce, as unyielding, as the creatures whose name they took and whose pelts they wore upon their backs. To their masters in the army of Rome, they were their eyes and ears in a dangerous terrain, where a savage enemy waited to seize on any opening. Scouts, wilderness men, who roamed the dense forests and deep valleys beyond the edge of empire, seeing all.

*Arcani*, they were called by the soldiers who manned the wall's defences.

The hidden ones.

Lucanus, known to all as the Wolf, held up his hand and the thump of feet slowed, then stopped. His bones were aching from the biting cold, which penetrated even his furs and his oiled leather armour and his breeches. He tugged his grey woollen cloak tighter, although it would do little good. Around the hearth-fires, folk were already grumbling that this winter would never leave, as they said every cold season. Perhaps this year they would be right.

'What do you say, Bellicus?'

The Wolf watched his second in command crouch down. Bellicus, wise counsellor, sometimes foul-tempered drunk counsellor. He often wondered what he'd do without his friend. Be found out as not quite good enough to fill his father's shoes, he supposed.

Bellicus hunched shoulders broad enough to bear a stag, and shook his long red hair and beard, both now streaked with silver. 'See, here,' he boomed, waving his hand towards a trail of broken stalks in the long grass. He looked back, eyes the colour of a winter sea in a face whipped to leather by the harsh northern wind. 'Five men would do it.'

Lucanus nodded, pleased. 'Mato?'

The tallest man there flexed a body as slender as a sapling. Pushing his head back, he flared his nostrils and breathed in. 'Smoke, upon the wind. Cold now, though.' He flashed a grin, eyes sparkling in the first light.

'If the Ravens have been taken by surprise out here, they won't be coming home,' Solinus snorted. Ah, Solinus, so much acid dripping from every word. Lucanus wondered if he'd been so sardonic before he got the scar that quartered his face.

'Let a little sunshine in, brother,' Mato said. 'Sometimes hope is all we have.'

Solinus crooked an eyebrow. 'See what hope buys you next time you're pleading with Amarina at the House of Wishes.'

Mato laughed at that.

Lucanus cracked his knuckles. Twenty-eight summers and he felt like an old man sometimes. At least he was still getting stronger, still wiser. If he was to keep the respect of these fine men, he would need to become as good a leader as his father had always been.

'Do we turn back?' The voice was almost lost beneath the moan of the wind. It was the fifth of them, Comitinus, a worrier, but that brought caution and it had probably saved his life on more than one occasion.

Lucanus searched the treeline. No sign of movement, anywhere. If there were enemies, they would be deep in the forest.

'Bellicus, Mato, with me,' he commanded. 'Solinus, Comitinus, stay here and watch our backs.'

The three scouts loped through the thigh-high grass. As they neared the trees, the wind whined among the branches and in it Lucanus could hear the voices of the spirits warning him to slow down, take care: death waited. Perhaps even his father's voice.

Heeding the warning, he lurched to a halt. The dark swelled among the ghostly skeletons of the ash trees. The silence was strained, as if the whole forest were holding its breath.

Once he felt certain they were safe to proceed, he raised his left hand and snapped it forward. The Grim Wolves edged into the trees. There, Lucanus could smell the hint of smoke in the air. Mato had been right: a fire had burned hard, now dead.

As his eyes adjusted to the gloom, his thoughts drifted back to Micico, the leader of the Ravens, hunched by the hearth at the fort at Banna, nursing the leg wound that had prevented him from going out beyond the wall with his brothers. The Ravens were another of the bands of *arcani* scouts – a unit was stationed at each of the forts along the wall – and they had already lost one man, mauled to death by a bear in the hills beyond the forest. The remaining three were scouting closer to home, following a trail of whispers of a Pictish war-band threatening an attack on one of the settlements.

Lucanus recalled the note of worry in the Ravens' leader's voice. His men should have been back by sunset. They could well have been pursuing the trail deep into the north. But Micico was old and seasoned, and he trusted the tightening of his gut, he said. When he pleaded for aid, how could Lucanus ignore him?

Cocking his head, the Wolf listened for the crunch of feet upon hoar frost among the trees. The barbarians were rarely silent. Most of the time you could hear them across vast tracts, lumbering like cattle through the vegetation, chattering and cheering and singing.

Only the soughing of the wind reached his ears. He felt his shoulders loosen and his fingers slipped away from his sword-hilt.

As blades of pale light eased among the shadows, the Grim Wolves crept to the edge of a large clearing. In the centre the black bones of charred timber pushed up through a sea of ash. Stumps dotted the ground all around, the creamy wood splintered by axe strikes.

'They cut down trees for this fire, made it a big one,' Bellicus said.

'And made the clearing bigger too.' Mato looked around at the way the vegetation had been flattened deep into the gloom beneath the canopy. 'This was no protection against the cold of the night.'

'A gathering,' Lucanus said. 'A council. But why here, why now?'

Mato strode into the circle. 'With keen eyes, we should be able to make a wager on the numbers who came. Not a few, I would say.' His words drained away as something caught his eye on the far side of the cold bonfire.

Lucanus recognized the way his wolf-brother's body stiffened and he drew his sword. Bellicus prowled to the edge of the folds of ash.

'Here are the Ravens,' he said.

Three bodies were strung among the trees, wrists and ankles bound to the trunks, slaughtered like cattle for the pot. Lucanus let his gaze drift across the ragged remains, legs hanging by a flap of skin, arms gone here and there, the severed limbs tossed into the trees.

The heads had all been taken. They would be on stakes somewhere, their magic conferring power on the victors.

Lucanus felt a cold sweat trickle down his back. The *arcani* never fell to the barbarians. The scouts were too skilled in creeping and hiding and watching, their senses too sharp to be caught unawares by the men of the north.

'Wait.' Mato's warning rustled out, almost lost beneath the wind's moan. Crouching in front of one of the corpses, he circled a finger in the air above a gaping wound.

Lucanus dropped to his side, seeing instantly what the other man had noticed. 'Teeth marks. No beast did that. A man.' Craning his head up, he saw the remains in a different light. Here and there the flesh had been pared away by a sharp blade. One of the arms lying on the cold ground had been gnawed.

The Wolf jumped to his feet, his levelled sword swaying from side to side. This was not the work of Picts or Scoti. They did not eat the flesh of men.

'Wait,' Bellicus said. Lucanus glanced back and saw him crouching, his head cocked to one side, his brow furrowed.

'If not the Picts, then what?' Mato's face had hardened like stone, but his darting eyes revealed all the horrors that danced through his head.

Then *what*. Not *who*.

'Wait,' Bellicus said again, louder this time. He was on his feet, backing away, searching the woods.

Before he could urge his companions to stay calm, Lucanus glimpsed what Bellicus must have sensed: movement away in the trees. Shadows flickered in the silver light, flitting from oak to ash to holly. Turning slowly, he could see the forest coming alive on all sides.

Silent as the *arcani*, silent as the grave.

'Away!' Lucanus' voice soared through the stark branches. 'Away!'

# CHAPTER TWO

# *Falx*

'TELL THE OTHERS NOTHING.' LUCANUS GLANCED BACK ACROSS THE grassland. Nothing moved along the treeline. He breathed more easily; they'd escaped by the skin of their teeth. 'For now, at least. I need time to talk this over with Atellus before Solinus blurts it out when he's at the bottom of his cup in the tavern.'

'What did we see?' Mato gasped, his breath ragged from the sprint up the slope towards the wall.

'The Eaters of the Dead.' Bellicus shook his head. 'Stories to frighten children. We thought.'

'Why here?' Mato pressed. 'Why now?'

Lucanus had no answer to that.

A lightning-blasted oak loomed up on the ridge ahead, alone in that grassland like a twisted old man with his skeletal arms outstretched. Lucanus broke off a knob of bread from the provisions in the pouch at his hip and set the morsel among the tangled roots. Kneeling, he bowed his head in silent prayer. If the god of this place accepted the offering, all would be well.

They heard the others bickering long before they crested a ridge and saw them. Lucanus loosened his shoulders and put on a grin.

Solinus was following the passage of a kestrel sweeping overhead, the scar quartering his face crinkling as he squinted into the sun. 'Look at that wind-fucker. I wish I was up there with him, not down here with you, you miserable bastards.'

'You're talking about me, aren't you?' Comitinus glared.

'You are a miserable bastard, that's true.'

Lucanus wagged his finger at Solinus. 'What did I tell you? Don't bait him.'

'Let him fight his own battles. I'd be happy to give him a kick up his arse.'

'You'll get a kick up the arse,' Bellicus growled and Solinus instantly fell silent.

Mato stepped in and put his arms round the shoulders of the two men. 'Brothers, we are all weary, with little to show for it. Save your arse-kicking for the tavern.'

'Of course, he'd lose.' Comitinus arched a brow.

Bellicus turned and looked out across the sea of swaying grass. Lucanus watched his friend's hunched shoulders, his lingering stare, unease in every line of his body, but the others were too caught up in their conversation to see.

'No sign of the Ravens?' Solinus asked. 'I tell you now, those three bastards are warm by a fire, tupping Pictish girls.' He pulled out the knife he used for whittling and began to clean under his nails.

'Back to the fort,' Lucanus called in a cheery voice to end that strand of conversation. 'You've earned a night of comforts. We'll talk more tomorrow.'

He felt a stab of pride as he watched the tight-knit band move off. All of them had proved themselves. They'd faced their wolf and won. Drenched in its blood, under the light of a full moon.

Bellicus the fierce. Mato the light-bringer. Solinus the sardonic. Comitinus the worrier. All so different that if they'd met in another life they would never have been friends. But now they'd become of one mind, one spirit, with the eternal pack.

His thoughts flew back to his own day of death and rebirth. He became something better then, he had no doubt about that. The night had been as cold as this one was, ten days after his father had disappeared in the Wilds and they could all be certain he wouldn't be coming back. For hours he'd tracked his beast into the darkest depths of the forest. It was an old wolf, a seasoned hunter, its fur streaked with silver, as was right. Lucanus was doing the pack a service by ending its time upon this world in glory and allowing a new, younger king to rise up.

The moment had come, in a clearing surrounded by ancient,

twisted yew. The wolf was exhausted, old legs worn, snorts of breath long and juddering. And then it had turned and those amber eyes had locked with his. In that stare he was sure he saw understanding, as if it knew what was to come, and accepted it as part of the endless cycle. Its time was done. A new power would rise.

Slaked in its blood, he'd loped home and found his bed. In that sleep of the bone-weary, he dreamt that the great wolf came to him and welcomed him into the pack. Just a dream, the folk in the settlement had said with a laugh.

But everyone who underwent that rite had the same dream.

Gold rimmed the orange roof tiles of Vercovicium. Lucanus shielded his eyes against the glare from the low sun of the new day and picked up his step. Although frost still glittered in the long shadows cast by the fort's stone walls, the greens and browns and purple of the rolling countryside floated under hazy light.

South of the fort, the *vicus* rolled out, the township's ringing shouts and laughter and reek of filth already thick in the air. Near two and a half thousand souls carved out a living there, as dependent upon the good graces of the army as the soldiers were on the services the citizens offered them.

From the edge of that sprawling settlement, mounds and the stumps of walls were almost lost beneath wild grass, bramble and elder, the ghost of the old township, abandoned some hundred years ago. Lucanus had heard many a story why – fire, plague, famine – but no one seemed to know for sure. And in the hazy distance he could see the Stanegate, the great stone road that ran almost the length of the wall from west to east, was free of traffic.

The Grim Wolves trudged through the twin arches of the *porta praetorium* into a storm of hammers and cursing. A team of soldiers, carpenters and masons was busy shoring up a sagging wall. Further on, part of that same wall had already collapsed into a pile of rubble. Lucanus swept his eyes across the missing roof tiles, the crumbling masonry, the rotting timbers, and then to a *cornicularius* outside the granaries, bellowing at a merchant about the poor quality of the latest grain delivery.

'The whole fort's falling down around our ears,' Bellicus muttered.

Many thought Rome had all but forgotten them. The camp commandant, Lucius Galerias Atellus, had sent message after message along the supply lines. Over time his demands for repairs, reinforcements, better supplies, more timely pay, had all turned to pleas. He was answered, intermittently, but the gap between responses was growing.

Rome's attention was elsewhere now, everyone said: in Gaul where the Emperor Valentinian fought the Alamanni along the frontier; in the east, where the Emperor Valens struggled with restless Goths; and on rebellion, not the least within its own city walls where Christian battled Christian after the contested papal election. But the forgotten men here at the final outpost did their duty and held the line.

Once they passed the first line of barracks and stables, Lucanus and the Grim Wolves tramped into the Via Sagularis, where the soldiers of the near four-hundred-strong Cohors Primae Tungrorum gathered when they were readying to march out to repel a Pictish raid.

Turning to Bellicus, he whispered, 'Fill their bellies. Give them as much wine as they can drink. We'll talk over what we found when they're rested.'

Bellicus nodded. 'I'll send them out to the baths after that, and then to the House of Wishes. They'll be ready for anything after a night between warm thighs.'

Once the Grim Wolves had departed, Lucanus strode to the crossroads of the Via Principalis and the Via Praetoria and swept into the Principia, where the business of the fort was conducted. Before he could enter the camp commandant's quarters, he heard his name called. In a doorway, Quintus Domitius Falx was glancing round to make sure he was not being observed. He beckoned furiously.

Centurion Falx: pale skin awash with freckles, piercing eyes the colour of a winter sky. A hard man, so everyone under his command said, but quick to laugh.

Lucanus stepped into a small, low-ceilinged room filled with scrolls and Falx closed the door behind him. A tall, insect-like man skittered along the far wall stoking the brazier. Carbo, the optio, had the face of someone who'd just swallowed a wasp. Lucanus forced a tight smile of greeting.

'Here. Try this.' Falx thrust a cup into Lucanus' hand.

Lucanus swilled back a mouthful of sweet wine, no doubt freshly imported along the sea-roads from the lush valleys of Gaul, a world away from the rough draught they were usually forced to drink.

'Should have been on its way to Vindolanda,' Falx said with a sly grin. 'Somehow the amphorae were left behind here.' He flashed a glance at Carbo, and his optio looked away uncomfortably. 'That bastard Stolo will be spitting blood when he finds he'll have to endure more of the usual ditchwater for the rest of the spring.'

'You'll have a lot of friends when you share your good fortune.'

Falx frowned as if Lucanus was stupid. 'Share? This good fortune will make me a better fortune when it's sold to all those families with fat purses and enough land to keep them from having to smell the reek of the *vicus*. Perhaps Menius and Amatius, eh? Will you have a word with that brood you're so friendly with the next time you're enjoying their hospitality? I'd think they'd have enough coin to buy an ocean of this fine wine.'

'What do I get in return?'

'One amphora, of course. Enough for you and your men.'

'Two.'

Falx cursed under his breath. 'The cold wind beyond the wall has made you hard, Lucanus, that you'd do this to a good friend. Two, then, though you'll beggar me.'

Lucanus nodded. A good deal. Comforts were hard to come by these days.

The centurion leaned in and said, 'This is only the start of good times, mark my words. Last night a messenger brought word about a rich merchant arriving from Rome.'

'Why would he be coming here?'

'Who knows? Perhaps he's addled. Perhaps he thinks it's a sunny land of olive groves and sweet-smelling flowers. The point is, he wants to conduct some business. With willing men. Like me. And you, of course. And he's prepared to pay a small fortune if we help him.'

'What does he want? In my experience, a small fortune usually involves something that puts necks on the line.'

Falx shrugged. 'We are men who get things done, Lucanus. Whatever it is, it won't be beyond our abilities. I'm offering you an opportunity here. Don't bite my hand. Are you in?'

'We'll see. I'll hear it from his own mouth first.' He took another sip of wine and decided to change the subject. 'I've heard grumbling from some of the *arcani* along the wall . . . the Crows . . . the Hounds . . . They say they're not getting paid on time. And sometimes purses arrive light.'

Falx refilled Lucanus' goblet to placate him.

'It's true that the pay is sometimes a little short. We all suffer from that,' he said. 'The *arcani* have to bide their time. All will be made right.'

'This isn't a good time to be angering the *arcani*. At dawn we found three of the Ravens butchered. And someone had been feasting on their flesh.'

Falx frowned. 'The barbarians are beasts, but they don't eat the dead.'

'Stories for children,' Carbo said from the back of the room. 'Tales of the Eaters of the Dead have been whispered since I was a boy. But that is all they are . . . whispers. All trace of them disappears the moment anyone investigates.'

Lucanus looked from one man to the other. 'I saw this with my own eyes.'

'Strange that we hear this now,' Carbo said, his voice ripely sardonic, 'when the *arcani* grumble about pay. What better way to show that they're needed more than ever? The Eaters of the Dead will come to devour your old grandmother. What do you say, Falx?'

The centurion shrugged. 'Perhaps you were mistaken, Lucanus. The bite of a wolf—'

'Isn't like the bite of a man. Do you think I'm a fool? I live my life on the land, in the sun and the rain and the snow, surrounded by the hoots of owls and the shrieks of crows. When I smell the wind, I can tell what's wolf and what's wildcat though they're an hour's march away. I know what's man and what's beast.' He looked to Carbo. 'And you're accusing me of lying for gain?'

The optio only smiled.

Lucanus wrestled his frustration under control. 'This vile deed took place less than half a day's march from here.' He selected one of the scrolls from the wall, unfurled it and pointed to the location on the map. 'Here. Whoever did this is still there; we saw the signs.'

Falx stared at the map, thinking. 'Don't spread this around. You know how superstitious people are here. First it's barbarians, then ghosts, and monsters, and then the gods have unleashed all their furies upon us and we are damned. We'll have everyone in the *vicus* hammering at the gates.' He pursed his lips and muttered, 'And some of the men too.'

'Mark my words, this is a bad business. We might not yet see where this road takes us. But something so savage and against the ways of men, an attack upon the *arcani*, coming so close to the wall, now? Things like this don't happen by chance, in my experience. It will only get worse if we don't put it to the sword now.'

The centurion nodded. 'You make a good case. Let me have a word with Atellus. Send out a few men, cavalry, perhaps twenty, or call in some of those hard bastards from the Hnaudifridi company. If the enemy have a greater number, there's no need to engage. A sign that we're looking their way will be enough, for now. Then we can decide our next step.'

Lucanus leaned into the wind as he crossed the fort and heaved himself up the worn steps to where the sentries watched the Wilds. Yes, he felt a little more reassured there. How could he not, looking along that line of stone into the hazy distance?

The wall was everything for those who lived in its shadow. That's why he'd been taught its history when he was a boy and could still recount the names of all the forts and the location of all the mile-castles along the eighty-mile length. Falx had said the *arcani* kept the army safe, but the wall was the true saviour, and had been for the near two hundred and fifty years since Hadrian had dragged it up out of that desolate land. The height of four men, as thick as two carts, with a huge defensive ditch behind it.

Let the Eaters of the Dead look upon it and weep.

And there in Vercovicium they were safer than anyone. He looked down the steep crag of whinstone on which the wall was perched, a mile long and flanked by two bleak moors.

Ahead there was a wide expanse of grassland, long since cleared of trees, and beyond that the vast, gloomy forest of pine and ash and holly that seemed to go on for ever. In the far north was a land of snow-capped mountains and purple hills and great lakes, so he had been told, but the *arcani* rarely ventured that far.

To the west were the Scoti, to the north and east, the Picts. A few Britons lived there too, ones who had fled the rule of Rome. The Votadini. The Selgovae. The Novantae. The Caledonii. So many, the names became a blur. The tribes of the Picts had joined together under a single king, but the others had their own chieftains and their own arcane rules. Sometimes they were at each other's throats, sometimes they worked together. The uneasy truce with the empire ebbed and flowed, but no one was in any doubt that there would be blood in days to come.

Out there he had always found a deep loathing for Rome and all it stood for. For now, though, their merchants paid to travel through the gates to the south to trade, and trekked back at nightfall.

They were called barbarians, but they were not, really, in any way he understood the word. They had their gods and their art, their songs and stories and dancing. They were good fishermen and farmers, valued their women and had their own laws that were strictly kept.

His father had taught him the tongues of the tribes, and over the seasons of his travels beyond the wall with the *arcani* he had learned their ways. The Grim Wolves posed as traders and merchants when they ventured into the villages, and they had always been well met. If they had been exposed as spies or scouts, it would have been a different matter, he knew. He had seen more than one captured Roman soldier gutted and left to hang in a tree as a warning.

'The watcher on the wall sees far, but nothing that truly matters.'

He hadn't heard her come, but there she was. Amarina, wrapped in a fine cloak the colour of moss embroidered with golden spirals. Anyone would have thought it cost more than a few coins, but Lucanus knew better. Amarina came by many gifts. Her auburn hair tufted out of her hood, pulled low against the blast of the wind. Emerald eyes flashed from its shadows. She came and went as she saw fit, even there in the fort.

'More word games?'

'How does a woman confuse a man, Lucanus?'

'I don't know.'

'She talks to him.'

The Wolf saw the ghost of a smile in the depths of that hood.

'Don't you have anything better to do than torment me?'

'I can always find time for that. You are the best for games, Lucanus. The others get angry and storm off. But, no, you try to *understand* me.'

The Wolf grunted. 'Perhaps I'm playing games with *you*.'

Amarina looked out over the rugged land. After a while, she asked, 'What do you see there?'

He shrugged. 'The Wilds. Grass, trees, bog, heather, lakes, rivers, stone. The same as you see.'

'This wall divides two worlds. Yes, there is the empire and the barbarian lands. The civilized and the Wilds. But it's more than that.'

He searched the landscape, trying to understand what she was saying. Amarina leaned in and with her thumb and forefinger closed his eyelids.

'Now you'll see better,' she murmured.

He rocked against the buffeting wind and grabbed to stop himself falling.

'Two worlds, Lucanus. The world of men and the world of the gods. We stand at the point where they meet.' Her words rustled around him, barely louder than the moan of the breeze. 'Gods and daemons. Here, we rule, as much as we can. There . . . different rules exist. Why, they're like the *arcani*, are they not? The secret folk, the hidden ones. They live under hill and lake, on the top of mountains and in the deep forests. Rarely seen, always watching, listening, leading men by the nose. This whole island was once their home, so I'm told, and it will be again. They're everywhere.'

'Daemons?' The Wolf wondered if this was another of her games, twisting his thoughts to see how much she could make him believe her words. He decided to play along. 'Where did you learn of these things?'

He felt her breath on his ear. 'A woman cannot learn? Or a woman like me cannot learn?'

He thought it better not to answer these questions.

'Some say we all have our daemons, Lucanus. Our higher selves who watch over us. Others say the daemons are the gods' tools upon the earth, carrying out their wishes, guiding men and women, thwarting them, destroying them. They are the agents of the Great Plan that none of us can see.'

'What plan would that be?'

'Rise up, look down, look back, look ahead, then you'll know.'

'Then we're nothing more than rats being run by the mill dog.'

'Here, on the edge of all things, the daemons have been shaping us for a long time, wolf-brother. Vercovicium is an island in a stormy sea. The ocean washes in the boats of the ones who twist our lives, they do their business under cover of the night, and they are away by the morning tide. And we wake and look around and are none the wiser. But we do their bidding, none the less. When your eyes are opened, you'll see their mark. So wiser folk than us say.'

Her elbow jabbed him in the ribs and his eyes snapped open. The gates were grinding apart. Twenty men on horseback were readying to ride out into that twilight world. Falx had been true to his word.

'Or else it is just like here. No gods, no daemons, and all we have in the battle to survive is whatever is inside us.'

Lucanus eyed her, unable to tell if she believed this bleak account as well. 'You keep me sharp, Amarina.'

'A good day's work, well done.'

The auxiliaries rode out. Their mail shirts and helms glimmered in the low winter sun. Their javelins poked out of the leather sheaths strapped to their mounts, swords snug in their scabbards. Lucanus knew no better warriors than these. Whatever flesh-eaters roamed those wild lands should beware.

Hooves thundered on the frozen earth. The line of horsemen rode out towards the charcoal smudge of forest, towards the daemons or the savage men, towards whatever the gods or the Fates decreed.

## CHAPTER THREE

# *Catia*

THE HOWL ROLLED OUT FROM THE ANTEROOM OF THE MITHRAEUM and Lucanus winced. Locked beneath stone slabs in the dark of the ordeal pit, some poor soul was being tormented by fire, or cold, or water again. Only the followers of the God of the Invincible Sun knew what really went on in that stone temple, but listening to that grim noise Lucanus could think of better ways to spend a day.

Yet the cult of Mithras seemed to have no problem recruiting soldiers from the fort. Perhaps they'd got so used to hardship in those barracks, they didn't mind suffering when they were bowing their heads to their god. He screwed up his nose. One deity, they said, only one. What use was that for all the obstacles on life's road?

The commandant, Lucius Galerias Atellus, walked from the shadowed entrance of the temple of Mithras, a swarthy-skinned man, his hair now grey. Though Lucanus had heard he was brutal in battle, age had given him a permanent air of wistfulness.

'Have you thought again about joining us with Mithras, Lucanus?' he said.

'It's not yet my time, Praefectus. But if I feel my heart moved, I'll come, head bowed.'

The other worshippers were filtering out of the temple, swathed in the sweet scent of incense. One man was naked to the waist, perhaps the supplicant who had been lifted from the pit. Sweat dripped from him, and his eyes were staring as if he were still haunted by what he'd discovered there. On his back the Wolf could see a raw patch where he'd been freshly branded with the mark of the bull.

'There are secrets here, Lucanus, mysteries that would turn your head.' Atellus looked up to the sky, staring hard as if he could see through that blue vault to the gods themselves. 'Secrets hidden in all the stories we tell ourselves. Greater truths. Knowledge of all there is, waiting for those who can unlock it.'

'One day.'

Atellus nodded. 'I pray that day will come. We have our gods and they shape our lives. This church of the Christ, you know of it?'

'Aye.'

'Their priests have set their heads and hearts against Mithras. They won't rest until all this is destroyed and our god forgotten.'

Lucanus laughed. 'Mithras will never be destroyed. He's been worshipped the world over since the oldest times.'

'The Christians have already started to build their churches upon our temples. They take what we have by degrees. We've been sheltered from it here, so far from Rome. But they'll come for us, soon enough, mark my words, and for all the pagans too. The gods we Romans worshipped in days gone? All will be forgotten. Their names scratched out. A new age is coming and it will not be good for the likes of us.'

The Wolf nodded, though he couldn't believe any of it.

He heard Atellus' voice harden when he continued. 'And their Messiah, he is no more than Mithras by another name. They would steal all that we have.'

'The Christ and Mithras . . . ?'

Atellus wagged a finger. 'Mithras, born of a virgin. A life of celibacy. We baptize our followers, so do they. We eat bread marked with a cross, and drink wine as the sacrificial blood. These Christians too. We worship the birth of Mithras upon the twenty-fifth day of December . . . the birth of the Invincible Sun . . . and now they say their Christ was born on that same day?' The Wolf heard incredulity in the crack of the voice. 'All their mysteries, they were ours first. Mark my words, Lucanus, they will not rest until they have destroyed us, so they can lay claim to this as if it were their own.'

Lucanus caught sight of a small, familiar figure watching him from the shadows along the side of the temple.

'Praefectus, you've spoken with Centurion Falx?' he asked, trying not to be distracted.

'About what you Grim Wolves found in the Wilds?' The commandant nodded. 'Bodies defiled. Men eaten. I've never heard the like, in all my time as a soldier. I've seen barbarians slaughter men by the score . . . ram the heads of women and children upon poles . . . but this . . .' Lucanus could hear the disgust in his voice. 'I've sent a messenger along the frontier, to warn the other forts, and to find if any of them have heard of such a thing.'

'They killed three of the *arcani*, Praefectus. That's never been known.'

'The season is turning, Lucanus. All the things we've known are falling into decay. Is this another portent of what is to come?' Atellus looked up to the walls of Vercovicium. 'We strip stone from our own fort to repair our defences because there's little left in the coffers to pay for repairs, and little hope of more to come. Sagging gates are stopped up with timber. We're short of food, short of new men to bolster our ranks. Pay comes late or not at all. And in Rome . . . in Rome . . .' Lucanus watched him struggle to complete his thought. 'We've brought order across this world.' Atellus' voice grew wistful as he turned and looked across the green lands to the south. 'But now I see the sky shading to black. Night is drawing in. Beyond the frontiers of the empire, there's only chaos and madness. Barbarians who don't think like us, who place no value on the things we treasure, who would see all of this civilized world reduced to ashes and blood. Would we lose all that we've built? Is that to be our legacy?'

'We stand firm here in Vercovicium, Praefectus. We will not be defeated.'

The commandant forced a smile. 'When the messenger returns with news, I'll summon the Grim Wolves. You'll find what new threat waits out there beyond the wall, I have no doubt of that.'

The Wolf watched the other man trudge away, and then he beckoned to the figure hiding by the Mithraeum. A boy ran out of the shadows towards him. He looked like a small storm cloud with his black hair and eyes too dark and intense for a lad of just eight summers.

'What is it, Marcus?'

'Will you hide me?'

'From the other lads?' He'd never known Marcus to flinch from a fight.

'Mother searches for me.' The boy bit his lip, hopeful. 'I've worked hard all morning, and now she wants me to study more.'

'And why do you think I'd stand in the way of your mother?'

'You didn't waste your days at your books.'

'And now I sleep in ditches and eat raw meat and wait for a barbarian sword to end my days.'

Lucanus saw Marcus wince. The boy hadn't yet grasped the closeness of death, not for the people for whom he cared. He'd known Lucanus all his life and saw him as as much a part of his family as his own blood, Lucanus knew. 'Come,' he said, trying to make amends. 'You can hide in my house, but make sure you're back home before dark. And if your mother finds out I've helped you, that barbarian's sword will be the least of my worries.'

On the edge of the township's main street, a crowd surged around two men grappling with each other, barrel-chested and bare to the waist despite the cold. A wrestling exhibition. Lucanus saw the glint of coin changing hands as the onlookers wagered on the outcome. Outside the tavern, Qunavo was on his hands and knees, throwing up his stomach of ale. He was always drunk these days and survived only through the kindness of his neighbours. Behind him, Falx bowed his head in intense conversation with Docca the tavern owner, a big-bellied man with a wild mane of blond hair. The centurion was whispering, no doubt conducting another illicit deal. Further down the street, a group of men were racing dogs, and in the lulls in the din Lucanus heard the twang of bowstrings and the thud of arrows hitting a target.

As he turned away, two gamblers on the edge of the crowd watching the wrestling bout started throwing punches at each other. A moment later, they were brawling on the ground beside the competitors. Lucanus pushed Marcus into the narrow ways at the back of the workshops. At the other end of the track, they slipped back on to the main street where his house leaned against the fence of a reeking pigsty. It was little more than a shack: mud walls and old timbers with a turf roof.

As they reached the door, Marcus' eyes widened. 'Quick. She's coming.'

Lucanus saw a blonde head bobbing among the throng on the main street. He shoved the boy into the dark interior and went to meet her.

'Catia.' He grinned at her, ignoring her stern expression. However much she pretended to be the cold, disapproving mother, he knew the truth. During their childhood, they'd barely spent a day apart. An odd couple, everyone agreed, she with her wealthy family and he learning to be a wolf-brother, crawling on his belly through the Wilds. But he'd never forget the time, when he was barely big enough to lift a sword and out in the Wilds on his own, when he hadn't heard his father creep up on him – a test, to discover if he was ready for a life where a lack of attention could see him dead – and his father had boxed his ears as a lesson. When Catia found him, she'd taken him to the stream alongside the Stanegate and bathed a cut above his eye from the silver ring his father had worn – a dragon with a studded ruby eye, he remembered. Though they'd heard her own father calling for her, she'd stayed with him until she was sure he was recovered, knowing full well it would mean a beating for her too.

He was a boy then, and he thought the world went the way he wished it to go. Now he knew better.

'Have you seen Marcus?' Catia narrowed her eyes at him.

'I'm fresh back from the Wilds. Why would I—'

Catia wagged her finger to silence him. 'Don't play games with me. You know that boy sees you as friend, protector, teacher and counsellor. That's why he must study more – to get some sense into his head.'

Lucanus knew the true story: Marcus came to him because he couldn't rely on his father. And Catia was more than aware of her husband's failings. He stared at another new bruise marking her face, this time above her left eye. Forgetting himself, he reached out to it.

Catia recoiled as if she'd been burned. 'I don't need you to protect me.'

'Wolf-sister . . .'

'Don't call me that! I'm not a child,' she snapped, pushing past

22

him. 'And I can endure a little hardship for a greater good.'

Caught up in a whirl of emotion, Lucanus only realized Catia was heading towards his house when she'd reached his door. By the time he caught up with her she was standing in the middle of the solitary room, looking round. With relief, he saw Marcus wasn't there. There was no bed to hide under, merely rushes and straw in one corner. The boy must have run away again, fearful that his mother would sniff him out.

'You live like a pig, Lucanus.' He watched her turn her nose up at the dried remnants of stew in the pot on the cold hearth, and the whetstone lying next to where he slept, and his old tunic still streaked with mud and wood-green from the last time he'd travelled beyond the wall.

'I live like a beast in the wild. Which is what I am.'

He saw a hint of tenderness in her eyes. She rarely let herself show it these days, as if it was too harsh a reminder of what she'd lost. Once she'd said to him, 'I must become like the stones of the earth.' At the time, he hadn't understood what she'd meant. Now he thought he knew.

'You're a good man,' she said, looking away. 'Everyone here is grateful for you and the Grim Wolves. You let us sleep well in our beds, we all know that.'

He knew she meant to be kind, but her words still stung. *Grateful.*

Catia must have seen his thoughts in his face. She stepped to the door, saying, 'Come to our house tonight. Eat with us. My father would be happy to see you.' As she slipped out, she added, 'And I would too.'

He felt a pang of regret as he watched her walk away. She wavered by a broad strip of land next to the stonemason's, where a group of archers were thumping arrows into a target, the sound he had heard earlier. Even before they hailed Catia, Lucanus knew what she would do next.

When she was a girl his own father had taught her how to use a bow, much to the annoyance of her family – it was not a suitable pastime for someone of her standing – and she'd taken to it better than anyone he knew. He smiled as he watched her grab a bow from one of the men and nock her shaft. For a moment she stood there, string drawn, arms rigid, her keen eyes judging the target. Her arrow thudded into the wood dead centre. Cheers rang out around her, and he saw she was flushed and smiling. He realized with a note of sadness that he hadn't seen her so alive in a long while.

As he turned away, he sensed a shadow darken the door and for a moment he thought she'd come back to him. Instead, it was her younger brother Aelius.

'Don't take her words to heart,' Aelius said. 'You know there's a good reason she's so harsh.'

'You were listening?'

'I hear everything, I see everything. That's one of the few advantages of being someone who is not seen or heard.'

Aelius was sixteen, his hair sleek and black, his jaw square. He was really Catia's half-brother, though no mention was ever made of his mother – one of the women at the House of Wishes, Lucanus guessed – but he had been raised as a full member of the family. He always turned his face to hide the side scarred from the pox that had afflicted him when he was a child, yet it was the withered right arm that diminished him in the eyes of many. Useless, it hung loosely at his side, a defect that had been apparent the moment he was born. It was not that he was sorely crippled – he'd learned to use his left arm effectively – it was that many said he'd been cursed by the gods. The girls ignored him, the young men taunted him. However skilled he was, that judgement hung over him like a cloud. Eternally damned, he said, even if he fought a hero's battle.

'Do you follow your sister round all day now?'

'I was helping her search for Marcus. It's not as if I'm over-burdened with responsibilities.' Aelius held up a sack hanging from his shoulder. 'And I have bought a new book for my father's library. It's a door through which I will escape from this world for a while.'

'You like your books.'

'One of the rewards of my family's riches. My life with books is better than my life without them.' Yet for all his words, Lucanus heard a sour note in his voice.

Aelius wandered around the hut, examining the patched ceiling where the rain came through in the storms, and the few possessions scattered here and there. 'Well, you live like an emperor, Lucanus. A home befitting a hero of the empire.'

'The Wilds, that's my home. The ditch my bed. The sky my ceiling.'

Aelius chuckled to himself. 'Oh, how your masters must love you. They give you . . . this.' He swept his good arm round the space. 'And all you give them in return is . . . everything. The days of your life, your good years, perhaps your neck, all to keep them safe and rich.'

'I'm happy with my lot.'

'And there is your curse. A life of sacrifice allows lesser men to prey upon you. You should be with Catia, you know that.'

'The wine's addled you.' Lucanus could smell it on his breath. Slumping on his straw bed, he picked up the whetstone and began slow, steady strokes along the edge of his blade. He didn't like where this conversation was going.

'Everyone can see it. Even Amatius, I'd wager. But Amatius is a complicated man,' Aelius continued. Lucanus could hear the sarcasm. 'He's filled with a raging jealousy. That bruise above her eye? Payment for the lascivious look the merchant Magiorius cast her way, as if she had summoned it herself. And yet he takes pride in showing off the most beautiful woman here around. A contradiction? Not in his mind. When she's on his arm, it's his worth that increases, for owning a thing of such value.'

'Catia chose Amatius.'

'Yes, yes. We all know our history, Wolf. A transaction. Her body for saving her family from ruin. Her choice. Even my father, for all his many flaws, would not have asked that of her. But Catia isn't a mewling child. She's got more fire in her heart than most men I know. More than me, that's without doubt. But she found she had agreed to much more than was ever in that original bargain. No life to call her own. Why, she is his plaything now.'

'Don't say such things.' Lucanus focused on the strokes of the whetstone.

'Fists,' Aelius continued, seemingly oblivious. 'A foot in the ribs. A punch in the belly. Some nights he takes her so roughly her screams ring through the house. My father . . . all of us . . . must lie there and listen to her suffering.'

'Still your tongue.' Lucanus hurled the whetstone aside and stood up.

'Would you rather not hear these truths?' Aelius did not retreat. Instead, he stepped forward, almost challenging. He raised his head, smiling. 'Would you prefer to pull that wolf pelt over your eyes and run back into the Wilds, where all is good?'

'Don't push me. I'm not a good man.'

'Ah, but you are, Lucanus. You are. Too good. And therein lies the problem.' Aelius turned away, slinking around the hut once more. 'Children can always see the truth. We lose that skill, when life sours us. But Marcus thinks you're a great man. I saw you with him earlier. He knows the real you.'

Lucanus bunched his fists, but there was nothing there deserving of his frustration. He knew everything Aelius said was true, and that he did his best to pretend it wasn't so. 'This is how things are. It can't be changed.'

'You could run Amatius through with your sword.'

'Murder?'

'Is it a crime to prevent a greater crime?'

'I see no crime. Catia is Amatius' wife. She serves him as he sees fit.'

'Easily said, if your heart's as cold as stone.' Aelius' stare was piercing.

Lucanus held it for a moment, then looked away. 'I will not murder a man.'

'I would, if I could.' Aelius' words were as light as if he'd asked for another cup of wine. He threw his cloak back to reveal his withered arm. 'But one good arm is not enough for such an act, not with a man like Amatius. A sword in my left hand would prick him like a needle, and my head would be off my shoulders before I had another chance. There is poison, of course. But where does one find such a thing? And how to feed it to him? Fire? Doused in oil and set ablaze?' He shrugged. 'I've thought of these things, and greatly, of late. I can see only one answer. One man capable of such a thing. One great hero of the empire who could commit such an act and escape judgement.'

'Return to your wine, Aelius, and don't speak of these things again, lest *you* be held to judgement.'

'Oh, I've already been judged by the gods and found wanting. Haven't you noticed?' Aelius swayed to the door, resting for one moment upon the jamb. 'Think on what I've said, Lucanus. But don't think too long.'

And then he was gone.

Lucanus slumped back on to the straw, feeling the weariness flood his limbs. As he lay there with his hands behind his head, his eyes fell on something swaying in the shadows above the door.

Hanging from the timber that supported the roof was an unfamiliar construction: twigs bound with grass to form a double cross with a square upon it, threaded on a leather thong. Feathers and small animal bones were fastened into the design. It was like one of the bird-frighteners the slaves hung around the fields.

Uneasily, Lucanus contemplated what hung from the bottom: a baby's skull with a triangle in a circle scratched in black on the forehead.

For a moment, he stared at the creamy bone swinging gently in the breeze. That unease was settling deeper into him. Who had left it there? And was it a charm?

Or a curse?

# CHAPTER FOUR

## *The House of Wishes*

GOLD AND PURPLE STREAKED THE WESTERN SKY. THE LAND WAS darkening fast.

Bellicus sucked in a deep, steadying breath. Behind him he could hear the Grim Wolves' raucous laughter as they weaved a drunken dance through the *vicus*. He was not as deep in his cups as some of them – Comitinus stumbled into walls every few paces, laughing, and sharp-tongued Solinus and the always sunny Mato exchanged merry talk. Lucanus had been right. The wine had washed away all their worries.

Not his own, though. He couldn't forget what he'd seen in that clearing at dawn. And the cavalry still hadn't returned. They should have been within the gates by sunset, that was the command.

In the huts and workshops, faces floated in the drifting smoke of the hearth-fires as the Grim Wolves passed by. Vrocata, a pretty girl with hair as red as his own, flirted with the twins Map and Lossio. They managed to flirt back with her while bickering between themselves. Old Gavo hammered new tiles on to the roof of his house in the last of the light, cursing loudly with each mistimed blow of his mallet. Qunavo the drunk danced a jig. Two laughing lads chased an escaped pig. Someone was singing away in the dark, the melody soaring above the rooftops.

For a moment, all was right with the world.

Comitinus flung a bony arm around Bellicus' shoulders – something he would never have dreamt of doing when wine was not flowing through his veins.

'Better days lie ahead, brother,' he slurred.

'Not for you, if you don't remove your arm.'

The other man did as requested, but his grin never dimmed. 'Let me tell you my wisdom,' he said, throwing his hands towards the heavens.

'Ugh,' Solinus grunted. 'I prefer you when you're a miserable fucker.'

'To appreciate all that we have here, a man has to look death in the eye,' Comitinus continued, undeterred. 'When I was a lad, I fell into a bog and spent three days and nights up to my neck. I thought my days were done. More so when the rats came, and tried to eat my face off. But I was saved, brothers, by a hungry hawk who chased those vermin away. The lesson here—'

'There's always a lesson with you, you whiny bastard.' Solinus swung a foot at his companion's arse.

'The lesson here—' Comitinus began again, narrowing his eyes.

'Even a rat thinks you're not worth fighting for,' Solinus said with a firm nod. 'We learned that lesson long ago.' Mato threw back his head and laughed. Bellicus knew that would only encourage Solinus.

'The lesson,' Comitinus all but shouted, 'is that when things are darkest, there's always hope. I'm wasted here. Wasted.'

Bellicus snorted, but as he strode on his instincts flickered towards figures approaching through the wisps of smoke. From the way they moved, shoulders low, balancing on the balls of their feet to be ready to react in an instant, he could see they were not the lowly folk of the *vicus*.

Mato edged beside him, his grin fading fast. 'The gods must have decided we were having too much fun,' he breathed. 'That's Motius and the Carrion Crows.'

'What are they doing here, so far from home?' Bellicus murmured.

As the band of *arcani* drew near, he could see they were dirty and bedraggled, their hair clotted with mud. Cold eyes glowed in faces blackened with soil. They had been long in the Wilds, Bellicus could see from those stares. They hadn't had time to throw off the beast and return to the ways of men.

'Grim Wolves,' Motius said. His hair hung in braids knotted with

29

beads, the left side of his face a swirl of black tattoos. At a glance he could pass for one of the barbarians. 'Your leader is not with you?'

'He has business in the fort. What brings you to Vercovicium?'

'We needed to break our journey before the long trek back to Vindolanda. And to hear what news there is, when we're fed and rested.'

'News?'

'When we'll receive the coin we've long been promised.' Behind him, his men began to shift. Someone spat on the ground. 'I'd share a cup with Lucanus and talk of these things. Do they keep your purses full here in Vercovicium?'

'Lucanus is the man who counts the coin. I'm only good with a sword.'

'Usually the one between his legs,' Solinus said. The Carrion Crows remained sullen.

'We'll share what we know,' Bellicus said, 'no doubt of that. But first, share your news with us. You've roamed far and wide beyond the wall. Have you found anything . . . out of kilter?'

'The land is empty.'

'No signs of war-bands?'

Motius shook his head. 'The land is empty,' he repeated. 'We saw nothing for four days' march north.'

'Is that not strange?' Bellicus pressed. 'The barbarians are never far from the wall. Even if you can't see them, you can hear them or smell them.'

'They'll be back soon enough. We'll always be needed.'

Bellicus wanted to say that was the least of his worries, but he could see the Carrion Crows were ready to move on to the world of men. With heads low and eyes searching the shadows on every side, they loped away into the growing gloom.

'Such a sour band,' Mato mused. 'Even if their purses were full, they'd still complain.'

In the shadow of the bath-house, they hurried up to a sprawling line of linked huts that seemed to be growing each time they visited it. New extensions flourished on the sides and back. Carved in the door jamb, a red-dyed budding rose shone in the flickering light of a torch.

Bellicus closed his eyes and breathed in a sweet scent of spices and lavender.

'The House of Wishes,' Comitinus slurred. 'The house of wonders.'

Before Bellicus could hammer on the wood, the door swung open and he reeled back in surprise. A soft golden glow formed a halo around the red hair of the woman who faced him. Her emerald eyes matched the colour of her dress, but it was her familiar smile that warmed Bellicus' heart.

'You think we're deaf?' she said. 'It was as if all Rome's enemies were marching to our door.'

'Take us in,' Bellicus said. 'I've had my fill of the world out here.'

Amarina crooked a finger to beckon the Grim Wolves inside. Bellicus had known her for four summers now, but she was still a mystery to him. As mistress of the House of Wishes, she chose only the best girls. They were well fed and always smiling, not like some of the scrawny, miserable whores he'd met along the wall. But Amarina was never available to guests. Those who regularly visited had learned not to ask.

Appearances were deceptive; he'd seen her slit a customer's throat after the man had taken his hand to one of the beauties there. The girls themselves had disposed of the body in the swamp beyond the *vicus*, with rocks fastened to drag the remains down to the depths. Bellicus wondered how many corpses lay there, all the men who had wronged Amarina and her girls.

'You've got rooms for all of us?' he asked.

Amarina smiled. 'We always have rooms for the ones who keep us safe. You're our defenders, Bellicus. You are emperors here, each one of you.' She shrugged. 'Besides, it's been quiet these past days. Few travellers on the Stanegate. Perhaps it's the cold.'

'And news?' he asked. 'You hear everything.'

'No news worth speaking of. All is quiet.' Her expression shifted in the torchlight, so quickly that few would have noticed. But Bellicus caught it. She was lying, he was sure of it, but he couldn't guess why.

'Come,' she said, beckoning them into a large room, snug and warm from the fire blazing in the hearth.

The women were already gathered, no doubt at Amarina's order when she heard the approaching commotion. They were a comely bunch, Bellicus had to admit: different shapes, sizes, skin colours, hair; something to please every man. Feigning shyness, they smiled and fluttered their eyelashes, as Amarina had taught them, for all men were children and easily swayed in the presence of women.

But sometimes he caught glimpses of flint in those eyes that chilled him. The younger Grim Wolves no doubt believed these women were here to be adored, but for the girls this was work, and at times grim work. Only a fool would forget that.

As his brothers made their choices, Bellicus looked across the faces, trying to hide his disappointment. When he moved to select one of the girls, Amarina took his hand and gently tugged him back.

'Forgive me,' she breathed in his ear. 'I'm guilty of teasing you.'

She pulled him to a chamber on the far side of the house. Inside, candlelight danced over the naked form of a woman on the bed. Black curls, now starting to streak with silver, tumbled across the pillow.

'Did you think I would not save Galantha for you?' Amarina whispered. Her tone was warm and as kindly as he had ever heard. She slipped out, closing the door behind her.

Bellicus stood at the end of the bed, looking down on the woman he'd known for so long, the only woman he would ever lie with, were it left to him. He tried to feign an aloof expression – he knew he would lose his power if she was aware of the depth of his fondness – but it was impossible.

Galantha patted the bed beside her. 'Lie next to me. It's been too long since we've been together.'

Bellicus stripped off his furs and his leather and clambered beside her. Enveloped in her sweet scent, he wrapped his large, scarred arms around her and held her close. 'Too long,' he breathed. 'But know this, in all the time I crawl through that hard, cold land, with death close at my heels, there's never a moment when you're not in my thoughts.'

Galantha kissed him long and soft, and for a moment he thought he sensed a fondness in her too. Or perhaps he was just a fool.

After their love-making, they basked in the warmth of the room

while the sweat dried on their bodies. At peace, for once, Bellicus'
gaze drifted around that familiar room. He'd lost count of how many
happy times he'd been there. But then he found himself staring at a
carving on a beam on the far wall. He'd never noticed it before, but
this night the candle had been placed at such a point that it picked
out the details in relief. It was the face of a man, staring at the bed,
but instead of hair and beard it had a tangle of branches and leaves,
as if the figure itself was peering out of the dense greenwood.

'What is that?'

Galantha followed his gaze. 'Nothing.'

'Has it always been there?'

'It has.' She pressed the tip of one finger against his nose. 'You
didn't notice it because you were lost in . . . something else. As well
you should be.'

Bellicus frowned. 'My drunken wits tell me I've seen it somewhere before, but I can't place where.'

'Shh.' Galantha kissed him into silence.

For a while, he floated in the dark behind his eyes. But then the
sour thoughts began to crawl up from the deep parts of his head and
he stiffened, hating the fact that even there he couldn't escape
them.

Galantha felt the tightness in his muscles. 'What's wrong?' she
asked, concerned.

'You hear tales from across the empire here.'

'Men speak of things they wouldn't utter outside. Important
things, things that matter not at all. Lies, stories.'

'Tell me . . . what have you heard about the Eaters of the Dead?'

Galantha furrowed her brow. 'I've heard some tales. A sailor,
whose ship was wrecked in a storm. The gods looked kindly on him
and sent great waves to wash him on to a beach in the far north. He
spoke of them.'

'They're real, then? Not tales to frighten children?'

'Men like to spin stories that will make a woman think more
highly of them, but I could hear the truth in this one.' Galantha ran
her fingers through his hair while she remembered. 'He was given
shelter by people who spoke a strange tongue. When darkness fell,
he crept out of his hut and explored the edges of the village, and
what he found there all but drove him mad, so he swore, and this

was a hard man who had sailed the sea-roads for many years and seen many terrible things. On spikes around the boundary were human heads, or what was left of them. And close to them was a pile of bones, a mountain, soaring up higher than his head. Human bones. These had the marks of butchery on them, and all around were leather pouches, and coin, and combs, and rings. He ran for his life, with the whole village at his heels, and only escaped by throwing himself off a cliff, back into the sea. This is how he told it to me.'

The room fell silent. Through the walls, the moans of the other girls echoed.

Bellicus closed his eyes, weighing what he had heard. 'This sounds like a tale told to frighten children.'

'It's true. He swore. You wouldn't doubt if you could have seen the terror in his eyes. As he spoke, he was back there, in that village.'

'And these Eaters of the Dead—'

'He called them the Attacotti.'

'The Attacotti.' Bellicus thought on this for a long moment. Half-remembered stories slowly surfaced. It seemed that he had heard of this tribe before, long ago, in a different place. 'But their land is far away. They would never have ventured here, so close to the wall.'

Bellicus felt Galantha stiffen at his side and he realized he'd said too much.

'You've seen them? Here?'

'No. But a good scout must always be prepared.' Before she could ask any more questions, he rolled on top of her again, and soon her body was singing to his touch. But the peace he'd felt had long since drifted away. Behind his eyes, once again he was standing in that clearing, looking at the swinging bodies of his fellow *arcani*. On the breeze he could taste ashes.

The wind had dropped and a stillness had descended across the dark grassland. Along the wall, the wavering light of the torches washed over the line of men staring out into the Wilds. For a while, nobody spoke. They only watched.

Lucanus tried to read Falx's features, but they were like stone, his brow throwing pools of shadow around his eyes.

'Where are you?' the centurion muttered.

Lucanus looked to Atellus beside him. If there was any hope of reassurance it would be there. But the commandant's brow was furrowed. No doubt he was beginning to conjure up explanations for the lateness of the cavalry. None of them would ring true. The auxiliaries had not ridden out with the necessary supplies to spend a freezing night in the Wilds – tents, greased furs, basic provisions. It was supposed to be a simple expedition, out and back, both a show of strength to any roaming barbarian band and a way to collect new information.

'If they don't return?' the Wolf asked.

'We send more men out to bring them back.' Atellus ground his teeth.

Lucanus felt his shoulders tighten. The auxiliaries were seasoned fighting men. There was not a threat among all the barbarian tribes they couldn't defeat or ride away from. No, Atellus, Falx and the other men there were haunted by deeper fears. Visions of monsters consuming human flesh played in their minds, he knew, though they would never admit to such superstitious doubts. To them, what lurked out there in the ocean of night, in the heaving, endless wilderness, was no ordinary mortal threat.

As if he could read Lucanus' thoughts, the commandant croaked, 'There is no fouler crime than the consumption of human flesh. Those who can commit such an act are capable of any horror.'

'Why have they come now?' Falx grunted.

No one answered. Falx shifted from foot to foot.

'Wait,' one of the men called from further along the line. 'Is that a torch?'

Lucanus leaned on the parapet. His eyes were not as good as Bellicus', but he thought he could see something. He sensed the soldiers around him stiffen and hold their breath.

A light bobbed, a single star in that vast gulf. It was drawing nearer, the Wolf could see now.

'They're back,' someone exclaimed. Along the line, murmured prayers rolled out.

'Come on.' Atellus pounded a fist into an open palm.

Lucanus found he couldn't take his eyes off that approaching light. One torch. Only one, for twenty men? He felt his initial elation ebb.

Atellus must have considered the same thing. The Wolf watched his shoulders sag and his smile fall away. The other men looked towards him, but there were no answers.

Then there was only silence once more and that wavering flame sweeping towards them.

'It is, at least, being carried on horseback,' Falx growled, estimating the speed of approach.

Lucanus frowned. The nature of that light troubled him. Now it seemed too large to be a mere torch, although it was hard to be certain in the featureless, swimming dark.

The men on the wall jerked as one, as if they'd all had the same revelation, and the Wolf raced down the stone steps with them. At the gate, Atellus barked for it to be opened and they flooded out into the Wilds.

Lucanus only had eyes for that nearing light. It *was* a horse, only one. He could hear the pounding of hooves on the frozen ground, but it was the sounds of terror the beast was making that set his teeth on edge. And as the flame swept towards that knot of anxious men, he felt the blood drain from him. His fear, all their fears, were confirmed.

The rider was ablaze.

Roaring flames surged in the wake, a thick, tarry smoke billowing out behind. The horse's mane had also caught alight, the orange of the inferno shimmering in its wide, wild eyes. The soldier must have been strapped to his mount, for he didn't fall however crazily the beast galloped.

'Bring it down,' Atellus commanded, his voice drained of all emotion. 'Put it out of its misery.'

# CHAPTER FIVE

## *Somewhere a Wolf Howls*

THE SOLDIERS SWARMED AROUND THE FLAILING HORSE. THEIR swords flashed and hot blood gushed from its throat. It was a merciful killing. The Wolf knew each man there would feel that death as deeply as if they had lost a brother. The cavalry horses held a special place in all their hearts.

Once the steed had fallen, the soldiers ran forward, lashing their cloaks on their burning comrade to try to extinguish the flames. Lucanus choked down acid as he smelled the reek of burning flesh. All could surely see it was far too late, and the fire was burning too hot to be put out.

In silence, they stumbled together in a crescent, watching the bodies being consumed.

For a long while, no one moved. Twenty auxiliaries dead. Twenty of the finest soldiers the empire had, brought down by . . . he did not know. None of them did.

He turned and looked into the dark. Perhaps Amarina had been right after all. Beyond the wall daemons had been summoned by the gods to carry out their Great Plan, one that ended with the destruction of them all.

The hoar-frosted grass crunched underfoot as Lucanus trudged with the others back to the gate. 'What is our next step?' he asked.

'We cannot let this attack go unchallenged,' Atellus said. In the glow from the torches along the wall his mouth looked like a slash in stone. 'We must ride back out, with more men next time. The whole army if necessary. These monsters must be wiped from the face of the earth.' When the commandant turned to him, Lucanus could see he hoped for reassurance. 'You saw no sign of any great force in the Wilds?'

'A campfire, the signs of a council perhaps. We saw some among the trees, but not an army, a war-band at best. More than us, so we fled.'

'What did they look like?' Falx asked.

He was, perhaps, praying for some description that wouldn't match the ghastly visions running through his head. The Wolf couldn't help him. 'Shadows. That was all we saw.'

'Shadows,' the centurion repeated, his voice low and wavering, as if Lucanus had described something far worse.

'What troubles me,' Atellus continued, 'is that the *arcani* have been thick on the ground in the Wilds along the whole length of the wall, yet not a single band has reported anything out of the ordinary. If any had found something like this, the messengers would have been racing from the other forts long ago.'

'Perhaps they're ghosts,' Falx croaked, 'who melt away at the first light of dawn.'

'Enough of that talk,' the commandant snapped. 'These are men. Barbarians. The worst kind, yes, barely more than savage beasts. But they are men, have no doubt of that. And we will do to them what we do to all our enemies.' At the gate, he paused and looked back. 'There's nothing more we can do tonight. Go about your business. Try to forget what you have seen. Tomorrow we make plans for a campaign that will destroy these Eaters of the Dead once and for all. They have woken the bear.'

He stormed off towards his rooms. Falx continued to stare into the night and then shook himself from his reverie. 'This is a bad business, but we have better ahead. I've already spoken to your friend Amatius about the wine and we're in agreement. But when the merchant from Rome gets here, there's a greater deal coming.' He tapped the side of his nose. 'We'll be awash in gold soon, Lucanus, mark my words. Go see your friends. Keep them sweet. And we'll talk on this soon.'

The centurion ambled away, everything he had just seen seemingly forgotten. Falx was a simple man, that was for sure. As he went, he whistled one of the soldiers' bawdy songs about a girl who enjoyed the pleasures of the legion's best. 'A Hundred Times A Night', they called it. Lucanus had always thought that couldn't have been particularly enjoyable for either party.

Lucanus shivered as he tramped up the slope away from the fort. Frozen puddles cracked under his feet. Before he'd gone far, he sensed movement in the corner of his eye, what looked like a giant crow pecking at the marshy area near where the spring trickled out of the ground. It was a woman, swathed all in black, her back twisted with age. Her hand hovered over whatever she was searching for, and then she craned her head towards him as if he'd hailed her.

Lucanus shrugged and marched on, but when he glanced back he saw she was still staring. He shuddered, not sure why. As he climbed the slope, he could feel her eyes on his back, and only when he reached the higher ground did he again allow himself to look over his shoulder. This time she was nowhere to be seen.

Away in the gloom, a wolf howled. Lucanus pushed back his head and bayed in turn, in salute to his brother.

He felt a yearning to be back in the Wilds. The folk of the civilized world could never understand what it meant to be *arcani*. They thought that all things were what they appeared to be. Out there, the scouts shucked off the skins of men and became the beasts they had pledged themselves to, putting on fur, seeing with amber eyes, their senses afire with new sights and sounds and smells. They could hear the beating heart in the ground and the whispers in the branches.

Civilized folk didn't know what it meant to be alive.

Vercovicium was a ship sailing upon the vast sea of night, its lamps glittering in the dark. The watch upon the wall would be changing their shift now. New eyes turning towards the north, trying to pierce the black veil.

Lucanus trekked on past the marker stone at the boundary of Catia's family's land. A little further and he was comforted by the soft glow of the lamps at the gates to the villa. Now he could smell the stew of smoked fish simmering in the pots in the kitchen. After the hardships of the *vicus*, it would be good to rest for a while on couches imported from Rome, dazzled by gold everywhere he looked and breathing in the perfume of lavender and rose.

The villa loomed out of the dark, with its two new wings enclosing a forecourt, and the farm buildings and brewhouse silhouetted against the starry sky. It hadn't always been so grand. Lucanus remembered a house that resembled a filthy beggar winding down towards death. But that was when the family had split in two, and the ones left here had been beaten to their knees.

How much wealth had been frittered away to turn this place into a palace, so far beyond the cold stone roundhouses that sat at the heart of most of the other farmsteads? To show their recovery from destitution, the patriarch, Menius, had insisted it be reconstructed in the modern Roman way, like the villas he had heard tell of in the south. It had its own baths, and a library. Lucanus still marvelled every time he stepped through the door. There was no more comfort in all of the north, he was sure of it.

His shadow danced ahead of him through the gates. Somewhere nearby, a creaking voice conjured an old song, the maudlin melody plucking images of when he was a boy, squatting in fear by the fireside out in the wilderness as the wolves howled in the distance. Perhaps he had heard the song then, too.

In the centre of the forecourt, an old man craned his neck to watch the moon appear from behind a cloud. Menius was like one of the wind-blasted trees that clung on to the thin soil of the high land in that place. He'd always been the sternest man Lucanus had known, but in recent times he'd softened a little.

'The Wolf,' the old man called. 'It's been too long since you graced our halls.' He surprised Lucanus with a hug. 'I promised your father I'd treat you as one of my own blood, and you are, you are. You will always be like a son to me.'

Lucanus heard an odd note in Menius' voice that he couldn't quite identify. 'The Wilds called to me. I couldn't deny them.'

'The Wilds always call to you, brother of wolves.' The old man rested a frail arm across Lucanus' shoulders and guided him towards the villa. 'The family has been abroad, looking for Marcus. He abandoned his chores and went out to play this morning. No one has seen him since.'

'He has a fire in his belly, that one. I wouldn't worry yet.'

'And in that, he's a lot like you when you were that age.' Menius peered up at the moon once again and mouthed something. A prayer, perhaps. 'When you walked through the gate, I thought for one moment that it was Lucanus the Elder. I think of your father from time to time, and more as the years lie heavily upon me, remembering the days we shared as children. I would see him again before I die.'

'My father is dead, Menius.' It was his standard response. He'd often prayed that some miracle would happen and his father would walk back into his life, but that was the dream of a child. And if his father had taught him one thing, it was that he was a man from the moment he could lift a sword.

'Have you seen his body? Have you seen his blood spilled upon the hard ground? No—'

'I watched my father walk away into the mists that morning, into the Wilds, to do his work as one of the *arcani*. If he chose not to return to me . . . if he preferred a life alone . . . then that is worse than his passing. No. He would have come back to me, if he could. He's left this world.'

Menius seemed on the brink of saying something else, but then he caught himself and smiled and nodded. 'Let us speak of brighter things. We have good food for the table, and wine. Falx was here. He reached some agreement with Amatius. I imagine both will have seen their purses swell. They are much alike, those two. Gold and gold, and gold.'

Lucanus couldn't deny that. Amatius was clever, but his wit was far exceeded by his cunning, and his greed. He'd married Catia when she was twelve and he seventeen. That marriage was the first step back from the miseries that had befallen her family, a joining with another family of wealthy merchants. Both sides had done well out of the arrangement.

Lucanus pushed aside the wave of bitterness.

At the threshold, they heard footsteps behind them. Catia appeared out of the night, her golden hair glowing in the circle of light under the lamps by the door. Lucanus winced when he saw the lines furrowing her brow and the dullness of her eyes.

'Have you found Marcus?' he asked.

'He's punishing me. I know he's hiding out there . . .' she waved a hand towards the dark, 'hoping to fill me with worry. And then he'll dance back when his belly is rumbling, filled with some tale of magic and murder.'

'You let that boy run wild,' Menius scolded. 'He'll be the ruin of you.'

'Father, he's eight. There's plenty of time to learn responsibility.'

'I learned responsibility when I was a boy younger than that, and then again when I was a man and my brother stole everything I had. Lucanus, did I tell you how I fought to claw this family back up out of the mud?'

'You've told him so many times he can probably recount it word for word,' Catia said with a sigh. 'Come. I won't play Marcus' games. The slaves will continue the search.'

As Lucanus entered the largest room, his feet echoed on the marble floor and he lowered his eyes against the glare from the white walls. After the silence and shadows of the Wilds, this world felt alien to him. But the scent of the pungent fish stew was stronger there and he breathed in a deep draught.

Aelius lounged at the low table, watching their guest over the rim of his goblet, with one eyebrow crooked and, Lucanus was sure, a hidden sardonic smile.

'Entertain us with tales of the Wilds, Wolf,' Aelius said.

'It's cold. The forests are dark. There are things that will eat you. Will that do?'

'Stay anyway. As long as you don't drink all the wine,' Aelius said.

Lucanus hoped that was all of them, but a moment later Amatius breezed in and kissed Catia on the cheek in passing. When he saw Lucanus, he pounced forward with a grin and loomed over him as he clapped a hand on his shoulder.

'My friend,' he gushed.

The Wolf forced a smile. Behind him, he could hear Aelius' hollow chuckles.

'Falx told me you suggested he bring the wine to me,' he said. 'I thank you for that. We'll do well out of this trade.' He swept to the side of the room, poured a fresh goblet of wine and proffered it to Lucanus.

Menius popped a fat olive in his mouth and rolled it around with his tongue so that his words sounded muffled. 'You'd do well to take care when you play these games. Here we survive at the mercy of the army . . . and men like Lucanus. If word got out that you were robbing them of good wine, and all the other fine things that find their way across our land, we'd pay a high price.'

'Word will not get out. Besides, Falx will always protect us. We pay him well enough.'

Lucanus took the wine and sipped it. 'Falx has only one interest at heart . . . his own. Don't forget that.'

Amatius shrugged. 'And you . . . you'll always look out for this family, too. You're one of us.'

'I'm one man.'

'Not to hear Falx and the other soldiers speak of you. Ten men, they say, ten men or a cornered wolf.'

Aelius waved his goblet in the air for Amatius to fill it, not even deigning to glance at the older man. 'I'm bored,' he sighed.

'You're always bored.' Catia eased her husband out of the way so she could refill her brother's cup. Lucanus watched her fix an eye on Aelius, silently warning him not to cause trouble.

'You've lived your life in peaceful times.' Menius wagged a finger at his son. 'An attack here, an attack there, but nothing that keeps you from your wine. Don't wish for the kind of excitement that was seen in times long gone.'

Aelius leaned back and rolled his eyes.

Lucanus watched Catia staring at the space at the table where Marcus usually sat and wished he could comfort her. 'I want to say a prayer at the shrine before we dine,' she said. As she moved away from the table, she glanced at him.

'I'll come with you,' he said, understanding that look.

The villa was quiet, but he could hear the questioning cries of the slaves out in the night as they searched for the boy.

'Sometimes I wish I could be a world away from here.' Catia hugged her arms around her as they passed the grand mosaic of Artemis, the old man's pride. 'Perhaps in Rome, with my mother.'

'Don't let your father hear those words.'

'Oh, I don't mean with my mother. But Rome . . .'

'You're not happy here?'

One look was enough. He felt foolish for saying it.

By the niche where the bronze statues of the family guardians stood, Catia lit three candles and murmured a few words to the *penates* to look after her son. But that was not enough, it seemed. Breath steaming in the open air, she strode across the gardens, past the spectral bulk of the mausoleum, to the *lararium*. Inside the shrine, Lucanus shivered as Catia lit a fourth candle and a mosaic shimmered out of the dark, the *genius* hovering over a coiled serpent. After another prayer, she turned and looked up at him. In the confined space, Lucanus smelled the scent of rose petals on her skin. Her eyes were black pools.

'I'm afraid,' she said, her voice barely more than a whisper.

Before she could continue, he heard cries echoing across the grounds outside.

'Oh,' Catia said. 'They've found Marcus.' Her face flooded with relief and she slipped out of the shrine, leaving Lucanus swimming in questions. He hurried after her into the villa. Low voices droned.

A blast of chill air cut through the warmth from the hypocaust. The door to the courtyard hung open to the night, and beyond the circle of lamplight he could just make out a line of figures. The family had abandoned their meal.

'Is it Marcus?' Catia called. 'Has he returned?'

As Lucanus caught up with her the family drifted apart, and now he could see lowered eyes and taut mouths. Beyond them stood five soldiers; at the front was Falx. He flashed the Wolf the irritated look of a man who thought he would get no rest that night, but when he turned back to Catia Lucanus saw his expression change.

She looked into the centurion's face, reading it, and her hand flew to her mouth.

# CHAPTER SIX

## *The Trail*

THE TORCH ROARED IN THE WIND BLASTING OVER THE WALL. Lucanus braced himself against the gale, snarling his fists in his billowing cloak, and looked down at the silver-haired woman huddling at his feet. He'd expected her to be afraid, surrounded by those stone-faced soldiers. But though one eye was milky, the other gleamed with a cold, confident intelligence.

'I saw you earlier this night, in the marsh by the spring.' The crow who had been watching him.

'Speak, you old crone. Tell them what you told my men.' Falx leaned over her, scowling.

The woman pointed a trembling finger towards the moonlit Wilds beyond the wall. Gusts of snow swirled above the long grass.

'Out there. That's where I saw him. The boy.'

'Alone?' Lucanus snapped.

She shook her head and he felt cold in the pit of his stomach.

'Who was with him?'

'I could not see. It was dark by the wall. But he was being led by the hand.'

Lucanus could sense the family at his back. Catia had choked back her sobs, and he was proud of her for that, but he could feel the weight of their fear. 'How could they leave?' He looked along the wall, past the watchtowers. Torches glimmered into the distance, soldiers standing here and there.

'The gate was left open.' Falx shifted and looked away. 'Perhaps after the . . . ah, the fire, earlier. When I find out who's responsible,

45

I'll have their bollocks.' Catching himself, the centurion glanced back at the family and said, 'Apologies.'

Amatius shook a finger in the centurion's face. 'You tell me one of those barbarians could have slipped in, found my son playing in the dark, and taken him away. One barbarian? When they come, they come in war-bands. This is unheard of.'

Falx snapped round to the old woman. She cowered away from him. 'Or perhaps you're lying, is that it? Perhaps you've taken him?'

'No!'

'I've heard the stories. Blood for the pot. Whispered spells—'

Catia cried out.

Lucanus held up a hand to silence the centurion. 'If she'd taken the boy, would she have come to you and told you she'd seen him?' He looked out towards the black band of trees on the horizon. 'I'll go after him. Now. Before they've gone too far.'

'If you go, you go alone,' Falx cautioned. 'This may be a trap. Lure out my men, or the Grim Wolves, and those barbarian bastards will descend upon us. After what happened earlier, we can't take any risks.'

Menius pushed his way forward, shaking, whether from the bitter cold or with emotion Lucanus couldn't be sure. 'This is madness. You can't abandon the boy to his fate.'

'I'll send out men at first light to search for him,' Falx said.

*By then it might be too late.* They all knew that.

Lucanus turned to Catia. 'I'll leave now, and I won't return without Marcus.'

Blinking away a tear, she smiled, but though her lips worked she couldn't find any words. He nodded. None were needed.

As he turned back, Amatius clasped his arm. 'You're a good man. We'll never forget this.'

Menius almost shoved his son-in-law aside and leaned in, trembling. 'Your father would be proud.' For Lucanus, those words were payment enough for whatever was to come. He turned to Falx.

'Send word to Bellicus, but leave it a while,' he said. 'He'll try to follow me, and he'll disobey all orders not to do so. If you try to stop him, he'll throw you on your arse, and that won't end well for either of you. Don't let him know what direction I went in. But tell him I'll see him soon. And Menius, take Catia home and give whatever prayers you can find in your hearts to the gods. There's still hope.'

At the gate, Lucanus bowed his head in his own prayer. He had to believe. That Marcus was still alive. That he could be saved. That he could escape whatever held him out there in the dark.

The barbarians had never done anything like this before. They came in waves, screaming, and hacking with their blades. Sneaking in to steal a boy was not their way. This was something new, and all the more worrying for it.

The gates groaned open.

For a moment he stood there, staring into the endless dark. The Wilds had been his home for as long as he could remember, but now his bones ached with a cold dread.

One more step and he would cross the threshold. Behind him, the world of men. Ahead, a haunted country, home of daemons and gods and the Eaters of the Dead.

# CHAPTER SEVEN

## *The Deal*

S OMEWHERE AN OWL SCREECHED.

'You have given me a night of such joy,' Mato said as the mournful sound died away. He grasped Decima's hand and kissed it, breathing in the strange spices from the unguents she massaged into her skin.

They were standing under the torch on the doorstep of the House of Wishes. Despite the cold, the night seemed to sing, rich and clear, although that was probably just his romantic soul.

The woman's eyelashes fluttered down. He traced a finger along the dark skin of her cheeks, remembering how she'd told him about her journey from the hot lands far to the south, from Africa perhaps. She kept her secrets close, did Decima, but he imagined she was an escaped slave, perhaps one who had killed her master for the abuses he heaped upon her.

'You are a kind man.' Her hot breath bloomed on his ear. 'If only there were more like you. Why, I don't think I've ever seen you without a smile on your face.' As she pressed close to him, Mato felt the hard edge of the knife she kept hidden in her dress, and he smiled. Innocent eyes, full lips and cold steel; a dangerous combination.

Decima pulled his cloak tighter around him. 'You must keep warm or you'll catch your death. There's no meat upon you.' She slid her fingertips across his chest. 'So tall and thin. Why, I would think in any battle you'd snap in two at the first blow.'

'Ah, but I'm light on my feet, and faster than any man alive. I can always run to save my neck. Run like the wind.'

The woman pressed the tip of her finger on the end of his nose. 'You wouldn't run. Your speed is matched only by your courage. Now go, before we both freeze. I'll keep the bed warm for your next visit.'

They kissed and Decima slipped back inside. Mato closed his eyes, sinking into the joy of the moment one last time, then whistled sharply. A figure separated from the dark among the clustering huts of the *vicus*.

Comitinus was stamping his feet and rubbing his hands. Such a sullen expression. He was not in good spirits now the glow of the wine had faded.

'Why wait out here in the cold? Amarina would have let you warm yourself by the hearth,' Mato said.

'And listen to the rest of you grunting like hogs and rattling the beds until it seemed the roof was collapsing?'

'This is the price you pay for finishing too soon.'

Comitinus wrinkled his nose at the taunt. 'Why do you treat Decima as if she were your love? She's only a whore. You are nothing more to her than a bag of gold.'

'Only a whore? She's a woman, Comitinus, and she spends her nights with foul, filthy, sweating men, slobbering and groping. She deserves our kindness, if not our pity. I'd rather crawl on my belly through a shit-reeking bog than do her job. Wouldn't you?'

The owl screeched again, overhead this time.

The track through the *vicus* glittered in the moonlight, the smoke from the home-fires stinging the back of his throat. He cocked his head, listening to the music from behind the doors they passed: the grunts of love-making, the cry of a baby, snores so loud they sounded like a prowling beast.

Mato came to a halt and raised his head to the sweep of stars. Comitinus looked round at him. 'What is it?'

'What wonders there are.'

Comitinus stamped his feet even harder and muttered something Mato couldn't hear.

'When I was a boy, a god spoke to me. A god or a sprite, a nymph, a dryad . . . a messenger.' In that moment Mato was back in the balmy warmth of the woods with the fireflies glimmering in the shadows, lying on his back in the grass. 'Fourteen summers ago, it was, when you were little more than a babe. The great general Magnentius had rebelled against the Emperor Constans and conquered Britannia. You know your history?'

'I've heard some,' Comitinus replied, 'and forgotten more. What use is it to us now?'

'Be wise, brother, be wise,' Mato cautioned with a smile. 'Days long gone shape days yet to come. If you don't know what has been, you will not be ready for what is yet to be.'

Comitinus rubbed his thin wrists.

'When Magnentius was defeated, an agent was sent to Britannia to crush any lingering support. Paulus Catena was his name, though they called him the Chain. I remember seeing him once, face like a hawk, eyes filled with hunger. A cruel man, hard as stone. But you don't send a kindly man to crush resistance, eh?'

'The Chain,' Comitinus repeated, remembering. 'I've heard of him. Blood everywhere.'

'Blood everywhere. Innocent and guilty alike, common man and noble, hunted down and slaughtered to send a message that no resistance would be tolerated.' Mato paused, surprised by the rush of emotion so long after the fact. 'His men cut down my sister Aula. Ran her through on a sword and left her in the street, with her blood leaking from her. Eleven summers she'd seen.'

'Oh.' Comitinus' voice was small. He let his arms fall by his side.

'This life is a rushing river and we're carried along by its flow. We make our plans, and shape our dreams, and pretend we have some control. We have none. A death like that . . . someone who had done no wrong, who had played no part in any resistance, who was merely wandering from her home to see what all the clamour was . . .' Mato shook his head. 'I found her there, after the men had ridden on, and I held her in my arms as her life ebbed away. After that, the world is not the same. The sun shines, but it is not the sun. The wind blows, but it is not the wind. There's no sense to any of it.'

'I'm sorry to hear this.'

Mato closed his eyes, remembering. 'It was the night of mid-summer. I was filled with such grief I thought it would take me too. There was talk among the old folk that if you went into the woods at that time, you'd see those you loved who had crossed over to the

Summerlands . . . see them one last time to say your goodbyes and to hear what message they had for you. I didn't believe, even as a boy, but I hoped. Do you understand that? How you can not believe, but still hope? And I so desperately wanted to see Aula one last time.'

'And did you see her?'

'No. Not Aula. But still . . .' Mato tried to find the words. 'In my grief I couldn't tell, but there was magic in the air. I had a sudden sense that there were people in the trees around me, a vast multitude. But when I opened my eyes no one was there. And then I heard the words in my head and in my heart.'

'What words?' Comitinus had stopped stamping his feet.

'I cannot say.' Mato opened his eyes and looked at the other man, smiling. 'They were for me alone. But they were a truth, and they made me see the world through different eyes.'

'You saw nothing. You heard the words *in your head*. You are mad.'

'Grief drives men to madness, that's true.' Perhaps it had been a dream, a wild vision of a boy who had lost his wits. It hardly mattered. It was still a truth. 'Britannia is filled with sprites and gods, watching and waiting. Listen, Comitinus. Use your eyes. Become wise. Know this: we're surrounded by death, but there's joy everywhere.'

'When I was up to my neck in that bog with the rats coming closer, I didn't see much joy. We're scouts, not priests.'

'We're both. We live with death at our heels every day. We walk between two worlds, we wolf-brothers, like priests. The world of men and the world of the Wilds, the world of gods and magic. Men here have no time to pay attention to what's around them. They hunger for gold, but that hunger turns them to lead. We've been freed from that life, little brother. We can listen to the whispers of the wind and the voices of the birds and we can hear the gods speak through them. Look around you. There's magic everywhere, if only you'd see it. Nothing is as it seems. A wise man would look past the surface and see the truth beneath.'

'You're still drunk. Or still mad.'

Another owl shrieked as it swooped overhead and Mato felt a shadow fall across him. 'Three screeches. That's an omen.'

'Omens, now. Are you priest or scout? Decide now, Mato. I would like to know for the next time I have you watching my back in the Wilds.'

'Both. Neither.' Mato looked back across the township to the walls of the fort. His neck was prickling, a familiar sign, and there was a weight in the air, like the feeling before a summer storm. Vercovicium was quiet, but he saw three torches more than usual flickering along the wall.

'Come,' he said. 'I need to find Lucanus.'

Before Comitinus could reply, Mato was loping back along the track to the fort. He'd already forgotten his wolf-brother, and left him far behind by the time he slipped through the gate and headed for the Principia. Comitinus caught up with him there, his breathing ragged.

Raucous conversation echoed from the centurion's room, punctuated by bursts of laughter. Mato pressed a finger to his lips and crept up to the door. He recognized the voices of Falx and the husband of Lucanus' friend Catia. Amatius' voice was pitched higher than most men's, as if he were always on the brink of laughter.

'Then we are agreed. This deal will seal our fortune,' Falx was saying. 'When the great merchant Lucius Sentius Varro arrives, will we see a river of gold streaming along the Stanegate, I wonder?' The centurion laughed long and hard.

'He's been in the west, arranging to ship tin back to Rome?' Amatius said.

'Aye, and in Londinium and Verulamium and Ratae and Mamucium too. He has more riches than you would see in ten lifetimes, and still he wants more.'

'And we are just the men to help him achieve his dreams.'

Mato jumped as angry voices echoed from outside the Principia. Grabbing Comitinus, he shoved him into the adjoining room. A moment later braided hair and tattoos and fierce expressions blurred past the door. Motius and the Carrion Crows crashed into the centurion's room, bellowing.

Through the din, he heard Falx roaring, 'Are you mad? I could have your heads for this.'

'You think it wise to make enemies of the *arcani*?' Motius' voice cracked with emotion. 'We're like ghosts. You hear and see nothing. And then death is upon you.'

'You dare threaten me? Guards!'

Mato's hand fell to his sword, unsure if he should intervene.

'Wait.' It was Amatius' voice. 'Stay your hands. What ails you?'

'This one steals the coin that is meant for our purse,' Motius said.

'Lies,' Falx snapped.

'Gold, wine, anything of value . . . strange how it all goes astray when it passes through Vercovicium,' Motius sneered. 'We are sick of it. We risk our necks every day and we are as nothing to you. We've had our fill!'

Mato heard the sound of more running feet. The guards had heard the disturbance.

'This is a warning,' Motius snarled. 'If we don't get our dues, there will be blood to pay.'

The Carrion Crows hurried away before the guards arrived. In the lull that followed, Mato heard Amatius whisper, 'Now, more than ever, we need what Varro is offering.'

# CHAPTER EIGHT

# *The Arrival*

'**H**o!' Bellicus' voice boomed over the throb of life in the *vicus.*

In his long leather apron, Ovincus stooped over his table outside his workshop, a half-butchered carcass in front of him, his cleaver embedded in the meat. He was tearing the ribs apart with his red-stained hands. Blood dripped from the table edge into the ditch that carried it straight to the drains.

'You still live, then?' Ovincus threw back his head and laughed, even though he said the same thing every time Bellicus returned from a sojourn in the Wilds. 'I suppose you'll be wanting Catulus?' He whistled and a dog bounded out of the shadows of his workshop.

Bellicus crouched to greet it. The hound ran in rings round him before falling on its back. It was an Agassian, small, slender and shaggy-haired, but fast enough to bring down a deer, and fangs sharp enough to rend through flesh.

'He's been well fed,' Ovincus said. 'Too well fed, with scraps from the table. Bring him back when next you go. It's too quiet without him.'

'You should get your own dog,' Bellicus called as he walked away.

'Too much work. I'd rather have one that visits from time to time.'

Back at his hut, Bellicus slumped on his bed and smiled as he watched Catulus investigating the scents along the walls. 'You'll be with Ovincus by nightfall, and more pampering,' he murmured. 'But when I'm back we will go out hunting, you have my word.'

Catulus did a circuit of the hut and flopped down beside the bed.

Bellicus looked down at the hairs of his red beard, spread out on his chest. When he saw that colour he could think only of the fire that night, flickering in the dark, far beyond the wall.

'There is no good in me, Catulus,' he said, closing his eyes. 'I have blood on my hands and a black rot in my heart. But you know that. You've heard it a hundred times. More. And now you'll hear it again.'

The fire blazing in the night. A beacon, one that still lit the road from then to now, much as he did not want to walk it.

'There were two of us. We'd scouted towards the west until we could smell the salt in the air. The land was empty and we were on our way home so we made camp on a crag above a river valley and drank a skin of wine between us. I can be a foul drunk, Catulus. I'm not proud of that. Sometimes I fly with the birds and sing with them too, but if worries or doubts or fears eat away at me, I can be a sour bastard. That night I was sour.'

Bellicus opened his eyes and stared into the shadows among the rafters. His bones ached from the chill. Perhaps he was getting old. He dropped a hand down until he found Catulus' head and scrubbed his fur.

'We'd been arguing, he and I, about a woman, as is usually the case. I was a fool, then, but still too old to be a young fool. I should have known better, but she'd stolen my heart. And yet she was more interested in him. Jealousy ate away at me like a sickness. I think I went mad for a while, eh, boy? Mad. That's no excuse, though. So we sat by the fire and drank and talked and drank and talked, about the woman. And then we argued, until, finally, we came to blows. I remember . . . I remember . . .' He closed his eyes, the vision of that night rushing back with queasy familiarity. 'My fist, crashing into his thick skull, again and again. My knuckles splitting. Blood flying. His and mine. For a while, I was lost to my rage. Then my eyes cleared.'

Bellicus swallowed. It sounded too loud in that still, cold room.

'I couldn't recognize who swayed before me. The face of the man

I'd called friend . . . best friend, for many a year . . . was a mask of blood. I don't know if he would have survived that night . . . perhaps not. But then he staggered back, and back. Over the crag.' Bellicus fell silent for a long moment. 'I clambered down, but it was too dark to see anything. Still, I searched the riverbank till dawn, feeling with my hands, but there was no hope. He'd gone into the water and been washed away. The next morning I found blood on rocks at the river's edge. I killed him, Catulus. I murdered my best friend.'

The dog twitched, sniffed the air.

'I murdered Lucanus' father. And I'm too much a coward to confess my sin to the man I now call leader. This is what I've become, a shadow, a half-a-man, limping towards death, consumed by his own weakness. I've done what I can to be the father Lucanus lost, but it's not enough. It will never be enough. And now he's gone off into the Wilds alone and we may never see him again.' Bellicus closed his eyes again, listening to the thump of blood in his head. 'You have heard this tale before, Catulus. You'll hear it again.'

After a long moment, he heaved himself to his feet and found the pouch of coins under the stone in front of the hearth. Stooping under the door jamb, he heard Catulus scamper at his heels as he walked out into the *vicus*.

On the narrow track by the tavern he found the widow Elsia outside her home, her dress speckled with flour, her face as drawn as it had always been since her husband had died. Bellicus pressed a coin into her palm as he passed.

'Thank you,' she called after him. He could hear her voice breaking.

'Go back to your oven, old wife,' he shouted back, in case she should chase him to thank him more.

Bellicus flipped another coin into the lap of a beggar who had lost a leg during a battle with the barbarians, and a third went to a young couple – he didn't know their names – who had welcomed a new baby only a week before.

The father looked shocked when he held the coin up to the light. 'Why?'

'My belly is full, I have all the wine and ale a man could want

– what need have I of gold?' Bellicus grumbled, not meeting their eyes. 'It only makes me prey for thieves and fills my home with things I have no time to use.'

As he strode on, Comitinus ambled up calling his name. 'We have visitors,' he said. 'Three wagons and men on horseback coming along the Stanegate from the west.'

'That merchant Falx and Amatius were so intent on meeting?'

'I'd think it likely. Who else would be travelling to this forsaken part of the empire? If you have nothing better to do, let us watch the arrival.'

A small group had already gathered on the south side of the *vicus*. Bellicus saw Mato perched on an outcropping of stone, his face turned to the sun. Solinus stood beside him, one eyebrow cocked in a wry manner as he peered into the distance.

Bellicus watched the merchant's *rhedae* drawing nearer along the Stanegate, the drumming of hoofbeats echoing through the crisp air. The wide stone road was unlike any he had heard tell of, winding its way around the hills and hummocks instead of ploughing as straight as an arrow across the landscape. Running south of the fort, it stretched from the river crossing at Corstopitum in the east to Luguvalium in the west.

At the fork, the riders slowed their pace and turned towards the fort.

Bellicus smelled a flowery scent on the breeze. Amarina and some of the women from the House of Wishes were swaying towards him, the golds and emeralds and ochres of their finest dresses bright in the muddy landscape. Amarina had a regal look about her, Bellicus thought. Her chin was up and she ignored the glances of the men as she watched the world through half-closed lids. The other women followed in her wake, whispering to each other and giggling behind their hands.

'Greeting new customers?' he said when Amarina arrived beside him.

'I go where the gold is.' A faint smile played on her lips, but her eyes were like a raptor's as she watched the new arrivals draw nearer.

'And there's plenty of gold there, I hear tell.'

'Men and their gold are easily parted where women are concerned.'

'You have a low opinion of us.'

'No, only a true opinion. You are all vile things when your mind is upon one thing.'

Bellicus thought about this for a moment, then nodded. 'True. We are foul beasts, chariots of lust.'

The other women preened, twisting locks of hair and brushing away smudges. They chose the best positions to present themselves and waited.

'I've often wondered,' Bellicus mused, 'what makes a woman as clever as you become a whore.'

'My father raped me when I was a child.'

Bellicus eyed her, frowning at what he'd heard, but Amarina's face remained as tranquil as a pool.

'Only once, though. I poured molten lead in his ear while he slept. That put an end to it.'

Now he stared at her, but she kept her gaze on the trundling wagons. Before he could ask her any more questions, they were engulfed in the thunder of hooves and the creaking of wheels. The caravan rumbled to a halt, and the riders slipped down, stretching the kinks from their muscles after a long ride. They all carried short swords and wore helms and breastplates under their brown woollen cloaks.

The lead wagon was a palace on wheels, the gold edging its roof afire in the sun. The two *rhedae* behind it were smaller and plain, filled with supplies, no doubt. One of the aides swung open the doors on the front wagon and set a wooden box at the foot of it.

Bellicus waited, intrigued. Around him, all eyes were gripped by that open doorway.

The wagon creaked on its axle, and lurched to one side. A hugely corpulent man hove into view, legs and arms seemingly too small for his vast belly, white toga glowing in the morning light as if he were a priest at temple. A clipped black beard edged his jowls and a fringe of hair fell from a bald pate. He wavered at the top of the steps, then lumbered down to the ground. The aide offered him an arm, but the merchant flapped a hand to dismiss it, gold glinting from all the rings on those chubby fingers.

Turning his head slowly, he surveyed the desolate landscape, the township, the fort beyond. His face remained like stone, his mouth a pink slash in those black bristles. He did not look like a man who loved life much, Bellicus thought.

A dwarf with a twisted spine and a face that looked like a melted candle staggered from the *rheda* behind him, and squinted into the light. He was dressed like a Briton, with bound breeches under a tunic of gold and black. Pushed back on his head was a conical Phrygian cap made of soft leather, which Bellicus had seen some of the followers of Mithras wearing.

Without looking round, Varro twitched his fingers and the dwarf scampered to his side, searching the faces in the gathered crowd, seemingly weighing each one. He looked Amarina up and down and then moved that lizard stare to Bellicus. They held each other's eyes for a long moment, the giant and the dwarf, sizing each other up. But whatever thoughts passed through the small man's head, Bellicus couldn't read them.

'Look.' An elbow nudged his side. Mato had risen from his rocky seat.

Bellicus followed the other man's gaze. Amatius was striding from the *vicus* with Catia by his side. A broad grin cracked his face, and his eyes gleamed as if he could already see the gold. Catia was looking down, her face ashen.

Amatius greeted Varro with a clap upon his shoulder. They leaned in, exchanging words, and then Amatius pushed Catia up to the wealthy merchant. She bowed her head, polite even then. The dwarf danced round her, lifting the hem of her skirt to peer under. Amatius and Varro laughed as Catia yanked her dress away.

'The dwarf is one of the *scurrae*, yes?' Amarina said. 'I've never found them amusing.'

'They're supposed to speak great truths,' Comitinus muttered. 'The gods have given them wisdom to make up for their cursed bodies.'

'What is this?' Amarina was looking towards the last of the wagons.

Bellicus followed her stare. A slave was walking towards the doors of the rear wagon with bread and a skin of water, or more likely wine. The doors of that *rheda* had been sealed shut with rope. The slave shook the fastening free and clambered inside with the provisions.

'A mystery,' Amarina mused. 'It seems the merchant Varro has a prisoner.'

# CHAPTER NINE

# *Corvus and Pavo*

*The Northern Frontier, Gaul*

BLOCKS OF GRANITE RAINED FROM THE HEAVENS. SOARING PINES shattered into splinters as the missiles laid waste to the snow-bound woods. Fires raged and the ground shook, and for the howling Alamanni warriors scrambling away from the onslaught it could have been the end of the world.

But not for Lucius Aurelius Corvus. He urged his horse on through a wall of acrid smoke, laughing; a madman, any observer would think.

The onagers had been pounding for an hour now and charred flakes and glowing sparks drifted across the snow. Though the Roman cavalry soldier was far behind enemy lines and as likely to be crushed by the stones as any of the fleeing barbarians, he dug his heels in his horse's haunches. It was too late to turn back now.

In the skirmish he'd drifted to the flanks, and while the other men were hacking down the Alamanni with their long, straight *spatha*-blades he'd followed a barbarian into the forest. His prey was still ahead, somewhere at the end of the trail of footprints in front of him.

Away from the raging fire, the icy wind sliced into his face, but he still screwed up his nose at the sweat flooding beneath his mail shirt and tunic and his leather trousers. Fear-sweat. How could he forget the risk from an enemy attack while he was isolated from his brothers? But the rush from that sense of danger was exhilarating too. He lived for moments like this.

61

Glancing back, he saw that any pursuers had fallen behind. Only his friend and co-conspirator rode with him. 'Let's get this done and return to where it's safe,' he called.

Tiberius Annaeus Pavo pulled up beside him. Smaller and stockier than his companion, he squatted low on his mount, huge hands gripping the reins. Corvus nodded, pleased that the other man was by his side, as he almost always was, whether they were fighting or feasting, matching him blow for blow and drink for drink.

'Savour the moment. After this you will be proclaimed hero,' Pavo told him.

'If only my mother saw it that way,' Corvus grumbled. 'I could bring back a mountain of gold and she'd still think my brother had a hand in it.'

'Ah, Ruga. A wonder to behold. Tall and handsome and wise. So much greatness lying ahead of him,' Pavo taunted. 'And you're just a filthy soldier with a knack for getting dirty jobs done.'

'True. All true. I can't argue with that.'

Corvus guided his horse on through the drifting snow, pushing aside the distant screams and the thunder of the assault. The last few months had been hard. While Valens, the emperor of the east, was putting down the revolt by the traitor Procopius, in the west there had been nothing but war against the Alamanni kings. They were a wild band of loosely linked tribes – the Lentienses, the Raetovarii, the Brisigavi, the Bucinobantes – but they fought with one mind.

He remembered returning to his bed night after night drenched in blood. The first time he'd seen them massed among the trees, their hair dyed red for battle, most of them drunk and roaring oaths to their pagan gods, he knew the threat was greater than most in the army believed.

Corvus shook his head, but his mother's warning still rang there: *All that we have fought for can be snatched away in the blink of an eye. We must fight and fight and fight and never stop to keep our hands upon our prize.*

The Alamanni had learned a powerful lesson. Only by banding together could the tribes have the strength to defeat the army of Rome. And they were well organized. That chill morning, when the first force had emerged from the mist, his friend Theodosius had told him what he'd learned from his father, the general. There were two superior kings overseeing the whole territory, and many lesser kings, and beneath them princes who ruled the smaller districts, the *pagi*. Each *pagus* provided a thousand fighting men. A thousand! For too long Rome had underestimated the barbarians. All it took was for those wild men of the forests to start acting together.

And so it had proved. The summer before last, after they had finished sowing the spring crops, they raided Gaul. The army had been defeated.

Blame Valentinian, the emperor in the west, a new and arrogant ruler, that's what the Alamanni said. He'd not given them the traditional gifts, and the kings needed that gold to pay their troops. One victory had been enough to make them believe Valentinian was a poor military leader. Together they could win more.

One year gone, they'd invaded Gaul with three great armies and many smaller tribal groups who smelled a chance they had never known before. Battle after battle had followed.

Corvus could count every scar across his arms and legs, each one marking a struggle where his life had hung in the balance. There were times when he thought the fighting would never end. But in the end they had claimed victory and the Alamanni had paid a terrible price. Thousands dead; the sky black with crows feasting upon the remains.

But that could not be the end of it.

Valentinian accepted, as they all did, that the barbarians had to be punished so that never again would they consider an attack upon the empire. Plans were made to invade. Corvus knew that, and the Alamanni knew it too. The skirmishes along the border, like this one, had escalated. Soon the time would come.

Corvus pushed up high on his horse and looked through the smoke and the swirling snowflakes. 'Now would not be the time to get lost in the woods. You would freeze and starve.'

'Never mind get captured by the enemy and have your bollocks cut off or be ransomed back to Theodosius the Elder like some slave girl,' Pavo added.

'The trials a man must face while fighting for the greater good.'

Corvus rode on a little further and then brought his mount to a halt. 'What's this?' He wiped the stinging flecks of snow from his eyes. Dropping to the ground, he followed the trail to a confusion of footprints by the tip of a rock protruding from a billowing snow-drift. He wiped away the folds of white to reveal a marker stone, carved with a man's face made out of leaves.

'A sign,' he murmured to himself. 'I know this.'

As he studied that graven image, a cry rang out. Corvus jerked up and drew his sword, holding it loosely at his side.

A moment later a bloody clot appeared in the white. The Alamanni warrior he had been following stepped out of the gusting snow, his dripping blade held out before him, his red hair stark in that black and white world. He was dragging a woman of perhaps twenty by the wrist.

Her blonde hair was a wild mane, matted and greasy, her face and arms streaked with dirt. Tracks of tears cut through the muck on her cheeks. Though she was filthy and untamed, she had a raw beauty to her, Corvus thought. Large eyes, full lips, a delicate jawline. Washed and groomed, she could pass for any noblewoman in Rome.

Corvus flashed a look at Pavo, and a nod, and then his feet flew across the snow. He watched the barbarian's eyes widen and a strange hint of incomprehension cross them as the man saw this Roman soldier bearing down on him. The warrior opened his mouth to speak, but before a sound came out Corvus rammed his sword into the man's gut.

The woman wrenched free and ran.

As the Alamanni fighter slumped down into the bloody splatter on the virgin snow, Corvus craned his neck round to his friend. 'Well, we can't turn back now.'

Corvus followed the trail of small footprints to the top of a ridge, from where he looked down on a hut so ramshackle it seemed little more than a pile of branches heaped against a tree. Two bodies lay in crimson slush beside it, an old crone and a dumpy, grey-haired woman. He understood the tears he had seen on the younger woman's face.

Descending the slope, he pushed open what he presumed to be a door and entered the hut. Embers glowed red in a circle of stones in the centre of the beaten-earth floor, but Corvus still shivered; it was as cold inside as out. His nose wrinkled at the tang of unfamiliar spices, no doubt rising from several rough clay pots set around the wall, but then his eyes fell on the young woman cowering in one corner and he forgot all else.

'Don't be afraid,' he said in a gentle voice. 'I'm here to help.'

Her eyes were wild and her lips were pulling back from her teeth as her hand crept towards a pile of rags. A hidden weapon, no doubt.

Kneeling, he looked at her through the blue wisp rising from the hot coals. 'I won't hurt you.'

She only glared at him, tears still brimming.

'Your sisters are dead.'

'Murdered.' The woman spat into the embers.

'I'm sorry about your suffering,' Corvus said. 'I can't put right what you've lost, but I might be able to bring a little light into your days.'

'You? A Roman bastard?'

'Was it a Roman who killed those dearest to you?'

Her eyes closed. A stray tear streaked her cheek.

'You can't stay here.'

'There is no other place for me.'

Corvus held her pale eyes. 'You don't have to be alone.'

She swallowed. 'I will not betray anyone.'

'Nor would I ask you to. I'm an honourable man, and I'm a good judge of a person. Though we have only just met, I can see you're honourable too.' He smiled his winning smile and he saw it pull a flicker of a response despite herself.

She narrowed her eyes at him. 'You are a Christian?'

'I follow Mithras. But we have much in common, you and I. We have to hide our true selves away. The Christians will come for both of us, sooner or later.' He held out both hands. 'I suggest an alliance. Equals. Friends. What's your name?'

'Hecate.'

'Then, Hecate, hear my vow. War is coming to these parts, but I'll keep you safe, even at the cost of my own life. I'll keep you well fed and give you all the gold you need so you can . . .' he looked round at the dismal surroundings, 'build a bigger hut—'

'I need nothing.'

He could not leave her here, he knew that. He had a responsibility. 'Then come with me, and we'll see what common ground we have, and what we can do to make things right.'

'And where would we go?'

'Rome.' When her eyes lit with fear, he said hastily, 'I've made a vow – I'll keep you safe. And should you decide at any time that our ways must part, I'll deliver you back here.'

He watched her making her calculations, but he knew she could not refuse. She must know she would struggle to survive in this dismal place on her own.

Once Hecate had nodded her assent, he left her there to gather whatever she needed, though he could see nothing worth bringing, and hurried back up the slope to Pavo. His friend was leaning against an ash tree, looking bored.

'Lead the way,' Corvus said, 'and make sure there are no enemies lying in wait.'

'Oh, good. You get to ride with a woman's arms around you and her breasts pressed against your back, and I get to be a soft target for spears and swords.'

Corvus sighed. 'If I bought you a drink for every complaint, you would not be sober for the rest of your days.'

Pavo grinned. 'A drink. That'll do to begin with.' When the woman joined them, he climbed on his horse and set off back the way they had come.

The walls of Reims loomed out of the snowstorm. It was night and the torches above the gate roared in the wind. Corvus flexed his frozen face, cracking the rime on his eyebrows. Some warmth at last, hot mulled wine, roasted lamb.

In summer, the green Gaulish land was pleasant enough, a patchwork of forest and grassy plain. But it was a hellish place in the grip of winter. On the ride from the frontier, the wind had blasted and the snow had cut like knives. Five days it had taken, five bitter days, begging a seat by the fire and any food that could be spared in the villages they passed through on the way.

Swaddled in a thick cloak, Hecate hugged tight against his back. Her head bobbed against his shoulder. Sleeping. At the start of their journey, she'd been silent and suspicious of him. He was sure she carried a knife on her somewhere – he'd felt her digging deep in the folds of her clothes whenever her body stiffened. But on the road together, especially in the heart of winter, two people found common ground quickly enough. She would tell him nothing about herself – the ways of her kind were secretive, as he knew. But they'd talked about small things: the light off the snow, the sound the crows made in the stark trees, like angry old women, the faces they saw in the clouds. Once she'd even laughed.

The guards swung open the gates and instantly he was swallowing the stink of rotting food and fish sauce and shit and smoke and a hundred other odours. Hecate cried out. She'd never left the forest before, and this sprawling city was strange and terrifying. A hundred thousand sheltered there behind the walls, or so he'd been told, and more were coming by the day now that Valentinian and the court were in residence. It was the home of the Remi, once, and they'd long since proved their loyalty to Rome, and been richly rewarded for it.

'What is this place?' she whimpered.

'All will be well,' he murmured as he helped her down from his horse outside the tavern. He felt pleased that his voice seemed to soothe her a little, though her eyes still darted.

'I do not like it,' she breathed. 'I cannot hear the wind in the branches and the smell makes me sick.' She rubbed her belly.

'My brother keeps a room here where you'll be safe.'

Her eyes flashed. 'I can look after myself.' That hand in the folds of her cloak again.

'I have no doubt. But I'd be a poor host if I didn't provide you with some small comforts.'

She shrugged, pretending not to care. He had decided he liked her insouciance; liked her, too, for all her wild ways.

'The owner will keep watch over you to make sure you're not troubled,' he continued. 'Don't answer the door, though. And keep away from the women – they're more dangerous than the men here.' He bowed, which seemed to surprise her. 'Rest. We have a long journey ahead of us.'

Once she was safely in her room, he came out into the cold night to find Pavo waiting for him. His friend was stamping his feet and clapping his hands to keep warm. 'Any more punishments to inflict on me, or can I call for wine?'

'Soon. First I have to see my brother.'

'Don't expect any praise.'

'I don't need to have my head swelled. A job well done is reward enough.'

'Liar.'

Corvus and Pavo splashed through the grey slush past the jumble of houses and workshops to the centre of Reims, where the large stone administrative building loomed up above the surrounding roofs. Oil-lamps still glowed in many of the windows. Valentinian and his senior advisers had taken over much of the building since he'd moved the court to the city while he plotted the destruction of the Alamanni.

'Good luck,' Pavo said at the door. 'Best if I'm not around while you talk to your exalted brother. It will only make things worse. Ask him about all those mysterious plots he and your mother seem to hatch together.' He laughed. 'Or perhaps you'd rather waste your breath another way.'

'You're a funny man, Pavo. If only your abilities as a soldier matched your wit and your mouth.'

'Hurry, I beg you. If we're not quick, the wine may all be drunk.' Pavo grinned, but added a nod of silent support.

Corvus clattered up the steps. On the next floor, he heard a rumble of voices, and through an open door he saw a group of men poring over maps. The emperor was there, pacing around the room. Valentinian was a tall man in the second half of his fifth decade, hollow-cheeked and prematurely wrinkled. Corvus thought how ill he looked. Balancing the demands of the western empire with his need to support his younger brother Valens during the tribulations in the east was taking its toll.

A man with a severe expression was stabbing the tip of his index finger on a map to make his point. The emperor valued the guidance given by Flavius Julius Theodosius the Elder, and had made him Master of the Horse. He was a good strategist, Corvus had heard many say. He would rise even higher.

'I thought you dead.'

Corvus turned to see Theodosius the Younger gaping at him. In that light, he thought how much his friend looked like his father, with his long face and bulging eyes and close-cropped sandy hair.

At least he hadn't yet developed the Elder's constant severe expression. It would come; that was religion for you, or at least this clan's particular kind.

'Hard to kill. You should know that by now.' Corvus didn't have to look to know the other man was clutching the crucifix he carried almost everywhere.

Theodosius beckoned him away from the door so they wouldn't be seen. 'I thought only your brother would be travelling to Rome with me.'

'Do you think I'd miss a chance of a civilized life? I've had Gaul under my fingernails for too long now.' Corvus was thinking of good wine, good food, and women who didn't keep pigs by day.

The other man nodded with enthusiasm. 'There's a new teacher at the church, so my father said. He's arranged for us to sit with him and hear his wise words on our Lord's guidance.'

'Exciting,' Corvus replied. 'I can barely contain myself.'

'There's bloodshed on the streets, I hear. Though Damasus was elected pope, his rival Ursinus will still not give up his claim. Their followers battle on a daily basis.'

Corvus had drifted out of the conversation momentarily, but he jerked himself back and said what he hoped was the right thing. 'I can see how that must be hard.'

'It is. It is. My prayers are with both sides. We must not allow any schism. Christians have to stand strong, together. Otherwise where will we be?'

'Exactly. Divided, I would think.'

'And if a house is divided against itself, that house cannot stand. The gospel of Mark. Of course, you know that.'

'Of course. Now, if you'll excuse me, I have to spend some time in prayer, and then find my brother to make arrangements for tomorrow.'

Theodosius bowed deeply, an odd form of expression between soldiers, Corvus thought, and then hurried away with more enthusiasm than any man could surely feel at that time of night.

Corvus ambled along the corridor to the room where he knew his brother would be working and worrying and plotting, despite the lateness of the hour.

The chamber was filled with scrolls and he breathed in their earthy smell in the dry, dusty atmosphere. At a podium, Servius Aurelius Ruga hunched over a scroll by the light of an oil-lamp. Though he was only a year older, silver strands gleamed in his black hair and lines webbed his eyes. The price he paid for the weight of his responsibilities, as he never tired of telling people when they commented on Corvus' youthful appearance.

He looked up, and made a grunt deep in his throat that could only have been some form of greeting.

'You'll go blind, reading by this light,' Corvus said.

'There's work to be done. There's always work to be done. Of course, you wouldn't understand. Why would I expect you to?'

'Valentinian's work, or the family's?' Corvus prowled by the podium, looking around the chamber to see if an amphora of wine had accidentally been left there.

'The family's. That is of paramount importance at this time.'

Corvus shrugged. 'It would help if you let me in on all those little secrets you share with Mother.'

'You?' Ruga sniffed. 'These are serious matters, and the less you know the better. We can't have you blurting them out in some tavern somewhere.'

As expected. Ruga was the serious one, feted from birth and steered towards the heights. Corvus was always and only the second son in all that that phrase meant. Not quite worthy enough. Good for the dirty jobs, but that was all. He'd never let it trouble him greatly. His life was too good for that.

'I rescued a woman from the grip of the enemy,' he mused, flicking papyrus with his fingertips dismissively.

'A woman?'

'A very special woman. One of three sisters.'

Ruga jerked his head up. 'Why didn't you say?'

'I just did.'

His brother made another strange noise in his throat, a hissing, like a snake. Condemnation? Weariness? Corvus wasn't quite sure. 'One of three sisters,' Ruga repeated, his voice quiet.

'There was nothing to keep her there.'

Ruga stared into the flame of the oil-lamp, lost to his thoughts.

'She's good-hearted,' Corvus continued. 'I wouldn't go so far as to say kind, but she's pleasant enough to be around.'

'Then she'll make a good wife for me.'

Corvus stiffened. 'This is not how you find a companion of the heart, brother.'

'Heart? A wife would serve me well . . . a wife like that. Who cares about heart?'

'Ah. She may not be aware of this part of the agreement.'

'She has no say in the matter.'

'I think she will have some say.'

'No say.' Ruga rolled the scroll back up and set it on one side. 'You will give her up to me. I'll marry her, honourably, and she will get all she wishes from life. Status, even.' He pursed his lips. 'And a wife like that will serve me well if I am to rise high within the order of Mithras. There is more to it than simple ritual. Of course, you would never understand that.'

Corvus frowned, not quite sure what he was hearing. 'I made a promise to her that if she wasn't happy with our terms I'd return her to her home.'

'That was a foolish thing to do.' Ruga picked up the lamp and walked towards the door. Without looking back, he added, 'Whatever the future holds, she won't be leaving Rome. Her days as a free woman are over.'

## CHAPTER TEN

# *Foul is Fair*

*North of Hadrian's Wall*

T HE WILDS WERE AS EMPTY OF MEN AS LUCANUS HAD EVER SEEN
them.

No hunters or traders moving between settlements. No smoke
caught on the breeze. No distant echoes of harsh voices. It was as if
he were all alone in the world and the barbarians had been swept
away, destroyed, driven into the snow-bound northern lands by the
judgement of angry gods.

Five days he'd been tramping, and the grassland had long since
been swallowed by the endless forest. In that other world, still and
dark and mysterious, he heard only the crunch of his feet on the
hoar frost beyond the shrieking of crows.

The more he had trespassed into this place, the more he sensed the
nearness of the gods, or daemons, or both. He blamed Amarina for
putting the thought in his head. But now he felt sure they were speaking to him through signs, if only he could understand their tongue.

Five birds had watched his passage from the branches, the first
four crows, the last a magpie. Five bones had been scattered across
his path, four the skulls of birds, the final one the skull of a fox. And
more, so many instances that he'd lost count. Always four the same,
one different. Five faces hidden in the gnarled bark of trunks, five
rocks protruding from the frozen earth. Five streams that he had to
cross. His neck prickled, but he could not yet understand what he
was being told.

This part of the forest was a dense tangle of ancient trees. Trunks too thick for three men to reach around. Gnarled fingers of roots creeping across the hard ground. Walls of thorn and holly. He could only stumble along narrow tracks made by deer or wolf to find a way through.

But he could see the trail left by his prey as clearly as ever, since he'd found it within moments of passing beyond the wall. Grass flattened, twigs broken, leaf mould turned over. Whoever had taken Marcus had made no attempt to cover their tracks. Perhaps Falx had been right and this was a trap to lure the army away from its defences. Yet how could he turn back and look Catia in the face?

As he pushed through a bank of brown bracken, his neck prickled. He whirled, searching among the trees. Nothing moved. Was he now becoming scared of his own shadow? He'd never scouted so deep into this part of the forest, and he couldn't shake the dark mood that seemed to stifle him, as if it were seeping out of the very ground itself.

Beyond the bracken, he came to an area where outcroppings of rock reared up among the trees, casting odd shapes on the edge of his vision. Lucanus slowed his step.

Sniffing the wind, he thought he smelled the boy's sweat, and a sourer reek, like vinegar. Something was here, he was sure of it. His eyes darting all around, the Wolf prowled forward.

Five steps on, the ground fell away from him. A cover of interwoven branches and turf tore past him and he slammed into the bottom of a pit.

For a moment he swallowed his anger that he had been caught like a novice and stared up at the square of grey sky above, his chest burning where the breath had been knocked out of him. At least it was not much of a trap. He could claw his way out, cutting handholds into the hard earth.

Yet as his eyes grew accustomed to the gloom, he saw a tunnel running into the deep dark ahead of him. He smelled scents caught on the air currents: herbs and spices, a hint of woodsmoke, and that vinegary reek of human musk.

Lucanus edged along the burrow, ducking under the thick roots of the trees above, which plucked at his hair like the hands of hidden enemies.

The gloom turned to grey and then he was squinting into clear daylight ahead, though not much of it, and a series of chambers carved out of the earth, each one screened by a curtain of ivy. In the one he could see, daylight was shining down from a small opening above a hearth of grey ashes. Dry grass and rushes were scattered here and there across the floor, and the walls visible between the hanging ivy were a mass of twisted roots and packed earth.

Lucanus padded in. He levelled his blade, swinging it from left to right, ready for any attacker who might emerge from one of the other chambers. He smelled rosemary, thyme, and other scents he didn't recognize, drifting off bunches of dried herbs hanging from hooks driven into the low roof. Amphorae clustered along the walls. He plucked up the lid of one and recoiled from the foul stench.

Who would choose to live here, in the most forbidding part of the forest, far from any human comfort?

Rattled, he started to scan the walls of roots more closely, unsure what had caught his attention. He searched the patchwork of shadows and light until his gaze settled on two small almond-shaped mounds in the brown earth among the mesh of tuberous growths. He leaned in to the gloom, trying to see more.

The eyes snapped open.

A shrieking apparition thrust out of the tangle of roots, a young woman, her hair a wild mane of filthy curls. Naked, her skin was caked with the brown earth that had disguised her. Bands of charcoal swirled across her body, helping to hide her in the gloom, and where the mud cracked he could see spiral tattoos on her pale skin.

Shocked, Lucanus barely had time to raise his sword.

The woman unfurled her right hand level with his face, a pile of white dust on her open palm. She blasted it at him with one breath and he winced at the bitter taste as the cloud filled his mouth and nose.

A moment later he crashed on to the mud floor, his arms and legs like stone. Cold dread gnawed at his heart. He was dead yet still alive, unable to lift a finger though he could see and hear all.

The woman's face floated above his own. She was smiling now, her eyes the colour of a forest canopy.

'Sisters,' she called.

Lucanus heard the sound of curtains of ivy being dragged back and feet padding nearer. His attacker eased to one side, revealing two other women, both of them naked. Their skin was cloaked in that same mixture of mud, charcoal and tattoos, their hair clotted with earth and dry leaves. One was dumpy with age, hair beginning to grey. The other was the withered old hag he had encountered at the wall.

His heart thundered. A trap, of course it was. But how could she have reached this place ahead of him?

'Lucanus, the Wolf,' the youngest of the three women breathed. He saw a dark humour in her flashing eyes.

Questions flooded his brain, but his mouth wouldn't move. The woman pressed one earthy finger on his lips to stop his struggle.

'My name is Hecate.' She pointed to the crone. 'And hers.' And to the third woman. 'And hers too. And our daughters will be called Hecate, and their daughters too. And in that way the weft and the warp will be woven together.'

The Wolf felt a chill reach deep into his bones. Was he dying?

She leaned in close, her hot breath washing over his ear. 'Would you be king, Lucanus?' she whispered. 'You could if you wished, of a kind. Would you be the warrior who guards the blood of the king? That too. That too.'

The other women were stalking around his frame of vision. The hag had fetched what seemed to be a coil of thread, and the mother was helping her measure it out. For some reason he could not explain, Lucanus felt troubled by the sight. It fell out of view when the youngest one straddled him, grinding her groin into his. She bent towards his face, her breasts scraping his chest.

'We are going to fly this day, Lucanus, and while we sweep through the heavens we will sing you our song. You will hear the prophecy, and you will see the road ahead, if you choose to walk it.' Leaning forward, her pink tongue curled out and she licked his face slowly from chin to forehead. 'Fear not, brother. This day we are not here to bring harm to you, or to anyone. The boy yet lives. But you still have a way to go to find him.'

The crone knelt next to him. From the corner of his eye, Lucanus could see the length of thread she had stretched out between her two hands. 'There is a weft and a warp to everything, Wolf. A pattern, hidden to all but those who fly. We tug on a thread here, and another there, and then . . .' She glanced from one sister to the other and gave a gap-toothed grin.

Lucanus felt a tingling in his legs. Whatever spell these women had cast upon him was already starting to fade. Soon he'd be able to show them a length of steel. Then they would tell him what they had done with Marcus.

The mother grasped a small amphora. Removing the lid, she waved it in front of Lucanus' eyes so he could see the contents: a creamy white paste.

The youngest woman lay flat upon his body, pressing herself into him. The tip of her nose almost brushed his own. 'We are wise. And our wisdom is of days long gone. Much of it has been forgotten now, Wolf. But we keep our secrets well, and renew them with each turn of the season. We keep the old names, that men like you no longer know. Beltane. Samhain. We hear the whispers of the old gods. Cernunnos. He stands deep in the forest and howls at man. You will hear his name again.'

Lucanus felt his head swimming. He could no more understand her words than the reason why he had been chosen to hear them. But his blood was pumping now, and he could feel the fire in his heart. Soon.

The young one dipped her hand into the mother's amphora and scraped out a gobbet of the white paste. She wafted it under Lucanus' nose. If he could have recoiled from the bitter reek, he would have.

'This is our magic,' she breathed. 'This is what makes us fly. This is our secret.' She flicked her tongue over her crusted lips. 'Lamb fat. Herbs picked in the light of the moon. The blood of a crow. And one more thing: the flesh of the toad's-stool, picked in the blood-month, and dried, and boiled. This is the secret we have guarded since the first man walked beneath the stars, the secret of the fruit of the soil. It is how we speak with the gods. Not just here in Britannia, Wolf. The world over. Even the priests of the new Christ use it, in the hot lands to the south, when they would plead with their sun-king.'

Her other hand prised open his mouth and he felt a wave of revulsion at the touch of her filthy fingers on his lips. Her face swam in his vision. Her pupils were wide and black and her eyes ranged with madness. It was the look of someone who saw things of which he could never dream, who thought thoughts he could never divine. Unreadable, unguessable. For a moment, he was not sure this even was a woman lying atop him.

'Eating the flesh of the toad's-stool is good. Drinking its sweat is good. But letting it soak into soft flesh, that is the best.' Thrusting the dollop of paste into his mouth, she smeared it on the inside of his cheek, then pressed her lips on his, a parting kiss. 'But even this way is too slow. We have a better way by far, Wolf. We will ride, and ride, and though you have gone first, we will catch you up as we fly and see the world as the gods see it.'

The woman slid down his body and out of his frame of vision. He could feel the life creeping back into him, but his head swam with other sensations. His mouth began to tingle and he tasted iron. All of the sounds in the room boomed louder, echoing. The scrape of a foot on the floor. The smack of lips. His sight blurred around the edges.

Through the haze, he caught sight of the three women holding broomsticks one of them had fetched from the corner of the chamber. They were smearing the white paste on the gnarled ends of the wood.

Lucanus' spirit was rushing up through him, or so he imagined, into his head, and then out of his skull, and up, up through the earthen chamber ceiling, and the tangled roots, out into the forest. And still he was racing ever up, past the highest branches of the trees and into the sky. Though it had been daylight a moment ago, he was now flying under the vast vault of the night. Stars glittered coldly. The full moon lit the forest to the mountains in the distance.

In the rush of euphoria, one thought flickered: was this all a dream caused by the potion? But even that thought died as he was caught up in the buffeting wind roaring past his ears and the sensation of soaring. He felt he could keep flying higher for ever, up even to the gods themselves.

He sensed he was no longer alone. On the edge of his vision, the three women swirled around him, their manes of hair lashing in the wind. However hard he tried, he couldn't seem to look directly at them.

'Where are we going?' he shouted. He felt no fear. He was drunk, ecstatic.

'We could fly to the great black ocean and walk upon its shores.' The voice of the crone floated to his ears. 'And visit those who passed to the Summerlands before us.'

'Not now, not now.' The mother was speaking. 'We must show the Wolf the road that lies before him.'

'The prophecy.' The voice of the youngest rang out as clear as a bell.

'Aye, the prophecy.'

'A king will come who will lead the people and unite this land. A king born of fire. In the time of greatest need, he will fight, and lead. And he will never die.'

Lucanus felt the blood pump in his temples. He had heard this prophecy before. A story, an old, old story.

'Am I to be this king?' he shouted above the roaring.

'Of a kind.' The youngest woman swept by. 'You will lead, and you will fight, and you will sacrifice greatly. And when the time comes, you will fall. But the king will live on, the one true king.'

'You will kill any who stand in your way,' the mother continued. 'Even if they are your friends.'

'War is coming. A war that will make this land run red for a hundred years,' the youngest cried out. 'Britannia will burn, Lucanus. Would you turn your back upon her? Or will you embrace this destiny that the gods have presented to you?'

The mother whisked past him. When she spoke there was a strange sibilance to her voice. 'To walk thiss road, you musst abandon your masterss . . . your dutiess. Your duty now will be to what musst come to passs.'

'You are traitors.'

'Aye, we are.' The hag cackled. 'Rome does not rule us. We will never bow our heads to the emperor.'

'Then you stand with the barbarians.'

'The tribes fight their fights, but rarely see beyond the day's end.'

'But you do.'

'Would you be your father's son, Wolf? Would you save the woman you love?' the youngest demanded.

How could they know so much about him? 'You cannot make me betray my masters, or kill the people I know.'

The women laughed among themselves, a musical sound that seemed to tinkle on too long. 'Words change the world,' the mother said when they were done. 'Tell a man he will be a king, and a king he may well be.'

And then he jerked, and convulsed as if he had an ague. Acid burned in his throat. When his vision cleared, he was lying on his back on the floor, where he had been before he flew in the night sky, if it had ever happened. A thin grey light fell through the hole above him. It was darkening. How long he had been caught up in this spell he could not tell.

The three naked women were squatting around him, blinking with hazy eyes, beatific smiles upon their lips. As one, they turned their heads towards him. He shivered under their otherworldly stare.

'All you said to me is true? The prophecy, the war, the part I should play in it?'

'It is.' The youngest rocked forward, balancing on her fingertips.

Lucanus shuddered, and realized that all life had returned to his limbs. He could draw his sword and loosen the tongues of these women with threats. And yet the urge to exert his power in this place had ebbed away. Whatever spell they had cast upon him had changed him. He could feel it, as if someone had planted a seed deep in his head. As the light flooded in it was beginning to grow.

'The boy was stolen to lure me here? How did you know I would be the one searching for him?'

'We know everything, Wolf.'

'Why have I been chosen?'

'Why you?' They laughed as one, just as they had done when they were flying. 'There will be blood, and fire, and the end of many things. It is too late to turn back.'

Lucanus felt sick and confused. 'The boy,' he croaked. 'Where is he?'

'Ahead, on the road you must walk,' the mother replied. 'It is still within your power to save him.'

'If you did not take him, who did?'

The mother smiled. The hag smiled. The maiden rocked on her haunches next to him. Her tiny fist was closed. When she opened it, a small pile of powder lay upon it, grey this time.

'Now you must sleep,' she whispered.

She threw the powder into Lucanus' face. He coughed and spluttered, but it flew deep into his throat. He smelled roses, sickly and sweet. A great weight crushed down on him.

As he drifted into drowsiness, he heard a voice speaking, but he could not tell which woman it was, or perhaps it was all of them speaking as one.

'You have met the company of women,' the voice said. 'But now you must find the company of men. Now you must find the king-makers.'

# CHAPTER ELEVEN

# *The War-Band*

L
UCANUS WOKE IN THE COLD DAWN. HIS BREATH STEAMED AND HIS
body felt like the grave. Surrounded by the birds' chorus, he
peered up through the high branches to the silvering sky and
wondered if it had all been a dream.

But there, turning slowly in the breeze, was something very real:
twigs tied into a double cross with a square upon it, festooned with
feathers and bones. A sign, one that linked this place with the
moment in his hut when Marcus had vanished. But what it meant
he could not be certain.

Sitting up, he looked along a track heading towards the north-
east. If the women had left him here, that was the way he was surely
expected to go.

'Run.'

He jolted at the exhortation in the stillness. A male voice, low and
rumbling.

'Run. Or die.'

Jumping to his feet, Lucanus whirled, but whoever was there was
hidden in the trees.

'Run! They're coming!'

A mournful lowing drifted through the forest. Though Lucanus
was half frozen, he felt the chill run deeper into his blood. He knew
that sound too well and the danger it heralded: one of the horns the
Scoti war-bands used to call to each other across the trackless
Wilds.

His heart thundering, he threw himself along the track. Now he could hear the yapping of the hounds the warriors bred to run down deer. But such curs were just as useful for scenting human prey.

On he raced until he glimpsed a sea of sedge next to a bog by a stream. Kneeling, he cracked through the frosty crust. A blast of rot and damp flooded his nose. Plunging both hands into the icy mud, he dragged up two gobbets from the sucking depths and smeared the stinking sludge on his face, in his hair. Then he was running once more.

His pursuers were closing, he could hear from the blasts of the horn. His legs burned and he knew he would not be able to escape them, not after the night he had experienced. Only one hope remained.

With barely a moment to spare, he crawled behind a fallen tree. In no time he was breathing in the musky scent of sweat, damp furs and meat. If he hadn't caked himself in that foul mud, the nearing barbarians would have been able to smell him too.

Figures eased out of the gloom among the trunks. They looked like bears, Lucanus thought, heavy with furs and leather, wild manes of hair, black like ravens' wings or a fiery red. Grey woollen cloaks flapped around them. The warriors kept their heads down, their eyes pooled in shadow. At first he thought he was watching a procession of the dead, those heads skulls. But as they neared he saw the impression was caused by black tattoos etched on their faces. Black circling the eyes, black along the cheekbones and between nose and lips.

The sound of slashing and hacking echoed through the stillness and he realized some of them were cutting through the undergrowth.

*Searching.*

He had been too confident, he knew that now. While he was following Marcus' trail, the barbarians had been following his own.

Lucanus fingered the hilt of his short sword. It would be next to useless in a face to face battle with these heavily armed foes. Some of them carried wide blades designed for gashing and stabbing, and others held square-headed axes hanging loosely in their right hands.

Dropping to his belly, he slithered beneath the fallen tree, past tiers of creamy-white fungus, and wormed his way along a natural furrow under a tangle of bramble. The thorns snagged on his wolf pelt and tore the exposed skin on the back of his left hand. He could smell the blood, as his brothers of the wilderness would be able to smell it. But these Scoti's senses were not as sharp as his, or the wolves'. They moved through the Wilds, but they were not a part of it, as he was. But what about the dogs?

Once he was ensconced in his briar nest, he stilled his breathing. His cheek was pressed against the cold earth, his body like wood, the grey pelt and crusted mud letting him fade into the background of that brown and dark green world. He listened to the pounding of his heart. He was afraid; that was good. Fear would put fire into his heart if he came to make his last stand. He would die like a fighting man, not a whipped cur.

Wood crunched nearby. A whistle rang out barely a spear's length away.

Screwing his eyes shut, Lucanus thought of Marcus and felt a wave of despair that there would be no one to bring the boy home. And then he thought of Catia and his regret, if anything, bit even deeper.

A moment passed with no cries of alarm and he stirred and looked out from under his lids. Through the mesh of bramble, he could see the warriors moving past him, steps slow and steady, heads turning as they searched among the trees.

At least they were not good trackers, these Scoti, not like the *arcani*. He hadn't tried to hide his path through the forest. If he escaped this, he wouldn't make that mistake again.

Yapping rang out, drawing nearer, and he heard the beat of paws upon the hard ground. Two shaggy brown dogs bounded in front of his hiding place. They were scrawny curs, their bellies hollow. Their masters kept them hungry, keen for rewards. The Wolf watched them sniff the air, then press their noses to the earth as they followed winding, invisible paths. They spiralled ever closer.

Voices barked and two men ran up, their cries and whistles whipping the dogs into a greater frenzy of searching.

The barbarians began to hack at the undergrowth nearby.

Lucanus folded his fingers around his sword-hilt. He was ready.

But then, when he could hear one of the dogs scrabbling only a blade's length from where he lay, one of the men whistled again and the dogs bounded away. The Scoti warriors followed their hounds, grunting as they cut a path through the thorn.

The stinking mud had done its work. He sucked a breath of air into his burning lungs.

The dark shapes drifted slowly by until they were swallowed up by the trees.

As he began to dare to hope, he heard two heavy warriors tramp up. Lucanus looked out at a pair of boots and woollen leggings. One of the men was slight, the other larger, like a bear. This one had a scabbard inscribed with interlocking spirals of shimmering gold, some of the finest work the Wolf had ever seen. A mark of status. Was this the leader?

'What do you say, Erca?' the smaller man said in the Scoti tongue. His voice was a little reedy, with a sardonic edge to the words.

'Keep hunting, for now,' the bigger man rumbled. 'I wouldn't think a scout would venture this far north. A beggar, perhaps. Or a thief, on the run. But if it is a scout, we must have his head. He must not be allowed to return to the wall.'

Lucanus was puzzled by the strength of conviction he was hearing. True, the Scoti hunted scouts the way others hunted deer. But this sounded weighted with some importance.

When the two men strode off, he pushed himself up to get a better look. Erca was indeed a big man, a head taller even than Bellicus. His wild black hair was wound into small plaits and into them were tied small skulls, of birds, and mice. A faint jangle echoed with each heavy step. The warriors disappeared into the gloom before he could see more.

Once he was sure they had gone, he slid back out from under the briar wall, sucking the blood from his scratches. The gods had been kind, this time, but he had to be more cautious from now on.

'Beware.'

Another male voice rustled out from the dark of the woods, gruffer than the one he had heard before. Once again, he searched the trees to no avail, but he caught himself before he called back. Cocking his head, he listened.

At his back, he heard ragged breathing and the crashing of feet in the undergrowth.

Around the edge of a hawthorn a young barbarian pounded, his mass of blond ringlets flying. A straggler, hurrying to catch up with the rest of his warrior-brothers. Lucanus watched the man's jaw go slack as he attempted to understand who this stranger was in front of him. Then his eyes hardened and his mouth began to open. A cry of warning was forming in his throat.

Slamming his hand across the barbarian's mouth, the Wolf thundered into him. They crashed into a sea of rust-coloured bracken. Underneath, the warrior bucked and thrashed, the strangled sounds vibrating against that muffling palm growing more intense. Lucanus could smell the man's sweat and the reek of raw meat coming off him.

He locked eyes with his foe, and a silent understanding flashed between them. There was only one ending here. The Wolf could not let this man escape to raise the alarm.

With his free hand, he pulled out his short knife and slid it under his opponent's jaw. Hot blood bubbled out over his fingers. He held his gaze on those pale blue eyes until the light in them died.

Pulling himself up, he wiped the back of his trembling hand across his mouth. How long would it take before the rest of the barbarians missed this straggler? One day? And then another day to come back and find the body.

Then they would be at his heels, and they wouldn't rest until they had hunted him down to gain their vengeance.

'My thanks,' he said to whoever had warned him, but only silence answered.

On he prowled until the forest began to thin out. Leaning against a pine sticky with sweet-smelling resin, he looked out across a grassy plain. Rolling hills reached up to the lowering sky, three peaks side by side, their tops glittering white in the shafts of thin sunlight that managed to break through the cloud cover.

Now he had his bearings. The foot of the largest hill was the site of the old fort Trimontium on the banks of a meandering river, long since abandoned when the army retreated. He squinted, picking out the ramparts and the remains of the signal tower, now little more than a stump.

The barbarians had tried to settle there more than once, he had heard. He remembered his father telling him it was a haunted place. Voices echoed from deep in the earth, blue flames flickered above the bogs near the river, and in the trees on the lower slopes it was said that the dead walked on moonless nights.

That was where he would rest.

# CHAPTER TWELVE

## *The Dwarf*

THE CANDLE FLAME FLICKERED INTO LIFE. AS THE SHADOWS swooped away from the shrine, Catia watched the god of the household appear. Guardian of the hearth, walker of boundaries, the Lar was perhaps her last hope.

'Please,' she whispered, swimming in the scent of sweet incense from the silver bowl, 'bring Marcus back to me.'

She set the flatbread and green olives on the offering plate. After a moment's pause, she added, 'Bring Lucanus back to me too. Watch over them both. Keep them safe.'

She felt a pang of guilt. Whatever the harsh reality of her married life, it still seemed as if she was betraying her husband, even though there were times when she lost herself in dreams of retribution, yes, and even cold-blooded murder. The touch of Amatius' calloused fingers on her smooth skin sickened her. The brush of his thin lips, the trace of his spittled tongue upon her cheek, her breasts, her belly, all of it made her gorge heave.

His fists, in some perverse way, were lesser torments. They only harmed her body, and the pain and the bruises faded. With each blow, her loathing hardened, and that gave her strength to fight on.

One murmured word of thanks, and then she stepped out into the cold morning.

The garden had been swallowed by white, the ghosts of paths and beds and box hedges waiting to rise up. Finding a smile, she looked up to the grey sky. This was her time of year, when the air was sharp as a knife and the ground like iron. On days like today, her father would call her the Winter Queen, with a gentle laugh and a twinkle in his eye. It was a more affectionate nickname than wolf-sister, which had been used as much to wound as it had to celebrate her heritage.

'Catia? Catia?'

She flinched at the sound of Amatius' voice and crouched behind a mulberry bush. Her husband was wandering along the rear of the villa, wearing the scowl that he always hid behind a jovial smile whenever he met others.

His dogs bounded at his side. She gritted her teeth as she watched them run. He would have told the slaves he was taking them out to stretch their legs. But she knew, if there was no one watching, her husband wouldn't think twice about setting them on her to bring her down. She'd run from him on more than one occasion rather than give in to his fists, and she was light on her feet, perhaps as fast as Mato. Amatius had soon learned the dogs were the only way to keep his power. She'd lost count of the number of bites she'd had to bathe.

So much misery and pain would be saved if she allowed him to guide her back into the house. But to torment him? That felt like a victory, however small.

Creeping to the door in the garden wall, she opened it a crack, and once she was sure the way was clear she slipped out and hurried along the path down to the township, plumes of snow rising from her heels.

Shortly after she'd been born, during the coldest winter they'd known in those parts for many a year, she'd disappeared from her crib. Grumbling soldiers had been brought out of the barracks into the vicious night to help with the search. Neighbours had told her of how they had stood at the gates and watched a river of fire rush out of the fort, breaking up into a constellation of orange stars drifting into the *vicus*, along the tracks and up to the wall.

A babe could not survive long in that bitter chill. And then a trail had been found heading out into the Wilds and the final torch of hope seemed to have been extinguished.

For three days the search party had plunged into deep valleys and dense pine forests, descending on villages, demanding to hear gossip of a stolen child, or a new babe that had not been expected, or anything. Just when they were about to give up, the tolling of a bell had echoed through the vast forest, so the legend said. Five times it rang out. The men were cold and hungry and exhausted and determined to return home to the fort. But their leader was convinced the ringing had been a signal from the gods.

They pushed on until they came upon a wolf pack surrounding a new mother suckling her cubs. And there she was. Even now, so many years later, she still smiled in amazement at this miraculous story. The wolf-sister, kept warm and fed in the harsh midwinter by a pack of wolves.

The soldiers must have seen it as some kind of blessing from the gods too. By all accounts, they fought like devils against the savage pack to take back that child. Three men died that day.

So many mysteries still remained, ones that now would never be answered. Who had taken her, and why she had then been abandoned.

And one more thing, that still troubled her more than most. When she had been returned to her parents, they had found that a mark had been branded into her back, a dragon curled into a circle, eating its own tail.

Catia reached behind her to touch her left shoulder blade. As she'd grown, the brand had become distorted, but in the scar tissue the ghost of it still remained. What it meant no one knew, nor why such an act of cruelty had been inflicted upon a babe. But she'd always taken it as a mark of a secret destiny, a sign that she was special.

She winced at the thought. In the end, all that she had come to be was the property of Amatius. That felt like the grandest betrayal of all.

A scarlet banner emblazoned with a falcon in flight fluttered above a vast amber tent. That could only be the merchant Varro's, Catia thought. A bonfire blazed in the centre of the camp. A few slaves wandered around, but the rest of the men seemed to be in one of the ten smaller tents, keeping warm.

Her gaze drifted past the settlement, to the blue sky, and beyond. She'd heard stories of distant Rome from travellers like these. In her mind's eye she could see across the green and purple moors, past the wind-blasted highlands and the sapphire sea, to the city of gleaming marble, vast monuments and soaring towers. The majestic golden eagle, ablaze in the sun. She could hear the talk of learned men, wise in their debate, and the tramp of immense armies keeping the empire secure.

There was a world where women could win respect and power and were not treated like beasts of the field. Where her mother was.

She wondered sometimes if the sour emotions that had their origin in that time when she had been taken had been responsible for the rift that had developed between her mother and father. Whether in some way she was responsible for all that had come to pass. For her own dire fate.

'I would not venture closer, if I were you.'

Catia whirled at the voice at her elbow and looked down on the dwarf who had taunted her when Varro had arrived. His conical Phrygian cap was pushed back from his face.

'Am I not allowed to visit our new guests?'

Beckoning, the dwarf hopped away out of sight of the camp. When he found a sheltered spot, he said, 'I didn't mean to frighten you.' He pulled off his cap and wrung it in his hands. 'Poor wretch. Myself, I see as a . . . giant among men. A warrior of the byways. Others . . . only as a scavenging rat.' He dropped his head as if he were being crushed by the weight of sadness. 'I am harmless, see.' He did a little dance, kicking up clouds of snow, and ended it with a deep bow. 'My master calls me fool. Bucco, the fool.'

Catia bowed in turn. The dwarf had irritated her when they first met, but she'd understood he'd been playing up to his master and Amatius. Now he seemed amenable enough. 'Why aren't you by the fire, keeping warm?'

'Sad life, sad life. But no, I must not burden you.' Then, 'But if you insist. My master wants me hard. To deal with life's travails. So he beats me. Morn, noon and night. Beats me so I cry like a babe. Like a babe, lady. One who has not been fed. A cosy fire in bitter winter? Softens the mind. I need to be hard. Hard.' He slapped his cheek, and again. It glowed red.

Catia felt a wave of pity for this poor soul. 'If I could help you, I would.'

'I carry misery in my wake. It's my curse. Oh, how I hate myself.' Fat tears rolled down his cheeks.

'Please, don't,' she begged.

Bucco dried his eyes with the back of his hand. 'What kindness you show me. A helping hand to a drowning man. What kindness! My heart sings. See?' He crooked his fingers in the corners of his mouth and pulled it wide in a show of a cheery grin. 'Why would a kindly woman like you visit this foul place?'

'It is a long way from Rome,' she agreed, looking over the dwarf's head as she ordered her thoughts. One thing had drawn her here, a whispered conversation she'd half heard on the day the merchant had arrived.

'In one way. Not another.'

'How so?'

'Men and women want the same things. There, and here. Here and everywhere. Power. Gold. To be spent.'

Catia felt herself blush. 'Your master is building his own empire. He wishes to reach agreement to trade with everyone along the wall, I hear.'

'That, and more.'

'More?'

Bucco shrugged. 'He always wants more. More food, more gold, more women.'

'Yesterday morning I heard him asking my husband about boys. What did he want, I wonder?' She hoped that perhaps Varro had heard something about Marcus. A rumour, gossip, anything that could ward off despair.

'Not boys for his bed. No, no. Not his tastes. Girls. Women! Rose blossom. Ample thighs. Honey kisses. Ends well? Not always. Very rarely. Some weep, some bleed. Some die.'

Catia felt revulsion but no surprise. She watched Bucco tap his chin with his forefinger, making a play of reflecting. 'Sly boys, shy boys. Brave boys, cowardly boys. Ones that thieve, and ones that fight. By the boy do we know the man. Do you have one? A boy?'

Catia flinched. Worries about Marcus rushed back in and she swallowed.

'Have I saddened you?'

'My boy has been taken by the barbarians beyond the wall.' She forced a smile. 'But he will be returned to me, I have no doubt of that.'

Bucco bowed his head. 'What a beast I am. To stir up such sadness in you.' He began to beat his chest.

Concerned, Catia held out a hand. 'Please. Don't blame yourself.'

She could see the dwarf squinting at her from under his lids. 'Thank the Lord. Oh, thank Him. But what a poor wretch I am, still. The misery-bringer. Every word.' He paused. 'You wonder if my master knows? Something about your son? If so, he has not said. But I will ask him.'

She shuddered, and not just from the cold. But here was hope, however thin. She turned back towards the villa, ready to face whatever awaited her.

At the house, Catia slumped on to a *sella* with her elbows on her knees and her head in her hands. After a while she plucked up a needle and began to sew the spiral design on the breast of her new dress. Her fingers slid across the fine silk that had been imported from the east and collected from the merchant only three days gone. There was a time when she would never have imagined such luxurious cloth against her skin. So many comforts in that house, yet she did not feel comforted.

Around her, the shadows lengthened. She thought about calling one of the slaves to light the lamps, but the growing darkness was a place to hide away from all that assailed her.

When a figure loomed in the doorway, she winced.

Amatius strode into the centre of the room. He was smiling, his arms thrown wide as if he were a loving husband greeting his wife. 'A kiss,' he murmured. 'And then to business.'

'Business?'

'I'm taking you to see the merchant Varro.'

'What concern is he of mine?'

Amatius smiled, the hateful smile she knew so well, cruel and cold. 'Why, any concern of the husband is the concern of the wife, is it not? And you are a dutiful wife, yes?'

Catia did not reply.

She saw that Amatius had been holding her cloak, and now he tossed it to her feet. 'Put that on.'

A wave of weariness washed over her. 'It's bitter out, and night is drawing in. Would your business not be better conducted by daylight?'

'Perhaps I didn't explain myself clearly,' he said, watching her. 'The business has been concluded. Now it is time for the payment.'

Catia furrowed her brow, trying to make sense of what he was saying. Before she could reach any conclusion, he lunged, snatching her wrist and yanking her to her feet. She cried out, despite herself.

'With this, our fortune will be sealed.' He seemed to see the confusion in her eyes, for he shook his head in clear contempt. 'You are the payment, you slow-witted sow. You. A night with the merchant Varro, for him to do as he pleases. And tomorrow our bargain will be struck.'

As realization dawned, dread crushed her heart. Was her husband truly capable of this? Of course he was.

A shadow appeared at the door: her brother Aelius. For a fleeting moment, she thought that he might rush in to save her, but how could he? Amatius would beat him to his knees. He slipped away before he was seen, and she felt relief that he at least would be safe.

'I would not wish to present you to Varro covered in bruises,' her husband said. 'But you will be presented, one way or another.'

# CHAPTER THIRTEEN

# *The Serpent*

LIGHTS WERE FLICKERING TO LIFE ACROSS THE *VICUS* AND A howling wind threatened more snow. Beyond the humble dwellings, silence hung over Varro's camp and now only embers glowed in the fire in the centre of the circle. Catia could see shadows moving across the cloth of the tents. From entrances that still hung loosely open, blades of light from the oil-lamps carved across the slush.

Amatius pushed her up to the large amber tent and called Varro's name. The merchant boomed for them to enter.

Inside, a brazier hissed, the coals red, and Catia choked on the spicy incense the merchant was using to mask the fire's acrid reek. Sheets of silk drifted in the air currents, dividing the tent into smaller rooms. She winced as Amatius slammed a hand between her shoulder blades to guide her through them, past mountains of cushions, to the heart of the tent, where a low bed lay. Catia tried not to look at it.

Varro wheezed as he lumbered to his feet, his bulk draped in a long white robe like the kind the traders from Africa wore. Rolls of flesh rippled beneath. As he swayed towards them, he plopped black olives into his mouth from a small bowl nestled in the chubby fingers of his left hand.

In one corner, Bucco the fool squatted on a stool, his twisted face blackened by a scowl; a child chastised by his mother. Varro handed the bowl to the dwarf and turned to face his guests. His grin was broad, but Catia thought how cold his eyes looked.

'Amatius,' he said. 'And the fair Catia.'

The merchant's gaze slipped past her husband, and she shuddered as it swept up and down her body, drinking in every part of her form. Then he grasped her hand and kissed the back of it. His lips lingered a moment too long.

Catia gazed straight ahead, not even deigning to look at him. She would not be cowed, whatever was to come. Her husband's fingers fumbled at her cloak and it fell to the floor. He had insisted she wear her finest dress, silk from the far east, dyed the amber of the merchant's tent.

Varro flicked his fingers and Bucco scampered to pour a cup of wine. He presented it to Amatius with a low bow. 'Deep draughts, drift away. Wonder and madness beckon.'

Amatius took the wine and flapped a hand to dismiss the fool. 'We have much to discuss. A shining future.' A greasy greed oiled his words. Catia felt disgust.

'Aye, we do,' the merchant replied. 'But not this night. This night is for wine, and pleasure.' He eyed the dwarf. 'And for other things too, if the gods are willing.'

Bucco raised one hand high. 'The gods are smiling. Their light shines down. Glory. Revelation. Twisted bones, dwarf bones. But they feel it, deep. Yes, they do.'

Catia watched her husband frown. He had no idea what the man was saying. Nor had she, but none of it mattered. This night would end the same way.

She looked around the tent for something she could use to fight the merchant off. She would never succumb willingly, even if it cost her her life. But there was nothing, and she was too slight to repel a mountain like Varro.

The merchant pushed Amatius' cup to his lips. 'Drink,' he said, 'and be gone.'

Sickened though she was, she couldn't help but smile at that demeaning dismissal.

'Have no fear,' the merchant continued. 'Our bargain stands. You and that dull-witted soldier will be my sole agents here in the north. For that prize, I would have demanded a coffer of gold. But you have brought me something of much greater value.'

From the corner of her eye, Catia could see Amatius' sly grin as he handed his empty cup back to Bucco. 'Then we will meet again in the morning and celebrate the rising of a new dawn.'

Catia watched her husband slip out though the folds of silk, knowing that he was thinking only that he had got all he wanted. She crooked her fingers into claws, waiting for her moment. 'I do not wish to be here,' she announced, 'and you would do well to let me go.'

'Your husband says otherwise.' Varro poured another cup of wine and offered it to her.

Catia made no move to take it.

Faster than she had ever seen a man his size move, he hurled the cup aside and lunged. His stubby fingers dug into the delicate silk of her dress and he ripped it free.

She cried out and clutched at the material to keep her nakedness covered, but Varro was still moving. Grabbing her shoulders, he spun her round.

'See, Bucco, see,' he exclaimed. 'We have found her.'

Catia wrapped her arms around herself, bracing for another attack, but Varro seemed spent. Wheezing from the exertion, he unfurled his fingers from her shoulders and stepped away.

'The Ouroboros.' The merchant's voice hissed with glee. She felt him trace the pink outline of the brand upon her back and she flinched, but there was almost tenderness in his touch. 'The dragon eating its own tail. Here . . . here . . . The eternal return. The phoenix that always rises. How long have I searched? How many broken women? How many dismal failures?' She was surprised to hear him choke back a sob, and wrenched herself away from his touch.

'Lay your paws on me again and I will kill you.'

'You have been marked, little sister. By the gods, or their agents. You have become a part of something greater. The Great Plan. The cycle of all the heavens. Rebirth!'

Varro wheeled away from her, rubbing his chubby hands together. She saw his eyes sparkle as he lumbered round the tent.

'That scar is from when I was a babe,' she said.

'Yes, of course. Hear, Bucco. Hear.'

'Harsh days. Fire and iron. Crying baby. The reek of burned flesh. But, then . . . a new age!'

Catia looked from the merchant to the dwarf, thinking for a moment that they might both be mad. 'How did you know about this brand?'

'I am more than a merchant, little daughter. Bucco?'

The dwarf searched through a pile of leather pouches in one corner and returned with a pin. 'To fasten your dress,' he said with a bow.

Catia snatched it and pinned the torn shoulder. 'What are you, then?'

'There are three worlds. Pay heed, for numbers are important. All that there is is built upon them, and odd numbers have the most power.' The merchant raised fingers one by one. 'Three worlds. The world of man that we all see around us. Then there is the secret world of man, the one that lies beneath the things you know. It has its own history . . . the real history . . . and its own rules. It is only for the enlightened. In that world you will find the true reasons for all that happens, the wars, and the crimes, the rise and fall of emperors, the rise and fall of religions. Everything that happens is decided in that world of secrets. Most people are never the wiser. They go about their business thinking they know full well why things occur. They do not. And the history of that world is never written down. None will ever discover it. But the keepers of those mysteries, they are all around you and you will never recognize them for who they are.'

'And the third world?'

'That is the world of the gods.'

Bucco brought his master a cup of wine. Varro continued to scrutinize Catia over the rim as he sipped.

'I am a man who seeks out the wisdom of that second world. By finding those secrets, the road to power can be seen. Power and riches. I seek to understand how to turn lead into gold.'

'Pfft. A tale for children and fools who wish the world were not the way it is.'

Varro laughed. 'But lead is not lead and gold is not gold. This is one of the secrets of that world, little daughter. Everything has two faces. What it seems on the surface, and what it truly is beneath.'

'Then what is lead?'

'Lead is a man. Say, your husband. Or that centurion, Falx. Or I.'

'And gold?'

'It is the enlightened man. One who has learned the wisdom of the gods. This is a great secret and tonight you have been allowed to know it. This is your first step into the second world. The search to transform lead into gold is the key to the second world.' He held out both hands. 'I am a humble man. All that I know of this, I learned in distant Alexandria under that hot sun, from the teachings of Cleopatra the Alchemist, one of the four great women of this world. Not Cleopatra, the queen, who died from an asp at her breast, no, no. This Cleopatra is greater by far. On her seal it says: "The divine is hidden from the people according to the wisdom of the Lord." True, all true.'

Catia wondered if by keeping the merchant talking, all night if necessary, she might be able to escape the fate he had planned for her. And when the sun was up, she could scream loudly enough to bring the entire *vicus* running to her aid.

'How did you know about this,' she repeated, tapping her left shoulder blade.

'The Ouroboros, the serpent eating its own tail, is a sigil. The serpent . . . the dragon! A sign that has great meaning and is known the world over. To the wild barbarians in the cold north it is the god-serpent Jörmungandr, who could circle the world. To Plato and the Greek wise men it is the first living thing, the spark, eternal. To the brown-skinned men in the east, it is the same. All there is, the gods and man, together, in the never-ending circle. Birth and death and rebirth. Destruction and creation. The turning of the seasons.' Varro's eyes gleamed as he recounted what he knew, a shine that Catia thought contained either madness or an all-consuming passion. 'We have been searching for a woman marked with this sigil since we first set foot upon this cold island, have we not, Bucco?'

'Shivering at night. Cold to the bones. Aching feet. Long miles. But now we have reached the end of our journey.' The dwarf danced, kicking his heels up.

'You're lying. Only my family knew of this brand,' Catia snapped.

'Only your family knew you had the brand. But a woman marked with the Ouroboros, that has been spoken of for long seasons. The sign of the dragon.' Varro found a heavy cloak lined with fur and pulled it over his shoulders. 'You have done well to live your life in this misbegotten place so far from civilization, avoiding all scrutiny. But that time has now passed.'

He pointed at Catia's cloak where Amatius had tossed it. She realized he wanted her to put it on and she fumbled for it, but she felt her thoughts racing too fast. How could she believe a word that the merchant was saying? And yet he seemed to accept it completely.

'Where are we going?' she asked as she threw the cloak over her shoulders.

'I need to know for certain,' Varro replied. 'This is a matter of such importance there can be no room for error.'

Bucco danced ahead of them, holding back the panels of silk to allow them to pass. Outside in the dusk, Varro led the way over the grey ridges of frozen snow and ice towards the wagons, keeping just close enough to grab her if she attempted to run away. What did he think was so important? How could men a world away have been searching for her? She felt excited by those questions and that confused her. Now she wanted . . . needed . . . to know more.

'You're still loath to give up your secrets,' she said.

The merchant grunted. 'They are hard-earned. A man like me would never have been privy to them. I have had to fight to glean what little knowledge I have. It has cost a great deal of gold. And some blood. But a new power will rise, so we are told, and I will hold it in my hands.'

'And who would not?' Bucco chuckled. 'Be lead, or be gold. What a choice!'

'Who keeps these secrets?' she asked.

'Priests. Seers. Wise men, wise women. The voice of Mithras speaks loudly of these mysteries in his temples. The priests of Jupiter and Apollo too, and the barbarians' priests. Even the Christians have learned a thing or two of them, cunning as they are.'

Varro heaved his bulk past his own wagon, and the one that carried supplies, to the third one. Catia looked at it, puzzled. The doors at the rear were bound with rope, but neither the merchant nor the dwarf made any move to open them.

'Lean in,' Varro said. He pressed his ear against the wood. After a moment, Catia followed his lead, wondering what she should be hearing. The dwarf did the same. What a strange sight they must seem, she thought. In the cold night, the three of them leaning against a wagon door.

'Stir yourself,' Varro barked. 'I would have words.'

Catia jolted. The wagon shifted and she heard a dragging sound as if someone was pulling themselves across the boards to the other side of the door.

'Speak.' It was a man's voice, low and throaty and weak.

'We have a woman with the Ouroboros branded upon her back,' Varro boomed.

'She has a child yet?' the voice croaked.

'A boy. A shy boy, a sly boy,' the dwarf chanted.

'How did she come by the brand?'

'Tell him.'

Catia felt the merchant shove her more roughly than he needed. This was a private thing, something she rarely discussed, but she sensed Varro would not allow any dissent. At least once she'd spoken perhaps she could get some explanations.

'When I was a baby, I was stolen from my home. Taken beyond the wall, into the Wilds. Most feared me dead, but I was found three days later, protected by a wolf pack, with the brand upon me.'

A long silence followed. Catia could sense Varro growing more tense. But then the voice rustled out, so low it was almost lost beneath the whine of the wind, 'She is the one.'

Catia shivered, though she didn't know why. Varro clapped his hands.

'We have done it, Bucco,' he whispered. 'Now destiny is ours.'

He grabbed Catia's arm and pulled her away from the wagon. 'Now,' he said, 'we will drink some wine together. And then I will see what pleasures you can offer.'

# CHAPTER FOURTEEN

# *The Old Gods*

A s Lucanus crossed the floodplain in the dying light, fingers of fog began to reach among the trees on the slopes of the three hills ahead. Now, at the river's edge, he could see no more than a few sword-lengths ahead of him.

For a while, he trailed along the bank until he found a bridge wide enough for one man to cross, just a few timbers, some of them rotten, others missing. Sliding one foot in front of the other, he edged his way over the slow-moving waters.

On the other side, the ruined walls of the fort loomed out of the shifting cloud. Trimontium had been abandoned long since, during the army's retreat. He picked his way over stones and shattered bricks scattered across the frozen ground, remembering how his father had told him that the Scoti had tried to build three villages there over the years. Ghosts had chased them out.

Clenching his hand around a raven's skull hanging from a leather thong at his neck, he muttered a prayer, and scrabbled over the crumbling outer wall. Inside, he watched the spectre of the fort emerge from the fog. Stumps of walls, blackened areas where fires had once been, cracked stones hiding the hypocaust, fragments of mosaics, the mysterious shapes revealing nothing of what they had once portrayed.

Lucanus wound his way into the centre of Trimontium.

Settling into one corner of what had once been a room, he hunched over his knees, listening. The skin on his arms prickled to goose-flesh at the sensation of being watched. His mind playing tricks with him, he told himself.

He imagined what a sight he must present to any who dared venture near, caked with grey mud from head to toe, white eyes wide in his crusted face. He must look like some revenant that had clawed its way out of the grave. He chuckled to himself, enjoying the feeling of humour after the hardship. That would teach those who sought him to venture into such a haunted place.

Once he'd collected what wood he could find from the surrounding area, he pulled his flint and cracked out sparks. Soon he was rubbing his hands in front of a small fire, almost overcome with joy as the ice crept from his bones. If he had been as cold as this before, he couldn't remember it. Once he could feel his fingers, he gnawed on some of the ruby deer meat from a carcass he'd found at the side of the track, and the growling in his belly stilled.

For a while, he drifted.

The warmth of the crackling fire tugged at his thoughts. Catia's face floated in his inner eye, and then his father's stern features, both of them lost to him, though in different ways. His eyelids were heavy. But he knew he had the senses of his brother wolves. A footfall a spear's throw away would have him on his feet in an instant, sword in hand.

Night fell.

As the flames flickered low, Lucanus raised his head. The shock thumped him and he jerked back against the remains of the wall.

A man was sitting across the fire from him.

Thrusting himself to his feet, the Wolf snatched out his blade. 'One move and I'll gut you. Who are you and what do you want?'

The smoke from the fire drifted and Lucanus could see this was no barbarian warrior. The man wore only a plain brown robe under a great cloak hanging loosely over his shoulders, his black hair twisted into ringlets and tied at the end with leather thongs. A hooked nose, a thin face, dark eyes that burned with intelligence. A tattoo of a black snake curled along his cheekbone and down to his jawline.

The Wolf looked him up and down, but couldn't see any weapons beyond a long staff lying on the ground beside him.

'My name is Myrrdin.' Lucanus heard a wry humour in that voice. 'It was my father's name and his father's before him. And it shall be my son's name, and all the sons unto the end of this world. What do I want? To meet you, Lucanus the Wolf.'

'Everyone in the Wilds seems to know who I am.'

'And with good reason.'

He levelled his blade. 'No more secrets or twisted words. If you're part of this plot to draw me north, speak now.'

'Sheathe your sword. You don't need to threaten me.' It was a command, but the stranger made it seem like a jibe between old friends.

For a moment, Lucanus studied the face before him, and then, satisfied, he put his weapon away and sat down. 'I want the boy back, unharmed.'

'Not a hair on his head has been touched. Nor will it be.'

'Then bring him to me and let's put an end to this.'

'I don't have him.'

Lucanus clenched his teeth. He was too weary and cold for these games. 'Where is he?'

'North.'

'Then you want me to go into a place thick with my enemies? You wish me dead?'

'You know that's not true.'

Fresh wood cracked and a shower of sparks swirled up. 'You lead me by the nose, as if I were a child.'

'You are. A child knows little and has much to learn.' Lucanus watched Myrrdin lean back, relaxing a little. 'The choice was well made,' he added with a nod. 'You followed the boy. That was the first test.'

Lucanus snorted. 'Any man would have followed the boy.'

'Into the heart of the enemy? Where death is only a whisper away?' Myrrdin shook his head slowly. 'Most would have left him to his fate.'

'Why are you playing these games?' Lucanus eyed the stranger. Perhaps he could take his blade and carve out a few chunks to get to the truth.

'Games? This is serious business. Nothing happens by chance, Wolf, remember that. Nothing ever, anywhere, happens by chance. There is always an invisible hand behind it.'

Lucanus watched a faint smile flicker on Myrrdin's lips. He

seemed to be enjoying this taunting, two warriors circling each other, seeking out the other's strengths and weaknesses. But here the weapons were words.

'Your life is not important. Nor mine,' the other man said. 'This game is greater than all of us.'

'On the road, I met three women. Witches. They cast their spells and set me flying, though I couldn't tell if it was all a dream. But they talked about prophecy and war and the blood of kings.'

'They shepherd lives, those three. A man thinks he chooses his own path, but they are cunning. They shape many things to their will.'

'And you?'

Myrrdin shrugged.

'They bade me seek out the company of men . . . the kingmakers. You're one of them?'

The other man nodded. 'In days long gone, my brothers and I wielded power across this land, and beyond. We chose the kings. We spoke with the gods. The old gods, who still watch, who still hear our prayers, who still guide our hands.'

Lucanus struggled to recall the name the youngest woman had told him. 'Cernunnos?'

'He is one. Cernunnos stands deep in the forest and howls at man.' He smiled and the Wolf felt his irritation bubble. 'Your memory's short. You only know what you've lived. But there were other gods here before the Romans brought their own. Those old gods didn't go away. They're still worshipped, in secret, away from the eyes of the invaders. In the villages, in the groves. If you're wise, and careful, you can find their altars along the great wall. Here in the Wilds and on your side too. These are humble folk. But they scribe the altars in the Roman tongue, as best they can. *Dibus veteribus.* To the old gods. If you were of a mind, you could find these signs, Lucanus, and you'd know another world, an older one, hides behind the one you see around you.'

'And you're a part of this older world?'

'Aye. You are *arcani*. And we are too, in our own way.'

With his foot, Myrrdin pushed a log deeper into the flames, sending the sparks showering once more. The Wolf listened to the fire crackle, but the fog that pressed hard around them muffled the sound.

'Let me tell you a story. So you know who we are, and the power we wielded, and which we still wield, in the shadows. A story of an age long gone. Before your father was born, before the Romans came to this island. When your kind roamed free, and you were not forced to kiss the feet of any master.'

Lucanus could see no threat in the face opposite him, but he trusted no one, not in this world beyond the wall. He slid his fingers close to his sword, ready to strike if necessary. 'Tell me, then. Who are you, kingmakers?'

'Druids, we were. We are.'

The Wolf frowned. He'd heard this name somewhere, once. 'Priests?'

'Priests, aye, and more than that. They called us wood-priests. Teachers. Guides. Wise men. We know the movements of the stars, and the plants that heal, and the speech of birds, and the ways of the beasts. In the wind we hear the whispers of what has once been, and read the omens of what is to come in the crows' flight. We speak with the gods and they speak with us. We were here when the first men walked upon this land and we are here still. We are everywhere, in all parts of Britannia and Hibernia, and beyond. When the Romans came for us with their swords, we slipped back into the forests, where our sacred groves were, into the wild places, the mountain tops, the moors. We became ghosts among the trees, speaking only to those we could trust with our lives.'

'Why do you hide?'

'When the Romans invaded, they wouldn't rest until they'd cut out the heart of what they found here. Crushed all resistance and slayed all druids. They knew we would never bow our heads to them. The kings of the tribes would always heed our words. The warriors would always fight. There would be never-ending rebellion.'

Lucanus heard Myrrdin's voice harden. A thick seam of loathing lay there, crushed down and made harder by the many seasons that had passed.

'The Romans marched north and west, seeking out the island that was our head and heart. Sacred to us, it was, Ynys Môn, for it had been given to us by the gods and they came to us there in our groves. And our school was there, where the youth learned our great wisdom, so they could follow in our footsteps. When we heard word the army was marching upon Ynys Môn, we prepared our defence as best we could. But we knew their might, these Romans: swords and javelins and horses and armour. We knew this could be our last stand. And so we sent out the wisest and the strongest, to the hills and forests, where they could keep our wisdom alive and pass it on to new blood. Our ways would not die. The wood-priests would live on. But they would bide their time, stay strong, stay hidden, until the time was right to return.'

'Your brothers stood against the army?' Lucanus looked the other man up and down, baffled.

'Men will fight hard for what lights a fire in their hearts, even unto death.' The Wolf watched him swallow a deep breath. 'We waited on the beach of Ynys Môn, knowing our season was about to end. Wood-priest and warrior, men, women and children. We cried to the gods to send down storms to destroy our foes, but there are times when men must stand alone and be tested. And we watched as the Romans crossed the waters in their flat-bottomed boats, their horses swimming beside them.

'It was a slaughter.' Lucanus heard his voice almost disappear beneath the crackle of the fire.

'Though we fought harder than we had ever fought, every man, woman and child there was put to the sword. The sands of Ynys Môn turned red, and it's said that under the light of a full moon they are red to this day. And the Romans took the bodies of our brave brothers and sisters and piled them high and set fire to them. And then they warmed their hands upon the flames and laughed.'

Lucanus watched Myrrdin's head fall forward until his chin was almost upon his chest. He understood that ache and felt a moment of pity for those lost lives.

'We wanted nothing more than to be left alone. To teach, to guide, to eat and drink and hear the wind in the trees and feel the grass beneath our feet. We were no threat to Rome.' Myrrdin's voice was low and heavy.

'And those who fled to the hills and forests?'

'The Romans thought us all dead. They were fools. When we have been here for so long . . . in every village, in every part of this land . . . when we have held power in our paws, and shepherded and guided every man, woman and child who lived and walked here, why would they think they could destroy us in one battle? Yet we could see there was no safe place for us while the Romans brought down their fist. But we are patient. We could wait, and plan.'

'Like any man, I like a good tale, well told, around a fire on a dark night. But what does this mean for me?'

'The wheel of life turns slowly, Wolf, but turn it does. All things must change. And now the old season is passing and a new one abirthing before our eyes.' Myrrdin leaned towards him, the flames dancing in his pupils. The sadness had passed and now he was filled with fire and fury. 'The gods will call on many men and women to play their part in this. The wyrd sisters are already tugging on the strands. And you, Lucanus, have been summoned to help shape what is to come.'

'I don't want any part of this.'

'We expected you'd refuse.' Myrrdin smiled, his eyes narrowing. 'You think you have any choice? The weft and the warp of all things is decided by gods, not men. Or would you challenge the gods?'

'I . . .' The words died in his throat. He knew full well what happened to men who turned their faces against the gods.

'The power of Rome is waning. You must know this. In time, there'll be a call for new rulers of this land. But there will be fire and war and bloodshed and suffering for long seasons before the true king rises. The king chosen by the gods. The king who can never die.' He paused, and the Wolf watched a smile flicker on his lips. 'The Dragon, Lucanus,' he whispered. 'The Dragon will rise.'

'This is the prophecy?'

'The prophecy is clear. Many seasons will pass before the king who will not die is born. But his bloodline . . . that royal blood . . . must be protected if we are to be returned to greatness again. Don't you want greatness for your people, Lucanus? Don't you want to be a part of this new age dawning? To be one of the guardians?'

'The guardians of the royal blood?'

'The king's line must be kept safe. There are dangers everywhere, and many who do not want to see this greatness come to pass.'

Lucanus turned up his nose. Prophecies and magic and the will of the gods. This wasn't a world he knew. He was a plain man, who liked a full belly and wine in his cup.

'And where would a man find this royal blood?'

'Why, in a child, Lucanus. In a child who will grow to be a man, who will sire another child, and so on, until the new son rises.'

'In a child, you say?' The Wolf felt even more unsettled now, as if the fog that was blanketing them was slowly lifting to reveal another, stranger world. 'Marcus?'

He watched Myrrdin's mouth curl into a smile. 'We need a guardian who can keep the blood safe. A man who would follow this child into the greatest danger without a thought for himself. You've proved yourself.'

'Marcus has the royal blood? No. That can't be true. His mother . . .'

'. . . Catia . . .'

Lucanus choked on his breath. How long had they been watching, plotting? '. . . his father . . . they're plain folk, not royalty. Awash with gold, but still no greater than you or me.'

'No greater than you,' Myrrdin corrected, stifling a smile. 'The gods decide who will be the king who will not die. And that choice has been made.'

Away in the woods, across the wide river floodplain, the wolf-brothers were howling. Lucanus wanted to run with them across the forests and the moors, to return to the simple life he knew. 'And you want me to take up my sword against anyone who would harm Marcus? Even if he was my master, my friend? One man, alone? I wouldn't last long.'

'I told you, Lucanus. The hidden ones watch and see everything. In the same way you *arcani* see everything. Walk with us and you'll be safe, as will all the ones who walk with you.'

'You can protect me?'

'We are everywhere. Wherever men call to the gods, or call to the heart, we're there. Even in the new church of Christ, we are there. You will know us by the mark of Cernunnos. What is old will be new again.'

'What is this mark?'

'A face, surrounded by leaves and branches. Cernunnos lives in the heart of the forest, and in the wind, and in the cries of the beast. In the moon and the lakes and the rivers and the great wide ocean.'

Lucanus felt his resolve harden. These hidden people had their own plans, it was clear, and they wouldn't think twice about lying to him to encourage him to do their work. 'Where's the boy?' he demanded.

'Go north and west from here, and find a great lake, a lake that is almost like a sea. And there you must make an offering to the gods. And if it's a good one, you'll be rewarded.'

'With what?'

'A sword. A weapon of power, blessed by Cernunnos himself. A blade that will lay waste to all your enemies, and unite your allies. A sword that will find its way to the hand of the king who will not die.'

'And that's where I'll find Marcus?'

'He'll be waiting for you when you arrive. The trail begins to the north of here. It's marked with stones, and if you look carefully enough you'll see the face of Cernunnos peering back at you from the rock.'

Standing, Lucanus jabbed his sword at the other man. 'I'll return with the boy, but I don't want any part of these plots. Find another fool to do your bidding. And heed my words: if you stand in my way . . . if the boy is harmed . . . I'll take your head.'

Myrrdin levered himself up and leaned on his staff. Why couldn't Lucanus see any disappointment in that face, any anger? Only a faint smile on those lips?

With a curt bow, the wood-priest turned and strode away from the fire. The fog swallowed him, and then there was only silence.

# CHAPTER FIFTEEN

## *Ghosts in the Night*

'THIS IS A FINE TIME FOR TREACHERY.' MATO TURNED HIS FACE towards the full moon and smiled. These nights were his favourites: the world transformed by snow and moonbeams.

'You'd probably marvel at the flight of a bird while they string us up and cut off our balls.' Bellicus loomed at his shoulder. His dog was squatting by his feet, looking around the knot of men. 'Treachery is no excuse for your poetry.'

'There's wonder everywhere, brother, if only you would open your eyes.'

Mato eyed the other Grim Wolves. They were showing confident faces, but that was uneasiness he saw in their eyes, he knew it. Yet what choice did they have? When Aelius had dashed into the tavern to tell them of Catia's plight, they all knew what Lucanus would have expected of them.

'Was it your bright idea to bring that dog?' In the moonlight, the cross-scar on Solinus' face was even more pronounced. 'If it barks, it'll bring every sword in the area down on us.'

'Catulus is better behaved than you,' Bellicus replied. 'I've seen you eat. Like a pig rooting for apples.'

'Let me tell you my wisdom for a night like this,' Comitinus began.

Everyone groaned.

'Have it your way, ' Comitinus grumbled, his hollow eyes pools of shadow. Mato thought his face looked even more skull-like in that stark light. 'If you don't want to learn, then don't. Let's be done with this and away. The longer we waste, the more chance of being caught.'

As one, the Grim Wolves edged out of the cover of the *vicus*. In the camp, the fire was a heap of cold ashes and a low chatter droned from the tents where the guards and slaves rested.

Mato loped across the ridges of frozen slush, his brothers beside him. At the entrance to the large amber tent, Bellicus tapped the shoulders of Solinus and Comitinus to keep watch. They were the best fighters among them and they would at least give Varro's guards pause. And they wouldn't be able to bicker out there. Each man drew his short sword and turned to face the camp.

Mato pulled back the tent flap for Bellicus to slip inside. Once they'd crossed the threshold they breathed in sweet incense, but they could smell bitter sweat beneath it, and their skin bloomed at the uncomfortable warmth. Sheets of silk swayed in the breeze. Mato leaned forward, listening to the purr of a man's voice deeper in the tent. Varro, most likely, was commanding someone – Catia? – to take off her dress or he would rip it from her.

There was still time.

Drawing his sword, Mato pushed through the first sheet of silk.

The dwarf was squatting on a stool in front of them, his eyes widening in shock. Before he could call out, Bellicus whisked the tip of his blade to the fool's throat. Mato hunched down in front of him, grinning, and pressed a finger to his lips. Bucco nodded.

Mato flexed his fingers and the dwarf slipped off his stool and turned. Bellicus prodded him forward with his sword.

A keening cry rang out.

Mato bolted through the remaining sheets.

In the glow from the oil-lamps, Varro slumped on a heap of cushions, his stare fixed on Catia. She loomed over him, snarling, her fists bunched, and Mato could see blood streaming from the merchant's nose.

He chuckled. 'This wolf has teeth, merchant. Be careful what you put near its mouth.'

'I should cut your throat now,' Bellicus snarled.

'You dare threaten me,' Varro blustered. 'I'm an honoured guest of Lucius Galerias Atellus. Once he knows you've raised your weapons against me, he'll have your heads.'

Striding forward, Bellicus flicked his sword in front of the merchant's face and waved it from side to side. 'Here's how it will go. We will take the woman. You will not try to stop us. You will not raise the alarm. If we hear the tread of one guard's foot at our back, we'll return, cut you into pieces and feed you to my dog.'

'Do you think you can walk away from this?' Varro levered himself up on his elbows. Catia glared at him and he slipped back down.

Mato sighed. 'The way I see it, this works well for you. You escape having your balls ripped off the moment she finds them under those rolls of flab.' He held out one hand towards Catia. She was still glowering at the merchant and in that moment not a man there doubted that she would have done it. 'You lose no face,' Mato continued. 'You can still hold your head high and wield all the power you believe your status deserves. And you'll still come out of this ahead, I have no doubt. This woman's compliance is the agreement Falx and Amatius reached with you, I'm certain, and they will have no choice but to crawl on their hands and knees begging for some new bargain. Now you can demand as much gold as you want.'

Mato could see Varro weighing his words. One thing lay in the Grim Wolves' favour. He was a merchant, not a warrior, and he knew a good deal when one was presented to him. After a moment, he grunted, 'I've had all I need from her. Take her.' He added, 'Don't call this a victory. It will not end well.'

'Nothing ever does,' Bellicus grunted. 'But give me a few days of drinking first and I'll die a happy man.'

Catia stepped over the merchant's splayed legs and plucked up her cloak. As she passed Mato, she whispered, 'You have my thanks. I wouldn't have been able to hold him off for long.'

'Modesty,' he murmured back. 'I'd have wagered good coin that you'd come off best.'

Catulus sat with his front paws on the dwarf's chest. When Bellicus whistled, he bounded after his master, and then Catia was hurrying with the others out into the bitter night. Only when they were stumbling through the maze of the *vicus* did anyone speak again.

'Varro was right,' Bellicus said. 'If we think we can leave this behind us we're all ale-addled.'

'We could have killed him,' Solinus mused. 'And the dwarf for good measure.'

Mato clapped a hand on the other man's shoulder. 'We are civilized men, not barbarians. We don't kill without good reason. A man with a fast tongue can win more battles than one with a fast sword.'

'I thank you all,' Catia said. 'I thought I had no friends left at all, but now . . .' Mato watched her choke down her emotion, and she looked away so they wouldn't see her emotions spill over.

'Aye, well, Lucanus would have kicked us from here to Rome if we'd let anything happen to you,' Bellicus grunted, pushing back his wolf pelt and scrubbing one hand through his wiry hair.

'Here's an idea. Let's stand here talking as though we're on the way to the tavern while that fat bastard sends his men after us,' Solinus said.

'He's right,' Mato said to Catia. 'We have to get you to safety.'

'If you take me home . . .' She swallowed, trying to find the right words. 'If you take me home, I will be back with Varro before dawn.'

Everyone there knew what she meant. 'We're the Grim Wolves,' Mato said with a grin. 'Do you think we'd have ventured out without a plan?'

## CHAPTER SIXTEEN

# *A Small, Dark Room*

'WHAT SHALL I DO WITH THIS?' DECIMA DANGLED THE BLOOD-soaked cloth.

Amarina turned up her nose. 'There's no saving it. Burn it.'

'Is that all of it?' Galantha asked. 'Soon there'll be no cloth to be had anywhere.'

'He did bleed a lot,' Decima replied with a shrug. 'But then most of his blood was in one place.' She screwed up the rag and tossed it into the flames in the hearth. The scent of rosewater and lavender stifled the stench of the burning.

Amarina studied the dark-skinned woman as she swayed back to them. 'You'll need to wash that fine dress too, before it stains.' A spray scarred the front, down to the hem.

Decima looked down and grimaced. 'Like a girl on her first day.'

A thunderous hammering sounded at the door. The three women jumped, and then each one made a face at their reaction. They were all acting like girls on their first day.

'He's still in your room?' Amarina asked.

Decima nodded.

'Come. I'll help you.' Galantha shook out her tumbling black curls, the hint of silver glinting in the light from the single oil-lamp.

Once the two women had disappeared into the deep shadows that always swathed the House of Wishes, Amarina sucked in a deep breath. Sometimes she wondered if there were better ways to make a living. The regulars all understood the rules of the house and behaved accordingly. But the strangers . . . there was always one in any group who thought their coin bought them the right to be emperor of all they surveyed.

With one hand wrapped around the hilt of the dagger hidden in her dress, she put on her most welcoming smile and swung the door wide.

'I smell trouble,' she said, her smile growing tighter when she saw who was standing on the threshold.

'That's a fine greeting,' Bellicus said.

Mato was grinning as if he could read every thought passing through her head. The two men flanked the woman Lucanus seemed to like so much, the gods knew why. Amarina leaned out and looked around. They were alone. That was good. With unfinished business in one of the rooms, the fewer prying eyes the better.

'No visitor to the House of Wishes is ever turned away. Even beggars, dogs with fleas and barbarians. As long as they have the necessary coin.'

Once the three visitors were in, she swung the door shut and leaned against it. Folding her arms, she studied their faces. 'How honoured we are,' she said, her gaze settling on the woman.

Catia narrowed her eyes. '*This* is sanctuary? I'd rather go into the Wilds.'

Amarina made to open the door again. Mato pressed one hand against it. 'We wouldn't dream of asking favours. You're a woman of business. Bellicus?'

The red-headed wolf pulled a leather pouch from under his cloak and jangled it.

Amarina eyed the purse, then took it and weighed it in the palm of her hand. 'What are you asking of me?'

'Hide her away. At least until Varro and his men have moved on. No one must know she's here.' Mato paused. 'Not her kin . . . her husband . . . no one.'

Amarina had seen the bruises upon Catia – who in the *vicus* had not? – and everyone knew Amatius' true face. 'Varro?'

'Would like nothing more than to get his hands on her,' Bellicus said.

'If he is anything like his men, then you've done well to escape him. One of them visited this night. He had to be dealt with in the customary manner.'

Bellicus and Mato winced.

Amarina eyed Catia. 'Hiding is not a solution, you know that? When the merchant leaves, there will still be a price to pay.'

Catia said nothing.

'You could bring your husband here. We would treat him with all the hospitality he deserves.'

'That may well be an answer for another night,' Mato said. *Trying to dismiss this talk of the bastard husband*, Amarina thought. Ah, Mato, always protecting the weak and wounded.

While scrubbing the fur on Catulus' head, she eyed Catia from under her lids. And yet this woman was not some cringing girl who ran after her man and meekly did all that she was ordered to do. She had fire in her belly; Lucanus would not value her so highly if that were not true. What drove her, then? Gold? That Amarina could understand, though no doubt this woman looking down her nose at her would not be flattered by any comparison between herself and the residents of the House of Wishes.

'We have an agreement,' she said. 'I'll keep her safe. And if anyone comes asking, I've not seen her, or you. You have your story straight?'

'We were drunk in the *vicus* and saw her flee the advances of Varro and his men,' Bellicus said. 'She paid good coin and has been whisked away to be with kin until she is sure she is safe.'

'A good enough lie. And Varro will doubtless have other things to talk about in the morning.' Amarina smiled, enjoying the woman's puzzled stare at her cryptic comment. She swung open the door and waved her hand a few times to usher the two men out.

Once they were gone, she turned back to Catia. 'You have good friends there.'

'I know.'

'I'm not your friend. But you will be treated like a queen while you're here.'

'All I ask is a place to hide and some food. Can your girls be trusted?'

'With my life, and I don't trust lightly. You'll find them like sisters, though they'll cut you with their tongues if you presume to hold your nose in the air.'

Catia shrugged. 'I was suckled by wolves. I wouldn't know how to be regal.'

Amarina eyed her guest askance. She wasn't the only one who enjoyed cryptic comments. 'Good. Come with me.' She swept through the House of Wishes, past rooms that rang with cries of pleasure and one that was silent.

Far from the main entrance, she lifted one corner of a tapestry embroidered with spirals and stars to reveal another door. 'Should any husbands need to hide from wives, or girls from drunken men,' Amarina said.

She pushed open the door and the two women squeezed into a small dark room. Amarina lit an oil-lamp, and the shadows danced away from a pile of furs and little else. She watched the other woman turn up her nose at the vinegary smell of stale sweat.

'It's not much and it's rarely used,' she said.

'It will suffice.' Catia sucked in a deep, juddering breath. 'You have my thanks.'

Amarina watched the other woman's shoulders slump as the weight of her predicament settled on her. She nodded – what was there left to say? – and wandered back to help Decima and Galantha clean up. Afterwards, she sat with a cup of wine while she counted the gold that Bellicus had given her, then lifted the stone in the floor and tucked her earnings into the space beneath. A small fortune nestled there, but it was not enough. It would never be enough.

The world was shading towards darkness and there would be a long night ahead, that was the talk circulating far from the seats of power. Yet she had her wits and the fire in her belly, and men would always need to pay for warm thighs and the comfort of love without demands.

From the kitchen, she collected a bowl of cold stew and some wine and drifted back to the hidden room. Catia lay on her back on the furs, staring blankly at the ceiling.

'Something to fill your belly and raise your spirits.' Amarina set the bowl and wine down where the other woman could reach them.

'How many men have you killed?' Catia asked, from nowhere.

Amarina could see where her thoughts had been. 'I don't keep count. As I don't keep count of the meals I've eaten.' She paused. 'Men are not the problem. People who want power and will do anything to achieve it, they are the problem. Men. Women.' She shrugged. 'Most people are happy with their lot. Their currency is kindness.'

Catia studied her face. 'That gives me some comfort. You're not as I imagined.'

'A whore can't be wise?'

'Would a wise woman choose to be a whore?'

'You presume there's a choice.'

'Then what made you follow this path?'

'I was stolen from my village by pirates when I was a young girl. The entire ship had their way with me, time and again. A hundred times each. One night, when they were moored offshore and the men were asleep on deck, I turned over the fire-pot and set the ship ablaze. I swam for the beach and stood there watching them all die in flames. A girl alone with no kin . . . what do you do?'

Catia had no response.

'You escaped Varro's slobbering advances?' Amarina sat on the end of the pile of furs.

'By the skin of my teeth.' She hesitated, staring at her hands. 'This night was about more than that fat slug's hungers.'

'How so?'

'Oh, he was ready to defile me. There was no doubt of that. But that was at the end, after everything else.' Amarina watched Catia stare into the middle distance. She seemed to be talking to herself, trying to make sense of what had happened to her. 'He said I was special.'

'Every man says that to a woman. It's the cock speaking.'

'No. He said he'd been searching through Britannia for a woman with the mark of the dragon upon her.'

Amarina let this sink in. 'You have such a mark upon you?'

Catia half turned towards her and lowered the shoulder of her dress. Amarina leaned in and traced her fingers around the distorted scar. The circle sprang to life in the light of the oil-lamp. Unmistakably a serpent eating its own tail.

'It was branded upon me when I was a babe. Varro called it the Ouroboros.'

'Birth and rebirth,' Amarina mused.

Catia started. 'You know of this?'

'Am I not a little box of surprises?'

Catia's eyes flashed. 'Don't play games with me. I've had my fill of being pushed around by everyone I meet.'

Amarina pulled the shoulder of the other woman's dress back up. 'There are stories. Old stories. Told by the wise women who live in the woods. Like all old stories, the telling changes with the teller. Some say one thing, some another. But this . . .' She tapped Catia's shoulder. 'It's always been a sign of something great. Of the gods' plan, perhaps. The mark of the great architect who builds the temple of the world. The plans of men too. It would seem you've been chosen.'

Catia pulled up her knees and hugged her arms around her. 'Chosen for what?'

Amarina leaned back against the wall, calculating what advantage there was in this knowledge. 'There are secrets everywhere, hidden behind things we all know. You've heard the folk sing of King Barleycorn when the harvest has been brought in?'

'Of course. They sing about the reaping of the crop and the beer made from it.'

'That, and more. It's an old song. Very old. Suffering, death and resurrection—'

'The reaping, the malting, the new growth in the spring as it all begins again.'

Amarina smiled. 'And we are all revived by the drinking of King Barleycorn's blood.' She paused, plucking her words from the depths of her memory. 'There's one story that's been long told, as old as that song. Of the coming of the king who will not die. The followers of the Christ have a similar story, I'm told. Suffering and death and resurrection. The Messiah, they call him. The one who will return to unite the people and save the land. The followers of Mithras say the same. And . . .' she laughed silently, 'everyone. It's an old, old tale. All tell it.'

'What does that have to do with me?'

'The king who will not die is often called the Dragon.' She tapped Catia's shoulder blade again. 'Suffering, death and resurrection; the circle never ends.'

Catia shook her head. Until this moment her life had been small and she was struggling to accept what she was hearing, Amarina could see. 'Varro asked about my son,' she breathed.

'My heart's hard. When I hear these old tales, I don't think here is the saviour that will lead us all to a land of wine and honey-cakes. I think whoever owns the king, rules the land. Those people who want power, the ones we talked about just now . . . I would think they'd be keen to find and lay claim to this king, whether he is real or imagined. Even an imagined king has power, if his name is praised enough. Take your son and hide, that would be my advice.'

Amarina thought Catia was about to be sick. 'My son has been stolen. Taken beyond the wall by . . . I don't know whom. Lucanus has gone in search of him.' She bowed her head and muttered a prayer that Amarina couldn't hear.

'You're right. I'm a whore. I don't know anything. Do not heed me.' Amarina stood and stepped to the door. 'I'm sorry to hear about your son. If any man can bring him back, Lucanus can, you know that.'

Before dawn, she woke her girls and together they dumped the body in the bog, weighted down with stones. Afterwards, they finished their task by leaving a sign that would show the way forward; no Ouroboros this. Then they hurried back to light the hearth-fires and prepare new perfume and incense. The beds would be creaking soon enough. She sent food and ale to the hidden room, and then ventured out into the cold morning.

She smiled as the hubbub rising from the camp reached her ears long before she saw the small crowd gathered on the edge of the crescent of tents and wagons. Amarina pushed her way to the front and stood beside the Grim Wolves. Mato and Bellicus eyed her, but said nothing.

Still fastening his cloak, Varro stormed from his tent, with Bucco and one of his guards hurrying at his heels. He marched up to his wagon, studied what had drawn the attention and then spun back to the crowd. 'What is this?' he roared.

Amarina narrowed her eyes, scrutinizing the chunk of flesh nailed to the *rheda*. 'I would say it looked like a cock, if it were larger.'

Varro snarled, a bestial sound, and stepped forward. His fingers flexed as if he would strangle her. 'Whore. This is your doing.'

She raised one eyebrow, showing an unperturbed face, in the full knowledge that it would only whip his anger to greater heights. Before the merchant could advance, Bellicus and Mato leapt in front of her.

'Step back,' Mato commanded, raising a hand.

'You would defend this sow too?'

Amarina pushed the two wolf-brothers aside. 'I need no protection.'

'One of my men is dead. You must pay for this crime.'

'Dead, you say? That's news to me. All I know is that one of your men was little more than a wild beast in the House of Wishes last night, and he was sent on his way.'

She smiled as the merchant jabbed a finger at her. 'I will have words with Atellus. You will not escape judgement.'

From along the Stanegate came the thunder of hooves and Amarina turned to watch a group of perhaps thirty men galloping along the stone road and then turning towards the fort. Varro's furious expression softened into a smile. When he glanced back at her, Amarina saw a look in his eyes that troubled her. Sly, hinting of victory.

He hauled his huge frame away from the crowd and across to the track to the Stanegate, where he waited to meet the riders.

'What is this?' Bellicus growled.

'If you forced me to wager, I'd say Varro sent out word last night for more swords to serve him,' Amarina replied.

'That's more guards than he needs,' Mato murmured. 'He's building an army.'

# CHAPTER SEVENTEEN

## *City of Gods*

ROME GLOWED IN THE ROSY DAWN LIGHT. ABOVE THE WALLS, THE mountains of marble looked down, silent and ethereal, ready to lift a man up to the heavens or smite him down. Corvus pushed himself upright on his horse and marvelled at the vision.

'Remember the stories we heard at our mothers' knee, back home in Britannia?' He heard a rare wistful tone in Pavo's voice. The days of their childhood were hazy now, that cold land barely more than smears of brown and green, only half shaped before his mother and father had whisked him away to the east.

'Romulus and Remus,' Pavo mused. He was leaning forward across his horse's neck, his short stature emphasized by the hunching of his broad shoulders. 'The twins, suckled by the she-wolf. From the wilds they came, and turned their dreams into the stones that built this place.'

Corvus looked back at his own brother, Ruga, perched on the bench of the wagon, oblivious of the view. 'Just a story,' he said.

'In every story there's a truth. A lesson to be learned.'

'And what should I learn from Romulus and Remus?'

Pavo was grinning now. Corvus knew that grin. It said that whatever words came out of his friend's mouth, much more was lying behind them. 'So many lessons, but for now let us consider the wolf.'

'The wolf?'

'What does a wolf do? Why, in all the stories I've heard, he leads you into the forest where you face your deepest fears. The wolf has already conquered them. Learn from the wolf and you can conquer them too.'

'From anyone else, those would be wise words.'

Laughing, Pavo rode on.

Corvus dug his heels in the flanks of his own horse, keen to get home. The journey from Gaul had been wearying. High winter seas had almost dashed the ship to pieces. But when they sailed to the mouth of the Tiber and docked at Ostia, the sun came out, the breeze grew warm and all seemed right with the world.

From the port, they'd ridden through the night, with Hecate sleeping in the back of the wagon.

'Thinking about the witch again?' He sensed Pavo's eyes on him.

'Is it that obvious?'

'To me.'

'You know me too well.' Corvus chewed on his lip. 'I pity her. I don't know exactly what Ruga has planned for her, but it isn't going to be good. He's already been . . .' He bit off the final words, unable to say anything bad about his brother.

Pavo finished it anyway. 'A snake in the grass?'

Corvus shrugged. 'He loves to plot. The questions are spilling over in my head.'

'You could ask him about his scheming, of course, if you wanted to be swatted away like a fly, as always.'

'I can live with his intrigues when no one else is involved.'

'But this time he's dragging the witch into it,' Pavo said with a nod. 'And she's an innocent here, a country girl with mud under her nails, not used to you cunning civilized men.'

'And I was the one who lured her here.' Corvus sighed.

'Well, we've long since established that you're a bastard to all who cross your path.' Pavo shielded his eyes from the sun, judging the distance to the gate.

'I should have known better than to expect sympathy from you.'

His friend snorted. 'I'll show you sympathy when you've earned it.' He rode on.

'Now I feel even worse,' Corvus muttered to himself.

'The seven hills of Rome.' The younger Theodosius had ridden up beside him and was craning his neck. 'In the Bible, we're told that seven is the number of perfection and completeness.' The soldier pulled off his helmet and mopped the sweat dripping from his sandy hair.

'Seven wolves,' Corvus muttered to himself, 'that's what I need.' He glanced at his friend and said, 'You should be overflowing with joy, escaping from those icy forests back to civilization. At least here you won't have to crack the frozen snot off your top lip when you wake every morning.'

'I am joyful, and the first thing I'll do once we enter the city will be to visit the church and pray for our good fortune. Will you join me?'

'Perhaps later. First I must visit my mother. Ruga sent word ahead and she will be expecting us. Perhaps she may even be pleased to discover I'm still alive.'

Theodosius laughed. 'You have a wit, my friend. This world would be darker without you.' He patted the packed leather pouch hanging over his horse's flanks. 'This work may well take time. Preparing the supply lines for the campaign against the Alamanni won't be easy when there are so many demands across the empire.'

*The longer it takes, the better*, Corvus thought. Weeks of negotiations might dull the mind, but it would give him the time he needed to discover the full extent of his brother's plans for Hecate.

The Via Aurelia led them straight to the Pons Aemelius. Corvus shielded his eyes against the shimmering waters of the Tiber as he urged his horse across the bridge, past trundling carts and merchants laden with bulging bales. The city was already coming alive. The streets rang with voices, masters and apprentices whistling call and response, boys whirling by in search of supplies for the day's business. Corvus pushed on through the growing throng, around the slopes of the Palatine Hill alongside columns of creamy marble and porticos holding up the blue sky.

On the edge of the forum, dwarfed by the soaring arch of Septimus Severus, he tossed a coin to a boy to water the horses. When he looked round, Pavo had lost himself to the milling crowd, gambling or arguing or hunting for food. Theodosius soon followed him, in search of his conversation with God.

While Ruga and the driver stretched their legs, Corvus cupped

Hecate's hand as she climbed down from the rear of the wagon. He watched her eyes widen with either fear or amazement. A life lived in the forest had not prepared her for the bustle of Reims, never mind the vastness of Rome. This heaving mass of life, this stew of choking scents, this ringing, fierce, wild den of vices.

'I did not know there were this many people alive in the world.' She clamped her hands on her ears at the din. In awe, she craned her neck up at the towering stone buildings that clustered around the forum, the temple of Divus Iulius and the arch of Augustus, and then to the great white walls of the basilica of Maxentius, a wonder to anyone, the largest building in all the empire. She gaped, her hands slowly falling away.

'If it helps, not many of them are worth knowing,' he replied.

Her eyes darted around the ceaseless activity in the forum. 'I could never grow to like it here.'

Corvus flinched. 'You'll be well looked after during your stay,' he said, softening his voice.

She looked at him and he was pleased to see some warmth in her face. He felt responsible for her. Perhaps he felt more than that, but he wasn't quite sure. Not one for reflection, Corvus.

'Your brother is a sour man.' She glanced over at Ruga. 'He is not like you at all.'

'Crack that stone face and you'll find some kindness underneath.' *I hope.* Truth be told, he had not seen it himself.

'You are kind.'

He flinched again, this time at the honesty of her words. 'Let's not have talk like that here in Rome,' he said, sardonic. 'In this city, everyone wears a mask. Truth doesn't come to the lips easily.'

'You do not say what you feel?'

'Not usually, no.'

'Why?'

He thought for a moment. 'Survival.'

'In the forest, we must kill to survive. Beasts, for food, men who wish to take what we have.'

'I have a lot to learn from you, I can see that now.'

'Then keep your ears open and I will teach.' She half turned away, but he could see her watching him from the corners of her eyes, a faint smile on her lips.

'Corvus. Stop your gibbering. Bring her over here.' Ruga was scowling at him and beckoning.

Corvus sighed. As they walked, he could feel the warmth of Hecate's cheek as she leaned in to him. 'Where are we going?' she whispered.

'To see our mother. She comes here at this time every day to conduct her business.'

'And your mother will welcome me?'

'Of course. Gaia has a big heart.'

They pushed through the multitude towards the basilica of Maxentius. Corvus heard his mother before he saw her, her mellifluous voice floating at a pitch that carried above the rumble of the forum. She drifted among the men, elegant in an ochre dress, slender, still beautiful for all the lines on her face and the silver in her hair. A touch on an arm here, eye contact there. Laughter.

'She is a queen?' Hecate asked.

'In her mind.'

One of the men caught in Gaia's orbit locked eyes with him. Gnaeus Calidus Severus. Once seen, never forgotten. They called him the Hanged Man. His head was permanently twisted at an angle to one side, the result of a failed hanging when he had been waylaid in the countryside beyond the city walls by, some said, rivals who blamed him for a business deal gone sour. He loomed over those around him, needle-thin, with hollow cheeks and bulging eyes and a shock of white hair swept back from his forehead.

Once Severus had recognized him, Corvus watched his mother's eyes dart towards them. She smiled and babbled and charmed, winding up her audience without once letting the men around her realize they were being dismissed.

When she came over, she hugged Ruga to her breast, holding him there for a long moment, then whispering something in his ear. Always Ruga first.

Once she was done with him, Corvus returned her smile. She cupped his jaw in her hand and held his eyes. 'My son. My beautiful son,' she breathed. 'You have returned to me.'

'Mother. Still tormenting Rome?'

'Oh, Corvus.' A silent laugh, but he saw that her attention was

126

already moving on. She looked her sons' companion up and down. 'And you. Look at you.' A sweet, welcoming smile.

'I am Hecate.'

'Of course you are.' Gaia reached out to brush the strands of hair from the woman's forehead. Hecate recoiled. 'Indulge me.'

Hecate looked to him for guidance and he nodded. With clear reluctance, she held firm as his mother traced her fingers over hair, tweaked cheeks. 'You are a beauty,' Gaia said. Corvus watched her frown when she saw the witch's eyes become like grey pebbles on a winter beach. 'Please. Do not worry,' she said. 'You will be welcomed into our home like a daughter.'

A flicker of relief in Hecate's eyes.

'We were strangers in Rome once too, and we relied upon the kindness of others,' Gaia continued, her voice warm. 'You will be safe here, and well fed, and cared for, have no doubt about that.'

Corvus was pleased to see his mother's response, though he'd expected no less. She might at least take the edge off whatever Ruga had planned.

From the other side of the forum, a cry rang out. Corvus turned, trying to see past the bobbing heads straining to spot the cause of the disturbance. Merchants arguing over a price, perhaps, or a debate between friends that had turned sour.

Yet the trouble didn't die away, and within a moment he could hear that furious yell leaping from tongue to tongue until it became a wave crashing down across the great square.

'What is it?' Hecate exclaimed, frightened.

Before he could find an answer, the crowd surged in wild panic and he spun back, the flood of bodies thrusting him along in the flow. Through the confusion, he glimpsed Hecate's frightened eyes, and his mother, aghast, and then they both disappeared in the swell.

'Hecate,' Corvus yelled into the storm of screams. He felt himself lifted up, spun around, swept away. Finally he wrenched his arms free and lashed out. Thrusting bodies left and right, he carved out a space where he could stand his ground.

On the other side of the forum, he could now see fifty or more men wearing purple sashes, each of them swinging a cudgel. Heads cracked, blood spattered. Cold fury glowed in those faces, the kind he had seen in enemies ready to die on the battlefield.

Grabbing the arm of a terrified man, Corvus yanked him to a halt. 'Who are they?' he demanded.

The man flailed, fighting to wrench himself free. When he looked back at the carnage, he trembled. 'The followers of the anti-pope Ursinus, the bishop who did not win the election. They will not back down.'

Hurling the man off, Corvus dived back into the stream of fleeing people. Not far away Ruga was gripping their mother's arm, dragging her away from the fighting towards the basilica of Maxentius. Good old Ruga. He would be showered with gratitude later.

On he pushed, towards the sound of breaking bones and screams and thudding sticks. On every side, men and women, young and old, sprawled on the blood-spattered stones where they'd fallen and been trampled by the mob.

Ahead he could see the anti-pope's men drawing forward on three sides, cold-eyed fanatics all, chanting Ursinus' name with each step. Taking the brunt of the attack, a smaller group pressed forward, perhaps the followers of the elected pope. What madness was this, Christian fighting Christian in the heart of Rome?

And then he glimpsed Hecate, crouched on her hands and knees, looking round, dazed. Blood was trickling from a gash on her forehead.

Beyond her, the line of zealots advanced, like farmers beating the crops to drive the rats out.

Corvus threw himself forward, shielding the witch from the crashing sticks with his own body. The cudgels rained down and bolts of agony seared through him. Almost driven to his knees, he hooked one arm under Hecate's waist and dragged her free.

Away from the fighting, she fell into his arms. What was it he saw in her face when she looked up at him? Gratitude? Perhaps even affection? This was something he hadn't experienced before.

'Come,' he murmured in her ear. 'We have to find somewhere safe.'

Grasping her wrist, he pulled her up the steps of the basilica of Maxentius and into the central nave. The screams from the forum echoed through the vast space up to the vaulted ceiling high overhead.

By the apse at the western end, Ruga and his mother were crouching alongside other shuddering refugees from the bloody battle. Corvus knelt beside them. 'If they dare to break in here, I'll fight them off as best I can. Take the door to the Via dell'Impero and get away.'

'You cannot sacrifice yourself,' Hecate said, her voice heavy with concern.

'Corvus is a fighting man,' Ruga said. 'This is what he does.'

His brother was right, as always. That was his value.

Gaia held his stare as Ruga tugged her away. He felt a familiar frustration as he watched the three of them disappear out of the door to the Via dell'Impero, leaving him alone.

Once the sound of fighting had died away, he wandered outside. Men and women were lying in puddles of blood, their groans rising up in one rumbling exhalation.

Pavo was sitting on the steps, sunning himself.

'You survived, then,' Corvus said.

'Don't I always?'

He slumped down beside his friend. The followers of the anti-pope had melted away before they could be called to face the consequences of their actions.

'In case you were thinking of asking, my mother and brother also escaped,' he said.

'Your kin don't like me very much, you know that.'

'To be honest, very few do.'

'This is true.' Pavo closed his eyes, basking.

For a long moment Corvus watched the gulls wheeling across the blue sky above the blinding white stone of the temples. 'I'm a simple man, as you well know,' he said, 'and not given to much in the way of worrying, or deep thoughts.'

'But?'

'I worry for our new friend.'

Pavo turned on to his side. Corvus recognized the meaning behind the smile on the other man's lips. His friend was his conscience, always had been, and Pavo said things that he himself could never consider. 'You don't trust your own blood?'

'I trust my mother.'

'Ah, if only she'd given you the care and attention you truly deserved, instead of diverting it all to your brother, the favoured son.'

'I've made my peace with that.'

'And that is where you are wrong. You should be angry. You've sacrificed so much, fought so hard for your family, since your father died. You're owed some recognition, and some gratitude.'

Corvus flinched. Why had they ever fled Britannia? If they'd stayed at home, none of it would ever have happened. For a moment, he was clinging on to the rail of that ship on the heaving black seas in the middle of the night, the fire-pot trailing flames as it swung wildly in the gale. Soaked in brine, he was watching his father go over the side, watching one desperate hand reaching out before he was sucked down to the depths.

'I don't want to think about my father.'

'Think about the witch, then.' Pavo flipped back, slipping his hands behind his head. Always relaxed. Nothing ever seemed to trouble him. That was one reason why Corvus liked him so much. From when they were children, Pavo had been there, guiding him, helping him through the difficult times, and never once did he ask for anything in return.

'She seems to have a good heart. We've all heard tales about the Company of Women, how they live in the forests, clinging on to days long gone and gods that everyone else has forgotten. Plotting. Weaving their spells that bewitch good men. Agents of the fates. Cursing and hating and shaping . . . to what ends?' Corvus shrugged. 'And yet now I've met one of them, I see they're just women like any other.'

'Did you see Ruga's eyes?' That sly tone in his friend's voice. Corvus did not look round.

'They're blue, the same as mine.'

'The way he looked at Hecate. Lust, that's all there was.'

'Ruga has some plan for her, you know that.'

'That too. But answer this question: does he *deserve* her? You've seen the way Hecate looks at you. I spy an opportunity there. How many times have you deferred to your brother? He's risen up because you're too kind, too thoughtful. You've never demanded what is rightfully yours. Are you going to carry on down that road?'

'Ruga's my brother. I'm not going to pick a fight with him.'

Pavo shrugged. 'Then he wins again. And you're left with nothing. Again.'

Corvus felt something stir inside him. He liked Hecate. He didn't want to see her suffer. But what could he do?

He watched an oddly silhouetted figure shamble out of the glare of the sun towards them. Gnaeus Calidus Severus, the Hanged Man, came to a halt in front of them. Corvus felt unsettled by the scrutiny, something in the angle of the stare created by that twisted neck.

'Severus. You are well?'

'As well as can be expected.' He looked around at the men and women mopping the blood from their faces. 'The Christians fight among themselves now. But soon there will be a victor, and then they will turn their eyes back to the business at hand. They will not be satisfied until they have crushed the last of us. And only a few of us remain, you know that.' He sighed. 'Once the worship of Sol Invictus reached from the frozen wastes of the north to the hot lands in the far east. Now look at us. A frightened sect, clinging on to what we had. We are the *chryfii* now, the hidden ones, just like the pagans who followed the gods of the wood-priests. And the Christians will soon destroy all trace of them too. We are at war. Do you hear me?'

'Yes, Father,' Corvus said. Father. Priest. Wise Man. Did he harbour any suspicions about Ruga's intentions, or did he truly see the feted brother as a dutiful follower of Mithras?

'Good. Then know that this is not a time for faint hearts. Only boldness will prevail.' The Hanged Man looked round once more to make sure they were not being overheard and added, 'We are in a last desperate fight, Lucius Aurelius Corvus. The weeks to come will decide who survives, and who thrives.'

In those words he heard something that made his neck prickle. He glanced at Pavo, who nodded; he had heard it too. 'Plots, Father?'

The Hanged Man pursed his lips in thought. 'In a short time, your brother will ascend. You will be there to raise him high. And then perhaps we can discuss what is to come next.'

Corvus steeled himself and asked, 'Next, Father?'

Severus turned his head so that the sun threw his face into shadow. 'There is a mistake that all our emperors and our generals have made since Rome was first founded upon these seven hills. Things that are driven out of the light do not die. They hide in the shadows, biding their time until they can rise up again.'

'A secret world? What are you saying?'

'It is the arrogance of many to believe that the sun shines its light upon all. But there is much that is hidden from the eyes of men.' Severus folded his hands together in front of him. 'We are a civilized people, Corvus, and our wise men write down what we do so that it will be remembered. The Greeks did too, and the Persians . . .' He let the words trail off. 'But there is much that is never written down. In a hundred years there will be no record of those things and people will therefore believe they never existed. That there was only what the scribes put down. But those who do not write their histor-ies are the wisest of us all, for they live on into eternity.' He shifted his head, a bow, Corvus thought, but the twisted neck made it hard to tell. 'Some of those secrets will be revealed in due time, Corvus, and the world will change because of them.'

And then he was gone, lurching back across the forum, past the wounded.

Corvus was not sure why, but Severus' words troubled him deeply. He imagined great powers shifting away in the dark, things of which he had no knowledge, perhaps could never know. At that moment, he felt insignificant and perhaps a little unnerved. He didn't like to feel that way.

*A secret world, hidden from the eyes of men.*

'I'd planned to while away our time here in Rome with wine and women,' he said. 'But now I think it would be wise to turn over some rocks and see what scurries out from beneath.'

'You want to know more about what your brother plans,' Pavo mused.

'There's little point in asking him. He tells me nothing, even when he says he's telling me something.'

'Clever. Men who know things are powerful. Why, they might even become the favoured son.' His friend chuckled to himself. 'The invincible son.'

'The more we know, the more chance we have of keeping Hecate safe and well,' Corvus said, refusing to rise to his friend's baiting.

'A maiden who needs protecting,' Pavo said. 'It seems we have the beginning of a story.'

# CHAPTER EIGHTEEN

# The Lake

*Caledonia, far beyond Hadrian's Wall*

THE BARBARIAN'S DYING BREATH WHISPERED OUT. LUCANUS HAD curled one arm around his foe's chest from behind, the other hand pressing the knife hilt-deep into the throat. He let the lookout slide to the ground.

Here, deep into Scoti territory, this warrior would never have expected to encounter an enemy creeping alone and silent through the endless forest. And so he'd been in a reverie, watching the pink and silver streaks of the dawn reflecting off the placid lake's surface when Lucanus had ghosted out of the trees behind him.

The morning was silent, with barely a breeze soughing through the branches. Pearly strands of mist crept down towards the water's edge.

Lucanus slithered to the edge of the platform of scrubby grass and looked down a precipitous drop to the vast expanse of water that Myrrdin had described to him. An inland sea, the wood-priest had said, and he was right. The water was like polished steel reflecting the blue sky. He could dive in and fly there like a bird. On the other side of the lake steep hills rose up, slopes as dense with pine as the woods he'd trekked through for the last five days.

Nothing moved. No sign of where Marcus might be held. But that didn't mean he was alone. Since he'd left the ruins of Trimontium, he'd spent every waking hour creeping past his enemies. Scouts roamed through the woods. Lookouts watched the rivers and the crossroads. War-bands crashed across the land, their horn blasts ringing out.

So far he'd escaped discovery. The shadows of the dense forests had cloaked him and only three scouts had fallen to his blade. But that trail of blood would still be enough to bring vengeful Scoti to his location, sooner or later. He could not afford to waste any time.

By the time he'd crept along a deer track to the water's edge, a thick fog had blanketed the lake. He strained to listen, but beyond the muffled lapping no other sound reached his ears, not even the mournful cries of the gulls. He might have been alone in all the world.

Choosing a direction at random, he scrambled over the slick stones along the shore towards the east. After more than an hour of fruitless searching, he felt the hairs on his neck prickle erect and he drew his sword. Smudges were appearing in the mist among the trees, figures taking shape, silent, like ghosts. Lucanus watched them drift down the slope towards him, the fog rolling away from their feet in wreaths. There was no urgency to their movements.

On the brink of emerging from the mist, they came to a halt and stayed half swathed by the white strands. Though their faces remained hidden, Lucanus thought he could sense their implacable gaze upon him.

One of the strangers continued walking. With each step, the mist folded away from him until Lucanus realized he was looking at Myrrdin. How the wood-priest had kept pace with him he did not know. As *arcani*, he was a seasoned scout, used to long, fast marches across the wilderness, barely pausing for rest. Yet the druid looked as fresh as if he had woken from a long sleep in the comfort of his home.

Lucanus waved his blade at the wise man. 'More games?'

'We are here to greet you, Wolf, my brothers and I.'

'I said I wanted no part of your plot.'

'You say and you say, but here you are, and here are we.' Myrrdin leaned on his staff and looked him up and down.

'Where's the boy?'

'Here. Waiting for you.'

'Don't make me any more angry than I already am. You've put the lad's life at risk, and my own. If any harm comes to Marcus before I return him to his mother, I'll hunt you down and kill you.'

'You think you have some power here, Wolf?' The wood-priest was smiling, his tone wry, but Lucanus stared into eyes like nail-heads. 'Do you think you can threaten me and not pay a price? You've entered a new land now. Here your sword means nothing. You stand before the power that has guided the men of this island since the dawn of all there is.' He lifted one hand as if he were pluck-ing an apple from a tree and slowly closed his fingers. 'Your life can be crushed in the blink of an eye.'

'You think I haven't heard threats before? Give me the boy and I'll be on my way.'

'First, you must do what I asked of you in the shadow of Three Hills.'

Lucanus shook his head to try to shake that conversation free of the sludge in his mind. All he'd dwelled on over the last few days was staying alive, and the cold, and the hunger, and wondering how much longer his aching legs would be trudging through that endless forest. 'An offering, that's what you said. I should make an offering here at the lake. For good fortune.' He gritted his teeth, his frustra-tion rising.

'My words didn't fall on deaf ears, then. I struggle to tell what goes in and what bounces off that thick skull of yours.'

'And what prize must I offer the gods? One mud-stained cloak?'

'Your sword, Wolf. That's your most prized possession, yes? The gods would surely look fondly on you with such an offering.'

'Are you mad? Then what would I use in a fight?' Another frag-ment of memory surfaced and he nodded. 'Oh, that's right. The gods will give me a magic sword.' He laughed, without humour. 'You're wasting my time with stories for children, Myrrdin. No, I think I'll follow my own path. I'll keep searching for the boy.' He waved his sword. 'Go back to the woods and your hiding places.'

'There is no time, Lucanus. Your enemies are just beyond the hill behind me. A horde of Scoti, with vengeance in their hearts for the man who killed their friends.'

'You lie. They're a day away.'

'We see everything, Lucanus. The Scoti didn't need to follow the track, like you. They know quicker ways through the wilderness. They'll be here in no time. And then you will be dead, and so will the boy.'

The Wolf felt a rush of rage. Levelling his sword, he strode towards the druid.

'Kill me if you will,' Myrrdin said, 'though I cannot say I'm filled with joy at such a prospect. But I will not tell you where the boy is.'

Lucanus threw back his head and let out a roar. 'The gods couldn't blame me if I took your head now and kicked it into the lake.'

'Here?' Lucanus asked. He frowned at a narrow pier leading out from the rocky shore, ancient, by the look of it, the timbers cracked and splintered, some of the boards shattered.

'Walk to the end, say your prayer and make your offering.'

'I pray to your god?' Lucanus heard the hesitation in his voice. 'Cernunnos?'

'There are many gods, Wolf. Some of them you know by different names.' From the corner of his eye, Lucanus saw the other man purse his lips, thinking. 'Say your prayer to Lugh. It's his temple where you have to venture, and you'd do well to earn his approval.'

'Lugh.' Lucanus turned the word over, but it sounded strange on his lips.

'That's one of his names. The Romans call him Mercury. You have heard of him, of course?'

Lucanus eyed the other man.

Myrrdin nodded. 'Good. Lugh is the god of the sun and the sky. He walks the boundaries between this world and the next and he likes his games. Walk carefully under his stare – he plays tricks on even the most devout. We hold his feast when the season is hot and the harvest is about to begin. Lughnasadh. In days long gone, all the tribes would come together to make merry and prepare for the cold months to come. But now . . .' Lucanus heard a momentary note of sadness in the man's voice. 'All seasons turn, and his time will come around again.'

Lucanus nodded. He'd petitioned many a god in his time. Some listened, some had little time for the ways of men. It would be good to see if this new god . . . this old god . . . would give him aid in this time of testing.

The fog had crept back to the hillsides now and he could see clearly across the vast lake. Still and quiet as it was, he understood how the wood-priest considered this a temple, one built by the gods, not man.

He strode out along the pier, feeling the planks give under his feet. Despite his doubts, it held, and when he reached the end he drew his sword.

For a moment, he turned the blade in his hand. Was he a fool for trusting Myrrdin? What if there was no great sword beneath the waters and he was left with only his knife to defend himself – and Marcus – on the long trek back to Vercovicium?

But time was short and he had run out of choices. Raising the sword over his head, he said, 'Here is my offering to you, great Lugh. My sword, a warrior's weapon, the most valuable thing I have. I give it to you. And I pray you will guide me back safely, with Marcus by my side.' He lowered his voice until it was little more than a murmur. 'And bring Catia to me.' He felt a pang of guilt the moment he had uttered the words, but by then it was too late.

He hurled the sword. Over and over it turned, barbs of steely light glinting off it, and he watched his prized blade splash into the grey waters. The glimmering ripples rushed back to him. He waited until all was still again and then walked back to Myrrdin.

'I've done as you asked. Don't make me out to be a fool.'

'You are wise,' the druid replied. 'Wiser than you look.'

Before Lucanus could draw offence, Myrddin walked north along the shore. Lucanus watched him go for a moment, and then decided he was supposed to follow.

The fog came and went, pale fingers probing the edges of the lake. When the wood-priest came to a halt, he pointed out across the water. Lucanus followed the direction he was indicating and saw an island swathed in mist. It was long and narrow, three low hummocks covered with long grass and hawthorn. At the centre, two yew trees stood proud.

'That is Inchlonaig,' Myrrdin said.

Lucanus thought how odd it appeared, those two yews standing there.

Myrrdin saw him looking. 'Would you hear a secret?'

The Wolf nodded.

'Two yew trees, that is a sign.'

'Of what?'

'Yews mark places where the world is thin. Places blessed by the gods. See how they bend together there, side by side? Do they not look like a door?'

Squinting through the drifting pearly strands, Lucanus had to agree. The thick, gnarled trunks, as old as anything in that land; the way the branches met above. He could imagine walking between those trees and entering . . . what?

'Aye, 'tis a door,' Myrrdin continued, 'to the Land of Always Summer.'

'We are travelling to the Summerlands?' Despite himself, Lucanus felt uneasy.

The wood-priest laughed. 'That is not a place for men. But on that isle we will find what the gods would give you.'

Pulling aside the dead bracken that came almost to the water's edge, Myrrdin revealed a small, circular boat. Seasoned hide had been stretched across a frame of ash-wood. An oar rested on the bottom.

'Stir yourself,' he commanded.

Lucanus dragged the vessel across the shingle and on to the water. They clambered inside, the Wolf holding out his arms to steady himself as the boat rocked back and forth. It was less stable than the flat-bottomed vessels he was used to, and he felt sure it would flip over and send them both to the bottom.

Once they were both sitting he released a taut breath as the rocking ceased. With slow, steady strokes, first one side, then the other, the wood-priest rowed out towards the island.

The stillness settled on them. Lucanus listened to the beat of the oar licking into the water and felt a fleeting peace.

'Lakes, and rivers, the ocean, hilltops, barrows, these are thin places where it's possible for the brave to pass between this world and the world of the gods.' Myrrdin's voice rolled out, low and calm. 'And where the gods, when they felt the urge, could travel to the world of men.'

'You've met the gods?'

'They've been long absent from this place. But they will come again.'

Lucanus watched the island draw out of the shrouding fog, a black slash in the white world.

'In times long gone, folk would travel here and make offerings,'

Myrrdin continued. 'A shield, a sword, an axe, a comb . . . a sacrifice. If the gods were pleased, they would look kindly on the giver.'

Lucanus glanced over the side of the boat. For a moment he thought he saw a face looking back up at him from the grey depths, but it was only his own.

At the island, he splashed into the shallows and pulled the boat up on to the stony shore, and then he stood for a moment, listening. No birds sang there. He found that strange and unsettling. An odd mood hung over the place, like the heaviness before a storm, or perhaps it was just his mind playing tricks upon him after all the wood-priest's talk.

Myrrdin crunched along the stones, beckoning. Lucanus followed him to a finger of rock reaching out into the water. At the end a cairn had been raised. He squatted in front of it, his fingers tracing the lines that had been carved in the surface. A man's face peering out of a halo of ivy and branches.

'Here is where you will find if Lugh has answered your call.' Myrrdin swept out an arm, indicating the water beyond the cairn. 'Dive deep, Wolf. Seek out the weapon of kings. If it is there, Lugh will bring your eyes to it.'

'And if it's not?'

'Then take the boy and return to your life. Our search for the Pendragon will continue.'

Lucanus wanted to ask what that odd word meant – he had not heard it before – but his eyes were gripped by the calm surface of the lake. 'The water's too cold. The warm-sleep will claim me and I'll be in the Summerlands before I know it.'

'Wisdom only comes when a man walks close to death. The gods will not give gifts to one who is faint of heart.' Lucanus felt Myrrdin's hand upon his shoulder, and the wood-priest leaned in and whispered, 'Step up to the threshold of the Summerlands, Wolf. Find your fate.'

# CHAPTER NINETEEN

# *The Sword*

As the grey water closed over him, Lucanus felt the clash of bitter cold like the flat of a blade to the side of the head. Then he was plunging down, into the deep, into the dark, to the very edge of the Summerlands.

Faces flashed through his head. His father. Bellicus. But most of all Catia. He prayed he would see her again before he was taken.

The darkness swept in around him. Drifting flakes of peat added to the murk, but he pulled himself on with strong, rhythmic strokes, trusting his senses. Close to the shore, the bottom fell away only gently and his fingers were soon scraping the mud.

Looking around, he could just make out objects half submerged in the silt. As he heaved himself on, the wheel of a half-buried shield emerged from the gloom, the wood rotted and falling away. Bumps and mounds across the muddy expanse revealed the resting places of long-lost offerings, their true nature only hinted at by their shape.

Swimming as low as he could, he let his fingers scrape across the bottom. His nails hooked under something hard and a goblet popped up. Gold, by the look of it, its surface studied with jewels. Vast riches lay there. But these were the possessions of the gods. To steal from them would surely damn him for all time.

His bones were aching from the cold. He'd seen men claimed by the warm-sleep before, in the seas to the west, and in the snows in the Wilds, men who were not used to hardship like the *arcani*. But even though he knew he was stronger than most, he could already feel his light dimming.

*Turn back,* a voice in his head urged. *Plead failure. Take Marcus and be gone.*

But now he wanted that sword, wanted it perhaps more than he had wanted anything in his life.

He swam on, though his limbs felt like stone and his chest burned.

Ahead was an area of deeper dark where the lake bottom fell away, and on the edge of that abyss . . . something. Lucanus squinted, trying to draw the shape from the gloom. A spear, he thought, thrown from the cairn, the tip embedded in the mud.

But no. The shape was irregular.

Two more strokes and he felt a swell of disbelief.

An arm was reaching up from the silt, stripped to the bone by the fish and the years, the fingers still gripping the hilt of a sword. Though the rest of the body was buried in the brown muck, that blade stabbed up towards light and life. Weeds floated from the blade like banners at the head of a war-band. Shafts of sunlight punched through the water around it, as if it were a beacon lit by the gods for his benefit alone.

Surely this must be the prize he desired?

He grasped the blade and tugged, but the owner held tight.

Lucanus jerked, his head throbbing with panic. Was this Lugh the trickster's final joke, luring him to the edge of victory only to snatch away his life for daring to take such a gift?

But then a sliver of gold glimmered in a sunbeam and he looked down at a fine wire fastening the sword-hilt to the bony wrist. More wire coiled around the arm bones towards the elbow and beyond. This was the work of men, not gods.

He floated, darkness rolling in around the edges of his vision, fingers of warmth creeping towards his heart. He could hear whispers lulling him, and the slowing beat of a distant drum.

*My life is leaking from me,* he thought, and felt surprised that he no longer cared.

Yanking on the blade, he wrenched it free. The wire snapped. The arm bones felt apart and drifted down to the silt.

And then he was striking out for the surface, his body cold stone, the light only a pinprick at the centre of his vision.

★

The smell of woodsmoke. The crackle of a fire.

As he rose up from the darkness, back into the world of men, Lucanus could feel warmth flooding his limbs. He stirred, and the wool of Myrrdin's cloak was rough against his arms. The smell of loam and incense filled his nose.

'Not dead, then,' he muttered.

The wood-priest looked down the bridge of his nose at him. 'There's more to you than a first glance would suggest, it seems.'

The Wolf pushed himself up. His head was like a stew too long in the pot. Looking around, he saw the fog had drifted away and a wintry sun made the lake gleam like molten lead.

'We can't rest here. Our enemies will soon be on us.'

'That's true. Sometimes you can hear their hunting cries ring out in the distance. But even I've not found a way to make a half-dead man run like a deer.'

'What, then? We stand and fight an army?'

'We? You fight if you wish. I still have wits in my head.' Myrrdin threw more wood upon the fire.

Lucanus dragged himself to his feet. He swayed, his legs almost crumpling beneath him. Light flashed across his vision and the dark closed in again.

He felt a hand on his shoulder, steadying him. 'Take your time. Find your strength. You are *arcani*, Wolf. You have the stealth and cunning that allow you to melt into the land. If the gods are with you, you will creep back through those barbarians, however many lie between here and your home.'

A thought flickered up from the depths. 'The boy,' Lucanus said. 'Marcus.'

'In good time. You've kept your side of the bargain. I'll give you what you want, in just a short while. But first, see what you've claimed.'

Myrrdin swept out one hand. On the ground, on Lucanus' sodden wolf pelt, lay the sword he'd brought back from the edge of the Summerlands. The wood-priest had scrubbed away the weeds and must have spent some time polishing it too. The blade now had the brown sheen of bronze, not like the iron weapons Lucanus was used to. A sharper edge, a weapon that wouldn't bend or break so easily in battle. He could just make out thin black lines inscribed on the blade, but what those strange symbols meant he had no idea. The hilt was inlaid with gold, the pommel curling into the head of a dragon. This surely must be a weapon of great age, the sword of the gods, a blade of kings, as the wood-priest had said.

'What do you see?' Myrrdin asked.

'A sword,' he said as if the other man was a fool.

The wood-priest nodded. 'Good. That's what a warrior should see.'

Picking up the weapon, the Wolf weighed it in his hand, turning it so the thin sunlight gleamed along the edge. 'As swords go, it's not much,' he said with a shrug. Even as the words left his mouth, he knew he didn't believe them.

'Look closer. Many men would hold this weapon and each would see a different thing. It has a name. Caledfwlch.'

'And that's not much of a name.'

'Still, it is what it is – a gift from the gods. With this blade you'll carve out your days yet to come, Lucanus, and the days yet to come of all men. Here.' Myrrdin disappeared among the scrubby hawthorns beyond the fire and returned with a leather scabbard. He held it out. It was well crafted, stitched and branded with a design of interlocking spirals.

'Where did you get that?'

'We've been preparing for this moment for long seasons. Do you think this was just a new day unfolding as all days do? You've been shaped, and guided, and what has happened to you has been shaped and guided. We've waited a long time, Lucanus, but now the wheel is turning.'

The Wolf felt a shiver run down his spine. He didn't like the thought that his life was not his own, and that the gods, and the witches, and these wood-priests were moving him like a piece on a tavla board. He glanced around, half expecting to see the three women there among the trees, waving their hands and pulling on the strands of his fate.

'Now,' he snapped. 'I'm ready. The boy.'

Myrrdin nodded. Lucanus stumbled along after him on a meandering path through the dense hawthorn trees. The way led steadily upward on the central hummock of the island until he could see the two yews swaying ahead of him. How old they looked, he thought as he neared, the trunks so wide that two men could scarce encircle them with their arms.

'You would take me through that door to the otherworld?' He tried to hide any tremor in his voice. The stories he'd heard around the hearth-fire still haunted him. Men lured by the gods to a land where they whirled in dance for a night, only to find a hundred years had passed at home and all that they knew was long gone.

'Should the gods wish you to join them there, they will summon you.' The wood-priest leaned on his staff as he hauled himself up the incline. 'Though I would think it would not be for your silver tongue.'

Lucanus grunted. He thought he could sense Myrrdin smiling, though the man's back was to him.

At the summit, the yews swayed in a light breeze. The Wolf looked around. Were those the cries of approaching enemies that he could hear? Or perhaps it was just the shriek of birds.

Eyeing the space between the yews as if Lugh would come dancing out and steal him away, Lucanus trudged behind the wood-priest round to the other side. When he saw the small shape lying under the trees, he forgot all his worries in an instant. Scrambling under the branches, he dropped to Marcus' side.

At first he thought the boy was dead. Only his face was visible in the folds of a thick cloak, but his skin was like snow, his chest barely rising and falling.

But then Marcus' eyes flickered open and he smiled. 'Lucanus. I had the strangest dream.'

'You're well?' He rested his hand on the boy's forehead. It was cold, not feverish, and Lucanus wondered if the wood-priest had given him some potion that had stolen his wits.

Marcus sat up, almost banging his head on the overhanging branches. 'Where am I?'

'A long way from home. But soon we'll have you back with your mother. If Myrrdin has stopped playing his games.'

'Who's Myrrdin?'

Lucanus jerked a thumb over his shoulder. When he saw a blank look on Marcus' face, he looked round and realized they were alone. Crawling out from beneath the branches, he stood on the summit and scanned the island.

The wood-priest had vanished as if he'd never been there.

145

# CHAPTER TWENTY

# The Battle Lost and Won

*Vercovicium*

IN THE DAWN, THERE WAS ONLY SILENCE.

No hails of *well met*, no laughter, no hammers upon anvil, no whistles of masters to apprentices, no songs of mothers, no curlew-calls of pig-herders.

Amarina shivered and not just from the cold, though she was not sure why. Puzzling over that unnatural quiet, she clip-clopped across whorls of frozen mud towards the *vicus*. She had decided to spend some of her hard-earned coin on a piece of silver jewellery, perhaps a brooch, one imported from Rome and crafted with a delicacy she would never be able to find in her grim homeland. There were rewards to be found in this life here, if you had a full purse; comforts that warmed the heart on bitter nights.

But as she neared the entrance to an alley that ran between the tavern and the chandler's, she saw a crescent of bowed heads, about twenty in all. Clouds of breath drifted up, but no one moved, no one spoke.

Pushing through the stiff bodies to the front, she stood for a moment, taking in what she was seeing.

A body lay face down on the hard earth and ridges of ice, the third in as many nights. A large brown stain surrounded it where the hot blood had soaked into the earth and frozen. It had no head and the flesh around the raw wound looked to have been gnawed.

'What do they want of us?' someone muttered.

'How can they come and go as they please?' another asked.

'These cannot be men.' The final voice was little more than an exhalation.

*Daemons,* Amarina thought.

She understood the desperation she heard in those voices. They were wondering who would be taken next, and where it would end.

A tramp of feet and clatter of metal echoed from the direction of the fort. Amarina turned to see Atellus, Falx and eight other men jogging down the slope. The commandant's face was like thunder.

The citizens parted to let the soldiers through and Falx dropped down by the body. Amarina watched his bovine expression flickering with confusion as he looked around for the missing head, and then his face falling further when he realized it had been taken.

'First at one of the villas, then in the fields, now here, in the very heart of the *vicus,* ' Atellus said, his jaw clenched.

*Closer with each step.*

The commandant grunted. 'They are testing our defences, and our resolve.'

'And they have found their answer,' Amarina said.

The people around her edged away. Atellus and the others glared, looking away when they saw who had spoken.

'Make no mistake, we will not rest until we have hunted down these barbarians and shown them what it means to challenge us,' the commandant said. 'If they came in numbers, there would be more dead than this. No, we can be satisfied only a few scouts crept in, perhaps only one.'

'One was enough for this poor soul. How did they get past the wall and all the men upon it?' Amarina pressed. Perhaps it was time for her to move away to a safer place, one where men were happy to pay for the beast with two backs instead of worrying about keeping their heads on their shoulders.

Atellus had no answer. He flexed his fingers and two of his men grabbed the arms of the corpse and began to drag it away.

As the soldiers made their way back to the fort, Amarina saw them pause to exchange a few words with Mato, who was coming in the opposite direction. His head was down, no doubt weary from another night out scouring the Wilds.

'I see a man in need of comfort,' she called.

'Men always need comfort. If we could choose our time we would have nothing but comfort,' Mato said, his grin lighting his face.

'That's because you grow beards, but never grow up. If not for women, where would you be?'

Glancing around to make sure they were not being overheard, Mato whispered, 'How is Catia?'

'As well as can be expected for a captive.' She shrugged. 'Though she hurts now, she'll grow stronger from it.'

'You speak from the heart.'

Amarina nodded. 'My mother and father were killed by wild dogs. I survived in the forest, feeding on roots and leaves until a kindly merchant saved me.'

Mato cocked an eyebrow and grinned.

'You are a wise man, Mato. You should not be living your life in the Wilds.'

'But where would my brothers be without my wisdom?'

A hubbub broke through the early morning stillness. Amarina turned to see men hammering on door jambs and barking questions at anyone they could find.

'Varro's guards,' Mato muttered.

Behind them, Amatius bowed his head in intense conversation with anyone who crossed his path.

'The merchant is searching for Catia.' Amarina watched the men progress methodically among the workshops and the huts.

'Why so much effort spent for one woman? You have a house full of more willing ones.'

'This is about more than where he puts his cock for the night. There's a larger web here than you or I understand, and Varro is a fat spider at the heart of it.'

The guards kicked their way through a brood of clucking hens, frightening a young boy who sat by the door. He began to bawl, but the men pushed on regardless.

'Leave me be!' The widow Elsia was cringing away from three guards snarling questions.

'Heed her,' Mato called. Amarina watched him march down to the three men, holding his arms wide. 'It's a cold day, but a good one, friends. Let's enjoy this morning, not sour it with harsh words.'

'This is not your business,' one of the guards said. He drew his short sword and pointed it at Mato. 'But if you want a fight, we're happy to join you. All three of us.'

'I'm a poor fighting man. My skill with a sword is like that of a one-armed drunk,' Mato replied, still grinning.

'Then leave,' the guard said. 'Before I teach you a lesson.'

Amarina stepped forward. 'I'm good with a blade.'

The guard looked her up and down. 'Ah. The whore. You would be skilled at handling blades.' The other men laughed.

'I would rather be a whore than a man without a cock.'

The guard sneered. 'I have a cock.'

'Now.' Amarina held the guard's gaze.

'These numbers are not right.'

She glanced back at the booming voice. Bellicus was making a show of cracking his knuckles, his dog, Catulus, bounding at his heels. He winked at the widow Elsia, who beamed at her saviour, and then he loomed over the guard who had spoken, who took a step back now his advantage had gone.

'No fighting. No blood.' Seemingly out of nowhere the dwarf danced between the two men. 'We are guests here. The master's name dishonoured? Will he reward for that? No, I say, no.' Bucco turned to Bellicus and took a step back himself, craning his neck up, and up. 'Head in the clouds. Hello. Hellooo.' He cupped his hands around his mouth, shouting, 'Can. You. Hear?'

The tension broken, the guards grunted and moved on.

'You have some skill there,' Amarina said.

'Not much of one, Domina. No. But little men learn. Make big what little things you have.' The dwarf eyed the disappearing guards, and when he was sure they were too far away to overhear he turned back to the others. 'Save me, kind people, save me,' he pleaded. 'I have a cruel master. He beats me long and hard. Take me with you, brothers and sister. Hide me away, like the fair Catia. Save my hide. And I will show you how to save yours.'

Amarina smiled, tight and hard, and she knew the dwarf would read her eyes. There'd be no saving him.

The north wind whined across the grassland, flecked with snow, and a waning moon silvered the frost. With her hood pulled low over her brow, Amarina strode away from Vercovicium. Far behind her, the torches over the gates of the fort were little more than twinkling stars in the dim reaches of the night.

She felt a slow-burning anger that had to be addressed, not caused by Varro or any of his men. No, it was the sense of the ground shifting under her feet that truly annoyed her. She'd worked hard to earn a little security and she would not see it all torn away from her. But now plots were circling away in the dark, and people far greater than she were playing games that would disrupt her life as if she were nothing.

When she reached the Blood Spring – so-called because the waters trickled with a rusty tint – she turned towards the south and marched up the gently rising incline until she reached the high ground. There, at the flat summit, in the centre of a wide area of blasted grassland, was the Birthing Stone, a jagged tooth of granite, lichen-dappled and flayed by the elements. Away in the dark, six other stones circled it, smaller ones that came midway up her shin, not to her waist like this one. Old stories said they were six warriors and their king, turned to stone for defying the gods.

Amarina traced her fingertips across the rock's rough surface, remembering other nights like this.

She struck a flint and the torch she'd been carrying flared into life.

How long she stood there she didn't know, but her body felt as numb as the stone beside her. For a while, she thought her call would not be answered – the wyrd sisters were mercurial and mysterious in their ways. But then she caught sight of movement away in the dark.

Amarina raised the torch higher. The wavering light washed out to where three women waited.

'Hecate,' she said.

'Yes,' they replied.

They had always been strange, but Amarina expected no more of women who lived their lives in the Wilds, with only wolf and crow and fox for company. They consumed their toadstools and set their thoughts to flying, and bubbled up pots of herbs and roots that twisted their minds. They spoke to the gods and the daemons and both spoke back. Madness for them was an old friend. But they were wise too, with knowledge passed down from mother to daughter from the earliest days. They knew secrets of which she could only dream.

'What do you want, sister?'

Amarina could tell from the softer voice that it was the youngest of them speaking. 'The Ouroboros, sister. The dragon that eats its own tail. You know this sign and what it means.'

'Aye. The season is turning. What once was will be again.'

'This is happening now?' Amarina stressed. 'As it was foretold . . . as it was hoped for . . . by you . . . by the wood-priests. Now, not in days yet to come?'

Wind blasted and the torch roared. Amarina's cloak lashed around her.

'The whispers beyond the wall have grown to a shout,' the youngest of the three women replied. 'Too much of our blood has been spilled. But now our time has come round again. We have been told the Dragon is rising, and that word has spread, beyond the wall, to Hibernia, Gaul, everywhere. The Dragon is rising, do you hear?'

'This can't be true.' Amarina reached out a hand to the three figures cloaked by the night beyond the torch's light. 'I've heard those old tales, so many times. They're stories to soothe children.'

'We have been told,' the second of the women repeated, her voice hardening. 'And now all Rome's enemies have hope. For if the Dragon is among us we cannot be crushed as we were that night on Ynys Môn.'

*Conspiratio.* The Roman word leapt into her mind. Amarina's thoughts flew back to her childhood, branches tearing at her face as she fled through the forest to escape the soldiers. When the shadowy figures among the trees slaughtered the men at her back and gave her a place to hide, she'd soon learned that the old ways had never gone away. They were still there, in the Wilds and the woods, in all the lands that Rome had conquered, a resistance surviving on old promises and prayers to old gods, waiting to rise up again, even though hundreds of years had passed since their defeat.

She shook her head. 'No. This is madness.' How many wood-priests and wise women still clung on to their beliefs? A handful here and there? Who would listen to them? 'This . . . this king that you have been promised for so long . . . you think he can challenge Rome? One man?' she said.

'Rome will be long gone by then.' This time it was the oldest speaking, her voice crackling with phlegm. 'The Bear-King will find a world burned clean, and he will remake it.'

'This is the time,' the youngest one continued. 'Rome is ailing, its power fading. If not now, then when?'

'And what power do you have? If you challenge Rome, you'll be crushed.'

'The Attacotti have come, sister.'

The words hung in the dark and Amarina shivered.

For long moments, there was only the howling of the wind. Amarina squinted to make sure the three women had not melted away into the night.

'Go back to your home and prepare yourself,' the youngest said eventually. 'All that you know will be burned away. Death is coming, and only the Bear-King will be able to lead you out of the long night.'

# PART TWO

# The Fall

*It is easy to go down into Hell; night and day, the gates of dark Death stand wide; but to climb back again, to retrace one's steps to the upper air – there's the rub, the task.*

Virgil, *The Aeneid*

## CHAPTER TWENTY-ONE

# *The Hunt*

THE BLAST OF THE HORN MOANED THROUGH THE FOREST. ANOTHER answered, closer still. Ahead of the wave of echoes, the man and the boy ran, as they'd been running for a day and a half now.

'How close are they?' Marcus blinked away tears, of fear or from the exertion, Lucanus wasn't sure.

'Close enough. Don't look back.'

The Wolf clawed his way up a steep slope, over snaking roots, under the grasping fingers of low branches. He'd tried to keep the lad's spirits up, but Marcus was no fool. He knew exactly what the barbarians at their back were capable of.

He watched the lad's trembling hands as he levered himself up, and the shudder that racked his legs. Exhaustion was setting in. Against his own command, he glanced back and saw movement in the half-light among the trees. Closer, now. It was only a matter of time before they caught up.

Once they'd scrambled on to a plateau, Lucanus grabbed Marcus' shoulders and looked him deep in the face. 'Time to use our wits,' he breathed.

Under the overhanging branches of a fir, a trench had been carved into the forest floor by the spring rains flooding down the hillside. Tufts of yellow grass edged the furrow. Lucanus pushed the boy in, then threw himself on top, pulling his wolf pelt tight over them. He prayed they would be unseen in the gloom.

For a while there was nothing. His skin bloomed at the warmth

155

of the body beneath him and the pattering of a small heart fluttered against his chest.

He mouthed another prayer, to Lugh, to Cernunnos, to any god who might be listening.

A branch cracked and he almost moved.

Feet tramped on frozen ground. A shout, a rumbling reply. And then the sound of laboured breathing, so loud it could have been at his elbow.

Lucanus stiffened. For what seemed like an age, his ears burned at the sound of that ragged breathing. A heavy hand was about to fall on him, he was sure of it.

At the moment when he thought his chest was ready to burst, the rasping floated away. Heaving in a draught of cold air, he loosened his muscles and felt the boy sag beneath him. A brief respite. He could still hear the war-band trundling all around.

The last day and night had blurred by. One moment he'd been paddling away from the Isle of Yews in the small round boat, with Marcus hunched behind him, and then he'd heard the barbarians crashing down to the rocky shores of the lake and there'd been nothing but running and hiding and praying as he picked a way through the enemy lines.

Why had the wood-priest abandoned them? Was this another test? The Wolf ground his teeth. He was sick of the questions and the plots, of being led on a dance that could cost him his life.

Through that simmering anger, he began to realize that all was now silent. Inching up his head, he peered over the lip of the trench.

'Do you hear anything?' Marcus whispered.

'No, but that's not a good sign. I don't hear the birds and they should be in full throat if the barbarians were far enough away not to be a threat. Stay strong. Soon.'

'I'm not afraid.'

Lucanus stifled a smile. He felt proud of this boy. He was tough and clever, not afraid of a little hardship, unlike many of the pampered children of wealthy merchants. There was a great deal of Catia's spirit in him, and he would need all of it in the days to come.

'Perhaps I'll teach you some of the ways of the *Arcani*, but you mustn't tell your father,' he breathed.

'Why?'

'He wants you to grow up to be a man with smooth hands, who reads and writes and lives a gentle life. And that's a good thing. Who'd wish to crawl in the mud and gnaw on roots and raw meat like a beast?'

'I want to do what you do, Lucanus.'

'No,' he said firmly. 'I'll teach you some things . . . ways that can help keep you safe should you find yourself in danger. But if I gave you any encouragement to become one of the *arcani*, your mother would beat me to death with my own sword.'

The boy chuckled.

In that moment, it was easy to forget that everything had now changed. Even if they survived this ordeal there would be no return to the peace of life in Vercovicium, not for the boy who carried the blood of kings and not for the man charged to defend him. If there was one thing he had learned about emperors and kings, it was that death always followed one step behind them.

The sun was already slipping towards the west when the slanting shafts of thin light breaking through the canopy began to wink out one by one. Lucanus craned his neck to look up through the high branches. Heavy clouds were banking overhead. Soon snow was falling, at first only a few large flakes, but then the flurries blew thick and fast and a white carpet unfurled across the forest floor.

The Wolf looked back along the pairs of footprints now chasing them along the trail and felt his chest tighten. It was as if the gods themselves were conspiring against them.

Beside him, Marcus stumbled, his exhausted legs giving out. Lucanus caught him before he fell and worried that the boy's hands were like stone. 'Here,' he said, stripping off his cloak and wrapping it around him.

'I'm warm enough,' Marcus protested, eyeing the Wolf's bare arms.

'You're a hardy soul, but it will grow colder still when night has fallen. My skin's thicker than yours and I'm used to being abroad in winter. The blood of wolves courses through my veins, you know that. Besides, if you freeze to death I'll only have to carry you.'

The boy nodded, sinking into the folds. As brave as the lad was,

Lucanus saw relief in his eyes. Marcus was too young for these hard-ships. It was a miracle he'd survived so far, and there were miles still to go, in the bitter cold, with scant food supplies to be found in the forest, and the barbarians relentless in their pursuit.

By the time the last of the light had faded, the snow was gripping their ankles and the crunch of their feet rolled out in a steady beat, too loud in the stillness. Lucanus leaned against a trunk to give Marcus a chance to catch his breath, and in the ensuing quiet cocked his head and listened.

When the wind in the branches dropped, he heard low voices somewhere ahead.

'Wait here,' he whispered.

Following the guttural conversation, he crept through the trees. Bursts of raucous laughter punctuated the conversation. These men were not trying to hide. He blinked away stinging snowflakes and saw a light glimmering ahead, a fire, another war-band at camp. How many of these bastards were roaming through the woods? Shouldn't they be at home by the warm hearth with their women?

Lucanus prowled as close as he dared. Crouching beside a fir, he watched perhaps fifty men in furs and leather hunched around three fires. His nostrils wrinkled at the sweet, sticky scent of roasting venison and his stomach growled in response.

Satisfied the Scoti had settled for the night, he followed his foot-prints back through the trees. But when he reached the place where he had left the boy, his heart thumped and he whirled around.

'Marcus,' he hissed, fighting back panic.

'Here.'

The lad was grinning down at him from the branches above his head.

Lucanus wagged a finger at him. 'You gave me a scare.'

'And wouldn't the great Lucanus have found a hiding place to keep himself safe?'

This boy continued to surprise him. A battler, a survivor. Perhaps the blood of kings *did* flow through his veins.

Once Marcus had clambered down, Lucanus lifted him on to his back and bowed into the gusting snow.

'We're taking a different path?' the boy asked.

'The barbarians are blocking our way and they may well have

watchmen far off on their flanks. I'm loath to waste more time, but we have to travel towards the west until it's safe to skirt them.'

Lucanus cursed under his breath. He'd wanted to make camp, light a fire for warmth, but now he couldn't risk that. They had to keep moving, put some space between them and their enemies.

After a while, he felt Marcus' head flop on to his shoulder and the boy's body grow limp. His breathing became regular, punctuated by low snores.

Lucanus' ears pulsed with the howling of the wind, but when the gale dropped for just an instant, he thought he heard something at his back. When he turned and listened, he felt his blood run cold.

A yowling rolled through the trees, the sound of the Scoti whipped into a frenzy of hunting. High-pitched whistles rang back and forth.

His trail in the snow had been discovered.

Lucanus thundered into a loping run. Marcus jolted awake at the sudden movement.

'What is it?' His voice was thick with sleep.

'Our enemies are upon us. Pray to the gods. We need their aid.'

'I'm weighing you down.' Though Lucanus fought him, the boy wriggled off his back.

'No. Your legs are tired—'

'I'm strong. I can run as fast as you.'

As they leapt a narrow stream trickling down from the higher ground, he caught the boy and yanked him back. 'Follow me,' he whispered.

Splashing into the water, he bounded up the brook. After a moment, he heard Marcus behind him.

'They will not be able to follow our footprints here,' the boy said, understanding.

'It will buy us a little time. But they're not fools, these barbarians. When our prints in the snow disappear, they'll guess where we went soon enough.'

As he stepped out of the stream and resumed the journey west, he heard baffled cries ring out away in the gulf of night. A moment later the howls and whistles began again.

'Look,' Marcus gasped after they'd raced on a little further.

When Lucanus raised his eyes from the ground, he followed the boy's pointing arm and saw flames dancing among the trees ahead of them. Torches.

'Another war-band?' he gasped. It must be. The ones at their backs could never have circled ahead of them in that short time.

Lucanus veered off the path he was on, listening to the howls and whistles sweep back and forth, fading out when the wind blasted stronger, only to return with greater force. They were deer, being run down by seasoned hunters.

'What can we do?'

Lucanus heard a tremor in the boy's voice. 'For now, run. We may find a place to hide somewhere ahead.'

They skidded up to the lip of a slope which plunged down into the dark. A valley. Scooping the boy up, Lucanus threw the two of them over the edge and they careered down the slope, a sea of bracken washing past his legs. Whipped snowflakes burned his eyes. A tree loomed out of the dark and he swerved at the last moment, the branches tearing at his face as he sped by.

And then they thundered on to the valley floor, steep slopes soaring up on three sides. Dropping Marcus to his feet, Lucanus plunged on into the dark along the only way open to him.

The howls and whistles died away and then there was just the thud of their feet on the whitening ground. Somehow the silence that pressed in was even worse.

When the fir trees thinned out, he thought he could make out a track disappearing into the night. Another byroad? That would allow them to move faster than the warriors trying to keep pace with them on the higher ground. As the wind whipped up a blizzard along the glen, he slowed his step, unsure.

'What if more wait for us ahead?' Marcus asked, reading Lucanus' hesitation.

'I'll fight them. I have a magic sword now.'

'A magic sword?'

'Aye. A gift from the gods, so fear not for me. Whatever happens, you must run on, though. Don't wait. Don't look back. I'll find you.'

He could feel the boy's eyes on him as he pounded on. Marcus was clever. He could see the lie.

'Keep running until you find a village,' Lucanus pressed. 'A boy like you, they'll give you food, a place to stay warm. Then keep going. See where the sun rises and mark its track in the sky. Head south. You'll reach the wall soon enough, if I've not found you by then.'

'I will not look back.' Marcus' voice floated to him, filled with determination. Somehow that made him feel worse.

And then the world fell away from him, just as it had once before.

Lucanus crashed on to hard ground, his breath smashed from him, and he was looking up at a square lighter than the darkness around him, snowflakes whipping across it. For the second time he'd plunged into a pit covered over with branches and turf, and hidden further by the covering of snow, an old hunter's trick. He roared his anguish.

The Scoti had herded him to where they wanted him to be, knowing full well he would keep on the track through the forest, for speed.

A silhouette appeared on the edge of that square. Marcus was looking down at him.

'Run,' he yelled. 'Run now. And may the gods be with you.'

The boy whisked away and the beat of running feet echoed into the hole.

Lucanus dropped his head into his hands, but only for a moment. Then he was on his feet, clawing at the side of the pit. A thin hope: the barbarians had dug their trap well. The sides were smooth, the ground so frozen he couldn't even gouge out a hand-hold with his fingernails.

'What have we here? A rat?'

Torchlight flickered around the hole, and in that orange glow he could make out a man crouching by the lip of the pit, grinning, the flames dancing in his eyes. It was Erca, the bear-like warrior Lucanus had glimpsed from his hiding place in the forest when the war-band had first passed him by.

'I'm a traveller, lost in the forest,' Lucanus began, in the Scot's own tongue.

Erca wagged a finger at him. 'Lost in the woods you may well be, for you're far from home. But I know your kind. I can smell the stink of you a day's march away. You have the blood of my people upon you.'

Lucanus looked up into that face, seeing the certainty there. What point lying? He must face his fate like a man.

'Say your prayers to your Roman gods,' Erca continued. 'Your days are done.'

# CHAPTER TWENTY-TWO

# *The Camp*

LUCANUS' EYES FLICKERED OPEN. A PUDDLED TRACK WAS trundling by beneath him. Sounds rushed in. Birds shrieking. The tramp of feet and the snort of horses, the steady drip of water from the high branches. He shook his head, feeling his senses slowly coalesce. Bolts of agony seared his joints and he realized he was hanging face down, his wrists and ankles bound above him.

Craning his neck, he squinted into bright sunlight slanting among trees. Through the flashes he could make out a Scoti warrior on each end of the branch on which he'd been strung. One of them saw him looking and laughed. 'Ah, you Roman bastard. Now you know what a deer carcass feels like.'

The Wolf glowered, hiding his bitterness that he'd allowed himself to be captured, but that only made them laugh harder.

He felt memories surface. That first night was little more than a blur. Once his enemies had hauled him out of the pit, they'd beaten him with such savage fury he'd lost consciousness. After that he'd drifted in and out of wakefulness, caught in a web of pain. He recalled blood caking his eyes so that he could barely force them open, and water from a hide sloshing on his cracked lips.

At some point, he'd been chewing on venison while he lay on the cold earth beside one of the fires, each new chunk forced between his lips. Through the smoke he'd watched his captors in the orange glow from the flames, hunched like bears in their furs and leathers, with their wild manes and beards. Sometimes he'd caught their coal eyes and felt a deep chill.

They were only keeping him alive so he could endure even greater agonies, he knew.

A hand gripped his hair and yanked his head up and he looked into the broad face of Erca, the features dashed here and there with scars. The Scoti leader's eyes sparkled.

'Still alive? That's good,' he said in his rumbling voice. 'You'll be of some use to us, at least for a short while.'

'Where are you taking me?' Lucanus winced when he heard his voice, so hoarse it was little more than a whisper. They had turned him into a ghost of his former self.

'Soon you'll see something one of your kind has never seen, and lived.' A sly smile.

The barbarian flung Lucanus' head down. Through slit eyes, the Wolf watched his tormentor stride to the head of the column of men. They'd been travelling a broad, well-used track through the forest, generally towards the west, so the shifting light told him. One war-band, around thirty men.

Colours and light surfaced from the constant gloom of the forest, and as Lucanus squinted ahead he thought that the trees were thinning. After a while the track passed the stumps of creamy wood still showing the marks of axes. Undergrowth had been cleared. His nose filled with sweet woodsmoke from smouldering bonfires of branches and brush.

Lucanus screwed up his eyes as they burst from the shadows of the forest into a sunlit expanse. When he looked again, he could see waving grass on either side and he breathed in the scent of roasting venison and the earthy reek of a great number of folk gathered in one place. The beat of hammers and axes rang out in the distance, accompanied by a chorus of raucous singing. Loud voices called from the front of the column.

'Wait.'

Erca strode back towards him as he swung to a halt.

'Raise him up. Let him see what is waiting for him.'

The two men heaved the pole upright and Lucanus stifled a cry as his shoulders wrenched. When the mist of pain cleared from his eyes, he looked out across a teeming tent-city filling a basin that reached to a row of low hills on the horizon. Under a thick pall of smoke, many fires glowed red. The sound of hammers he had heard came from forges; his nostrils flared at the bitter scent of those furnaces. When the wind shifted, he breathed in the musk of horses and saw that one side of the camp was given over to an enclosure; more mounts than he had ever seen in his life. Boys wandered among them, tossing handfuls of hay.

'What do you think of our moot, Roman?' Erca murmured close to his ear. He drew his long knife, leaned in, and Lucanus felt his bonds grow tight. First his legs swung free, then his wrists, and he tumbled forward on to the mud, too weak to support his own weight. The barbarians around him laughed and his cheeks burned.

'Crawl into our camp on your hands and knees so everyone can see you for the dog you are,' Erca said, 'or stand and walk like a man.'

Lucanus steeled himself against the agony in his ankles and hips. A cold anger froze his heart; his pride was all he had left and he would not easily give that up. Pushing himself upright, he swayed on his feet for a moment. The barbarians watched him, still laughing. One step, then another.

The Wolf swallowed his pain and trudged to his doom.

At the edge of the camp, a rotting head on a pole looked down its nose at two sentries warming their hands over a bonfire.

Lucanus stumbled past them into the throb of life, his ears ringing with the din of the hammers, the yapping of hounds, the bellowed conversations in tongues he could barely recognize, choking on the miasma of shit and piss and smoke, roasting meat, the tang of burned iron.

Faces flashed by him, and in the whirl a few moments passed before he realized what he was seeing. Unfamiliar tattoos, skin darker than any he had seen before, more as pale as snow with blond hair in long, tight curls, curved swords, long straight blades, axes large and small, tall thin warriors with olive-shaped eyes, short stocky men with black beards that came down almost to their waists.

He felt their eyes burning him as he passed, heard their braying laughter, understood their mockery even though he could not recognize all their words.

Erca must have seen his baffled expression, or have been waiting for it, for he stepped forward and said, 'See now, dog?' He fluttered his fingers in front of his captive's eyes. Lucanus thought how sly his grin looked.

'An army?' In all his time roaming north of the wall, he had never heard of so many tribes from so many far-flung lands gathering in one place.

Erca laughed. 'This is not an army. This is but a council, the last one of many, where agreements are finally to be reached. Differences have been fought over. At times swords have been drawn and men have been at each other's throats, but now we are all friends.' He chuckled and rubbed his hands together.

'Who are they?'

Erca jabbed a finger towards differently garbed warriors as he passed. 'The Scoti you know. And the Picts too, those savage, tattooed bastards. We have Saxons from Germania. The Alamanni from Gaul. And the Attacotti.'

Lucanus frowned. 'I have not heard of them.'

'You will meet the Attacotti. Very soon.'

The Wolf looked around, still not quite able to believe that these truculent peoples had somehow found common cause. 'If you think Rome will allow you to forge alliances—'

'Rome has no say in this, or in anything any more. Its time is done.'

Lucanus snorted. 'I've never heard that before.'

Erca shoved him, then spun away, raising his arms in greeting as several barbarians barged through the crowd to throw their arms around him. The Wolf watched them slap his back and roar their congratulations, another rabbit for the pot, more entertainment to be prodded with spears and swords and jeered at and humiliated.

Lucanus turned away, studying the crowd milling through the tents. He could see now that the majority were Scoti and Picts. Only a few of each other group ranged around, envoys most likely, sent from their tribes to agree terms.

Nearby, two dogs tore at each other, snapping and snarling. A crowd of men roared and shook their fists and broke off chunks of gold from the bands around their arms to wager. Beyond them, others wrestled and yet more fought bouts with their blades, the cheers of their supporters ringing out.

So many warriors. There was no chance of escape here.

As his gaze drifted over the tent-city, he caught sight of a knot of men striding towards him. Picts, by the look of them, their pale skin stained with black tattoos of spirals and circles and stars. He'd heard so many stories about these people: that they were the ones who had put up the stone circles and cairns that dotted the landscape; that they'd come from the hot lands across the sea when the world was young, that they were once Scythians or Basques or Chaldees.

All he knew was that these were the last warriors he'd want to face on the battlefield. They were as savage as beasts and filled with loathing for Rome. He'd once seen one of them hack away at a legionary, even though the Pict had been disembowelled and lost his left arm. Even after he was dead his eyes seemed to blaze with hatred. Atellus once told him that the Pictish navy was as fearsome as their armies. They were born to fight and kill, on land or at sea.

As the Picts came to a halt in front of him, Lucanus stared at one in the centre who towered over the rest. His head was swathed in filthy strips of cloth. Eyes the colour of a winter sky seared from the shadows of the sockets and Lucanus felt that he was being carved open by them and every part of him judged.

Erca leaned in and whispered behind the back of his hand. 'That's Arrist, the king from the south. The king from the north has sent men to speak for him. You do not want to make an enemy of Arrist, I'll tell you that for free.'

'What's wrong with his face?' the Wolf murmured, unable to break that icy stare.

'All the flesh has been burned away, or so they say, down to the bone itself. He chased down the man who did it for seven days and nights and chopped him into chunks as big as my thumb and fed them to his wife.' He shrugged. 'Or so they say.'

He turned to a short man with a ratty face, few teeth and long greasy hair. 'Take this Roman bastard,' he said. 'We will find out what he knows, one way or another.'

Lucanus felt strong hands grip him and then he was dragged away into the crowd.

## CHAPTER TWENTY-THREE

# *Eaters of the Dead*

LUCANUS CAREERED INTO THE HALL AND FELL SPRAWLING ACROSS the floor. For a moment he lay face down on the cold ground, listening to the footsteps of the two guards who had thrown him and silently cursing himself because he didn't have the strength to fight back. A shadow fell across him and he looked up at the rat-faced man.

'I am Logen. Logen of the Fire's Heart.' His voice was thin and reedy.

'Fire's Heart?' Lucanus repeated, looking around. The hall was little more than rows of logs resting on a frame of three jointed tree trunks, the centre of the pitch about twice his height. A fire smouldered at the far end.

With a gap-toothed grin, the other man thrust out his left arm. The flesh to the elbow was a mass of scar tissue. Logen unfurled the fingers of the hand to reveal a circle containing a cross burned into the palm.

'A man wagered that I wasn't brave enough to plunge my hand into the heart of the fire to find an amulet he'd thrown there.' He held his palm close to the Wolf's face. 'There is the mark of the amulet, branded into me. I took that man's gold. And then I killed him with a knife to his throat. Do you think you could suffer such agonies, just to win a wager? This night perhaps we'll find out.'

He crossed the floor to the two guards and they bent their heads together, whispering and flashing occasional glances at their captive. Whatever they planned, Lucanus' fate was no longer in his own hands. Instead, he thought back to all he had seen in the camp, still wondering what this new alliance of tribes meant. It was unlikely he'd live long enough to find out.

His three guards looked round at some disturbance outside, and a moment later Erca strode in, wiping the grease from his mouth with the back of his right hand. In his left he was carrying Caledfwlch.

'A fine scabbard but a poor sword. Old. Is this the best you can do, Roman bastard? Is your army so short of coin and supplies that you must rely on your grandfathers' weapons?' He tossed the sword into the corner of the hall and prowled around his prey. 'Lucanus,' he said, turning over the name he had learned not long after he had set off for the camp with his captive. 'The Wolf.' He flexed his broad shoulders, shook his large head in a manner that resembled the bear that he seemed, then cracked his knuckles. 'Let us be at it. I have much business to finish this night and I have little time for a flea like you.'

'You'd save time by killing me now. I'll tell you nothing.'

'You'll speak. All men do, in the end. The true question is, do you have anything worth saying? I'd wager not. We've learned all we need to know about your army, your comings and goings, your weaknesses and strengths. Mostly weaknesses.'

Lucanus laughed silently. The *arcani* roamed far and wide in the Wilds along the length of the wall. Everyone would know if the barbarians had got close enough to spy.

Erca grinned, reading his captive's eyes. 'There is much you don't know, Wolf.'

'How many times have your men attacked? How much of your blood must be spilled before you accept that you can never defeat the might of Rome?'

'What was does not always have to be.' Erca flicked the fingers of his right hand and Logen and the two guards came forward.

Lucanus braced himself.

'Why did you venture so far north?' Erca squatted, rocking on his haunches as he studied his captive. 'What had you heard of our business? What did you hope to find?'

The Wolf only grinned.

After he'd taken their boots and fists, he licked the fresh blood from his lips. 'You waste your time.' His voice was still hoarse, the words cracking. 'If I wanted to learn what games you were playing, I would have brought my men.'

'Easier for one man to venture so far into our land than ten.'

'I was searching for a boy. He'd been taken from his home and brought north.' It didn't matter that he told the truth. Marcus was dead, or, if the gods had swooped down and carried him to safety, he was too far away for this man to harm him.

Erca snorted. 'A boy. Now I know you're lying.'

'You wouldn't save a child?'

'I wouldn't risk my neck, not unless he had some value to me. Was he your son?'

Lucanus shook his head.

'Coming so far into our land, on your own, you must have known the chance of returning was slim. And you tell me you did that for some child that was not your own? You think me a fool?' Scowling, he pushed himself to his feet.

The Fates found laughter everywhere. Lucanus had told the truth and now he'd be punished for it.

Logen flexed the fingers of his burned hand. 'Leave him with us. We'll draw the truth from him soon enough.'

Lucanus watched Erca pace around, then glance back at Logen. 'No. I need you in the council with the Saxons. You're the only one who can draw sense out of that old man who understands their animal tongue. Keep watch over him,' he said to the two guards before turning back to the Wolf. 'You would have done better to tell all to me, here. What will happen now, you've brought upon your own head.'

Erca and Logen strode out of the hall and into the sun-drenched camp. Lucanus watched them go, trying not to dwell on what had been meant by those final words.

The Wolf swam up from a dream of witches and druids and Marcus dead in the snow, his unseeing eyes staring up at the circling ravens. Night had come and he could hear song and laughter and cheering ringing across the camp. Lying on his side, he looked past the two guards. Orange light danced everywhere, the sky alive with a thousand sparks glimmering like fireflies from well-stoked bonfires.

He smelled roasting venison and his stomach growled in response. A feast. A celebration.

A moment later, Logen swept in. 'Bring him,' the rat-faced man commanded the two guards.

Hands hooked under his armpits and he was yanked half up and dragged out into the night. After a mazy route among the tents, he crashed to his knees by a great fire at the centre of the camp, the flames the height of three men. He looked round at row upon row of glowing faces disappearing into the dark. Some of the warriors gnawed on chunks of meat, the juices coating their beards. Others swilled back wine or beer from wooden cups, immediately lifting the vessel to be refilled by one of the men moving through the crowd with hides.

When they saw him, the barbarians thrust their fists into the air and roared their approval. The two guards jerked him back to his feet and wrenched his arms behind him.

'Are you afraid yet, Roman dog?' Erca stepped forward. Shadows danced across his face.

'I made my peace when you had me in that pit. I knew I wouldn't live to see many new dawns.'

'It's not death that should fill you with fear. It's how you die.'

Erca looked to his left and beckoned. Supporting himself on a staff, a man edged into the wavering glow from the fire. At first Lucanus thought it was Myrrdin, the same robes, the same haughty tilt of the head. But this man's pate was bald, white hair flowing from the sides and back, his furrowed face a map of years of hardship. Spiral tattoos, now faded to mountain grey, cascaded down the left side of his features. Another druid, the Wolf thought. He had to be.

'Speak, Hadrun of the Hills,' Erca commanded. 'Let this Roman dog hear what you told me at sunset.'

'The prophecy?'

'Aye, the prophecy.'

Hadrun turned his gaze on the captive and croaked, 'The season is turning, and all must change.'

Lucanus could feel Erca's eyes upon him, but he was gripped by the familiar words.

'This is the hour that has been foretold since the first-times, when

171

the true power in this land will begin to rise. In days yet to come, a great king will be born, a king who will not die. All will fall before his sword. The riches of the world will be bestowed upon him, and power the like of which has never been seen before. He will unite all who have suffered in this isle and lead them to a golden age.'

'And whosoever stands with this king will share in that power,' Erca boomed. A stillness had fallen on the crowd, disturbed only by the crackling of the fire.

'Aye,' Hadrun replied.

'And why should we care now, wood-priest, if this king is yet to be born?' Erca prowled around the fire, disappearing from view behind the leaping flames.

'His bloodline is rising now from the sea of men, ready to take its place to rule.' The old man's voice rose, cracking. 'That blood of kings is here, in this age, lying within a chalice. And that chalice is a child. He will grow, and father a son who will father a son, and when the time is ripe the great king will be born. The Bear-King.'

The Wolf saw Erca appear from the other side of the fire. The flames danced in the Scot's eyes as he stared at his captive. 'When you told me you hunted a child, I thought you were lying, Roman bastard. What man would risk all to come to our land for such a one?' The barbarian held his arms wide. 'But now I see. A risk must be matched by the worth of the prize, and what greater prize than this? Is this the truth of your quest, Roman bastard?'

Lucanus glared at Hadrun, then forced a blank face, trying to hide the confusion he was feeling. What game were these wood-priests playing? First they tell him that he must be the protector of the bloodline, now they reveal all to his greatest enemies? He felt sick that he had ever trusted Myrrdin.

'It was the son of a friend, no more.' Words that managed to be both truth and lie.

Erca snorted. 'This is a game I would play too. That boy, raised by the Scoti . . . and his son, and his son's son . . . No one would dare challenge us then.'

'Rome will challenge you.'

'I think not.'

'You waste your breath. The boy's dead, and the king died with him. You saw to that when you trapped me in that pit. You think a boy could survive in the Wilds in winter?'

'On his own, no. But if your allies were there, waiting to take the boy back . . .'

'I came alone.'

'Would one of the great *arcani* be that foolish?' Lucanus watched Erca shake his head slowly, and when the barbarian leader cupped his hands to his mouth and bellowed 'Ho!' he realized that his fate had been sealed.

He looked around and saw movement in the dark far beyond the fire's circle of life. Someone was coming.

'I know your kind, Roman bastard.' Erca stepped in front of him. 'The *arcani* are hard like mountain stone. To live in the Wilds in winter, that is beyond the reach of most men, aye, even seasoned warriors. But you deal with hardship as you deal with joy. I know this. You will not loosen your tongue willingly. My men could try and they would succeed, but it would take too long, until your bones were broken and you could barely speak. Why waste that time when there are some here who are far more skilled in these ways?'

Lucanus broke the barbarian's stare and looked towards that movement away in the dark. Now he could see several figures picking their way through the men squatting on the ground. Though they were no more than shadows, he felt a chill begin to grow in the pit of his stomach.

One by one, they eased into the wavering light, ten of them, glowing white, like the ghosts that walked among the graves at midnight, their heads like skulls, only black holes where the missing eyes should be.

Lucanus stared, his skin prickling into gooseflesh. *Daemons,* he thought.

But as they neared he felt relief wash through him. They were men after all, naked to the waist, their bodies crusted with ashes and charcoal smeared around their eyes and along their cheekbones to suggest the skull beneath the skin.

'Look upon the priest-kings of the Attacotti,' Erca called above the roar of the fire.

Those staring eyes gripped him and in their black depths he finally understood. 'The Eaters of the Dead.'

His thoughts flew back to that clearing where the last council must have taken place, and the half-consumed bodies of the Ravens.

'What are you?' Lucanus breathed.

'You waste your breath. They do not understand your tongue, or mine, or any that we know, and only one man here speaks theirs.' Erca rested a hand on his shoulder and waved a finger towards the ghastly band. 'They are not like you or me, Wolf. Their home is far away from here, and they have kept themselves to themselves there, shut away from the outside world. They worship strange gods, and pray to them at altars made from the bones of their enemies. Their thoughts are strange too, and their secrets many. In consuming a man's flesh, they steal his power, that is what they believe. Once all men were this way, they say, but now only the Attacotti still cling to those old beliefs.'

Lucanus looked the Attacotti up and down. Parchment skin hung thinly over bone. 'There is nothing to them,' he said, showing a contemptuous face.

'Do not trust your eyes. There are no fiercer warriors on the battlefield, not even the Picts. And they are more than that, much more. You *arcani* are good trackers. The Attacotti are better. Silent hunters, these. You will never know they are there until they are upon you, and then it is too late. I am told they do not fear death – they welcome it. They believe that when they die, their spirits live on. That makes them strong.'

Lucanus watched the Attacotti drop their shoulders and lean forward on to the balls of their feet. He was reminded of nothing more than a wolf pack preparing to set upon a cornered lamb.

'Aye, they are Eaters of the Dead.' Erca's voice floated somewhere behind him. 'Yet they are more than that. They are the Eaters of the Living too.'

The nearest warrior lunged, the left hand snarling in Lucanus' hair and yanking his head to one side. The Wolf glimpsed the flash of a blade, a long knife, the edge badly chipped.

His vision filled with that ash-white face. Black-ringed eyes wide. Black lips pulling back from yellowing teeth. He smelt a gust of foul, meaty breath.

And then the gaunt spectre began to saw.

Lucanus howled until his throat was raw, but his ears only rang with the roaring of the crowd. Blood sprayed across his vision and filled his eye sockets. Agony punched through his skull.

He reeled. When his vision cleared, he was looking at a blurry red vision of the Attacotti warrior stepping back and holding his prize aloft.

Lucanus blinked away the blood. That prize. Pale. Clutched between thumb and forefinger.

His left ear.

The Attacotti warrior slipped the morsel into his mouth and chewed on cartilage and flesh, chewed hard, and swallowed. The roaring thundered anew, the barbarians leaping to their feet and punching the air.

And that was the last Lucanus saw.

# CHAPTER TWENTY-FOUR

# *The Blood Pit*

*Rome*

SHARDS OF GOLD GLITTERED ON THE SURFACE OF THE WATER. As Corvus closed the door, the torch on the wall guttered and those flecks of light swept in a constellation across the vaulted ceiling of the baths of Caracalla high over his head. The vast *thermae*, the second largest in all Rome, were deserted at that time of night, the shops along the north wall still, the libraries on the east and west sides silent.

'Where is the sentinel?' he breathed.

'Why are you whispering?' Pavo crooked one eyebrow. 'I swear you're scared of your own shadow these days.'

'There's only one thing I'm scared of, and that's listening to more jabbering from a small man with a big mouth.'

With a chuckle, Pavo flapped his cloak around him and swept out one arm to usher his friend ahead.

Corvus led the way along the edge of the *frigidarium*. Through the doors in front of him, he could see the moon floating on water. The *natatio* was open to the skies, and during the day bronze mirrors above reflected the sunlight down to the pool area.

His footsteps raced up the walls to the shadowy high spaces where they pattered for a while.

'In times past we wouldn't have been skulking in like thieves,' he sighed.

At a door, he paused. It had been a while since he had been here, but he seemed to remember this was the way. He swept past the *palaestrae,* the courts still reeking of sweat from the day's boxing and wrestling bouts, to another door that opened on to a narrow flight of steps. At the bottom, they found themselves in the maze of tunnels where repairs could be carried out to the hypocaust that heated the baths, and the complex network of pipes that carried the water from the Aqua Antoniniana aqueduct.

'There,' Pavo breathed at his back.

The door was smaller than all the others they had passed, the wood faded and cracked with age. Corvus hammered his fist three times and heard a low grunt in reply on the other side.

Moistening his lips, he said, 'I come with head bowed and eyes lowered, in awe of Sol Invictus.'

The door swung open.

The beast was already there.

Corvus tasted the heavy musk hanging in the air, and when the thrum of voices died away he was sure he could hear the snort of hot breath.

For a moment, he stood on the threshold of the underworld, settling in to the heat and the gloom. Two torches flickered on opposite walls, but the shadows seemed to have the power to swallow the light. Only a small circle glowed around the blood pit.

As he entered, his heels clattered on the bedrock, still bearing the marks where his predecessors had carved the vault out of the stone. Though the walls here had been dressed, some of the adjoining chambers resembled little more than caves, and that was right, for from the earth they all were born, and to the heavens they reached.

He pushed his head back, as if he could see through the ceiling, through the baths above and up to the night sky where the constellation of Perseus glowed, Perseus who slew the bull, Taurus, as the stars shifted. This site had been carefully chosen for that very reason; lines drawn, angles calculated, mapped and divined.

In the dimness, silhouettes shifted. Clusters of men, some standing, some seated on the stone benches along the walls. Though he couldn't see their faces, he knew who many of them were. The worshippers who bowed their heads in the churches above would be surprised if they ever learned the names of the ones who trudged down here under cover of night. Great men who still clung on to the certainties of the past, soldiers and butchers and blacksmiths unshaken in their belief that this place was a beacon lighting the way into days yet to come. All were equal in this brotherhood.

The beast snorted more loudly, the rumbling exhalation rolling through the secret caverns reaching deep into the dark. Voices ebbed away into silence.

Corvus held Pavo's eyes. Outside in the world they swaggered and bragged, but here he could see his friend was as awed as he was.

On the edge of the circle of light, he looked up at the ceiling, painted dark blue and spotted with stars to match the night sky above. Who could not be awed by the largest Mithraeum in Rome and the second largest in all the empire? Oaths had been made here, and sacrifices, that had shaped the face of the world.

Those days had all but gone. The Christians had seen to that. Though his fellows here now had to keep their secrets well away from the light, he had the sense that some of them, perhaps his brother among them, still thought there was hope for one last chance to put things right.

'All is well.'

The voice boomed from the dark and Corvus felt his neck prickle. Around him, the silence swelled.

Corvus squinted through the half-light to see the altar at the end of that claustrophobic space, a sarcophagus carved on the front with the image of Mithras slaying the bull. He could just make out the niches on either side, one containing the bust of Sol, the other the statue of Mithras *petra generix*, their god being born from the rock.

'All is well,' the voice rang out again, closer this time.

A figure stepped in front of the altar and pulled back its hood.

Gnaeus Calidus Severus, the Hanged Man, craned his twisted neck slowly so that he could let his gaze fall upon everyone there.

'Greetings, Father,' the congregation replied as one.

Corvus thought how impressive this deformed man now looked. Severus was wearing the cloak of Mithras, as black as the night sky, with stars and the signs of the Zodiac glimmering in gold upon the back. On his head was the red cap, on his finger the ring that the initiate would kiss, and in his other hand the shepherd's staff, for they were his flock and he guided them.

'Here we map the passage of the soul,' Severus intoned, 'from this world to the afterlife, as the Invincible Sun travels the sky from horizon to endless horizon. Is there a penitent who would make this journey before me?'

Corvus looked round until he saw his brother standing on the other side of the blood pit, swathed in a hood and a cloak.

'There is,' Corvus announced.

'Name him.'

'Servius Aurelius Ruga.'

'Is there a faithful Soldier who will offer up the penitent for judgement?'

'There is,' Corvus said again.

'Name him.'

'Lucius Aurelius Corvus.'

'Bring forth the penitent.'

Corvus grasped his brother's hand and tugged him in front of Severus. Once Ruga had shucked off his cloak to stand naked in front of the priest, two torchbearers marched from either side and lit another flame upon the altar. The shadows swooped away.

'Here we shall approach the great mystery, which only the most enlightened of us know in full,' Severus continued. 'Here, the soul of brother Ruga will descend into the dark, into the reaches of the underworld, and when he emerges from the earth he will be reborn.'

The beast snorted so loudly that Corvus almost jerked round, fearing it was behind him. He felt his heart pound harder, though he knew what was to come.

Severus raised his arms, so his hands hung above both their heads. 'Brother Ruga has made known his wish to ascend the seven heavens and return to where the soul is born. Do we all bear witness?'

The men swaddled in the stifling dark chanted, 'We do.'

Corvus saw that Severus had something in his hand which he pushed into Ruga's mouth, under his tongue. This was part of the ritual, he knew, but what the thing was remained one of the great mysteries. Ruga chewed and swallowed.

'Take the next step, brother.'

Ruga knelt and bowed his head.

Corvus pushed aside a pang of frustration. It should be him there.

Pavo told him that very thing after every one of these rituals. Sighing, he counted through the seven degrees of initiation, one for each of the steps through the seven heavens. This was Ruga's sixth, the Heliodromus, the Sun Runner.

To be a Sun Runner, one who has seen the sun and has grown close to it . . . Corvus sighed again. Ruga would be on the brink of true enlightenment while he had still only attained the lowly rank of Soldier.

Severus raised his hands to those painted stars and Corvus heard his voice tremble with emotion. 'We call upon all-powerful Mithras, born of the Virgin Mother. Mithras, who will be incarnated into the body of a man, a saviour who will lead us all out of the dark. Mithras who will live on in the blood of men.'

On the stone floor at his side, Ruga convulsed. Corvus watched his brother's head crane back and was shocked to see the eyes drained of all colour, so enlarged were the pupils.

'Around the Mother, we are told, the winged serpents coiled,' Severus continued, his voice beginning to boil. 'The great serpents, born of the earth, born of fire, who bring with them wisdom. The great serpents who fly from this world to the heavens. Who herald the king of kings, great Mithras made flesh. The Dragon.'

Corvus shivered.

Ruga thrashed around at his feet, clawing at his body, raising welts and drawing lines of blood.

Corvus began to feel queasy now. The rising and falling timbre of the Hanged Man's voice, the words, the heat, the dark. His head was spinning. He hadn't expected to be so affected.

Severus stamped his crook upon the floor. 'Our teachings must remain secret, only revealed to the initiates. But here, we know. We know. We must die before we can be reborn. But once reborn, under Mithras, we can rise up to reach the final secret.'

Corvus opened his eyes. His brother was on his hands and knees, vomiting. He swallowed and dry-retched as the acid stench filled his nose.

When his head cleared, he heard the sound of wings, or perhaps it was just in his mind.

'The raven, the messenger of the sun, has come,' Severus boomed. 'It is time.'

Corvus shook himself. This was his moment. He heaved his brother to his feet and dragged him to one side, though Ruga's head lolled and vomit still trickled from his mouth.

That heady musk filled the air. He heard the beast, snorting and stamping its hooves, drawing closer, and then finally he glimpsed its huge bulk in the shadows.

Two Soldiers dragged the great bull out of the adjoining cavern. They had brought it down the secret way to the temple, Corvus knew, and had given it the preparation of herbs that would make it docile, at least for a while.

'All things have two faces. The bull here is our lower self, and must be slain before we can rise to the heights.' The priest nodded to Corvus. 'This is the ordeal that must be faced upon the road to enlightenment.'

His brother was limp, his legs buckling, but somehow Corvus managed to drag him forward and press him down into the blood pit. All he could think was that it looked like a grave. Ruga dying . . . gone.

He watched, and thought, and tried to find his feelings.

The two Soldiers heaved the bull to the edge of the pit. Severus stepped forward and rammed a knife into the side of the beast's neck.

The hot blood gushed out, showering into the pit, swilling around Ruga, soaking him. He lay there, still now, as the thick crimson liquid flooded the hole, splashed across his face, filled his eyes.

Half drowned in the beast's life essence, he began to splutter and choke.

'In the tongue that was passed down to us from the east, Sun and Love are the same,' Severus all but bellowed above the beast's groans. 'And here we learn the greatest mystery – that Love moves all that there is under the heavens, and beyond. Love is all. The Invincible Sun, invincible love.'

The bull crumpled as its legs grew too weak to support it. Dying, dying, even as Ruga was gaining a new life.

Corvus watched, and wondered.

Corvus slumped on to one of the benches, swamped in the iron reek of blood and the suffocating heat from the braziers and the dying echoes of the bull's rumbling breath. He felt sick, but he knew something about this night had changed him, though he wasn't sure what.

For a while, he closed his eyes, listening to Severus' soothing voice, talking of Mithras, and the hope of days yet to come. When he opened them again, the beast had been dragged away and Ruga too was gone.

Plunging into the ranks of ecstatic men, he found Pavo at the back, leaning against the wall, arms crossed.

'Thank Mithras you are still here.' He clapped a hand on his friend's shoulder and saw that it was trembling.

'Old Severus puts on a good show, I'll give him that.'

'You're not moved?'

'I don't have much in the way of ambition, but that . . .' Pavo wiped the back of his hand across his mouth, his eyes trailing towards the blood pit gleaming in the torchlight. 'I felt something inside me. I felt . . . Mithras.'

'Yes. I did too.'

'That should have been you, brother. You're more deserving. Too many people are conspiring against you.'

Corvus took a step back, shaking his head. 'You say that . . . you've always said it, but—'

'Imagine if you were a Sun Runner,' Pavo said, cutting him off. 'You think your brother can do a better job than you?'

'Perhaps.'

'Liar.'

The sound of wooden tables being dragged in front of the benches echoed through the temple, followed by a loud cheer. Corvus turned to see Ruga walking back past the altar, grinning. He had washed off the gore, and was dressed in a pristine crimson tunic, the colour of the sun, and fire, and blood.

Corvus gripped his friend's shoulder again, leaning in to whisper, 'I have to sit with Ruga at the feast. I'm his right hand. But I need your advice, my friend. Can we talk later?'

Pavo nodded. He grabbed Corvus' wrist and held it for a long moment, a bond of trust that transcended the years.

Taking his seat at the long table, Corvus basked in the good humour of the worshippers. Ruga sat beside him, and for once his brother seemed to look on him in a kindly manner. He laughed long and loud, and clapped his arm round Corvus' shoulders.

In one of the other caverns, the bull had been butchered, and the aroma of roasting beef wafted through the temple. When the chunks of glistening meat were served up for the sacred meal, Corvus felt some of his doubts ebbing away.

Severus carried an amphora to the table. Setting a silver cup in front of Ruga, he poured the wine, then broke knobs off a loaf of bread. 'This wine is love,' he said. 'Drink deeply of it. Then take this bread, for it is not only bread. It is the flesh of Mithras. Eat it and you will be cleansed and transformed.'

As Ruga reached for the bread, a sound like thunder reverberated through the chambers. *Boom, boom, boom.* Shouts rang out, muffled by the walls, and all around the acolytes leapt to their feet, faces drawn.

Corvus gasped, stunned by the sudden milling crowd and the noise.

As he jumped up, Severus grabbed his shoulder and croaked, 'We are undone.'

As one, the worshippers rushed to the door. 'Hold it shut,' someone bellowed. In the spaces between the tremendous pounding from the other side, Corvus could hear the drone of angry voices. He caught sight of Pavo through the milling bodies. His friend was mouthing something through the rising din.

Before he could make it out, Ruga grabbed his arm, his face twisted by rising panic. 'The Christians have found us,' he hissed.

'We're doing nothing wrong.'

'You're a fool.' Ruga bounded past Severus, almost knocking the priest over, and disappeared into the shadows behind the altar.

A crack echoed, then another, and then that ancient door burst into shards. A mob forced the defenders back, jabbing cudgels into faces. Through the maelstrom of fighting men, Corvus glimpsed a familiar face, his friend, Theodosius, wielding a club, his face as cold as the grave. He'd always been as devout a Christian as any Corvus had encountered, but this?

Pavo was at his side. 'If he sees you, it's all over . . . for you . . . your mother, your brother. And Hecate . . . You know Theodosius well. What would he do if he found out your family harbours a witch?'

For a moment, Corvus hesitated, unsure if he should risk everything by aiding his brothers in the temple. But then his gaze settled on Severus, drained of blood and filled with horror, and he knew what he had to do.

Throwing himself over the table, he caught the priest's arm. 'We have to get you away from here, Father.'

'We must—'

'There's nothing we can do, you know that. But you must be saved, for the good of us all.'

Severus nodded, understanding.

'There's another way out of the temple? Where the bull was brought in?'

'This way.' The Hanged Man lurched into the gloom in Ruga's footsteps.

As Corvus followed, Pavo snorted at his back. 'Looks as though your brother saved his own neck. I expected no less.'

The three of them plunged into the dark. Corvus pushed himself close to Severus. He couldn't see a thing, but the priest knew the way blindly.

'Go on,' Pavo breathed. 'I'll watch your back. But if we get out of this alive we'll have words, you and me.'

Corvus and Severus burst out of the door behind the baths and scrambled into the shadows of the towering aqueduct. They ran alongside the great arches, south towards the Appian gate, until Corvus heard Severus gasp for him to stop. In the dark under one of the arches, the pair slumped against the stone, catching their breath. Corvus listened, but he couldn't hear any sounds of pursuit.

Severus shuddered. 'The temple is lost.'

'What will they do?'

'Fill it with earth and rock so we can never go down there again, as they have done to every other temple they have found.'

'But we have a right . . .'

'Not in their eyes. This is only the start. I had some hope when Emperor Julian tried to revive our fortunes. But once he was seen to fail, the Christians gained the upper hand. They will not let it slip away.'

Corvus thought of that cruel look in Theodosius' eyes, that cold determination. If even the son of one of Valentinian's most trusted advisers could lead an attack like this, then the persecution would only get worse.

The priest seemed to know what he was thinking. 'Valentinian and Valens both have too much on their minds to trouble themselves with religious strife. Valentinian has let this struggle between the pope and the anti-pope drag on because he hopes it will burn hard and then die. But one day we will have an emperor who will cleanse Rome of all who do not follow the Christian path, mark my words.'

Severus rubbed his twisted neck, and Corvus felt that there was more to the story of his disability than an argument between rival businesses.

'Already they destroy our temples, and all the pagan temples they find across the empire, and build their own churches on top of them, and they turn old gods into their saints. They are clever, these Christians. They steal what is not theirs and make it their own.' Corvus winced at the hollowness of the other man's laughter.

'But why?'

'Whosoever tells the story best holds power in his hand.'

Corvus thought how bitter the other man's smirk was. Here was someone who was fighting a war he knew he was losing, but could not see why.

Severus drew himself up and sucked in a deep breath. 'Enough of this. Dark thoughts will get us nowhere. I haven't thanked you for saving my life.'

'I did what I could, nothing more.'

The Hanged Man nodded, smiling. 'We are all grateful for your mother's work.'

'What does my mother have to do with this?'

'She came to us with an offer of gold when our temple had fallen prey to the Christians moving to deny us our rights.' He pursed his lips, remembering. 'And she told me she had heard talk . . . some rumour . . . some hidden knowledge she had discovered in Britannia . . . about Mithras incarnate.' Severus batted his thoughts away with a wave of his hand. 'Your mother is a woman who keeps many secrets. All I can say is that before he died your father accepted the light of Sol Invictus, and your mother wished to aid us on his behalf. She has given you and your brother into the service of the Invincible Sun, and she donates much to our cause. But sometimes I wonder if she plays another game entirely, one that none of us ever quite see.'

Corvus nodded. 'I am just a simple soldier. I know nothing of my mother's plans.'

Severus thought for a moment. 'There was a man who used to serve your mother. Titus Didius Strabo. He came with her from Britannia, and helped keep her safe when your father was lost at sea, if I recall. You remember him?'

Corvus pictured a gruff man with a face like knapped flint. 'I think I do.'

'I once saw him break the arm of a man who tried to snatch your mother's hand as she crossed the forum. After a while, she had no further need of him and he left her employ. The last I heard he was working in one of the taverns near the Pinciana gate, throwing the drunks out into the street. He may well know what your mother learned in Britannia, and what she plans, and if anyone's tongue could be loosened with a little gold, it would be his. Should it be of interest to you.'

'Thank you, Father.'

Corvus looked round the arch and saw a solitary figure trudging along the street. Pavo was searching for him. Now they would have to put off any drinking to celebrate their escape. They had work to do.

# CHAPTER TWENTY-FIVE

# *A Voice in the Dark*

THE NIGHT WAS FILLED WITH FIRE AND FURY.

Through the haze of pain, Lucanus felt hands grip him and drag him away from the heat. He heard the voice thick in his head as if bubbling up from deep water.

'Take a while to dwell upon what you have lost and what you have yet to lose,' Erca said. 'Then you will return here, and we will see if your tongue has been loosened. If not, then the Attacotti will find another morsel. And another. And more, until there is nothing left.'

And then those hands were pulling him through the flapping tents. He saw sparks swirling on the breeze. He heard the cheers of the warriors, as if a huge beast was roaring for blood.

The world blurred by.

Within a moment of reaching the wooden hall, he was tumbling across the cold ground. Blinking away crusted blood, he stifled the agony ringing in his skull and looked up at Logen and the two guards, silhouetted against the orange glow from the fire.

'Bind his feet,' the rat-faced man commanded.

As the barbarians yanked bonds tight around his ankles, Logen loomed over him. 'The night is long, but your time is short. Lie here. Feel the throb where your ear once was. Drink in that agony and learn from it. Then choose if you will speak to save the rest of you.'

The three men walked away into the gloom. Lucanus sagged down, willing the earth to open up and swallow him. Behind his eyes swam the ghastly white faces of the Attacotti and he knew there was no hope. Even if he told everything he had ever learned, he would still be offered up as the next feast for those Eaters of the Dead. He felt his stomach knot. Erca had been right. Death did not scare him, but to die that way . . . eaten while still alive . . . that was a horror he could not contemplate.

'Thank the gods.'

Lucanus jumped at the whisper rustling in from the dark at his back. He rolled over and hissed, 'Who's there?'

At first he thought he was seeing a spectre. A small figure separated from the dark and crawled towards him. Only when the light filtering in from the distant campfire hit the face did he see it was Marcus. At first he couldn't comprehend what lay before him – a vision caused by the pain, a visitation come to guide him into the otherworld? His lips worked but no sounds came out.

The boy smiled. 'I thought I'd never see you again.'

'You're alive,' the Wolf croaked.

'I disobeyed you, Lucanus.' Marcus' mouth turned down. 'When I saw you beaten and carried away, I knew I couldn't leave you. I followed. Here.' From somewhere he pulled out a knife and began to saw at Lucanus' bonds.

'How did you survive?'

'I'm quick. And cunning. I crept into the barbarians' camp at night as they travelled along the road. I stole food, and this knife. And while they slept, I slept too, by the dying fire. But with one eye open, as you taught me.'

'Good boy.' Lucanus could scarcely believe what he was hearing. When the bonds at his wrist fell away, he grabbed the knife and sawed through the rope at his ankles. Once he was free, he ruffled Marcus' hair, then pulled the boy to him and hugged him tight. 'You're a good boy,' Lucanus repeated, 'and your mother would be proud of you. I'm proud of you. But now we have to hurry before we're found.'

He lurched to his feet, swaying for a moment.

'You're weak,' Marcus said.

'My strength has deserted me.' In the gloom, and with his hair falling, the boy couldn't see his missing ear. Lucanus grabbed the lad by his shoulders. 'And this time you must swear to me. If I fall, you'll run on alone. They know of you now. They know of your value—'

'My value?'

The Wolf waved a hand to silence him. 'If I fall, there will be no saving me. Do you hear? I'll be dead in no time. You must save yourself. Swear.'

After a moment, the boy replied, 'I so swear.'

'Good. Now follow me.'

Lucanus snatched up his wolf pelt where it lay in one corner. When he slipped it on, he felt the fire in his chest blaze higher, and the spirit of his wolf-brother enter him. Immediately, he was stronger, braver. With a glance over his shoulder at the glow from the campfire, he prowled to the rear of the hall and beckoned for the boy to follow.

His eyes fell upon Caledfwlch in the shadows where Erca had tossed it earlier that day. He was minded to leave it there and spit on it as he passed. Could he believe a single word that Myrrdin had told him? But that would only spite himself. He needed a weapon. Snatching it up, he fastened the scabbard around his waist.

'This is a good time,' he murmured. 'All here are enjoying their feast. But soon they'll come looking for me. We must be fast.'

The boy nodded. In that moment, Lucanus could believe that the blood of a great king coursed through Marcus' veins. He felt a swell of pride, and then pushed the boy out into the night.

Through the camp they ran, keeping low, listening for any sounds of pursuit through the din of singing and laughter. When they reached the place where the horses had been penned, he pressed his finger to his lips to warn Marcus. The steeds snorted and stamped their feet, sensing someone they didn't know. Creeping forward, Lucanus made the low noise deep in his throat that he knew would calm them, and whispered soothing words.

Selecting one, a black stallion, he stroked its neck until it was ready, then hauled himself on to its back. Snarling his fist in Marcus' tunic, he lifted the boy behind him.

'Hold tight,' he whispered. 'When we are beyond the edge of camp I'll ride hard.'

His head still fizzing from the pain and the lack of food, he dug in his heels and guided the horse away from the tents to the road that led east.

★

As the track began to rise to the edge of the forest, Lucanus glanced back to where the sky glowed orange from the campfire. Now that he had some distance, he could see the flickering smaller fires in the vast bowl of night that revealed the scale of this council of barbarians, and he felt a rising chill at what this portended for the days yet to come.

Before he could begin to wonder what the tribes planned to do with their common cause, a cry rang out. It leapt from lips to lips, growing louder by the instant, and then the cheering at the fire died away. For a moment he could hear only the murmur of the wind in the branches, and then the roar rushed in with a vengeance, this time tinged with fury.

Lucanus kicked the horse's flanks. Hooves pounded the hard ground and he felt lifted up, the breeze tearing at his hair. In the dark of the forest, they would not be able to ride at this speed for fear of being brought down by the uneven track. But there were miles to go until they were safe and those barbarians would risk all to capture them.

Lucanus felt Marcus' arms wrap around him and the boy's head press against his back. He had to find a way to survive, for the lad's sake, and for all those at home who did not realize what was waiting for them in the cold north.

# CHAPTER TWENTY-SIX

# *Flight*

THE HOWL ROLLED OUT ACROSS THE FOREST, ECHOED BY ANOTHER, and then another. The barbarians were the wolves now, whipped into a frenzy by the scent of blood.

Lucanus clasped his arms around the horse's neck, his head flopping against the mane. For two days, they'd grabbed nothing but quick sleeps along the way, their bellies empty, their thirst quenched only by brackish water gulped from pools. He'd avoided the well-used tracks for fear their enemies might be lying in wait, and instead weaved through a world of shadows and dark green light. When night fell, they floated through an abyss.

His eyelids flickered. The few patches of thin light dappling the forest floor faded and the dusk pressed in on every side. He could sleep, deep and long, sleep for the rest of his days.

'Your skin burns. I can barely touch it.'

Lucanus swallowed, but there seemed no moisture left in his throat. He'd almost forgotten the boy was there, clinging on to his back. But of course that was why their enemies ran them so hard.

Whoever was master of the royal blood was master of the land.

'No,' he replied. 'I'm cold now,' and as he said it he shivered as if a blast of freezing air had rushed down from the northern mountains.

Marcus reached round and wiped his forehead. 'You're sweating.'

'Hard work makes a man sweat.'

'You're sick, Lucanus. When I'm unwell my mother always wraps me in blankets and sits me by the fire. "Sweat out the poison," she says.'

'Your mother isn't here.' Even as he said it, Lucanus saw Catia in his mind's eye, standing on the wall, praying for the return of her son. She was counting on him.

He pushed himself upright, forcing what little strength he had into his feeble limbs. What could he tell the boy: that he was probably dying? The wound on the side of his head had been left open to the elements. Soon the flesh around it would smell like rotten apples as the sickness ate its way through him until only black rot remained. He'd seen that terrible death more than once, and here there was no leech to try to save him.

The night came down hard. Everything rushed away, and he felt himself falling.

*Be strong, Lucanus. Be strong.*

Rough bark scratched his back and his nostrils were filled with the sweet scent of sticky resin. His fingers dug into the sharp pine needles on the ground where he sat, and through heavy lids he looked into a hazy light among the trees. It seemed to be that quiet hour of dusk, the one that Mato loved so much.

A light was dancing there in the gloom, a flame it seemed, but this had a sapphire sheen to it. He watched it slither towards him across the forest floor. At first he thought it looked like a river of fire, then a winding road; not the ones that Rome built, but the sinuous paths of old.

*We walked like serpents in those days,* someone had once told him. He could not remember who.

Where would this road take him?

Grey shapes flitted among the trees on either side of that sapphire glow. Gradually some solidified, took on form. Others remained mist-like, fading away when his gaze fell upon them.

*Ghosts,* he thought. *Daemons.* And then: *I'm dying.* This sickness was eating away at his thoughts, breaking them up into pieces.

Behind the misty shapes, other figures waited on the edge of the darkness that engulfed the rest of the forest. He thought he saw a woman there, dressed in black, her hair black too, surrounded by ravens that circled endlessly. A man who glowed golden, like the sun, like Catia. Another who seemed constructed from the very forest itself, bark and leaves and ivy and holly.

*Dying.*

His thoughts spun away. A procession drifted by, a king and queen and their court, and they looked at him with such sadness he felt tears sting his eyes. Bellicus and Mato were there too, and the other Grim Wolves, and his father, though his face was a blur. A bear trudged behind, walking like a man, its glassy black eyes flickering with that same blue fire. The bear was carrying his sword, Caledfwlch.

'That's mine,' he said.

'It is yours and mine,' the bear growled back.

As they all moved away into the dark, only one figure remained, a sentinel watching silently. He seemed to be judging, Lucanus thought. He was a warrior with a helm that covered all his face, and a long shield, and a great sword that he held loosely in his right hand, pointing towards the earth. His armour, his weapons, all were green, the deep green of the endless forest.

'Who are you?' Lucanus croaked.

The warrior did not answer. He only judged.

*Be strong, Lucanus. Be strong.*

He shuddered awake and realized he was no longer sitting at the foot of the tree, if he ever had been. The icy ground chilled his cheek and he breathed in a loamy odour, mingled with sweat, and a familiar spicy perfume, though he couldn't remember where he had first experienced it.

'Death was close, Wolf. You were almost lost to us.' A woman's voice, one he knew. Her breath warmed his ear.

'Catia?' he murmured.

Laughter. Three women's voices joined as one.

'Where is Marcus?'

'Near,' the woman nearest him whispered.

'Searching,' an older voice added.

Lucanus shivered as slender fingers probed where his ear had been. His skin tingled at the touch of something cold and wet and he breathed in a pungent aroma of herbs and lamb fat. After a moment the gash began to burn and he jerked up. A cool hand pressed him back down.

'This will help fight the sickness,' the woman said. 'Leave it there until you feel well again.'

Now Lucanus smelled a rich, sweet scent and he realized the woman was coating his wound with honey to seal it.

'Will I live?' he asked, not wholly sure if this was really happening or one of the dreams that had afflicted him.

'If the gods so wish.'

'The barbarians—'

'Your enemies roam the night, but they have lost the scent of you. They follow your horse, and that is long gone. You must make the rest of the journey on foot, unless death claims you first.'

'I have to get Marcus back to Catia,' he croaked, almost to himself.

He sensed the woman leaning in as if she were about to kiss him. It was so dark that he couldn't see her even though she was close, but the bloom of her skin warmed him. 'You must prepare the way for the Bear-King,' she whispered.

Something was pressed into his hand and his fingers brushed supple leather, a pouch perhaps.

'The fever will break soon,' she murmured. 'When it does, chew on these leaves. They will give you all the strength you need, and more.' As she spoke, her voice drifted away from him. 'From here, you are on your own, Wolf. We cannot watch over you. Live or die, now, that is down to you. But if you survive, you will be changed. Death changes everyone, Lucanus. Lead into gold. That is the secret that no one tells, but now it has been told, to you.'

Digging deep into what little strength he had left, he levered himself up on his elbow and looked around, but though it was too dark to see anything, he felt sure they were gone.

A moment later, he heard a voice calling his name.

'Here,' he croaked.

Feet pounded up and Marcus dropped down beside him.

'I went in search of food and then couldn't find my way back to you and you didn't answer.' The boy's voice was cracking with emotion.

'All is well now,' Lucanus comforted, praying that it was true. 'Rest a while, but only a while. We have a long march ahead.'

# CHAPTER TWENTY-SEVEN

## *The Season Turns*

'THAT CANNOT BE TRUE.' SOLINUS SCREWED UP HIS NOSE. 'FALX IS a sly bastard, but even he wouldn't steal gold from his own men's purses.'

'Have you been drunk for the last few years? Falx would sell his own mother,' Comitinus snorted. The two men had been bickering from the moment the Grim Wolves had left the shelter of the fort.

Mato searched the rolling grasslands in that curtain between wall and endless gloomy forest. When the moon eased out from behind the clouds, bands of silver and black sailed across the empty landscape and his heart beat faster. 'Enjoy this moment, brothers. Here, at least, there is peace.'

Comitinus jabbed a finger at Solinus, ignoring Mato's urging. 'The wagon bringing the wages from Londinium was robbed on the Stanegate, this we know. The thieves had cloths tied across their faces so they could not be identified. And Falx needs gold to complete his bargain with Varro the merchant.'

Solinus scrubbed the scar tissue on his face. 'If that were true and the men found out, they would hang Falx from the wall. It's been an age since anyone's been paid, and—'

'We're here to do a job,' Bellicus snapped. 'You'd do well to keep your minds on it.' He crouched, resting his fingertips on a patch of flattened grass.

Chastened, Comitinus rubbed his skinny wrists despite the spring warmth. 'I say the Attacotti have returned to whatever place spawned them. We should go back to our beds.'

Solinus sniffed the wind. 'You're a whining bastard, and I'm loath to say it, but this time you're right. If those flesh-eaters were camped out here, there'd be some trace. We're wasting our time.'

An owl swooped overhead, its screech mournful. Mato watched its silhouette sweep by. 'On a night like this, no one wastes their time.' He realized that Bellicus had fallen silent. The red-bearded man was still hunched over the patch of grass. 'What is it, brother?' he asked.

'Someone has passed this way before us. See? Here, and here. I would say four, perhaps five. They've not tried to hide their trail.'

Solinus crouched beside him. 'Bollocks. You're right.'

Mato turned to Comitinus, whose eyes were the sharpest. 'What do you see?'

Comitinus shook his head. 'Nothing, for now. They may well have reached the trees already. When I was a boy—'

'Not another of your stories,' Solinus grumbled. 'What, the Attacotti came to your house and thought you were too scrawny to eat?'

Comitinus cocked an eyebrow. 'If you don't want to learn, it's your loss. You'll be wishing you did, the next time you're looking death in the eye.'

Solinus thought for a moment, then said, 'Go on, then.'

'Too late.' Comitinus turned his back.

Mato sighed. Sometimes it was like shepherding children. 'We have no choice,' he said, standing. 'We follow the trail. But we keep our wits about us. If it is the Attacotti, we shouldn't get too close. Not unless we want to go the way of the Ravens.'

'Live to take the word back to the fort,' Comitinus affirmed. 'That's the wise course.'

As Bellicus loped ahead, Mato bowed into the breeze and ran after him. He heard the other Grim Wolves pounding tight at his heels.

On the edge of the woods, Bellicus held up a hand to bring them to a halt and they stood for a moment, listening to the screech of the owls and staring into the darkness among the trees. The wind had dropped and all was serene, yet Mato felt his neck prickle with unease. They could all sense it, he knew; instinct built up by years in the Wilds.

He sniffed the air again. 'Sweat.' His voice was a whisper but it seemed as if he had shouted.

Comitinus pushed his wolf pelt back from his face. 'We should turn back.'

'We can't.' Bellicus' voice was firm. 'Not until we know for sure.'

'You're whining like a babe.' Solinus swung a foot at Comitinus' arse. The other man jumped out of the way, cursing. 'The trail is clear. If we follow it with care we'll see them before they see us.'

'But if those bastards turn and look at us with their devil eyes, we run.' Bellicus pushed his way into the trees.

Another world existed in the woods, one of shadow and stillness. Sometimes Mato enjoyed the calm there, away from the buffeting winds of the grasslands. Not this night. It seemed as though all of the Wilds were holding their breath.

As the Grim Wolves fanned out and became one with the trees, Mato slipped to the right flank. When he glanced over at his brothers, he nodded. Any watchful eyes would barely see them, or would think them beasts searching for prey.

Silence.

He fixed one eye on Bellicus, watching for their leader's signals. Head down above the trail, Bellicus crept forward. The smell of hot bodies was stronger now. Whoever was there was not far ahead.

He frowned. If this was a war-band, there should be some other sign. Voices, the crunch of footsteps.

Far off through the trees, a figure hove into view in the centre of a moonlit clearing. Mato stiffened. The man was looking their way, seemingly waiting for them.

The Grim Wolves eased behind oak and hawthorn and grew still. Mato exchanged a look with Bellicus. For a while they waited, testing the moment.

The more Mato stared, the more he thought the outline of this man looked familiar. Bellicus must have seen it too, for he slipped out from behind an ash tree and edged forward. Mato watched their leader draw himself up as he neared, and then he raised one arm and flicked his hand to summon the Grim Wolves out of hiding.

At the edge of the clearing, Mato loosened his shoulders and sighed. Motius of the Carrion Crows grinned back, the black spiral tattoos on the left of his face stark in the moonlight.

'Brothers,' he greeted them.

'You are far from your grounds,' Bellicus said.

The Crow furrowed his brow. 'We were sent here by Blaesus at Banna, on the trail of Scoti scouts. Were you not told?'

'Atellus made no mention.' Bellicus looked around. 'Where are the others?'

'Searching ahead. An old wife in one of the villages to the east said the Attacotti had also been seen near here. We have found no tracks so far.'

'You heard us coming?' Mato said. 'Then we are a poor excuse for *arcani.*'

Motius smiled. 'I have good ears.'

'And you left a good trail,' Mato continued. 'That's not like the Carrion Crows.' He sensed his brothers shift as they all reached the same conclusion. Motius' smile hardened. He saw the conclusion they had reached too.

The Crow raised his right hand.

Mato backed away, feeling his heart begin to race though he was not yet sure why. As his eyes darted around, he sensed movement above him.

The Carrion Crows dropped from the low branches. When they hit the ground, they snatched out their short swords and threw themselves into a run. Mato gaped, trying to make sense of what he was seeing. Surely their brothers could not be attacking them?

But then Bellicus barked an order to flee and he was darting back towards the grasslands, the other Grim Wolves whipping through the trees on either side.

*What treachery is this?* His confused thoughts stumbled over each other. They were brothers, a bond built over long years. *Why . . . why . . . ?*

And then his feet were skimming across the forest floor, his head swimming with shock and his heart thundering.

As he crashed out of the blur of trees, he heard Motius' voice ringing out: 'All things are coming to an end, Grim Wolves. The season has turned.'

Mato raced ahead across the grasslands and felt a rush of relief when he glanced back and saw Bellicus, Solinus and Comitinus scrambling across the mounds and hollows behind him. With Motius at their head, the Carrion Crows bounded out of the treeline in pursuit.

The world had gone mad. Mato's head swam, but he didn't slow his step until he could see the torches flickering along the wall and he knew safety was in their grasp. Only then did he look back. No doubt realizing they had lost their chance, the Crows fell away and melted back into the night.

'The Crows lured us out there to kill us,' Solinus spat.

'This makes no sense . . . our brothers . . . *arcani* . . .' Realizing he was starting to ramble, Comitinus caught himself.

'They are always filled with vinegar, those bastard Crows,' Solinus continued, his fists bunching. 'Eaten away that they are never paid on time, grumbling and carping and looking for blame. They don't care for anything but their own comfort.' He grimaced as if he were thinking of clamping his teeth on Motius' throat. 'They'd kill one of their own for a pouch of coin.'

Mato saw that Bellicus was looking away into the dark, lost to his thoughts. 'What is it, brother?'

Bellicus began slowly. 'Everyone knows the frontier can't be kept safe without the work the *arcani* do. Yet are we treated with respect? No, we're treated like dogs, thrown crumbs of comfort. And for all that, they can't even pay us on time. So yes, that eats away at a man's guts, makes him question who his friends are.'

'You're talking as though you're in your cups,' Solinus said. 'Make some sense.'

'What if they found better work? Work which earned good coin, and paid on time?'

Mato watched Solinus' exasperation drain away and his brow furrow. He glanced at Comitinus and their eyes widened at the same time.

'You say the Crows are taking the pay of our enemies?' Mato said.

'They helped the Attacotti cross south of the wall. Did they bribe the guards?' Solinus continued, growing animated. 'Bastards. What fucking bastards.'

'They wouldn't.' Comitinus was shaking his head. 'Would they?'

'They sold us out, all of us in Vercovicium, I'm sure of it,' Bellicus said.

Mato paced, trying to bring some order to his racing thoughts. 'They lured us out . . . why would they lure us out to kill us? Not because they have any grudge against us, but because . . . because . . . we are *arcani*. And we see all. And we hear . . .' He clamped down on the word as another thought burst free. 'What if the Crows are not alone? If the scouts along the length of the wall have been in the pay of the barbarians and lying to the army, we have no true knowledge of what's happening in the north.'

Bellicus looked round at him. 'What did Motius mean, "The season has turned"?'

A moment later they were running to the wall. At the nearest crossing point, only one soldier peered down at them, his face sullen, and he barely passed a word when he cranked open the gate. On the road to the fort, Mato looked back, but the wall now looked deserted.

As they neared Vercovicium, voices rose up into the night.

'What in the name of the gods,' Bellicus breathed. 'Has everyone gone mad?'

Groups of soldiers roamed around the barracks, voices cracking with anger. From their flushed faces and clouded eyes, Mato could tell some of them had been drinking, but that was a sign of trouble, not the true cause.

'Where is our pay?' someone yelled.

'Good wine? Food that isn't foul?'

'The reinforcements we asked for months ago?' another shouted.

'This place is falling down around our ears.'

'Rome's abandoned us.'

Mato glimpsed Atellus in the midst of the mob. He was barking orders, his face red, but no one was listening to him.

Bellicus thrust his way through the crowd and grabbed the commandant's arm. Over the din, Mato heard his friend yelling about the Crows and the threat they posed, but Atellus only waved him away and plunged into another fit of shouting at his men.

'They're on the brink of rebellion,' Comitinus said, looking round. 'Everything is falling apart.'

Mato peered over their heads and past the barracks. 'Who mans the gates . . . the walls?'

As the words left his lips, a star shot up into the heavens out over the Wilds. He watched its arc and knew instantly this was no sign from the gods. It was an omen, though, but one from an earthly origin.

The blazing arrow lit the northern sky, and then fell to earth.

Mato scrambled up the steps to the top of the wall. He could hear the angry voices of the soldiers ebb into a rustle of querying cries.

Squinting against the gusting wind, he leaned on the parapet and looked out into the night.

'I see nothing,' Bellicus grunted.

Mato continued to stare. After a moment, he pointed deep into the dark. 'No. There.'

The forest was moving. And the hills, and the grasslands, the whole of the Wilds. Heaving, seething.

Beside him, Bellicus shook his head and frowned. 'What am I seeing?'

'Barbarians,' Mato uttered.

Thousand upon thousand of them, sweeping down from all sides, to bring judgement on them all.

## CHAPTER TWENTY-EIGHT

# *The Fall*

'Run, Marcus. Run.' Lucanus grabbed the boy's hand and hauled him so hard his feet almost left the ground.

They were halfway across the grasslands with the wall a silhouette against the starry sky ahead when the flaming arrow had lit up the night. The Wolf allowed himself one glance back and wished he hadn't. A sea of fire reached as far as the eye could see into the black gulf, torches raised high and sweeping southward.

He reeled at the sight, trying to comprehend the true size of this army.

Now he understood the meaning of that council where he'd been taken captive. Scoti, Picts, Attacotti, the envoys from so many tribes across the waves, all of them had come together to plan for this assault, an attack so immense that the empire's forces would be overwhelmed in an instant.

The ground shook and his ears ached with the din of the battle cries.

'What is it, Lucanus? What's happening?' Marcus' voice cracked with terror.

'Keep running,' the Wolf yelled. 'Don't look back. We'll be safe soon enough.'

Though his heart pounded fit to burst, he'd not escaped death by the skin of his teeth to lose everything now, not when he was so close to home.

His feet flew over the grass and he silently gave thanks for the pouch of herbs left by the three women which had put fire in his limbs.

'We won't reach the gate,' Marcus cried. Lucanus sensed the boy flagging. The long journey had taken its toll.

'I won't leave you. I'll fight them all if I have to.' Lucanus swept the lad up into his arms as the roar of the army engulfed them. Growing closer by the moment, it sounded as if the very world was coming to an end.

He fought to keep his eyes on the torches hissing above the gate, so tantalizingly close, but then his heart sank when he saw no soldiers stood guard there, none anywhere along the wall as far as he could see. Had they all already fled in terror?

No one to open the gate. No escape.

Lucanus pushed aside his fears. He couldn't let Marcus see them.

The final leg blurred past. In the circle of torchlight at the gate, he dropped Marcus and pressed the boy's face into his chest so he wouldn't glimpse what lay at their backs. Drawing his sword, he hammered with the hilt on the wood and yelled until his throat was raw, but the roar of the horde drowned out all his efforts.

The gate stayed closed. No one had heard, or no one was there.

Lucanus felt despair clutch at him, not for himself, but for Marcus and what would lie ahead for him if he fell into the hands of the barbarians.

Clutching the boy to his chest, he rested his back against the gate and gripped his sword, knowing full well it would do no good.

That endless sea of fire, that incalculable army, the entire world shaking in its death-throes.

Lucanus reeled backwards as the gate swung open. Hands grabbed him, supported him. Someone snatched Marcus from his chest and carried him away. In an instant, the gate slammed shut again. The great bar across the inside crashed back into place.

He wrenched the hands off him, his thoughts still outside the wall, waiting to be crushed beneath the iron wave of sword and spear.

'You're safe,' someone bellowed above the roaring from beyond the wall. 'Lucanus. You're safe.'

Faces swam around him. Bellicus, Solinus, Comitinus, Mato clutching Marcus tight.

'You bastard. The gods must smile upon you.' The Bear heaved him up in a rib-cracking hug.

The gate thoomed, jolting them all from their jubilation, and then again, bodies pounding against wood that now seemed too fragile.

'To the walls,' Lucanus yelled. 'We have to hold them back.' Even as the words left his mouth he knew how futile they were.

Mato set Marcus down. 'Run to the House of Wishes and ask for your mother. She'll keep you safe.'

'No,' Lucanus shouted. 'Marcus stays by my side at all times.'

He saw the puzzled looks on his wolf-brothers' faces, but this was not the time to explain.

Inside the fort, Lucanus left Marcus crouching at the foot of the steps and clambered to the top of the wall. Atellus was marching back and forth, bellowing orders. Though he showed a determined face to his men, the Wolf glimpsed flashes of the drawn look of a leader who could see the end.

Soldiers swarmed along the wall, finding places where they could make a stand, and the Grim Wolves pushed in among them. Time and again, Lucanus watched features grow ashen as the men peered over the edge and saw the true extent of what they faced.

He shivered with that same sense of hopelessness when he looked down. The heaving sea of barbarians slammed against the wall, faces burning with fury, roars merging into one terrible bellow of rage, a vast beast ready to crush them all in its claws.

Ladders sailed across heads towards the front of the army, and they crashed against the stone one after the other. Atellus barked the command to repel the invaders and his men braced themselves, swords raised.

Bellicus grabbed his arm. 'We have no hope of winning this.'

'What choice do we have?' the commandant yelled back. 'We fight or we die.'

As the barbarians began to climb, the sky burst into fire. A thousand burning arrows whined down.

Lucanus dropped down, with Bellicus beside him. The arrows punched into the chests of soldiers who had reacted too slowly, into their faces, tunics and hair bursting into flames. Screams rang out as they flailed along the wall, staggering into neighbours, setting alight their brothers. Some toppled backwards, crashing down to the ground in a stream of gold and orange.

At a thunderous battle cry, he jumped to his feet. A shaven-headed Pict lunged over the top of the wall, hacking with his blade to clear a path to climb over.

From the corner of his eye, Lucanus saw the same scene repeated along the length of the defences.

He danced out of reach of the tip of that blade, his heels teetering on the edge. And then all his senses drew in and he stared into that one weather-beaten face. He felt the wolf in him, one that would fight to the death with fang and claw if it was cornered.

As the shaven-headed warrior swung one leg over the wall, Lucanus thrust Caledfwlch. Sparks flared as iron clashed against bronze.

His best chance was now, he knew, before the barbarian found his footing. As his foe tried to right his balance, Lucanus lunged, driving his weapon into the man's throat.

Shock flared in those eyes, but only for a moment. Then the Pict was clutching at his neck, blood spraying as he wheeled back, away from the wall, away from the ladder and down into the sea of warriors below.

Lucanus whirled. Bellicus wrenched his dripping sword out of his own enemy and heaved the limp body over the edge with a triumphant roar. But he could see Mato staggering back under a blur of blows – he was not a good swordsman. The Wolf lunged, stabbing his blade into the enemy's guts. Bellicus rammed his shoulder into the warrior and pitched him over the side.

Mato wiped the back of a trembling hand across his mouth. 'You have my thanks,' he gasped.

But there was no time.

More flaming arrows flashed through the dark. They all dropped to their knees, and when they rose again new faces hove into view over the wall.

As Lucanus gutted his third foe, he glanced along the walkway and felt the cold rush through him. Gaps were beginning to appear in the line. Soldiers sprawled on the ground below in a growing lake of blood. Others hung half over the edge, their life fluid leaking away.

And further along the wall, a knot of Picts hacked and thrust, back-to-back. Other barbarians were clambering over the ladder into their midst, their numbers multiplying by the moment.

'This is madness,' Bellicus shouted. 'The barbarians can afford to lose ten men, fifty, for every one of us they kill.'

Lucanus couldn't deny it. It was only a matter of time before they were overwhelmed.

Further along the wall, a column of flames roared up into the sky. The soldiers near to it were shouting something he couldn't hear, but he could smell the sticky scent of pitch amid the burning.

'They've set fire to the gate,' Comitinus yelled. 'They're setting all the gates ablaze.'

Lucanus glanced down the steps and saw Marcus cowering in the shadows. 'There's no point waiting here to die,' he shouted to his brothers. 'There's a greater destiny in play.'

Their faces crinkled in confusion, but when he threw himself down the steps, they dived after him without question.

On the ground, he caught Marcus' arm. 'Come. We'll find your mother and be away.'

The boy buried his face in Lucanus' chest, for just a moment, and then they swept away among the barracks. They were not alone. Soldiers who had abandoned their posts streamed by on every side. It was only a matter of time now. As they hurried to the fort's gates, he heard Atellus shout the order to retreat.

An instant later, men were leaping from the walkway and throwing themselves down the steps.

The barbarians hauled themselves over the top, cheering and thrusting their swords into the air as they claimed the wall.

Lucanus waved his men on. Only a sliver of hope remained.

The gates crashed in with a gush of flames and a shower of sparks and the barbarians whipped themselves up into an even greater frenzy. And then the horde flooded in, a torrent that seemed never-ending.

Vercovicium had fallen.

## CHAPTER TWENTY-NINE

# *The Final Hour*

MATO SPRINTED INTO THE HAUNTED ATMOSPHERE OF THE *VICUS*, where pale spectres stared up, aghast, at the orange glow rising above the wall.

'Run,' Mato bellowed over the din. 'Run.'

Faces blank with disbelief swivelled towards him. He could see one question reflected in all those dazed eyes: how could they not be safe with a garrison of seasoned soldiers to watch over them?

'It's too late,' he shouted at them. 'For the first time in more than two centuries the wall has been lost.'

Mouths gaped stupidly. A babe in arms bawled, children sobbed, old men mouthed obscenities at the sky, all of it lost to the howling fury.

Mato swung his arms, exhorting them to flee, but they only jerked from their stupor when the soldiers scrambled past, shedding armour. When that river of iron and death finally began to flood from the fort, those confused expressions finally shaded towards fear. Only then did they think of escape.

And by that time it was too late.

The wave of panic swept Mato up and spun him around in a maelstrom of buffeting bodies, his ears numb from the screams and the yells. Flailing, he fought to claw his way free, but the flood rushed him along the street, dashing him against folk weighted by whatever meagre possessions they considered too valuable to leave behind.

Finally, a hand grasped his arm and wrenched him free. It was Lucanus, carrying Marcus in his arms.

Mato wanted to yell out that he was afraid, that he was a scout, not a warrior, but he was too ashamed to admit it. The Wolf seemed to understand. He held Mato's eyes in a silent communication of support, a kindness that Mato would never forget.

'This is madness,' Lucanus shouted. 'But if we are to survive it, we will do so shoulder to shoulder.'

Shoving his way through the melee, his leader carved a path for him to stumble to the edge of the street. There, Bellicus, Solinus and Comitinus hunched over their swords, faces twisted with fury.

Mato followed their gaze and saw Picts and Scoti stream into the outskirts of the *vicus*, harvesting men, women and children, young and old, without a second thought.

A blade sliced through the top of an old woman's head. Another plunged through a boy's chest. An entire family tumbled under those running feet. Mato gaped. These barbarians were not interested in a military victory. Their hatreds had simmered for so long, they saw everyone south of the wall as their enemy.

'We have to save them.' He blinked away hot tears.

Lucanus gripped his arm more tightly. 'Look at the numbers.' His voice cracked. 'There's nothing we can do for them.'

Mato felt acid rise in his throat as he cast his eyes over that army. He could see nothing of the ground beneath the *vicus* and the wall, just an ocean of heads and swords burning orange in the light of the flames. More were still pushing in through the gates, and more, and more.

Not far away, the twins Map and Lossio crashed to the ground, blades hacking into their backs, and a moment later a sword chopped down their love Vrocata, their affair never to be resolved. Mato cried out, then spun away, not wanting to let Lucanus see his despair. Friends, neighbours, all he had ever known, lost.

'We save the few we can, and flee,' the Wolf shouted. In a daze, Mato felt himself dragged away from the milling bodies towards the House of Wishes.

Bellicus erupted into life. 'Go,' he said, turning in the opposite direction. 'I'll find you.' He began to thrust his way into the flow of fleeing people.

'Where are you going, you jolt-head?' Solinus cried, clawing at the other man's arm to haul him back.

The Bear shrugged him off. Solinus yelled until his throat was raw, but by then Bellicus was lost to the crowd.

Catia could bear it no longer. She yanked open the door to the hidden room and peered outside, though Amarina had told her never to do that. But she'd been listening to the thunder of battle and the roar of voices and screams echoing through the walls for what seemed like an age.

Amarina's girls were rushing around the house, sweeping up armfuls of fine dresses and jewellery and whatever coin they had saved.

'What's happening?' Catia shouted.

The women flashed her blank looks, but no one answered. They had their own concerns.

Seeing the panic in their faces, Catia slipped out into the passage. 'Where is Amarina?' she demanded, and when still no one replied she grabbed Decima's arm.

The dark-skinned woman glared at her, then snapped, 'In her rooms.' She wrenched free and ran.

Catia raced along the corridor. She couldn't begin to imagine what was causing the din, but the girls were as frightened as anyone she'd ever seen, and nothing scared them.

She threw open a door to find Amarina loading coin into a leather sack from a hiding place beneath the floor. She glowered at Catia as if she were about to be robbed. A blade appeared in her hand from nowhere.

'I don't want your gold,' Catia spat. 'Tell me what's happening.'

'The barbarians have broken through the wall. An army of them. More than I ever thought existed.' Amarina scooped the last of her coin into the sack and stood up. 'Stay here and die. Or flee.'

Catia's thoughts flew to her father and Aelius, even Amatius. 'I must go to my family—'

'Go to them, then. Don't waste my time.' Amarina barged past her.

'We should stay together . . .' Catia began.

'You'll only slow me down. Go your own way.'

The red-haired woman ran from the room, the others joining her as she hurried to the door. Catia followed. She would not be told what to do by Amarina.

The women, all eight of them, crashed out into the night.

Catia recoiled from the deafening roar and the screams. She choked on smoke from the burning and tasted ashes on her tongue. A deluge of warriors surged into the *vicus*, so thick upon the ground she could not see past them. People running, terrified. Fighting. Innocents cut down as they fled.

Amarina gaped. Even she had not expected this madness, Catia could see.

'What now?' Galantha shouted. 'We'll never get through to the Stanegate.'

Before Amarina could answer, a gang of Scoti spun towards them. They laughed, eyes brightening with delight in the glare from the fires, and, as one, they ran towards the women.

Some of the girls screamed. In their fear, they were too slow. Catia watched them swept up by the attackers, and then dashed to the ground to be raped. The barbarians fell on them like hungry beasts.

Catia thought Amarina would flee. Instead, she darted forward, her face wintry.

Her blade slashed the throat of the nearest man. As he stumbled backwards, trying to stem the flood of blood, Amarina snatched his sword and tossed it to Catia.

'Here's your chance to prove me wrong,' she spat. 'Fight.'

Catia grasped the blade. The moment it was in her hands, she remembered every moment of the hours she had spent sparring with Lucanus when she was a girl. She was not a good swordswoman, but good enough to do some harm.

A barbarian charged at her, laughing as she waved the sword. She lunged, and though the strike was not perfect the blade skidded across his arm, opening him up. He spun away, howling.

Galantha and Decima waved their knives from side to side, spitting like wildcats, and as the four women advanced the Scoti stumbled back, cursing. They wanted easy booty, not having to fight for their prizes.

Two of the girls were dead by the time Catia and Amarina ran up to them. The snarling Scoti hauled off the other two, both of them screaming, their arms reaching out for aid. Catia felt sick to see the terror in their eyes. But there was nothing she could do to save them before they were lost to the churning mass of bodies.

'Now what?' Decima's voice trembled as she looked around for a way out, saw none.

'There.' Amarina stabbed a finger towards a circle of soldiers slashing any attackers who dared venture close, seemingly undeterred by the numbers swarming up to them. At the front, Atellus was a blood-drenched vision of madness, the centurion, Falx, at his shoulder guarding his commander's back. 'Let them protect us,' Amarina continued. 'It's the least they can do for all the pleasure we've given them.'

But as the four women hurried towards them, Catia heard Falx shout an order to the men around him, the words lost beneath the clash of steel, and a moment later he was running away with six of the men beside him. Catia gasped. Less than half had fled, but they'd torn the heart out of the carefully organized defence.

Atellus' face twisted in shock before hardening into grim acceptance. Throwing back his head, he roared like a cornered bear, a final show of defiance, and then the Scoti swords slashed down.

Catia sensed the other women stiffen around her and she wondered if they all felt as cold as she did now that the last meagre hope had drained away.

Heads swivelled their way, eyes gleaming with a sickening hunger that she knew only too well.

One foot stepped forward. Then another. Five. Ten. More.

Bellicus barged through the madness of blind terror, his ears aching from the screams. Bodies crushed him on every side and he smelled sweat and piss and shit, that battlefield reek. It shouldn't be here, in the *vicus*, home, safety. He squinted over the sea of heads jamming every street, all those poor bastards funnelling past the huts and the workshops in a desperate attempt to reach the open countryside beyond.

But what then?

Cursing, he elbowed his way to the side of the flow and kicked open the door of the wine merchant's. Before he dived inside, he glanced up the slope to the fort. Against the sheets of flame, silhouettes hacked in indiscriminate slaughter. He felt sickened. It was like seeing pigs being cut down for the blood-month feast.

Past the rows of amphorae he hurried, breathing in the sour wine scent, and out at the back. He scrambled over heaps of rotting vegetables and broken pottery, rats fleeing before him, and then stumbled through the dark faster than he ever could have done in that mad throng.

As he slipped through the dark, he glanced along one of the narrow alleys to the mayhem in the street. Framed in the wavering orange glow of that thin rectangle, he saw the widow Elsia sprawled on the packed mud. Feet sped by her face as she reached out a hand, sobbing in desperation for someone to help her up. Elsia, whom he'd helped time and again with a little coin after her husband died. Poor lonely Elsia.

A Pict lurched up, naked to the waist, his body black with tattoos.

The barbarian swung his sword down and split her head in two.

Bellicus choked down his despair.

*Madness, madness.*

Cutting through the back of a metalworker's on to the edge of the street, he skidded to a halt. Ovincus was standing outside his shop, a cleaver in one hand, an axe in the other. He was still wearing his blood-stained apron.

When he saw Bellicus, he nodded as if this was any normal day, his bald head glowing orange in the firelight.

'Vercovicium is lost,' Bellicus shouted. 'Get away from here.'

'And what? Starve? Be hunted down like the beasts I carve on my table?' Ovincus' eyes gleamed, and Bellicus could see he'd already chosen his fate.

The Grim Wolf felt a pang of sadness. They'd been friends for many years, and he couldn't imagine a life without seeing him again. But Ovincus had decided on his own way of dying and that was a man's right. He deserved no less.

Bellicus clapped a hand on his shoulder. 'I'll miss you, brother. Take a host of them with you.'

Ovincus grinned. 'I can cut a ram's head off with one blow. Let them taste that.' He looked round. 'Your dog's in the back. Take good care of him. I'll miss the savage bastard.' He flashed another grin, a sad one this time, and turned his back on Bellicus as if saying there would be no more soft-headed goodbyes.

For a moment, Bellicus watched him standing there like a sentinel, framed against the glow from the walls, and then he darted into the blood-fouled confines of the workshop.

'Catulus,' he called, and whistled. The dog bounded out to him, wagging its tail. He surprised himself with the rush of affection he felt.

'Good boy,' he said. 'Good boy, wolf-brother.'


Lucanus sprinted up to the door of the House of Wishes. Here, on the fringes, only a few of the invading army had ventured, for now, and the Grim Wolves had managed to slip by them.

Lowering Marcus to the ground, the Wolf ducked inside, calling Catia's name, but all that met him were echoes, open doors and ransacked rooms. Choking back his rising dread, he dashed back into the night and stared around.

'Where would she go?' Mato said, but all Lucanus could manage was an impotent shake of his head.

'Over here,' Comitinus shouted from the dark, and as Lucanus ran towards him he heard taunts and laughter somewhere ahead.

Racing around the bath-house to where the temples stood, he could see a group of four fur-swathed warriors advancing on four women. He couldn't make out their faces in the gloom, but when one of them spat an epithet he was sure it was Amarina's voice.

Putting his head down, the Wolf bounded on, knowing his brothers would be at his back. He rammed his sword into the side of the first warrior he came to, a Saxon by the look of him, and the Grim Wolves fell upon the rest, as did, he noted with surprise, two of the women. Amarina and Catia swung their blades awkwardly, but their ferocity made up for their lack of expertise.

Lucanus felt a rush of relief when he saw Catia standing over the bodies. How many times had he dreamt about her on the long journey into the north, never really believing he would live to see her again? He couldn't stop himself beaming, but somehow he found it in him to step back and wait.

'Mother.' Marcus rushed into Catia's arms, and she sank to her knees, her whole body heaving with silent sobs.

After a moment, Marcus prised himself free as if he'd only been away playing with his friends, and looked back. 'Lucanus saved me,' he said simply.

Catia looked up at her wolf-brother with tear-rimmed eyes and he saw such gratitude in her face – perhaps even love – that he felt shaken. She tried to find some words to thank him, but she could only swallow and nod.

Amarina hooked a hand under her arm and dragged her to her feet. 'All good friends, well met, yes. Now – shall we let our heels fly or wait here until we feel the prick of swords?'

'I must . . . I must save my family,' Catia said, almost apologetically, Lucanus thought.

'Good. You have horses – we'll need those if we're to have any chance of escaping,' he said.

Clutching Marcus by the hand, Catia set off along the track to the villa with Solinus, Comitinus and the other women close behind. Before the Wolf could follow, he felt Mato grab his arm. 'I can't leave without Bellicus.'

Lucanus held the other man's gaze. They both knew it was unlikely the Bear could escape the slaughter heaving in the *vicus* below them. 'The barbarians will soon turn their attention to the villas. If you wait here—'

Mato nodded, cutting off the words he didn't want to hear. 'Bellicus,' he said again, as if that were explanation enough. 'I can't leave him.'

Lucanus nodded. 'We'll wait as long as we can.' He turned and ran along the track after the others. When he looked back, he saw a lonely figure watching the destruction of all that he had known.

The villa was still and dark.

'Fetch the horses,' Lucanus commanded his wolf-brothers. While the women hung back, searching the night in case any of the barbarians had already ventured this far, he himself swept through the gates.

The merchants had built their villas far enough away from the *vicus* to escape the earthy aroma of a bustling township, but he could smell smoke and ashes on the breeze. The sound of the carnage was like the low rumble of a great beast, heavy with slumber after a bloody feast.

'Come out,' he yelled. 'Out now or die hiding under your beds.'

Catia caught up with him. 'They will be scared. Let me.'

When she finally stepped out of the villa, beckoning, Amatius was behind her, looking like a whipped cur, and then Aelius, his good arm supporting Menius. The old man was a grey shadow seemingly on the edge of death, Lucanus thought.

At the clopping of hooves, he turned and shouted to Comitinus, 'Keep watch.' His chest tightened as the others hitched a horse to a low, open wagon and he swallowed the urge to order them to move faster.

When a whistle rang out from the vicinity of the gate, he hurried over to Comitinus. The other man pointed to a line of torches bobbing along the track to the villa. Lucanus could hear voices, insistent, harsh, the guttural tongues of barbarians.

'Make haste,' he called. 'They're coming.'

He whirled back at the sound of running feet just beyond the villa wall. Comitinus drew his sword, but a moment later Mato and Bellicus scrambled through the gates with Catulus behind them. The two men hunched over, hands on their knees as they caught their breath.

'Thirty of them,' Mato croaked, waving a hand at his back. 'Perhaps more.'

As Lucanus raced back into the yard, Amarina plucked up her skirt and ran ahead to where Solinus and the family were finishing hitching the wagon. 'We must go. Now,' she insisted. 'There's an army outside the gates. Leave behind anyone who will slow us.'

'Does that include you?' Aelius spat.

'I'll be first out of here, little boy.'

Lucanus and Aelius heaved Menius into the back of the wagon. Catia, Marcus, Decima and Galantha clambered in beside him. Lucanus beckoned to Amarina to join them.

'I can ride,' she said, pulling herself on to the back of a horse with ease.

On the board of the wagon, Amatius, the *mulio*, lashed a whip and Lucanus gripped the sides of the *rheda* as it thundered out of the courtyard. Aelius and the Grim Wolves bounded on to the remaining horses and rode out of the gate.

What now was left for any of them?

215

★

Once he was sure they'd put enough distance between them and the invaders, Lucanus raised his hand to bring the group to a halt.

The villa was already ablaze. Everywhere he looked, more fires lit up the gulf of darkness. In the distance, to the west and the east, the sky glowed a dim orange.

'Vercovicium was only a part of it,' Bellicus said at his side. 'They've come through along the length of the wall, I'd wager.' Nestled in his lap, Catulus rumbled deep in his throat as if he understood every word.

Against those fires near the fort, Lucanus watched the silhouettes swarming like a disturbed anthill. More flowed through the gates from the northlands.

'Scoti. Picts. Attacotti. Alamanni. Saxons. Some I did not even know.' Mato's voice was strained. 'All of them, together? This is unheard of.'

'How long have they been planning it?' Bellicus asked.

'We've never met this before, you're right,' Lucanus said. 'This army . . . the size of it . . . barbarians who have hated each other since time began . . . this is not the end, I'm certain.'

How much of this had the wood-priests been involved in, he wondered? Was this part of their Great Plan? Drive out the empire so that this new messiah, this king who would not die, could lay claim to the land? Their king, their voice in his ear, their hand upon his shoulder. If that were true, the blood of all the innocents who'd died this night would be on their hands.

He looked to Catia in the back of the wagon, hugging her son to her breast, singing to him. The world might be ending around them, but she was lost to the joy of that reunion.

Now Marcus, and Catia, and all of them, were inextricably bound into this unfolding slaughter. The wood-priests, Erca and his men, all of them would be searching for this child.

There could be no rest.

# CHAPTER THIRTY

## *Escape*

BELLICUS CARVED THE END OF THE BRANCH INTO A SPEAR-POINT and looked up. He was perched on a fallen log, surrounded by curling shavings. 'I'll take Solinus. If we can find a deer or a boar, all the better. If not, a bird, or fish if there's some water near here. And if not that, we'll have to make do with worms and bugs until we can find something to give us strength.'

'Don't stray too far,' Lucanus cautioned. 'We don't know how fast the barbarians are pushing south, and there may well be cut-throats around these parts. Not that they would find much to steal.'

He looked around the camp, a small clearing in the greenwood, a little way off the track where they had left the *rheda*. Comitinus was blowing on sparks in a nest of dry grass and twigs and Catia and her family lay around it, trying to get some sleep. They'd ridden through the night, always heading due south. As first light painted the drawn faces and the shuddering bodies, Lucanus decided they could afford to rest, at least for a while, to build up their spirits.

Amarina, Decima and Galantha slumped at the foot of a gnarled oak, wrapped in thick cloaks, faces lost in deep hoods. Heads bent together, they were whispering, about what he couldn't tell.

Once Bellicus and Solinus had stalked off among the ash and the elm, he squatted on the edge of the clearing, breathing in the scents of a world about to burst with new life. When he looked up, he saw Catia watching him. She smiled and came over.

Sitting, she took his hand, something she would never have dared do back in Vercovicium. 'Thank you,' she said. 'Thank you a thousand times.'

'Marcus has been like a son to me. And you . . .' He let the words trail away, afraid he would say something he regretted. As he looked past her to the fire, he saw Amatius, his cheek pressed against the cold earth as he tried to sleep, but his eyes wide and staring. Gently, Lucanus eased his hand from hers.

'Your husband,' he breathed without moving his lips.

He watched Catia frown. 'Yes, he is my husband. But everything has changed. All of us here, we have nothing now. We're beggars on the land. I don't have to bow my head to him to ensure my father gets what he deserves.' She looked up, her eyes like pebbles. 'If he dares lay a hand on me again, he'll pay, and pay dearly, for all the times he's done it in the past. No more. No. More.'

Lucanus felt relieved to hear the defiance in her voice. 'You know how much it pained me to see you suffer so.'

She nodded, smiling again. He couldn't remember the last time he'd seen such simple joy in her face. How strange it was that it should appear now, when they were fleeing for their lives with all that they had known burning around them.

After a moment, he saw her expression grow grave and she said, 'There's much we must talk about.'

'I have much to tell you too. About Marcus. About why he was taken . . . his days yet to come . . . You won't believe it, I swear, this destiny the gods have planned for him, but—'

Catia pressed her finger against his lips to silence him, her eyes widening. 'You know?'

'*You* know?'

'A merchant came to Vercovicium . . . Varro was his name. He'd travelled all the way from Rome to find me, and he told me a story, from long ago – a prophecy, I suppose – that one day there'd be a woman marked with the sign of the Ouroboros, the dragon eating its own tail. You know of that.'

He did. They'd talked many times since childhood about what kind of person would brand a baby with that mark, and why.

'Somehow Varro was aware that this woman was alive in these times . . . and living somewhere along the wall. She . . . I . . . have a special destiny, he said.'

Lucanus let her words settle on him for a moment before answering. 'Witches and wood-priests, they can't be trusted. Men and women who've spent too much time in the Wilds in their own company. It drives you mad after a while; the madness of the woods, we call it in the *arcani*.' He shrugged. 'They would say it's the wisdom of the gods, who speak through the trees and the winds and the deep lakes. But they too spoke about this prophecy. I don't know if there's any truth in it, but they believe it, and it seems that everything they do is directed towards one end: making this prophecy come about.' He furrowed his brow, trying to make sense of what he'd heard. 'I'm a simple man. I can't read or write. And when they spoke of these things . . . of signs and portents . . . they seemed to be talking of one thing but meaning another.'

'*Everything has two faces. What it seems on the surface, and what it truly is beneath.* That's what Varro said.' He saw her wince. This memory was a hard one, for some reason.

'And nothing happens by chance.'

'The dragon on my back is not a dragon. It is a sign of . . . rebirth . . . of what, I can't be sure.'

'Of the old gods. The old ways. Of a time that the Romans swept away when they invaded Britannia. The wood-priests have been plotting since that time . . . preparing for the moment when the prophecy said all would be made right again. By one man. The king who will not die.'

Catia glanced back at the fire where her son was sleeping. Amatius' eyes were shut now too. 'Marcus?'

'His son. Or his son's son. He carries the royal blood.' He heard his voice soften, and he resisted the urge to stroke her hair. 'As do you. You were chosen, wolf-sister. The gods saw greatness in you. You're the chalice that holds the hopes of us all.'

Her eyes sparkled. That pleased him. 'It's a good destiny. A great one. To save everyone . . . to lead them out of darkness,' she breathed.

'A good destiny.'

'And you have a part to play in this?'

'The gods have given me a task too.' He slid Caledfwlch a little way out of its scabbard to show her the marks upon the blade, and he told her how he came to own it. 'I'm the guardian of the royal

219

blood, so Myrrdin told me. No harm must come to Marcus, so the seed will sprout and the prophecy will flourish.'

'Then you must stay with us.'

'For as long as I'm needed.'

For a while there was only the crackling of the fire and the bird-song. Lucanus liked the sounds of them. He could tell Catia was considering them too, but he couldn't see any sign of her thoughts.

'There are dangers now,' he continued. 'Before, you and Marcus went about your lives unnoticed. Now men who wield power have heard of you and they covet you both, for whoever has the king's ear—'

'Rules the land.' Catia bit her lip, starting to worry.

'I don't wish to frighten you, but it's right that you know these things so that you can prepare. The barbarians know of Marcus and his worth, and they won't relent in their search for him.'

'If Varro escaped Vercovicium, he will be looking for Marcus too.' She chewed on a nail, reflecting.

'Who knows how many more will want to lay claim to you and your son?'

'Wherever we are going, no one will know us.'

'For now. But this is a story that sets hearts and mind afire. Word will spread. Soon everyone will have heard of the woman marked with the dragon, and the son who will bring forth the gods-given king.'

Catia tugged at the new swards of grass poking out among the tree's roots. 'So many choices. So many dangers.' When she looked up, her eyes were bright. 'I'm glad you stand with me. I would not want this burden on my own.'

When everyone had woken, they took it in turns to go to a stream that Mato had found, to slake their thirst and wash the dust of the road from their faces. The water was a cold knife cutting through worry.

Back at the fire, Menius lay on his back, staring up into the branches, his face the colour of the ashes. Catia leaned over him, mopping the sweat from his brow with a strip she'd torn from the hem of her dress.

She looked round and her eyes summoned Lucanus.

He crouched beside her. 'How is he?'

'His brow is so hot. His lips are dry.' She leaned away so the old man would not hear and whispered, 'Is he dying? Please let it not be so.'

'Let me help.' Amarina was standing behind the Wolf.

'What can you do?' Catia snapped.

'I can stand here talking while your father weakens, if you wish.'

Catia hesitated, then moved aside so Amarina could kneel beside the old man. She rested one hand on his forehead, then peeled back his eyelids to reveal the yellowy whites. For a few moments, her hands fluttered across his face and neck and Lucanus watched the concentration in her frown.

When she was done, she pulled a leather pouch from the folds of her dress and delved inside for a handful of dried leaves. 'By rights, these should be left to steep in ditchwater for a night. But we can't wait. His light is dim.'

As she began to push the leaves between Menius' lips, Catia gripped her wrist.

'I am not going to poison him.'

Lucanus watched Catia trying to read the other woman's face before she relented. 'It will make him well?'

'It will help bring down his fever. For now, that's the best we can hope.' He noticed Amarina eye Catia and soften a little when she saw the other woman's worry. 'When we are on the road, I'll search for more herbs that might ease his sickness.' It was a kindness, though Lucanus knew she would never admit it.

Catia knelt back down to tend to her father and Amarina stepped away.

Lucanus walked beside her. 'Where did you learn these things?'

'A little here, a little there.'

'You have many secrets, Amarina.'

'Everyone has secrets, Wolf.'

'Still, the only women I know versed in these arts are the wise ones who live in the woods.'

'All women are wise, Lucanus. You would do well to remember that.' She flashed a smile, one that hid more than it revealed, and walked to the shady spot where Mato was making Decima laugh.

Amatius was waiting for him as he turned back. 'Beware of that woman. She can't be trusted.'

'Amarina plays games with words and foolish men. But I've known her since she arrived in Vercovicium, and I'm a good judge. I'd trust her with my life.'

'Then you are a fool.' Amatius bunched his fists. He had always been good at hiding his feelings – the mark of a man successful in business – but now he seemed a ball of rage. 'One more thing, Lucanus.' He tried to force a smile, but it flickered on his lips, making its insincerity even more apparent. 'I love my wife. I love her more than life itself. And if anyone came between the two of us, I would kill him.'

'Everyone knows you are husband and wife, Amatius. You have no need to worry.'

The Wolf walked away before any more could be said.

Bellicus and Solinus crashed into the clearing, their spears dripping blood, but Lucanus could not see any sign of meat.

'Come,' Bellicus called, beckoning.

At the note of warning in his voice, everyone except Menius and Marcus followed the two men back into the depths of the woods. The path meandered past dense clumps of hawthorn and bracken flecked with new green shoots.

Lucanus smelled the iron tang of blood in the air, but it was only the carcass of a boar, Bellicus' and Solinus' prey, no doubt. Or so he thought.

But then the two wolves came to a halt by a listing ash tree, and he realized there was more to it. Three bodies were littered at the foot of the trunk, cut down by swords or axes by the look of it, half an arm and a leg and the top of a skull scattered nearby. Each man had a bow and carried a quiver. 'Hunters,' he murmured.

But as he knelt to examine the kill, he saw what had truly concerned the other two men. Butcher's marks scarred the pale flesh of two of the fallen.

'The Attacotti,' he said.

'The barbarians are still moving south?' Galantha said.

Bellicus ran a hand through his red hair. 'It's more than that.'

Lucanus stood up and cupped his ear. 'No sound of an army advancing. This is a few men, scouts perhaps. The Attacotti are stealthy, we know that from the ease with which they moved through

Vercovicium. But . . .' He looked at Catia. 'They may be hunting us.'

'Why would those barbarians be interested in a handful of fleeing Romans? We have no gold,' Amatius demanded.

'Be that as it may, we should heed Lucanus' warning. We must not take any risks,' Catia said.

When the Wolf looked round at his brothers, he could see from their narrowed eyes that they knew there was something he had not told them. 'We'll speak of this later,' he said. 'For now, we should act as if they are hunting for us and will not relent. Bellicus, Solinus, hurry to the camp now. Guard Marcus and Menius.'

'We'll pick up the boar as we pass,' Bellicus said. 'Some meat in our bellies will not go amiss.'

Lucanus felt Catia's hand linger on his arm for an instant as she eased past him to stand on the edge of the blood-soaked area. She eyed the bodies for a moment, then plucked up a bow and a quiver.

'This will be mine. I want to be of some use on the road.'

'A bow?' Amatius said. 'You couldn't draw it, never mind loose an arrow.' Lucanus could hear the contempt in his voice, but Catia showed no sign that she cared, or even heard her husband any more.

She stepped up to Lucanus, slinging the leather quiver over her shoulder. 'Remember when we were children? Thumping shafts into the old oak? Your father was a good teacher.'

'And he cuffed me round the head because you were better with a bow than me.'

'But you were better with a sword.'

Lucanus shrugged. 'Not much, wolf-sister.' He sensed Amatius bristle at his words. But as he turned to make light of them, Catia's husband was already stalking back towards the camp.

## CHAPTER THIRTY-ONE

# *On the Trail of the Dragon*

*Rome*

A RABBLE OF LAUGHING CHILDREN ON THE WATER'S EDGE HURLED stones at the floating corpse. The gulls feasting on the remains soared up in a thunderous beating of wings, circled once, and then flocked back. More missiles, more shrieking, the cycle repeated.

'Another poor bastard executed at the Stairs of Mourning.' Corvus shielded his eyes against the glare coming off the Tiber. 'You spend all your life struggling and striving and you end up as bird food.'

Pavo cracked the knuckles of his huge hands. 'If you ask me, there are no good deaths.'

Corvus looked up past the Tabularium to the grim front of the Mamertine prison. That view was probably the last thing the dead man had seen before he ended up in the river. 'One thing's for sure. In a city founded by men raised by a wolf, you can't afford to be a lamb.'

'Then I'd suggest you grow some teeth, and fast.'

Sighing, Corvus drifted down a set of stone steps to the river. The sound of hammers beat out and his nose filled with the conflicting scents of pitch and fresh-cut wood. A little further along the bank, he could see their destination: a small boat-builder's yard that carried out repairs on the skiffs and smaller craft that were the only ones able to navigate the Tiber past the city.

He'd spent long days searching for the man Severus had told him about, the one who had once worked for his mother. Questioning suspicious owners of taverns near the Pinciana gate, convincing them he was not a debt collector or a man with a grudge, following the dismal trail through places where unskilled men found hard work for little reward.

Others would not have been so dogged, but he wasn't someone who was easily deterred. The secrets that his family kept drove him on.

'You're thinking of the witch again,' Pavo taunted. 'It's all over your face.'

'I'm worried about her.'

'You talk as if you've drunk too much wine. You and I both know you'd like to be holding hands and skipping with her through fields of corn.'

Corvus sighed again.

'Oh? The thought has never crossed your mind?'

'I'm not a boy still yearning for first love.'

Pavo snorted. 'Of course. How wrong I am.' There was a long silence, and when Corvus looked at his friend he saw how serious he'd grown. 'I don't want to see you hurt, you know that. But your brother—'

'Stop bringing up my brother.'

'I can't. He doesn't care about you.'

'Enough.' Corvus felt his anger mounting. At his friend for bringing up things he wanted to ignore. And at himself, because he knew that everything Pavo said was true.

'I'm going to talk to our man alone,' he said.

'Then I'll wait. Enjoy the sun. Torment the children. Sit here and be your conscience.'

Corvus strode on along the edge of the glittering Tiber, glancing back only once. Pavo was a smudge of shadow in the bright sunlight flooding the stone wall against which he leaned.

As he became engulfed in the sound of hammers from the boat-builder's yard, he thought how distant his mother and brother had grown since the raid upon the temple. Ruga had roamed around with a face like a man who had been stung by a bee, snapping at anyone who came near him. But it was his mother who troubled him the most. Whenever she was sad or suffering, he felt gloomy, as if he were responsible. That had always been the case, since he was a boy.

And now she looked on the verge of tears all the time. She sat in her room for long hours, emerging in the dark when the day turned only to huddle with Ruga. Their conversation always ended when he came near. That stung him too.

Skirting the heaps of ballast, he studied the boat-builders sawing fresh wood and stretching hide to dry. One caught his eye, a familiar face rising from his memory, though much younger then; not these crumpled features like a weather-beaten cliff face and hair more silver than black. He was stirring a barrel of pitch with all the enthusiasm of a man who had been told his balls would be fed to the yard dog as soon as he was finished.

'Titus Didius Strabo.'

The man looked over, shoulders growing taut. Someone used to being cornered, Corvus thought.

'It's taken me a long time to find you.' He bowed, trying to put the other man at his ease. 'Do you remember me?'

Strabo's eyes narrowed as he looked this stranger up and down. He shook his head slowly and returned to his stirring.

'You used to work for my mother, Gaia—'

The other man stiffened. Was that anger Corvus saw? Suspicion? Hurt?

After a moment, Strabo grunted, 'You were the strange one.'

'If by that you mean the witty, charming, courageous one who was filled with an unbounded sense of adventure, then yes.'

'Why are you here? We agreed terms. I have not gone back on my word.'

'Terms? My mother paid you?'

'Not enough.'

Corvus looked around the yard. 'All gone now, I'd wager.'

Strabo's top lip twitched, but he said nothing.

'A little more gold would not go amiss?' Corvus jangled a leather pouch.

The other man eyed it, unable to hide his hunger. 'What do you want?'

'To hear what you know. About my mother, and my brother, and the time you spent with us.'

Strabo took the skin hanging at his hip and swigged back the contents. Red wine trickled from the corner of his mouth. He wiped it away with the back of his hand and jerked his head, indicating that they should move beyond a heap of timber where they would not be overheard. As expected: loose lips, easily bought. Strabo slumped down in the shade and watched with wary eyes.

Corvus perched on the end of a half-cut log. 'You worked for my mother and father in Britannia?'

Strabo smirked. 'I did. But not for your mother and her husband.'

While Corvus was trying to make sense of this word-play, Strabo flexed his fingers. Corvus tossed him the purse and watched him inspect the contents. He seemed satisfied.

'Your mother was married to another in Vercovicium. A man named Menius. He failed her, or so she said. Too weak, too . . .' He waved a hand in the air. 'Who knows? She took up with his brother.'

Corvus flinched. This was news to him. He didn't want to think of his mother in that way. 'This can't be true.'

Strabo sniggered. 'Are you sure you want to hear more?'

His unease growing, Corvus nodded for him to continue.

'I worked for your father at the time. A strong arm when he needed it, some hunting. He was tupping your mother long before she left Menius.' He shrugged. 'Might be that he is the true father of your half-sister. Or sister. Or . . . families, eh?'

This time Corvus gaped, unable to hide his shock.

'Didn't tell you about her, I see. Aye, Catia's her name. I bet your mother didn't tell you that she robbed her old husband blind when she ran off with his brother, either. Took his gold, all his trade, his slaves, everything he had apart from a little bit of land. Left him to scratch his way back up or starve.'

'That I cannot believe.'

Strabo eyed him for a moment, then said, 'Oh, there's worse than that.'

Corvus slipped into the modest house on the Via Flaminia that his mother had bought with his father's gold when she had arrived in Rome. Gaia was sitting in her chamber, looking out of the window over the orange-tiled rooftops baking in the sun. She jerked round when he swept in.

'What's wrong?' she began, trying to read his expression. 'Is it Ruga?'

'It's not Ruga.' He pushed aside his annoyance that his brother was the first thing which came to her mind.

'What's wrong, my love? Come. Sit beside me.' She beckoned him over as if he would fall on to the floor by her legs as he did when he was a boy.

Instead, he prowled around the chamber, watching her. 'Do you remember Titus Didius Strabo? He remembers you well.'

Gaia's smile drained away. 'Strabo is . . . ?' The words died in her throat.

'I have a sister. Why didn't you tell me?'

He watched her flick her hair back from her face, composing herself while she bought herself time. 'What's gone is gone. It's too painful for me to think about the poor child . . . about what I have lost. And I wouldn't wish that pain on you, when you can never see her. Her father would not allow it.'

Corvus moistened his lips. 'You'll forgive me if I have some difficulty in accepting your hurt, Mother. Not after Strabo told me you ordered him to take my baby sister out into the wilderness to leave her to die. Your own daughter.'

Her eyes brimmed with tears. 'A lie.'

'Is it?'

'There's more to it than that. So much more.'

'Then tell me.'

'I cannot, I cannot.' She bowed her head, covering her face with her hands, in grief or shame, he couldn't tell. 'Nothing is as it seems,' she murmured through her fingers.

'Did you want her dead?' His voice was almost lost beneath the sound of voices and rattle of cart wheels rising from the street outside.

Gaia crossed the chamber to him, holding out her arms. 'Could you think that of me? After all the love I lavished on you? I sheltered you from the storms of life, I gave you all the hugs and kisses a mother could, and stroked your hair and rocked you in my arms whenever you were sad.'

Corvus took a step back and that seemed to cut her more than anything. 'Strabo told me the babe was saved by a pack of wolves.

Suckled by the she-wolf. An act of the gods, he said, damning you. And after that you couldn't live in Vercovicium any more. You ran away with my . . . my father to Banna, and then here to Rome, because you were too afraid to live in Britannia any more.' He couldn't bear to wound her further with talk of how she'd robbed her husband in the process and left him broken.

She whirled away to the window. 'Yes, I was afraid. When you and your brother were born at Banna, and when we fled by sea that night.' She paused. 'Afraid, even here.'

'Of what?'

She shook her head, still not looking at him. 'The less you know, the better.'

'You don't need to spare me. I can protect you now.'

Gaia looked back at him, her smile wistful. 'I will always fight to keep you safe. You were such a troubled child.'

'If Father were here—'

'Your father was a cruel man, a violent man. He took me, with force, time and again.' She swept across the chamber to him. 'If we are speaking truth now, you should hear me out . . .'

Corvus held up a hand to stop her.

'You knew. You saw once. You heard my screams, and found him upon me on the floor. And you fought to protect me, my love. But you were too small, too fragile.'

'I don't remember that.'

'Of course not. What boy would, seeing his mother in such a state. But a part of you never forgot, my darling boy.'

Corvus shook his head, trying to get the visions his mother had created out of it. 'Enough. You're telling me this to distract me.'

'No, my love, no. I tell you this because it is the truth, and a hard one. What son should think of his father that way? As a brute who rapes his wife. You were born from that violent congress. For that pain and suffering I was rewarded with you, my wonderful boy, and I showered all my love on you, and Ruga—'

*Ruga.* Corvus jerked back from her. 'Ruga was the one who had all the love, all the opportunities, I remember that.'

'No, my darling, no.' Gaia cupped his jaw in her hands as she had done so many times since he was tiny. He pulled back and jabbed a finger at her, then regretted it. She looked so frightened, as if she thought he was his father, about to attack her. 'I'm sorry . . .' he began.

His mother turned away, blinking back tears, her hand to her mouth.

'The plans you and Ruga have been concocting . . .'

'You are too delicate to be burdened with such a thing,' she interrupted, her voice a low croak.

Corvus stifled a smile. How many days had he returned from the front line drenched in the blood of the Alamanni? 'Delicate, yes. A little flower. But I've had my fill of being kept outside this wall you and Ruga have built around yourselves.'

'No wall, my love.' She tried to cup his face again, but he pulled back. His mouth was dry, and he hated how she made him feel, as if he were in the wrong here.

'I don't want to be excluded from your plans any longer. I want . . .'

He flinched at the sadness he saw in her eyes, and the rest of his words became a rock in his throat.

Gaia sighed. 'You must *trust* me.' A familiar smile. 'Have I ever lied to you?'

Corvus shook his head. He turned away, looking out on to the sun-drenched rooftops. 'I will see my sister one day,' he murmured to himself, trying to imagine what his sibling looked like. When he turned back, he said, 'One question, then. For now. What part does Hecate play in all this?'

For a moment, his mother weighed her response. 'You remember Varro the merchant? Of course you do, the foul man. He stole something from me, something of great value. For a while, all seemed lost. I could no longer see the way ahead. But now, perhaps, Hecate can help.'

'How? Ruga says—'

'Ignore what your brother has to say.' He watched her search his face and then a smile crept to her lips and she nodded. 'Know that I already love her as a daughter. You have no need to worry. She will be well taken care of. You are a good boy, pleading for her so. You always think of others.' She reached out to stroke his cheek. 'You must trust me. And let that be the end of it.'

★

Furious voices rang out over the rooftops of the grand houses of the wealthiest Romans. As Corvus hurried along the street, he realized they were coming from his destination, the camp of the strangers, the *castra peregrina*, high on the Caelian Hill. The barracks was an old building, but the camp commandants had kept it well repaired across the years, a monument to the most glorious days of the empire.

Corvus wheeled along its stone walls, glowing the colour of honey in the late afternoon sun, and slipped past the guards at the gate into what seemed to be a simmering battle between two groups of soldiers.

Since the return from Gaul he'd spent too long roaming this barracks yard while Theodosius conducted the Emperor Valentinian's business – sourcing the supply lines for the coming invasion across the Gaulish frontier into the territory of the Alamanni. It was this place the *frumentarii* called their home, the former wheat-collectors who travelled the length and breadth of the empire acting as spies.

And there was his friend, at the centre of the commotion, staring down a hook-nosed *magister* who loomed a good head above him. As always, Theodosius showed an emotionless face, seemingly unruffled. But Corvus recognized those eyes like nail-heads and knew he was simmering inside.

'Back down, I say.' The hook-nosed man's hand slipped to the hilt of his sword. It was an instinct, nothing more, Corvus was sure, but tempers were still high.

He pushed his way between the two men. His friend's opponent looked down that nose at him, his brow knitting.

'Who are you?'

'A wise man, a peaceful man, a friend in troubled times—'

'A man who likes to talk.'

'True. Talking is always better than fighting.' Corvus dropped his own hand to his sword, to show there were alternatives.

His intrusion seemed to have sucked the poison out of the confrontation. The hook-nosed man grunted and took a step back. Eyeing Theodosius, he said, 'This is not over, you know that.'

'As my friend said, we'll talk and find a solution.'

'Talking is all we do. I'm sick of it.' The hook-nosed man marched away, and the groups of opposing soldiers broke up and drifted off.

'For a man who talks so much about peace, you make a lot of enemies,' Corvus said.

Theodosius shrugged. 'He's an envoy from the Emperor Valens. His master needs supplies for his campaign against the Goths and he was sent here to secure a little more than they have in the east.'

'But our needs are greater.'

'Some of the Goths have accepted Christ into their hearts, but not all, by any means. Valens is keen to show them the error of their ways. That is a good cause. He's already replaced Sallustius as Praetorian prefect, ready for the attack upon the Tervingi.' Theodosius sighed. 'But you're right. We can't afford to give too much. Valentinian would never forgive me, never mind my father. I've no desire for another boot up my behind.'

'More talks, then.'

Theodosius laughed. 'I know they bore you. My abiding memory of you, Corvus, is of a madman riding into the enemy, laughing as you loosed arrows right, left and centre. You need that thrill of battle.'

'I like to think I'm more than that.'

'You're many things, true. But you're a good friend. You have my thanks for stepping in there and saving me from myself. However much I pray, I can't seem to stifle the anger that burns inside me.'

Corvus searched the yard for his brother. Ruga would be here somewhere, as he always was during the day.

'We're all slaves to what hides inside us,' he said, distracted.

Theodosius led the way to the shade by the walls. 'True. God sets his plan upon the world, but men will always fight, with themselves, or each other, to bring his vision into effect. This war between the new pope and the anti-pope – it troubles me. We Christians need to be united if we're to bring light into the world. But this fight seems to be more about power than anything.'

'Men fighting over power. No surprises there.'

'These are men of God.'

He heard an odd tone in his friend's voice and realized he had not been taking enough care when talking about his religion.

'Did you hear about the attack upon the temple of Mithras under the baths of Caracalla?'

Theodosius was watching the gulls swoop across the blue sky, pretending this question held no weight, but Corvus knew better. He'd stumbled around the edges of these traps before.

'The baths? No.'

'I was told you were seen nearby that night.'

Corvus felt the sweat begin to trickle down his back. 'If there are taverns nearby, then that's probably true. You'll find me wandering the streets most nights.'

'Less wine, my friend. It clouds God's vision.' Theodosius studied him for a moment. Whatever he saw, it seemed to satisfy him, for now. He slapped a hand on Corvus' shoulder. 'We don't talk enough these days. Let us pray together tomorrow and we'll eat afterwards. Remember our days of glory, like old soldiers.'

'All your glory lies ahead of you, if your father has his way. But that would be good. We'll pray together, then eat.' *And I will do my best not to choke on it.*

He caught sight of Ruga emerging from the row of offices. Theodosius followed his gaze.

'You have a love for life that your brother lacks. He's too gloomy.'

'One of us needs to be the serious one.'

Leaving Theodosius, he crossed the yard. The boys who fetched and carried called his name and with a grin he flicked them a coin. They scrambled in the dust for it.

Ruga waited by the last of the office buildings. He looked hunted, Corvus thought.

'Why don't you run into the middle of the yard and proclaim your love for the Invincible Sun?' Corvus said as they huddled together.

'Stop making light,' Ruga snapped. 'Are you thick-headed? Can you not see how things are going? The few of us who still follow Mithras are being dragged into the open. Informed on by our friends . . . friends! We break no laws. But those Christian zealots don't care about that. They see it as a badge of their faith to bring down unbelievers, and the authorities turn a blind eye while we are beaten and ruined and . . . and . . . worse.'

'You worry too much.'

Ruga glared at him. 'You're more mad than I thought. The Christians have even been killing each other in those bloody riots.

This is not just about being exposed. We could lose our lives.'

'You need to be stronger. Running scared will only make things worse.' How could their mother have put so much faith in such a coward, he thought? 'There's much we need to talk about.'

Ruga eyed him, suspicious now.

'I've spoken to Mother. About your plot—'

'That's none of your business.'

'There's no need for us to fight about this—'

'Then keep your mouth shut.'

As Ruga started to turn away, Corvus caught his arm, a little more roughly than he intended.

His brother glared at him. 'Would you strike me now?'

Corvus let his hand fall. 'I'm worried. Mother is frightened.'

'Our plans have taken a turn for the worse. It's nothing. We'll find a new road.'

'Let me help. I'm good with a sword, and a bow.' *And you are not.*

'This is not something for you.'

'What is this? Keeping all the glory for yourself?'

'This is not about glory. Mother chose me for good reason.'

Corvus felt the heat rise up his neck. 'Perhaps she chose the wrong brother.'

'She chose well.'

His irritation burned as Ruga looked him up and down with contempt.

'You? You drink too much, you . . .' Whatever he was about to say, Ruga caught himself and turned away. 'Leave, now, before I say something I regret.'

Corvus stood his ground. 'I won't let this drop.'

Ruga whirled, unable to contain his anger. He thrust his face forward until it filled Corvus' vision. 'No one likes you, brother. No one trusts you.' Spittle flew from his lips. 'Not me, not Mother. Not Hecate. Leave us all alone. This is a job for grown men.'

Ruga stormed away and Corvus watched him disappear into the churn of life in the barracks.

When he peered down the steps into the gloom of the cellar, Corvus smelled the reek of age in the dank air current that rushed up to meet him. No one should be living in a place like that.

'Are you there?' he called.

'Yes.'

Hearing Hecate's voice, he descended into the dark. Though he'd offered to give her his own room, the witch had insisted she found some comfort in that miserable cellar. It reminded her of her home, cold and filled with shadows.

As he reached the flagstones, he looked around and saw a single flame flickering in one corner. There, he breathed in other, more comforting scents from the herbs and spices that Hecate had requested in order to carry out whatever strange rituals she saw fit.

In the many hours he'd spent with her, he'd only heard her complain a few times. She felt lonely and adrift without her dead sisters, and at least here she believed there were people who cared for her.

As his eyes adjusted to the gloom, he watched a figure rise up and cross the floor to him. At first he thought he saw his mother standing there, the same face, the same outline, but it was Hecate. She was smiling at him. His brother had been lying, of course he had. But still the doubts had flickered at the back of his head.

'I wanted to be sure you have all you need,' he said.

'You are kind.' She looked around. 'I need little, but . . .'

'What?'

'Your mother is kind too. She takes me to the forum and buys me gifts and gives me good food. But still . . .' He heard a wistful tone in her voice. 'I am not sure this is the place for me.'

'You must stay.' He'd spoken more forcefully than he intended and he saw the surprise in her eyes. 'It's good to have you here. Who else would I talk to?' He grinned, making light.

'Your brother has asked me to be his bride.'

He flinched. He'd expected this, of course, but Ruga and his mother had never mentioned a word of it. Another sign of their pushing him out into the wilderness. Yet he could see in her down-turned eyes that this was not something she wanted. 'Have you answered him?'

'Not yet.'

'Bide your time until you give him an answer. That's your right. Let me think on this.'

He watched her frown, but he left before she could ask him any more questions.

Outside in the last of the sun, he hurried through the streets, searching for Pavo. He was sick of all the questions that continually raced through his head. Great things, perhaps dangerous things, were moving just beyond the edge of his vision.

He found his friend exactly where he thought he would, at a table near the window of a tavern, watching the sun set. He called for some wine, and turned to Pavo, who was grinning at him, puzzled. 'You look as though you're about to fall apart. What are you – angry, questioning, frustrated? Jealous, perhaps?'

'All of that and more,' Corvus conceded. 'You always give me good advice, and mostly I ignore it.'

'Probably wise. A lot of it comes from the bottom of a cup.'

'I need to hear some wise words now. Are you ready for it?'

Pavo raised his goblet, his eyes twinkling. 'Sit down, then. We have much to talk about.'

# CHAPTER THIRTY-TWO

## *Survivors*

FOR THREE WEEKS, THE GRIM WOLVES LED THE WAY SOUTH AND Mato found his spirits lifting. Lucanus had guided them along a winding route through the forests and the wind-lashed high land, avoiding the road from Luguvalium to Mamucium, or the road to Eboracum. But though they had encountered no one, at times they had heard cries swept up on the wind and tasted ashes on their tongues.

Then they came to a land of purple-topped mountains and steep-sided valleys where shimmering lakes reflected the clouds marching across the blue sky. The days were warm, the sun burning bright. Every tree was flush with green and flowers bloomed in the wood-lands, perfuming their passage. The birds sang and butterflies flitted across the grasslands.

As they stood on the summit of a high hill looking down on one of the biggest lakes they had seen so far, Mato turned his face to the sun and closed his eyes. There was peace here, even in the midst of war. This was why he was *arcani*. To be at the beating heart of the land.

Here he could still hear his sister's voice. Here his life had meaning.

'Folk.' Bellicus was standing beside him, sniffing the air. 'Shit and smoke.'

'I'd happily avoid all meetings. But the others will want to hear fresh voices, I'd wager. Some comfort. Some news.'

'I have a craving for good wine. Even poor ale. And if we could beg some skins, we'll not have to grub around looking for fresh water every step of the way.' Bellicus glanced back to where the others lay on the grass, basking in the sun. 'And if truth be told, it will be good to dilute the whining and the carping of some of those who travel with us. Come. Let's do this.'

The track wound along the side of the hill, moving past the weather-scarred upper reaches where chunks of granite punched through the earth, to a sea of swaying grass on the lower slopes, and then on to the lush valley bottom. Out of the wind, Mato's skin burned in the sun and flies droned lazily among the trees. After a winter that seemed as if it would never end, summer could not come fast enough.

On the banks of the great lake, the riders slipped to the ground and led their horses along the rocky shore. As they rounded a finger of land, the settlement hove into view: a pier reaching out into the water with several small boats moored to it; a few huts scattered along the shoreline. Mato could see a small boat-maker's yard next to it. Yet despite the small size of the place, he could hear the unmistakable throb of life, easily as loud as Vercovicium at its most raucous.

Puzzled, he trudged on, and as he closed on the edge of the settlement he felt astonished to see a sprawl of shelters stretching deep into the shadows beneath the canopy. Those huts looked as though they'd been thrown up in a day, with low mud-brick walls and roofs of interwoven branches that would provide little cover when the rains came. Clutches of people huddled around small fires, and as their heads turned to study the new arrivals Mato was shocked to see how some looked little more than bones covered with skin, eyes heavy-lidded, cheeks hollow. Children bawled everywhere.

'Hunger,' he said. 'Want.'

'Poor souls. They must be fleeing the fighting.' Mato could hear the dismay in Catia's voice.

'We'll not find much for us here,' Bellicus added.

Six men trudged out of the camp and lined up along the shore-line. Mato looked along the row of scowls and hooded eyes. Only one had a sword. Adzes hung from the belts of the others.

'What's your business?' The speaker's face was a spider-web of wrinkles, his long black hair streaked with grey. He had a hooked nose and dark eyes that made him look like a hungry falcon.

'The same as all those other folk, I'd wager.' Lucanus waved a hand towards the settlement in the wood. 'We are running for our lives.'

'There's nothing for you here,' the one who seemed to be the leader said. 'We can't feed you. We can't feed ourselves. We've near been washed away in the torrent, and more arrive every day, every hour.'

'All we ask is a night or two. We have no wish to stay long.'

Mato smiled, holding his arms wide. 'We are kindly folk.'

The leader peered past him to where the others waited in the wagon. 'Women. A child,' he mused.

'And an old man. He's been sick; still ails. It would be a kindness to allow him a few nights here to rest and recover, where it's safe,' Mato said.

One of the other men sneered. 'You think it's safe here?'

The leader weighed the request. Mato watched him look the Grim Wolves up and down, his attention lingering on their swords. Frowning, he reached out and rubbed Lucanus' wolf pelt between thumb and forefinger. 'What are you?'

'*Arcani*,' Lucanus replied.

'Fighting men?'

'Scouts.'

'But you're with the army? You know how to use those weapons?' Mato saw the leader's eyes gleam.

Lucanus said nothing.

'My name's Kunaris.' The leader held out an open hand. 'We have farmers and smiths, merchants and beggars. But we have no one who can defend us. Put those swords to good use and you're welcome here, for as long as you want. And if you show your worth, if there's any food that can be spared, it'll be yours.'

Mato looked to Lucanus. This seemed a fair deal. But he saw his leader frown.

'Defend you from what?' Lucanus asked.

The camp seemed to go on for ever.

Mato felt a pang of despair as he looked into the faces of the hungry, desperate people huddling near the entrances to their shelters. Most had nothing but the clothes on their backs, and those were filthy. A child ran up, begging for food, and Mato was sickened that he couldn't offer even a crumb. Some lay too weak from hunger to move. Others coughed, their tunics soaked with sweat as they slumped on their sides.

'Some hope, that is what these people need,' he said. 'A beacon. The lights are going out everywhere.'

'A war is coming that will make this land run red for a hundred years. That's what the three wise women said to me in the Wilds.' Lucanus looked around the misery gathered in that shadowy world beneath the branches. 'This is why the king who will not die is needed. The saviour. To lead these people out of darkness and into hope.'

'You still believe what those women said, then? And the wood-priest?'

Mato watched his friend's brow furrow. The Wolf didn't take his responsibilities lightly. When he'd confided in them what he'd learned north of the wall, about Marcus' destiny, they had all found it hard to take in. But every man in the Grim Wolves trusted their leader above all others, and he had told his tale with such passion they couldn't deny him. Every one of them had vowed to stand by him.

'These poor bastards,' Bellicus muttered. 'They need a saviour now, not in a hundred years' time.'

Solinus cracked his knuckles. 'We all need a saviour, but they're a bit thin on the ground right now. Still, if we can hold off those nightly attacks that worry them so, they'll at least be free to hunt, and plant crops.'

For three nights now, strangers had come in the middle of the night, dragging off a man or a woman each time. The victim's screams had drawn out the sleeping refugees, who had seen spectral figures disappearing into the dark. Superstition was rife there, as it was everywhere away from the biggest settlements. But Kunaris had his feet upon the ground, they'd all soon realized. He was convinced this was a band of barbarians, and Lucanus was convinced he knew which ones.

'We're not warriors,' Mato cautioned. 'Knowing which end of a sword to stick in a man may not be enough.'

'Not if it's the Attacotti.' Comitinus looked around as if the Eaters of the Dead might be at his back at that moment. Mato saw an involuntary shudder.

'They can be beaten, like any other enemy,' Lucanus said. 'I've looked in their eyes.'

'Should we fight here, that's the question? Or would it be better to flee and keep Marcus away from prying eyes?' Comitinus asked.

'These people need us,' Lucanus said. 'We can't abandon them.'

Catulus was sniffing around a pile of waste at the back of a hut. Bellicus whistled and the dog ran over.

'We'd have more food to go round if we weren't having to fill that hound's belly too,' Solinus said.

'He's as deserving of a meal as you.' Bellicus narrowed his eyes at the other man. 'More so, I'd say.'

Solinus laughed. 'Now I'm less than a dog. My life's journey is complete.'

Mato felt his spirits raised by the sound of that laughter. There had been too little of it of late.

As they passed the last of the shelters, Lucanus stopped and looked each way along the perimeter of the camp. Before him, the wood reached up the valley side, deep and dark and green.

'How can we defend this place?' Comitinus said. 'It sprawls for ever and there are only five of us.'

'You could stand there and whine like you usually do,' Solinus said. 'That would keep most away.'

'We need our own wall.' Lucanus drew a line in the air with his index finger. 'And ditches to slow the enemy's advance.'

'That will take days,' Bellicus said.

'And many are too weak to help,' Comitinus pointed out.

'True. But some are strong,' Mato said. 'Choose the best men. Working together we can solve this.'

Lucanus nodded. 'Aye. Working together. The leader needs to lead. Everyone who comes here is looking out only for themselves. But if some worked on the defences, others were sent out to hunt, or fish, so that everyone could eat . . .'

Mato pointed up the slope. A figure was staggering out of the shadows, a soldier, by the looks of him, though his helm and shield were missing.

241

'The army is coming?' Mato said with hope once the man had trudged up.

The soldier's dirt-streaked face crumpled. 'Defeated, everywhere. Forts burning. Those who didn't die have fled. No one was prepared for this.'

'The barbarians are still marching south?' Lucanus asked.

'The whole of the wall was overwhelmed.' The soldier leaned on a tree, catching his breath. 'I ran before the onslaught, I'm not ashamed to say. That saved my neck. On the road, I've met others who did the same. They told of messengers riding between forts to warn of ships sweeping in along the coasts in the east and the west. Barbarians coming from across the sea, all of them joining forces to destroy us here.'

Comitinus looked to the other Grim Wolves. 'No one is coming to save us.'

'Tonight I may die. But I can think of no better way to spend the last hours of my life.' Mato rolled on to his back and wiped the sweat from his brow.

'The gods are not ready for you yet.'

From the cover of his palm, he eyed Decima, lying on her side, head propped up on her arm. Her lips twitched into a smile, but it was the knowing look in her eyes that set his heart thumping. He could never get enough of her.

Kissing the tips of his fingers, he touched them to her lips. 'This life would be harder without you.'

Her smile broadened to a grin, her teeth white against her dark skin. She must have heard this from a hundred men, he knew. Still, that didn't make it any less true.

Knowing what was to come when darkness fell, the Grim Wolves had gone their own way for a while, to make peace with their thoughts, to drink deep of what this life offered, perhaps, to see the reasons why they were risking their necks. Lucanus was a good leader. He knew they all needed this time.

'This is a hard world we're moving into. I can't see many comforts in the days yet to come. And I worry for you.'

'I am well versed in looking after myself.'

He laughed. 'I have no doubt. But still, the laws of the land have gone now. There are only the laws of the strong.' He paused, choosing his words. 'If you want my sword in your service, it's yours. We have to watch over the people we care for, now more than ever.'

Decima stroked the hair away from his face. 'I'm fond of you, Mato. You're a good man with a big heart. If I accept your offer, I'll keep you warm at night in turn. That's a fair exchange. But you must know that I could never love you. I can't love anyone. I don't have it in me. That part is missing.'

'You're certain?'

She nodded. 'It is the whore's affliction.'

'Nevertheless, I didn't ask for your love, or your services. I offer my sword without any expectation of reward.'

Decima rolled next to him and embraced him. 'If I could love any man it would be you, Mato,' she breathed as she pulled away. 'But to be friends like this, that is a jewel in itself.'

When Decima made her way back to the lake to wash, Mato searched around for the Wolf. They would need to plan this night's business well if they were to see the dawn.

Bellicus was throwing a stick for Catulus and he pointed towards the shadowy reaches beyond the edge of the camp. As Mato prowled past oak and ash, he heard a faint sighing, and when he eased behind a hawthorn he glimpsed Lucanus lying with Catia, the rhythm of their love-making tender, restrained, no doubt, to avoid drawing attention. Mato pulled back and spun on his heel, pleased that the couple hadn't seen him.

As he hurried back to the camp he realized that deep down he was unsurprised. There was not a man or woman in Vercovicium who didn't secretly think that Lucanus and Catia should be together, he was sure. But still, he felt uneasy at this revelation.

His fears were confirmed when he caught sight of Amatius striding out of the camp with a face like thunder. 'Have you seen my wife?' he demanded.

'Aye. By the lake, not moments ago.'

Amatius looked back, and after a brief hesitation he nodded and grunted, 'Very well.'

Mato watched him set off back down the slope. Amatius sensed something amiss, he was sure. No good could come of this.

★

Fat and red, the sun slipped to the horizon and dusk crept through the woods. The birdsong ebbed and a stillness descended that did not bring peace.

Smoke drifted among the trees as the hearth-fires were stoked, and those who had foraged some food began to eat. Mato walked along the water's edge, trying to enjoy the last of the peace. He found Lucanus staring into the growing dark among the trees.

'Are you ready?' the Wolf asked him.

'Aye. But first a word.' Mato looked round to make sure they would not be overheard. 'There's no easy way to say this. I saw you with Catia, brother.'

Lucanus looked away, either uncomfortable or annoyed, Mato couldn't be sure which.

'I came across you by accident,' he continued, 'and if I could, so could Amatius. You must do what you will, of course – I don't judge. And it's true that it's far better for Catia that she is with you than a man who thinks with his fists. But I beg you, take care. This business could tear us apart, when we need to be standing shoulder to shoulder.'

'You don't need to say it.' Mato heard the snap in those words and he knew his friend would regret it later. 'I always take great care.'

'If I could—'

'No more. This is between Catia and me. Do you hear?'

Mato nodded.

Lucanus looked round, almost as if he expected Amatius to be watching him. When he turned back, Mato saw his brow furrow. He followed his friend's stare and saw someone walking through the woods towards them, as the soldier had done earlier. But Lucanus seemed to recognize this new arrival.

The darkness unfurled around the striding figure, almost, Mato thought, as if he were forming out of the very air itself. As he neared he took on weight and shape, and Mato saw a cloaked man walking with the aid of a staff. Ringlets of black hair snaking out. A hooked nose and a thin face. At first he thought the left side of those features had been burned. But as the man neared, he saw it was a black tattoo, a spiral that became a winged snake as it curled under his jawline.

'Myrrdin,' Lucanus whispered.

Then this must be the wood-priest that their leader had told them about, the one who he could not be sure was friend or enemy.

'How did you find me?' Lucanus asked when the druid stood in front of them.

'You are being watched, Wolf.' A smile crept across the wood-priest's lips. 'You are always being watched.'

# CHAPTER THIRTY-THREE

# *A Single Scream*

O NE BY ONE, THE TORCHES ALONG THE CAMP'S PERIMETER FLARED into life and a wavering band of light marched between the jumble of shelters and the endless dark.

Lucanus smelled the tang of the boat-builder's pitch curling up in the thick smoke as he looked along the faces of the few men who were strong or brave enough to hold that line. Yet the glow from the brands glimmered in eyes too wide, barely blinking, staring deep into the wood's gloom. Afraid to miss even a hint of movement. The defenders seeing, perhaps, in their mind's eye, horrors a thousand times worse than what waited for them.

The Grim Wolves patrolled the ranks, trying to keep spirits up. These men were farmers or merchants or smiths and they only brandished rough-carved spears. Beyond the sole soldier, there was not a seasoned fighter among them.

But Lucanus watched Mato's brightness sparking relief wherever he went. The message was clear: we have fought these bastards before and we have defeated them. A well-told lie was a powerful weapon in itself.

Lucanus felt unease spark pinpricks of sweat along his back. These folk were more than unprepared. They were ignorant of what might be demanded of them. And he was equally unprepared to lead such innocents towards their own deaths. Any life lost here would be a stain on him.

Bellicus strode over. 'This is as good as it gets.'

'Aelius is there?'

'Aye, though he has only one good arm to wield his spear. Brave lad.'

'Amatius?'

The Bear turned up his nose. 'He's chosen to stay by the lake with the women and the boy and the old man. To be the last line of defence, to protect them come the worst. He says.'

Lucanus shrugged. 'Better there than half-hearted when the enemy comes at us.'

'You still believe this is the right course?'

'What do you believe?' He tried to read his friend's face, but the dancing shadows hid more than they revealed.

'I think you are wiser than me, despite your years. And I think you have a good heart. I'm a sour bastard who should never be trusted to do the right thing.' He hesitated. 'Your father would be proud.'

Lucanus winced to hear that. He was not sure it was true.

Bellicus paused, seemingly searching for the right thing to say. 'When this is done, I would have words with you. About days long gone.'

There was a look in his eye, of worry, perhaps, or sadness. Lucanus felt even more uneasy at the thought of what was lying there. 'Don't trouble me with things done. I only want to hear of the now or the days yet to come.'

Bellicus held his gaze for a moment, then nodded his assent.

'Keep watch,' Lucanus said. 'I can't settle until I've given that bastard wood-priest the side of my tongue.'

He found Myrrdin warming his hands by one of the campfires, watching the preparations.

'You are on the side of the barbarians,' he snapped as he walked up.

'And greetings to you too.'

'Don't anger me, wood-priest. This is a warning. I'm close to taking my blade to you.'

Myrrdin shrugged, unbowed. 'The Scoti and the Picts sheltered us. As many tribes have, the world over. We walk our own path.'

'I saw one of your breed in the camp where the war-moot was taking place. He told them about Marcus and his worth.' Lucanus grimaced, trying to choke down his rage, but after all the miseries he had endured . . . all caused by his encounter with this man and his allies . . . he felt on the brink of being overwhelmed.

'I'd be lying if I said we didn't know their minds, or guide them. But we are not their kings. We are priests. They march upon their own road.' Myrrdin held out a hand, a gesture of conciliation. 'And between the two of us, they cannot see beyond the ends of their noses. Attack. Kill. Loot. Rape.' He sighed, shaking his head. 'A moment's thought, and listening to good advice, would not go amiss.'

'You make light. But now these bastards are hunting the boy down so they can claim a prize that will seal their victory. You did this. You and your talk of prophecies and kings.'

'Your words are like a knife to my heart,' Myrrdin taunted, pressing his right hand on his breast. 'Hear me, now. I am an ally, and, if you will, a friend. And if it were not Erca and his warlords, it would be someone else. You see only what's in front of your nose. But these stories about the prophecy and the king who will not die have been like a fish swimming in the deep for long years, slowly, slowly rising until it breaks the surface. From Caledonia to Rome and beyond, whispers are reaching ears, eyes are being raised and looking here, to the edge of the empire. Today . . . tomorrow . . . in days yet to come, they will come for him. The boy's time of peace is all behind him now.'

Lucanus weighed the words, feeling some of the edge leave his anger as he recognized the magnitude of what he was being told.

'There are many people who need a new saviour, Wolf,' Myrrdin continued, his voice softening. 'The Christians have had theirs and they are seizing power everywhere. All have seen how the words of the Christ, the voice and hand of their god, have bent emperors and kings to their will. There is a war being fought, one that uses no swords or spears. Long-held power is shifting. The sun goes down on dreams and hopes. And desperate men will do anything to keep . . . or reclaim . . . power.'

'I hear you,' the Wolf said. 'A boy, an innocent boy, is a tool in a fight between those who have no regard for him, or his life, or the lives of those who love him. So tell me why you are here now. To cause more trouble? To steal Marcus away? To lay your own grubby hands on this great prize?'

'I am here to save the boy's life. And the mother's, and yours, if I can.'

'I have the feeling that you're leading me by the nose to something else.'

'True.'

Lucanus bristled at the wood-priest's baldness.

'Who is to say my plan is not in your best interests too?' Myrrdin added.

'Tell me. Then I'll be the judge.'

'Wisdom learned by a man following his own path is better than knowledge told by a teacher. There are times when you have to see with your eyes to know what is right. And if you are determined to keep your eyes shut, that will never happen. So, you must be guided along the way. Until you are ready to see.'

Lucanus prowled around the fire, scrutinizing the other man like a hawk. 'You say you're always watching me. How can this be so? How many of you are there . . . your kind . . . druids . . . witches . . . ?'

'My kind? We are not all the same, Wolf. There is not some vast, hidden army. There are allies . . . friends . . . enemies who want the same thing. But we have eyes and ears everywhere. In towns thick with people as well as in the forests. The wood-folk have been hiding for a long time. They've learned to be stealthy, to listen and watch. Their lives have depended upon never being seen for many years now, since the Romans drenched the shores of Ynys Môn in blood. You have had someone at your back since you left the Isle of Yews.'

'Why?'

'Because you've proved yourself to be our road into days yet to come, and all our dreams re-made.' Lucanus heard the light tone in those words and once again couldn't tell if he was being mocked.

'Go to your work,' Myrrdin said. 'Let Caledfwlch be true and filled with all the power of the gods. Hear the howl of Cernunnos in the forest. Feel the light of Lugh shine upon you. Smite your enemies and live to see the dawn. For all the people of this land now count upon you.'

At the vigil by the torches, no man spoke. All heads were turned towards the wall of dark. At their backs echoed the cries of babes and the moans of the sick, a constant reminder of why they were fighting.

Lucanus walked the line. He saw from the eyes flickering his way that his presence seemed to do some good, as if those there had faith in him to lead and lead well. He nodded in turn, trying to stop his doubts playing out on his face.

Aelius held his spear loosely in his good hand. He'd not been drunk for days, and for a while it had left him like a hungry dog. Now his eyes were clear and he seemed a better man for it. If he felt any fear, he didn't show it. That was good.

Bellicus loomed at the centre of the defence, his long shadow reaching down the slope. 'Perhaps they will not come,' he said in a low, rumbling voice. 'Perhaps they've already moved on to torment some other poor bastards.'

'Perhaps.'

The night drew on.

As eyes were growing heavy and shoulders beginning to droop, Lucanus saw Bellicus stiffen. The Bear had heard a sound, or smelled an unusual trace on the cool breeze. He leaned forward, shielding his eyes from the glare of the torches.

'What do you see?' Lucanus whispered.

'We are not alone.'

The Wolf felt the hairs on his neck prickle. At first there was only the endless dark. As he stared into that void, he felt his vision swim, and then he realized he was seeing movement within it.

Keening whines rang out, rising and falling, like a baby crying or the shriek of mating foxes. Moans echoed along the defensive line. Lucanus understood his men's fear. This was a sound that could have come from beyond the grave, a haunting lament for what lay on the other side of death.

He drew Caledfwlch. Bellicus unsheathed his own blade.

Out of the night they came, spectral skin, skull-like heads, pale eyes glowing in pools of black.

'They are men,' the Wolf called to his sorry band of defenders. 'Only men.' To those faced with the sight of them, it sounded a feeble lie.

As the Attacotti neared, he could see that the deathly pallor came from crusted ashes, the impression of rot from the charcoal smeared around their eyes and along their cheekbones. But would even his own men see through their fears?

'Would ghosts need weapons?' he called again.

These Attacotti carried long swords, bronze by the look of it, and in the flickering torchlight he thought he could see marks on the blades, like the odd symbols etched into Caledfwlch. They had no armour, no shields. Each wore only a leather belt to carry the scabbard, and a strip of cloth that hung down across the groin.

He counted twenty of them, about as many as they had along the line. For now.

That whining cry rolled out again, and the Wolf winced. Somehow they drew it from their throats without moving their mouths, only adding to the otherworldly air that surrounded them.

At first, they prowled on the balls of their feet, shoulders lowered, heads shifting from side to side, so slow they seemed to be wading through water. Then both flanks surged. Lucanus felt his breath catch in his throat at the speed of that attack, one moment among the trees, the next at the line, two groups of three warriors swinging their swords as one.

Blood spurted and a man staggered back, half his head hanging. Another dropped on the other end of the line. Two dead already, and they had not even raised their weapons.

'Fight,' Lucanus bellowed. 'Hold them at bay.'

The two teams of Attacotti darted back as fast as they had come, and more rushed forward at different points along the line. This time the Grim Wolves were ready. Solinus threw himself into the path of one group, Comitinus dashing to repel another.

At their exhortations, the men around them stabbed with their spears, again and again. The Attacotti swept back.

Time and again, the pattern was repeated. The ghastly warriors rushed in, thrust with swift, precise strikes, then retreated.

For a while, Lucanus held on to the hope that they might be able to wear the Attacotti down. But then another defender collapsed back in a crimson spray, the soldier who had walked into camp earlier that day, one of their few skilled fighters.

And then he was darting back and forth along the line, throwing himself into the fray every time the Attacotti launched a strike. Caledfwlch raked across the shoulder of one pale warrior, blood streaking through the ashes. Small payment for his lost ear, he thought, but his heart thumped none the less.

His legs ached from the running. The line blurred. He saw only skull-like faces, piercing eyes, stabbing swords. Sparks flew as he clashed blades. His right arm grew weary.

As he reeled back from another fight, he heard Bellicus shout at him, 'You can't fight this battle on your own. If you try to save everyone here, you'll only lose your own life when weariness takes hold.'

His friend was right, he knew. But he couldn't bear to stand still if he could help, just a little, to save another life.

Finally, Mato caught his arm and yanked him to a halt. He grinned. 'Stay by my side, brother. You know I fight like a child. I need your magic sword or I will lose my head.'

Lucanus nodded. Though he knew what Mato was doing, he was too weary to resist. The Attacotti outnumbered them now, and instead of tiring, they seemed to have been whipped into a greater frenzy by the deaths.

'We can hold out,' Mato said, as if he could read his leader's thoughts.

The words had barely left his lips when one of the white warriors loomed in front of him, sword ready to slash down.

Time seemed to slow as the Wolf watched his friend speeding towards death. The thunder of his own heart swelled in his head.

As the sword began to swing, an arrow punched into the Attacotti warrior's right eye.

Back he wheeled, his sword flying from his hand. Though he clutched at the shaft protruding from his socket, not a sound escaped his lips.

*They are not men. They cannot be,* Lucanus thought, though he knew it was not true.

As he struggled to comprehend what was happening, another arrow whined by, slamming into the back of a retreating warrior, who crashed face down on to the ground. Two of his fellows rushed out, grabbed his arms and dragged him into the dark.

Lucanus felt his senses come back to him and he spun round, searching for the bowman.

Catia stood behind him, another shaft already nocked. One eye was closed, the other sighting down the length of the arrow as she looked to fire through any gap in the line.

Lucanus started to yell at her to get away from the fighting, but she flashed him such a fierce look he was silenced.

Another arrow thumped into the shoulder of one of the Attacotti.

Bellicus looked at him and raised one eyebrow. Lucanus nodded.

'Wolf-sister,' he called, grinning.

'Wolf-brother,' she called back. The excitable joy in her voice made his heart pound faster; he hadn't heard it since she was a child.

As he hurried along the ranks, urging the men to hold fast, he heard an alarmed cry from the end of the line. When he raced towards it, he saw Aelius shouting and pointing towards the enemy.

Two Attacotti grappled with a flailing man they had clearly wrenched from the defensive line, hauling him away from the band of torchlight into the dark. The captive's face was twisted with terror, but Lucanus recognized him – earlier that day his features had been lit with joy after his wife had given birth to a son.

Lucanus shook himself from his daze. Snatching up one of the torches, he threw himself beyond the line and raced into the dark.

The shadows swooped away from the circle of his torchlight. He half expected to see pale eyes reflecting that orange glow, a pack of those ghostly warriors loping towards him through the trees, but it seemed that he was alone. The Attacotti had melted away into the night.

Not long after, a single scream rang out. It seemed to go on for too long, grow too high-pitched, until suddenly it was snapped off.

# CHAPTER THIRTY-FOUR

## *The Chalice*

A S THE FIRST PINK LIGHT OF DAWN FILTERED THROUGH THE TREES, Catia stroked Marcus' head by the fire while she watched Amatius pacing around the edge of their camp. She felt his urgent glances in her direction, but she didn't meet his eyes.

Eventually he loomed over her. 'A woman with a bow,' he said. 'You bring shame on me and upon yourself. Even the barbarians do not have their women fighting.'

'And you bring shame on all of us by your cowardice. Hiding away instead of putting your neck on the line, like—' She caught herself before she said Lucanus' name. But Amatius' face flared with anger none the less, as if he expected it.

Fists bunching, he advanced on her, as he had done a hundred, a thousand times before. This time she eased Marcus aside and jumped to her feet. 'Lay one hand on me and it will be the last thing you ever do.'

Amatius gaped like a codfish. As the shock faded, he scowled, but she saw his eyes darting, assessing, no doubt, whether he could get away with striking her under the gaze of her family. Aelius was already on his feet, spear in hand, his lips pulling back from his teeth.

'Please,' Marcus begged, throwing his arms around Catia's waist. 'Don't fight.'

'See?' Amatius said. 'You have woken the boy and upset him. What a poor excuse for a mother you are.' He spun on his heel, beckoning for his son to follow. 'Come. Leave her. She only cares about herself.'

He strode away before she could answer, still, and always, the coward. Marcus skipped after his father, wiping away his tears as he ran.

'How long do we stay here?' Catia asked.

Lucanus stood at the line of torches, watching a group of men dig a long trench. With only a few shovels to go round, some were breaking the soil with sharpened sticks and scooping it out with their cupped hands. The spoil was being piled up along the perimeter, a wall in the making, but still far from being any kind of defence.

The Wolf shook his head. 'Not long. I don't know. These folk need us. I couldn't abandon them.' He forced a smile at her. 'Nor would you, I know.'

She thought how weary he looked. Tired eyes, new lines on his brow and by his mouth. True, he hadn't slept, but she knew it was the burden of responsibility that was wearing him down. Yet he'd never once complained. She felt her heart go out to him and wished she could show her affection, care for him in the manner that he deserved. But somewhere her husband was watching, she was sure of it, and Amatius had a streak of cruelty that would only cause more misery if he decided he wanted revenge, as he undoubtedly would.

'You're a good man,' she whispered.

Leaving the diggers to continue their work, they walked down the slope. Catia grasped Lucanus' hand and tugged him behind a bank of holly where she knew they would not be overlooked, and then she threw her arms around him, kissing him deeply. She felt like a starving woman who had finally been offered a meal. The heat rose in her, and she would have pushed him down and ridden him there and then if she could.

'We must take care,' he whispered when he broke the embrace.

'I know.' She rested her head on his chest. 'Sometimes I feel crippled with guilt. So many deaths, so many terrible things, and yet I feel happy that the world I lived in has gone. Happy. How selfish I am.'

'You did not have a good life.'

'I had friends. And a father and a brother who loved me. And a son who meant more than anything to me. That's more than most can hope for. Only one black cloud hung over me.'

'Don't belittle it.'

For a moment, one only, she closed her eyes, enjoying the smell of him, and dreamt of how things might be.

A sword's length lay between them as they wandered down the slope to the narrow line of pebbles at the water's edge. Myrrdin was leaning on his staff, watching Amarina, Decima and Galantha paddle through the shallows, their dresses pulled up to their calves. The three women laughed and chattered, oblivious, no doubt used to the eyes of men upon them.

'Hello, sister,' the wood-priest said to Amarina as she passed.

Amarina splashed by without meeting his eyes. 'I don't know you.'

'But I know a moon-child when I see one.'

Though Amarina ignored him, Catia sensed that some nerve had been touched. The wood-priest turned to her and bowed. 'The Chalice,' he said. 'An honour.'

'The Chalice?'

'You are the cup that holds the royal blood.'

Just as Lucanus had said. She felt unsettled under the scrutiny of those dark eyes, but she pushed her chin up and tried not to show it. 'I have many questions for you. About why I was chosen, and who took me into the woods when I was a babe. Who left me with the wolves, and how they knew I would not be eaten. Who branded me—'

Myrrdin held up a hand. 'And they will all be answered. In good time.'

'Don't waste your breath,' Lucanus sighed. 'He will only lead you round and round in circles, promising to tell you all, and when he's done and many, many words have been spent, you'll find yourself back at the beginning and none the wiser.'

'I'm wounded,' the wood-priest said. 'Truly.'

'No games,' Catia said. 'I only want to keep my son safe.'

'Then we are of like mind.'

'Lucanus tells me there are many people who would like to get their hands on Marcus.'

'And many of them do not have the charm that I do. They are . . .' he waved his fingers as he thought, 'unpleasant.'

'Dangerous,' Lucanus said. 'Men who will do anything to gain power.'

Myrrdin nodded.

'Then we need a sanctuary,' Catia said. 'Somewhere we can be away from prying eyes.'

'Your kind have spent an age hiding, wood-priest,' the Wolf said. 'I would think you'd be good at that kind of thing.'

The druid shrugged. 'There are such places. But this world is in flux. Power shifts, and no man can predict where it will end, and where will be safe.'

'What, then?' Catia tried to keep the worry out of her voice.

'For a while, we will be like a leaf caught in the wind. But if you put your faith in me, I will guide you.'

Catia looked from Myrrdin to Lucanus.

'And you'll protect us from the cut-throats who will want to steal Marcus from us every step of the way?' the Wolf said.

'That's your work, Lucanus. That is why you are here.'

Night after night the attacks came.

Every evening Catia would offer her prayers for Lucanus as he took his place at the centre of the defence and every morning she would see the scars of those long hours upon his face. She yearned to see the light-hearted man she had once known, and felt her heart break for the suffering she knew he silently endured.

Men died, good men, cut down by the barbarians. Every dawn their wives wailed and their children sobbed. This was not the way it should be. They had known peace for so long.

'The lights are going out,' Bellicus said, time and again, and she couldn't help but think he was right: a great darkness was sweeping in to swallow everything they had ever known. All she wanted to do was hug Marcus to her and run away with Lucanus towards the dawn, in the hope that they could snatch a little happiness in the midst of all this misery.

But the wall of earth was growing higher, reinforced with felled trees, and the network of ditches spread, some of them filled with spikes to catch any unwary barbarian who ventured too close. Every day Lucanus would oversee the works, grabbing fleeting sleep when he could. Catia watched the admiring looks that followed him and felt proud that everyone could see the truth of the man she knew.

On the third dawn, he had told her that the threat they faced was no longer just the Attacotti: that night he had seen Picts and Scoti. Only a few, he said, but he was worried that the numbers were growing. If that were true, what hope did they have with such a collection of unseasoned defenders.

Catia had no more arrows left, but she had set a man to whittling more for her and soon she would have a quiver full of well-fletched shafts.

But by then it might be too late.

As she tossed fitfully on the edge of sleep, Catia heard the cry ring out. She scrambled out of the shelter where Amatius slept the sleep of the dead and scrabbled up the slope to the line of defenders with Marcus trailing behind her.

Beyond the line of torches embedded in the wall, seven men watched from the edge of the wavering shadow. Not barbarians, these, she thought, even though they bore tattoos on their faces.

'Who is that?' she asked, pointing to the one who seemed to be the leader.

Mato leaned in and whispered, 'His name is Motius and they are *arcani* like us. The Carrion Crows. They are the reason why we are in such dire straits.'

Lucanus rested one foot on the wall, addressing the traitors. Catia could see the coldness in his face and the depth of his contempt.

'We are a brotherhood, Motius,' he was saying. 'We are forged by life in the Wilds. We are bound by blood. And you have sacrificed all that for a few coins in your palm?'

'You are blind, brother, and you always were. You trusted too much. Our paymasters thought nothing of us. They didn't care if we lived or died. We fought for nothing. We died for nothing. I am the honourable one here. I stand for the pride of the *arcani*. You . . . you are nothing but a lapdog.'

Catia saw Lucanus flinch. She wanted to rush to him, to calm him in the way that she always could. 'You speak of honour,' he said with a strained voice. 'But we would never see an innocent die. We would not sacrifice our own brothers. Lie to yourself as much as you want, but you've taken the gold of the barbarians for your own gain. You will grow rich on the bodies of the people who once counted you friends.'

Motius shrugged. 'We can argue about this until the world ends, Wolf. But we have work to do now. We want the boy and we will not rest until we get him.'

Catia felt her stomach knot.

Lucanus would not back down, though. She knew that. 'You fight for gold,' he said. 'We fight for something greater than that. You will not win.'

Motius smirked. 'But my message is not for you, brother. It is for those poor souls who are sacrificing themselves without realizing the truth of why they die.'

Catia watched him take a step forward and turn his attention away from Lucanus to address the crowd that had gathered.

'You have a boy there.' His voice rang out across the still, watchful crowd. 'A boy guarded by the man you have put your faith in. Give us the lad and you will live. Give us the boy and you have my word that we will leave this place and leave you in peace. If not . . .' He shrugged. 'Reinforcements are coming and you will be overrun.'

Catia sensed a stiffening in the people about her. As she looked around, she saw heads turn her way, stares growing harder, measuring, weighing.

Keeping Marcus tight at her side, she pushed through the gathered refugees and away.

# CHAPTER THIRTY-FIVE

# *Pendragon*

'WILL YOU LET ME SPEAK?' LUCANUS ASKED.

The residents of the camp stood in a wide circle. Heads bowed, they had been listening to their leader Kunaris plead with them not to dishonour themselves. That was good, Bellicus thought; not everyone there was a spineless bastard.

'Why do we need to hear from him?' someone shouted.

Kunaris whirled, his eyes flashing. 'Any man who has risked his life for us has earned the right to be heard.'

As the Wolf walked into the circle, Bellicus marvelled at his friend's easy manner. This was not a Lucanus he had seen before. He had grown into his role.

'Many of us are strangers here.' The Wolf's voice soared above the birdsong. 'But you know a man the moment you look into his eyes. And I would hope that all who have met me will have seen what lies in my heart, and know I always speak true.'

A few grunts of assent rolled around the gathering.

'A barbarian war-band is riding towards us even as we speak,' Lucanus continued. 'Many of you have seen what they can do. They are not ones to show mercy, even to innocents. We have been waiting here for the army to come and save us, but we can't afford to wait any longer. We must make a choice, now. You know giving up the boy is not the right thing to do. Once they have him, the barbarians will not leave you alone. They will come for your gold, or your women, and they will leave nothing alive in their wake.

'If we are to survive these dark days, we must stand together.'

Lucanus' voice grew harder, louder. 'That is the only way. The only way. We must be brave. Fearless in the face of the enemy. That is the only way we can hope to take back what has been stolen from us. If we are cowards, when the army comes and drives the barbarians back beyond the wall, we may gain back our homes, and our work. We may have enough food to mean we never go hungry, and enough wine to restore our spirits. But when we look in our hearts, we will know that something has gone which can never be replaced. That emptiness will nag at us until we are on our deathbeds. We will never be able to forget that we were found wanting. There will be no peace for us.'

Bellicus watched a few heads bow. Shame. Good.

'We can barely hold back the ones who already attack us,' someone said. 'What hope do we have when a war-band arrives?'

'Here is what I offer you,' Lucanus replied. 'We do not give up the boy. We will stand here tonight and fight as we have always done. And tomorrow, we will wait until the war-band is close enough to smell our sweat upon the wind. Then my men will ride out of here. We will lead the barbarians far away. And we will keep leading them, until their legs are so weary they cannot stand and they've been turned around so many times that they couldn't find the way back to you even if their strength allowed them to try.'

Bellicus grunted. The risks in this plan were too great. They could never afford to be so far ahead of their enemies that the trail would be lost and the war-band would turn back here. Yet if the barbarians were close on their heels so many things could go wrong – a track that led nowhere, a horse breaking a leg, another war-band cutting off their escape. This was a wager that might well result in disaster.

He saw Solinus frowning – he too knew the dangers they faced and that their chance of escape was slim. But Comitinus was smiling, relieved that they would be doing everything they could to help these people.

Bellicus watched realization dawn on the refugees' faces, and worry and doubt turn to warmth, then honest gratitude. Cheers rang out, catching fire as they ran round the circle.

He grinned at the surprise sparking in Lucanus' face, and then his discomfort as he squirmed and tried to leave the circle before Kunaris brought him back to shower him with thanks.

'Sometimes I wish we had a leader who was a bastard,' Solinus said with a sigh. 'Our lives would be easier by far.'

The dawn light crept through the trees, driving the dark away. Mist drifted across the lake. The woods were still and peaceful and only the first few larks had started their song.

Bellicus stretched and cracked his bones. For the first night since they'd arrived at the camp, no attack had come. Motius and his treacherous band were biding their time, knowing they didn't have to risk any more lives with reinforcements on the way.

He watched Myrrdin moving through the camp, a spectre in the dawn light, waking people from their slumbers, whispering soothing words as heads emerged from shelters. Bleary eyes looked around, glanced towards the lake when they understood what the wood-priest was saying. One by one they crawled out into the half-light.

Lucanus was walking up with Catia, heads bowed together, brows furrowed. Bellicus knew the difficult conversation they were having.

'Tell him,' Catia beseeched when she stepped up. 'You can't abandon us. We must travel with you.'

'You will. But not now,' Bellicus replied, trying to keep his voice low and calm to soothe her. 'If you come with us now, you'll risk all our lives. We must be ready to ride hard, to fight if necessary. You will slow us down.'

Catia clenched her fists at her sides. 'And who is supposed to protect Marcus?'

Bellicus smiled. 'I saw a woman with a bow who made fair work of slaying a few barbarians,' he said.

She turned to Lucanus, jabbing a finger towards his face. 'You would keep him safe. You. That's what you vowed.'

'We'll lead away the ones who want to steal him.' The Wolf's voice was calm. 'You'll be free to ride on and we'll meet further down the road.'

'Where?'

'Myrrdin will show you.'

'And what if we meet cut-throats and robbers first? What then? What if we meet more of the people who want to get their hands on Marcus . . . the many, many people, as you told me?'

Lucanus hesitated, choosing his words. Bellicus knew this was the hardest thing his friend would have to say.

'You will have to tell Amatius of Marcus' destiny.'

'Never!' Catia's eyes blazed.

'Hear me out,' Lucanus continued. 'Put aside what lies between the two of you. As I have put aside my feelings about your husband. For Marcus' sake.'

Bellicus watched her shoulders sag.

'Even if Amatius doesn't understand, Marcus is still his son. There's no better man to protect a boy than his father.'

'Heed him,' Bellicus said. 'In this he speaks true. This is the best way to keep Marcus, and you, and all of you, safe. If we don't do this—'

'Enough,' she snapped. 'If I don't agree you will all set on me with your words, words, words.'

'That is what we do when we cannot use our swords,' Bellicus said with a nod.

'You have to promise me that you'll do all in your power to come back to me . . . to us . . . all of you.' Bellicus saw her acknowledge him, but he knew her words were meant for Lucanus.

'You have my word,' the Wolf said.

Myrrdin strode up and wagged the tip of his staff in their direction. 'It's time.' Before they could respond, he turned and walked down the slope towards the lakeside.

'What is this?' Lucanus asked.

'Follow him, brother. Let's get this over with,' Bellicus said. He spun away before Lucanus could say any more and followed the druid down the slope.

At the lakeside, Myrrdin lifted his head and looked down his nose at the Grim Wolves, and Amarina, Decima and Galantha, and the refugees drifting down from the camp to gather in silence in a crescent around him. As Lucanus walked up, they parted. Bellicus held out a hand to guide his friend to the wood-priest.

The Wolf looked around, baffled.

A low wall of white rolled across the placid waters, tinged pink upon the top. So peaceful was it that even Bellicus felt the hairs on his neck prickle.

Then Myrrdin stamped his staff upon the stones and a flock of gulls took wing, their cries soaring with them.

Once the mournful sound had died away, the druid looked round at the crowd again. 'Some of you know of the wood-priests. What we once were to the people of this land. Guardians. Wise men. The voice of the gods and the shapers of all things. And what we once were, we shall be again. The season has turned, brothers and sisters. The old world falls away. A new world is dawning, a new world that is older by far. A better world.'

Myrrdin commanded attention, Bellicus saw. For the first time the Bear thought he could glimpse a hint of this man's true nature.

'You cannot see this golden dawn yet,' the wood-priest continued. 'For we are in the dark, before the sun rises. There is suffering, and there is blood, and there will be war, as there always is when the circle turns.' He beckoned to the Wolf.

When Lucanus shook his head and took a step back, Bellicus went to him as he had promised the druid he would. 'Do all that he says, and do it without complaining,' he breathed in his friend's ear. 'I will explain later. But for now, much rides on this.' With relief, he saw the trust in the Wolf's eyes. Lucanus stepped forward.

'In those days, long gone, the wood-priests were kingmakers,' Myrrdin said. 'And in times like these, we had another task too. To crown the war leader who would defeat all enemies, one chosen by the gods themselves to guide the people towards the light of that new dawn.' His voice rose, plucking at the hearts of those who watched him. 'This great war leader is called Pendragon – the Dragon's Head.'

Bellicus watched realization dawn on Lucanus' face. The Wolf narrowed his eyes at his friend, mouthing an epithet. Bellicus grinned and nodded, turning the blade, as friends do.

'It is time for the Dragon to rise. The circle must be completed once again,' the druid boomed. From inside his cloak, he pulled something that flashed in the dawn light. A sigh of amazement rippled through the crowd. Even Bellicus was surprised. Myrrdin had caught him off-guard with this.

The wood-priest held up his prize so that the light continued to glint off it: a circlet of gold, a crown by any other name, Bellicus thought, a sinuous winged serpent eating its own tail, ruby eyes glinting as if it were alive. And the Bear surprised himself once again as he felt a wave of pride when the druid set the crown on Lucanus' head.

'All hail the Head of the Dragon,' Myrrdin called. 'All hail Lucanus. First and Last and Always. The Pendragon.'

A cheer rose up. As Bellicus looked around the congregation, he saw how this ceremony had gripped everyone there. Shining eyes, bright faces.

Hope.

# PART THREE

# The Dark

*Give me where to stand and I will move the earth.*

Archimedes

# CHAPTER THIRTY-SIX

## *The Morrigan*

A PALL OF BLACK SMOKE DRIFTED ACROSS THE SUN AND THE WORLD grew dark.

On the high ground, Lucanus pushed himself upright on his horse and looked out across a hellish landscape of blazing villages.

'This is worse than any of us feared.' The whine of the wind almost swallowed Mato's voice.

'The barbarians never stopped.' Comitinus' face crumpled. 'We never knew . . . we never expected . . . They were not satisfied with breaching the wall.'

'And why would they?' Bellicus grunted. 'That would have been small revenge for those long years with a bitter taste in their mouths, all those lost battles. And once they saw how easy that victory was, they knew they had an opening.'

Solinus nodded. 'Keep going. Keep going. South. But how far? All the way to Londinium? To the sea? To the walls of Rome?'

'Their army was vast. But to take all of Britannia?' Mato said.

Lucanus felt a cold pit in his stomach. 'This was their plan all along . . . the Saxon fleets striking along the east coast, perhaps even the west . . .'

'A blacksmith's tongs,' Bellicus said. 'Squeezing the life out of the army. You know as well as I how tired and lazy they'd grown, always moaning about worn candles and lice-ridden tunics and sour wine. Not looking to the horizon. Never paying attention. Too confident by far that no one would ever dare attack them.'

For long moments, everyone fell silent, watching those fires burn.

Lucanus dug his heels in and his horse heaved away, slow steps, not even breaking into a canter. What point was there? Running from hell, or into its mouth, it mattered little.

For a while they had dared to hope.

They'd left the camp at the lakeside when the thunder of hooves from the approaching war-band rumbled through the trees. Lucanus remembered the last look he'd exchanged with Catia as Myrrdin had led the rest of their group away along the water's edge, wondering if he'd ever see her again. But then they were pounding through the trees, skirting just close enough to where the Attacotti and the Carrion Crows had made camp to entice them, but not close enough for them to see Marcus was not with them.

And from then on, there had been little time to think, to sleep, to eat. They'd ridden hard up steep-sided valleys into that world of wind-lashed hills and shimmering lakes, making sure their trail was clear. Mato broke branches. They guided their horses through oceans of long grass so their path was like an arrow pointing to where they were going. They rode along the muddy banks of streams.

Motius and his men would be suspicious of course that their trail was so obvious, but Lucanus hoped they would attribute it to desperation in their fear of being caught.

It worked. At times they slowed enough to make sure they did not lose their pursuers, but the din of the warriors at their backs never ebbed.

When they were certain Myrrdin and the others had had enough time to make good their escape, they charged on to rockier ground and rode along the leas of valleys so the smell of their sweat was not caught on the wind. Solinus and Mato galloped in opposite directions to set up false trails and then took their mounts along the shallows of water courses to leave no tracks at all.

It would not be enough, not for *arcani*. The Carrion Crows were too skilled in the art of hiding trails as well as following them. But Lucanus had hoped it would buy them some time to find a well-manned fort or a legion marching to repel the invaders.

Now, looking at the devastation on every side, he was not so sure.

★

The body slumped on the spike at the side of the track, a warning for anyone approaching: here was the land of the dead.

A crow perched on the head, feasting on one of the eyes. The other was already gone. It was a man, that much Lucanus could tell, but cheeks and lips had been pecked away, leaving only a bony grimace. One arm had been hacked off. The clothes were little more than rags, sodden from the last night's rain. A poor man, then, one who would have posed little danger to the barbarians. That had not saved him.

Already flyblown, the corpse reeked of rot. Comitinus covered his mouth and nose as he looked up at it. 'Soon there'll be nothing worth fighting for.'

Along the track, other victims waited to greet guests. The Grim Wolves rode on, looking straight ahead. Everywhere they went they saw slaughter. They reined in on the outskirts of a small village, no more than ten homes set around a green where two hens pecked. It was as still as they'd expected.

Rather than shout above the shrieking din of crows, driven to a frenzy by the carrion left for them, Lucanus flicked one hand towards the settlement. Mato slipped from his horse and crept to the nearest shack. He reeled back, barely before he even had a chance to peer inside, the back of his hand pressed against his mouth.

Each dwelling brought a similar response, and at the end he trudged back to the horses, shaking his head. 'All dead,' he croaked. 'Women raped. Children put to the sword. A baby cut in two. Men with their hands and their feet cut off . . . no eyes . . . butchered while they were still alive, from the look of the blood smeared around the walls.'

'Where are we going to go?' Comitinus said, asking the question none of them had dared voice until now. 'Where will we find sanctuary?'

'The army will have retreated . . . somewhere,' Solinus replied. 'We only have to find them.'

Once the village was far behind, they gnawed on some knobs of dry bread Bellicus had found in one of the huts. Along the horizon, a squall blew up and lightning flashed above the burning villages. The wind blasted, cold for that time of year, and they bowed their heads into it. But no rain came, and for that they were thankful.

When the sun again punched through the lowering clouds and drifting smoke, Lucanus could see how fortunate they had been. They rode the high ground towards the place where they had arranged to meet the others, a spine of brown rock and scrubby grass that ran south, cold and with little cover, but still the best place for them.

'Myrrdin was right to say this was the road to safety,' Bellicus said, following Lucanus' stare.

Where the hills reached down to the plains on every side of the ridge of rock, they could see war-bands riding south. The trail of burning villages stretched out in their wake.

'He knows this land well,' the Wolf said. 'For all his faults, he has wisdom and knowledge that reaches across the years.'

'Some of the barbarians must have ventured up here. The slaughter in that village tells us that. But I'd wager they found so little to kill or plunder in the hills that most of them returned to where there were richer pickings.'

'Anyone fleeing the north is likely to follow this same path, if they have any sense.' Lucanus looked into the distance, but he couldn't estimate how far this high land went before they would find themselves in the midst of the invaders.

'The army is going to have a fight on its hands to drive them back beyond the wall,' Mato said.

'Aye, well, the Britons have a war leader now, Mato.' Solinus grinned. 'The great Pendragon will be at the head of the army sending these barbarians to hell.'

'Where's your crown, Lucanus?' Without looking round, the Wolf could hear that Comitinus was smirking. 'Show us your crown. That fine gold crown.'

Lucanus eyed Bellicus. His friend was grinning at him. 'You're all bastards,' the Wolf said. 'I'll try to forget your mockery when you're on your knees pleading for mercy from the Head of the Dragon.'

Thunder rumbled across the heathland. Grey clouds lowered and the wind bit, yet there was no sign of any storm.

'This is a dismal place,' Bellicus grumbled, looking round at the featureless landscape.

Behind them, to the north, lay the high moors. All around, rough yellow grass reached across the plateau with barely a tree to break the view, the land as empty as any they had passed through in that wind-blasted place. But ahead Lucanus could see a charcoal line of gritstone, the cliffs he had been told to expect.

'It doesn't suit men well,' he replied. 'That's why Myrrdin chose it for our meet. Little chance of prying eyes, or robber bands.'

The thunder grew louder. Now the Wolf could see a sheet of white spray rising up from the line of rock, the edge of cliffs where the land fell away in a dizzying drop.

He lifted his weary head to look out across the grassland rolling into the misty south. No fires blazed. No pall of smoke. He felt a wave of relief.

'The barbarians may have reached the end of their ambition,' Mato said.

'Or else they're catching their breath and building their strength,' Solinus countered. 'The greater battles lie ahead. They'll not want to rush into them.'

The booming was coming from a waterfall cascading down the gritstone to churn into a meandering river below. A westerly wind was blowing and it whisked up spray vertically from the lip of the fall as if the world had been turned on its head.

'Myrrdin said this fall was called Kinder Scut,' Lucanus said. It was a good enough landmark, dwarfing any he had seen near the wall.

Slipping from his horse, he waved his wolf-brothers away to search for any sign that might have been left to show Catia and the others had been here. When they returned, their grim faces told him the answer.

Bellicus clapped a hand on his shoulder. 'It's a hard ride and they have an old man with them.'

'They should have been here by now, you know that.'

His friend nodded, slow and sad. 'We can't stay. There's no shelter.'

As he walked away, Lucanus started to follow him and then stopped. Turning in a slow arc, he yelled 'Catia' at the top of his voice.

The Grim Wolves waved agitated hands to quiet him, knowing full well his voice could carry for miles.

He called her name again, and again.

'Could you ride any slower?' Myrrdin appeared as if from nowhere two spear-throws away, his cloak billowing.

Lucanus sagged with relief.

The camp squatted in a hollow invisible to anyone looking out across the heathland. Black gorse bushes clustered around the edge and Lucanus breathed in the sweet aroma rising from their yellow flowers as he wandered down to where the horses grazed beside the wagon. Menius was sitting by one wheel, sipping from a skin. Amarina knelt beside him, no doubt tending to him with more of her herbs. Amatius was carrying an armful of peat, ready to make a campfire, while Aelius struggled to thrust a branch through the carcass of some fowl for roasting. Decima and Galantha knelt beside him.

Lucanus stopped himself from sprinting down the slope when he saw Catia holding Marcus' hand. All they could do was smile at each other. He looked away from her stare after only an instant, knowing that she did the same.

Amatius watched him, his thoughts writ large on his face too. Jealousy. Resentment. Perhaps even loathing. Their survival was no joy to him, there was no doubt of that.

'Rest and eat,' Myrrdin said, 'and then I will tell you what chance you have of living to see the winter's snows.'

As streaks of pink coloured the western sky, Lucanus wiped the grease from his mouth and tossed the bone into the campfire.

'Come.' Myrrdin passed him and kept walking as if Lucanus was Catulus who would follow him at will.

And he was a dog, clearly, for he saw no choice but to go after the druid.

The shadows were rushing over the heath like a tide coming in. After a short while, they came to a glassy pool that reflected the scudding clouds. As deep as the sky, Lucanus thought.

'Across this land there are places that have always been filled with the power of the gods,' Myrrdin said. 'In those places the otherworld is only a whisper away. Some say an unwise man can wander through to the Summerlands and never be seen again.'

'I have heard those tales.' Lucanus eyed the pool. *Like the Isle of Yews.*

'The wood-priests have been the keepers of those places since the first days. In our schools, this is the first thing a novice is taught. Where they are. Why we must be wary when we are near them. How they set our spirits afire and make us new again.'

He skirted the edge of the pool, staring into the shimmering waters.

The sun died and the dark swept in.

'We are told that a nymph lives here upon the heath. Every day, she bathes in this pool,' he continued. 'If a man meets her in this place, on the right night, when the stars are aligned and the moon is full, she will take him down to a cavern far below and there she will make him immortal.'

'You have many stories, wood-priest. I wonder how many are true and how many are part of that spell you weave to bend people to your will.'

'Oh, all are true, Wolf. In their own way.'

Lucanus gritted his teeth. For now he decided to play along, and after a moment's thought said, 'True, as in gold can be gold or a man grown wise. A dragon can be a dragon or a man reborn—'

'Or an idea reborn. A way of life reborn. Good. You're not as thick-headed as you look.'

The clouds drifted away and the moon came out. As Lucanus looked across the heathland, he jerked. In the lambent light, he thought he saw a figure watching them, silhouetted against the starry sky of the horizon. It was gone almost as soon as he looked at it, but some aspect of it was familiar, though he could not be sure why.

He grabbed Myrrdin's arm. 'We're not alone,' he whispered.

The wood-priest shrugged. 'We are never alone.'

Lucanus searched the dark landscape, but when he could find no sign of any movement he decided he must have dreamt it. 'Why have you brought me here?'

'Would you be made immortal, like the nymph's lovers, Wolf?'

'One life is enough for me.'

'You've already died once and been reborn, in the cold waters of the lake where you found your sword.'

'I did not die.'

'Your body did not.'

'More riddles? One day I'll fall into a sleep at the sound of your voice and never wake up.'

Myrrdin reached out his left hand. 'Everything that has happened to you has brought you to this place, at this time. One thing leads to another, then another, then another, and only the gods know where it all starts. There is a pattern, a warp and a weft, but we see only the strands around us.'

Lucanus watched Myrrdin's other hand disappear inside his cloak, and for a moment he thought the druid had brought him there to murder him, a knife in the gut, his blood drained, a sacrifice to those old gods the wood-priest revered. But when he withdrew his hand, he was holding a switch of hazel which he waved towards the still waters.

'The man you were is long gone,' he said. 'We have called upon Lugh's shining light. Now we must turn our eyes to the dark. Now we must ready for war. Now we must summon the Morrigan.'

Lucanus thought he heard a beating of wings, but it was only the wind in his ears. 'Another of your old gods?'

'The Phantom Queen has never left us, Wolf. She is a sister too, and like Hecate she comes three-fold. Badb, Macha and Nemain. Should you meet her, do not look her in the face, for your wits will be dashed from your head and you will be struck dead there and then. The Morrigan is doom, Wolf. Doom in all its forms. In the shape of a crow, she flies above the battlefield, foretelling who will be cut down. She brings night down upon the day, and winter to summer's end. She is the storm and the shadow and the blood.' Myrrdin bowed his head and muttered something more, but the words were snatched away by the breeze.

Lucanus shivered, from the cold, he supposed.

When he looked up, the wood-priest's face was drawn, his eyes coals, haunted. 'She is known everywhere. In Hibernia they call her the Morrigan, as do we. But she has other names. One and the same. Three as one. Now, when you see a crow upon your travels, it is the Morrigan watching you as you go. When you see a raven feasting upon carrion, it is the Morrigan. She is with you now and always, Wolf. And you will feel her might fill you up whenever you draw Caledfwlch, and you will hear her shriek for blood and death, and her fire will make you a warrior-king, ready for what is to come.'

'And what is to come?'

'War. A war the likes of which this land has never known.'

'I have four wolf-brothers, that is all. How can I fight a war?'

Myrrdin slipped the hazel wand back into the depths of his cloak. 'If you do not fight the war, you and all you love will be destroyed. The gods have already decreed this.'

Lucanus felt his anger rising. 'I will fight. For Catia, for Marcus, for my brothers. I've never said otherwise. But without an army? You're mad, wood-priest.'

'That may well be true.' The druid scooped up a handful of water and wiped it across his brow. 'But you are no longer merely Lucanus the Wolf. You are now the Pendragon, and that is a title which has long since carried some weight upon this island.'

Lucanus felt eyes upon him again and he whirled, but it was too dark to see far. All the talk of the Morrigan had unsettled him, he was sure, but still he wondered what secret allies the wood-priest might have.

'There is nowhere to run now, nowhere to hide,' the druid said.

'You think you're the hand of the gods,' Lucanus spat. 'You and your kind make your plans and believe you can bring about all that you hope for, through will alone. But you can't. That's been proved now. You have no power over the barbarian horde. They do as they wish. You never expected them to sweep on, destroying all they encountered. Say it.'

Myrrdin shrugged, not denying it.

'How many lives have you ruined in your arrogance? How many have been destroyed, and for naught? Because you thought all would fall into place as you wished. Any warrior . . . any man . . . knows the fates will decide those things.' He felt the heat of his anger.

'Be that as it may. Any hope for running . . . for hiding . . . that has all been dashed now. What point a king of this land if there is no land to rule? You must fight for it, Lucanus. You must lead an army, and die if you must, to save all there is for the sake of the royal blood.'

'And again, wood-priest, how?'

'I have sent out word to the four corners,' Myrrdin continued. 'The old names . . . the old tribes . . . they still live on. Some still remember what was and what will be again. And if they do remember, and they answer, then there will be a war-moot at the Heartstones, and your army may well appear, as if by magic.'

'And if they do not remember? If they do not answer?'

'Then you die, Wolf. And your woman dies. And the boy is taken. And the dream we all share dies too.'

## CHAPTER THIRTY-SEVEN

# *Old Friends*

BLACK WINGS BLOTTED OUT THE SUN. BELOW, THE SHADOWS OF those carrion birds swept across the green land, their shrieks drowning out all other sounds. Crows and ravens. The Morrigan was there to see what war had wrought.

Through a thick fog of smoke drifting across the landscape the dull orange of the fires glowed, and the air reeked of burning and blood.

Amarina was kneeling in a deep thicket, staring at the procession trundling past, her throat so narrow she thought she would never breathe again.

The barbarians towered on the backs of muscular stallions, spears tucked in the crooks of their elbows or swords in their hands. Faces like carved stone, eyes like coals, wild hair limned by the light from the burning homes. Stumbling alongside, half-naked women clutched on to the hands of children, filthy with soot and dappled with bruises. Looking around, bewildered at what had become of them. Men, bleeding and broken, their heads bowing so low in despair it seemed that with each step they would fall to their knees.

Amarina choked back a wave of pity that she thought had long since been wrung out of her.

Occasionally the barbarians would prod the captives with their weapons, to make them walk faster or merely for sport, and then they would bark with cruel laughter.

The invaders were making slaves of the conquered.

Amarina felt sickened by the depravities heaped on these poor souls, and she had endured many terrible things in her life. She saw some faces so ragged with despair she imagined they believed only death would save them.

Since they had descended from Kinder Scut to this blasted land, this was all she had seen – smoke and fire, ravens feasting upon the dead, and the free folk who had survived bound and forced to serve their new masters.

They had made their way through a lush land of thick forests and meadows and rushing streams, following the paths of steep, shadowed valleys. For a while, they had thought they might be able to creep past the horde by avoiding settlements, but soon they realized the numbers were swelling by the day as more flooded in from east and west. Now they were all but trapped, their route south blocked by the rampaging barbarians who were filled with such a blood-lust it seemed they would not rest until they had stripped the land bare of all that was civilized.

Her gaze settled on a girl who had seen perhaps seven summers. Naked and smeared with mud, her blonde hair hung in greasy coils around her frightened face. Amarina watched her, caught up in a storm of memories, and for a moment she thought her despair for this poor child would overwhelm her. What hope was there for her now? What hope for any of them?

Two horses rode up. On one was a man with a mane of black hair, the plaits decorated with the skulls of birds and mice. Beside him was a familiar smirking face: Motius, the Carrion Crow.

The black-haired man barked an order in a tongue she couldn't understand; he was the leader, she thought. Two of his men slipped from their horses and dragged one of the slaves out, throwing him to his knees. The leader climbed down and levelled his sword at the captive.

Amarina felt her heart leap when she saw it was a woodsman they'd met in a copse not two days gone.

Nearby the horses churned as if sensing the bloodshed that was to come. Their riders yanked on reins to bring them under control, but they too had the sniff of blood. Amarina could see it in their grins, the cock of their heads, and she hated them for it.

Their captive trembled as the leader questioned him in his guttural tongue. Motius appeared to be translating the words into something the slave could understand.

Whatever he heard, the Scoti warrior jabbed his blade deeper into flesh, drawing out a keening cry. For a moment, the barbarian hesitated, and then, with a shake of his head, he thrust.

Amarina felt fingertips brush her arm and she jerked and almost cried out.

Mato was beside her, pressing a finger to his lips. He flicked his hand to summon her, and together they wriggled back through a sea of bracken. On the edge of a valley shadowed by dense woods, Lucanus and Bellicus hunched, waiting.

'She was watching the war-band,' Mato said.

'Don't go off on your own again,' the Wolf said.

'Is that an order, Lucanus?' she replied. 'I would have thought you would know better than that.'

'You're wasting your breath. She will do as she wishes, you know that,' Bellicus grunted, though Amarina thought she could hear some admiration in his voice.

'I saw a barbarian there, one who leads them, I think,' she said, describing what she had seen.

'His name is Erca,' Lucanus replied. 'A bastard above all bastards.'

'That is no lie. Motius and his Carrion Crows were there too. They questioned the woodsman we met, then killed him. They're looking for us, I have no doubt.'

The Wolf gritted his teeth. 'We knew they wouldn't rest. Nothing is more important to Erca now the barbarians have routed any resistance to their attack.'

'What do we do now?' Mato asked. 'We can't go south from here. And every hour we wait they circle closer to us.'

'Erca is no fool,' Lucanus said. 'He knows our army, or what remains of it, will probably have regrouped somewhere in the south. Fullofaudes must be preparing for a fight. If not, he is not worthy of the title Dux Britanniarum. We only have to get past wherever he draws his line and builds his own army for the final battle.'

'Easier said than done,' Bellicus muttered.

Amarina thought her heart couldn't sink any lower, but suddenly her limbs felt so heavy all she wanted to do was sleep. 'I'm tired of talking,' she said. 'Words, words, words, that's all I hear these days. Let us return to the others and make a plan that will truly save us.'

They plunged down the steep valley side, weaving among the trees, until they reached the bottom. There they followed the line of a silver stream until they found where the others had made camp in the dark shelter beneath an outcropping shield of rock.

In the dank shadows, Myrrdin watched them draw near. Amarina could see he was reading their faces. Rarely did he have anything but a grin on his lips, yet now his face was like stone.

'Our way is blocked,' Lucanus told him. 'We must find another road or stay here and die.'

Lucanus thought he heard the temple calling to them as they made their way down through the steep valley of the Black Brook. Was it the wind in the branches or the seductive whispers of old gods?

Five days had passed since they'd witnessed the horde taking slaves, five long days of creeping through dense woods towards the south-west. Weary, wary, they had bickered and snapped. But Myrrdin had led them on, promising sanctuary and an ally. And the Wolf had to admit that decision was the right one. The smoke drifted away. The clamour of slaughter faded until there was only birdsong.

Swatting away fat flies, Amarina had long been complaining about the lack of any sign of their destination. The druid had only smiled. But now Lucanus could see it, or thought he could, a place hidden from anyone but those searching for it.

Deep in the forest a cleft gashed through the rock, as wide as a man, made all but invisible by trees and grass and moss. Steps carved into the stone disappeared into the cool dark.

'What kind of temple is this?' Amarina asked, her voice oddly hushed.

'The folk in these parts call it Lud's Temple, in their way,' Myrrdin replied. 'The true name is Lugh's Temple. Here in days long gone, the god was worshipped in the belly of the earth. Here, too, Cernunnos lives. But now it is the home of the Lord of the Greenwood.'

The riders slipped off their horses, the wagon abandoned to one side. The druid climbed to the top of those steps, and crooked a finger for Lucanus to join him. Together they looked down into the gloom.

The Wolf felt his skin turn to gooseflesh, though he wasn't sure why. 'What's down there?' he said.

'Your destiny.'

'That ally you mentioned?'

'Perhaps.'

Lucanus eyed him. 'More games?'

'This is not a place for games, Wolf.' The druid's voice was low, almost afraid, Lucanus thought.

With the tip of his staff, the wood-priest scratched a circle in the dry soil.

'You must venture down alone,' he said, 'with your head bowed and your heart open. Cernunnos will judge if you are worthy.'

'And if he doesn't?'

'We won't see you again.'

Lucanus stared into that swelling darkness, feeling his heart patter, despite himself. After a moment, he swung a foot over the first step, held it there for a moment, testing the dark and himself, and then he edged down.

His neck burned from the sun, but he felt it fade by the moment as the light fell away and the cool void swallowed him. His footsteps echoed off the stone walls, his nose filling with the dank air and the thick scent of soil and vegetation and cold rock.

Down he stepped, and down further, and gradually his eyes told him the shadows were not as deep as he believed. When he reached the bottom and looked around, he felt his skin prickle in a different way.

He marvelled at a green world. The light filtering through the vegetation and the moss that covered the sheer rock walls painted the refuge with an emerald tint. He craned his neck up and saw that the cleft – the temple – soared up the height of near ten men.

Cool. Silent. He shivered at the majesty of this sanctuary. A temple indeed.

'This is one of the old places.' Myrrdin's voice echoed down to him. 'And in every old place, the gods can be heard, aye, and spoken to, if the voice is right.'

In the centre of the temple, flat stones had been piled up, and on them nestled bones, dry flowers and herbs, and knobs of bread that had taken on the consistency of stone. An altar.

As the dark swept away, Lucanus could see he was alone in the long, narrow temple, yet he sensed something fading in the air as if a presence had been there only very recently. He breathed in deeply, letting the tightness ease out of his shoulders and the sanctity of the place settle on him, and he realized he had been unconsciously holding on to the hilt of his sword.

Reaching out, he scraped his fingers along the rough stone wall as he walked along the cleft. Images had been scratched there by unknown hands, some of them faded with great age, and he leaned in and squinted. His fingertips traced the faint outline of writing, runes, of the kind that had been etched into Caledfwlch, and surrounding those unreadable messages from times long gone, drawings. He followed the patterns and gasped when he saw they swept up high over his head, higher than any man could reach. He saw clouds throwing lightning bolts, and what looked like a boar bristling with spears; a man's face formed from leaf and branch; swords and axes, bulls and crows and snakes, and two figures of differing sizes, which he took to be a man and a boy. That one had a sharper outline.

He shrugged. The work of idle hands, scratched out by firelight during long nights, perhaps. Yet he sensed a reverence in the careful strokes of those delicate designs, work that held a meaning for those who had laboured over them, but one which escaped him.

Walking to the centre of the temple, he looked up once more to that emerald slash high overhead where barbs of glinting sunlight broke through the vegetation. 'The Lord of the Greenwood,' he murmured. 'Where are you?'

Jerking from his reverie, he strode to the foot of the steps and shouted up, 'There's no one here.'

A moment later he heard tentative footsteps trudging down.

'Where is this ally?' he said, when the others had reached the bottom and were gazing around the temple, mouths slack.

Myrrdin walked along the narrow cleft, looking round. 'He is not here now, but he will come. And then I will petition him for aid. This is the most dangerous time, for all of us here, and for what we hope to achieve. All will be lost if the barbarian horde cannot be resisted.'

'Not just your plans, or the lives of those here, wood-priest, don't forget that. This is not a conquering army of the kind we've heard about in times past. The slaughter of all the folk who live in Britannia will not stop, and those who do survive will become slaves. Rome did not unleash a tide of blood when they first sailed to these shores.'

The druid's eyes narrowed. 'You say. The wood-priests would disagree.'

Lucanus nodded. 'That is fair. But now everything we have known stands to be lost.'

'Yes, this is a war that will shape the fates of all who live here. But we must get to the Heartstones without being captured or killed, and begin to build an army. We can't do that alone.'

Lucanus raised his head so the others could not see his doubts. The army was fragmented, perhaps already crushed, and the chance that they could raise some fighting force from lazy merchants and farmers was beyond his dreams. But the others needed hope if they were to keep their spirits up. 'Then let's find this Lord of the Greenwood,' he said.

'If he is not here, he will be heeding the call of Cernunnos, for this day is Beltane, the fire festival. Summer is a-coming in.'

The dark deepened in Lud's temple. Myrrdin demanded firewood and by the time dusk drew in Lucanus had helped the others build a small fire at one end of the cleft. They all had to help; the druid had insisted on that. As the flames licked up, the wood-priest stood behind the blaze and raised his arms to the sky. The Wolf watched his shadow swoop up the rock walls as if rising to the heavens themselves.

'We call to Lugh,' Myrrdin said, his voice ringing off the stone. 'We call to Cernunnos. As the wheel of the year turns, and the land gives up its bounty, we raise our faces to the sun and give thanks for all that will be.'

The druid said much more, but Lucanus found his thoughts turning to gods and daemons and the Fates and how they ran men like dogs toying with a nest of rats.

He slipped from his thoughts when the wood-priest commanded, 'Pick up your torches, then walk around the bonfire as the sun crosses the sky. Wolf, you must go last.'

Lucanus watched as first Amarina, then Decima and Galantha picked up the pieces of wood they had chosen earlier and processed around the fire. They plunged their torches into the golden heart, and when they were alight the three women walked to the foot of the stone steps and waited. Catia and Marcus followed, then Aelius, Amatius glowering, and Menius supported by Solinus and Comitinus, and Mato and Bellicus. Finally, he walked up himself.

Myrrdin rested a hand on his shoulder and leaned in. 'The Dragon is born from fire,' he whispered, 'and this Beltane you shall be reborn, finally. I will tell you one of the great secrets.'

He opened his palm and Lucanus saw what looked like a shrivelled piece of bark. He tasted iron on his tongue as the druid pushed it into his mouth and commanded, 'Chew.'

He chewed and swallowed. 'What is it?'

'The flesh of the toad's-stool.'

'Are we flying? This is what the witches gave me.'

Myrrdin smiled. 'Not flying. But you will meet the gods and see the daemons. That is the secret, Wolf. That is what our novices learn. And not just wood-priests and witches. The toad's-stool is sacred to all, the world over. Every religion. Mithras. The Greeks, the priests of Rome. In their holy places, in their houses of mystery where they keep their secrets tight to their breasts, learned only by the novitiates, they eat the toad's-stool. It is part of their rites. And in this isle, this Albion, we are told that it has been sacred since the first men walked. The ones who put up the stones. And now you will undergo the Beltane rite, and the next step of your journey will begin.'

'What if I do not want to hear the gods?'

'You will be changed, Wolf. The man you once were must die so that the dragon may rise from the ashes. You wear the gold crown of the Ouroboros, but now you must become the Pendragon.'

'Then let's be done with this. I have a war to fight.' Lucanus thrust his torch into the flames.

'You still have much to learn. This is not one night. This is for all your days. The toad's-stool and the Pendragon are bound together. In battle, it will make you a great warrior. You will fear nothing. You will have the strength of a hundred men. You will not tire. And in your darkest nights, and there will be many, it will give you wisdom.'

The wood-priest gave his shoulder a squeeze. He thought he felt something honest in that touch, a first for the druid. Was it concern? Or pity?

'The voices of the gods can bring a man to terror,' he said. 'But fear not, I will be at your side. For all time now. We are joined too.'

His words seemed to throb and twist. The crackle of the fire whirled around him. As he peered along the cleft, Lucanus thought each of the torches held by his friends now burned like molten iron in the smith's forge.

'One thing leads to another, Lucanus. Always remember that.' The words seemed to hang over him, uttered by no mouth. 'There is not a single choice that a man makes that does not roll off into days yet to come.' A whisper as loud as a shout.

He felt a hand on his arm. Myrrdin guided him away from the bonfire, past the others, and then up the stone steps. At the entrance, he saw the yellow forest flowers, the Beltane blooms, that Catia and Marcus had picked earlier and arranged to the wood-priest's design. They swirled out into the dark.

'Follow the spiral path,' Myrrdin murmured. 'This is life, and this is death, both joined, never ending. And at the end you will be renewed, ready for what is to come.'

'Where is our ally?' Lucanus said, distracted.

'He's watching you, Wolf. He is always watching you.'

The night was warmer than he expected, the forest rich with scents he had never smelled before. He looked around in wonder. The torches swept out among the trees, fireflies dancing in the dark.

'See, Wolf,' Myrrdin whispered. 'See the majesty.'

And he did.

How long he was there, he didn't know. At some point Myrrdin must have left him, for he found himself on his own. He thought he saw ivy-twined figures emerging from tree trunks, watching him with eyes flickering with emerald fire. Away in the night men and women processed, their skin shining with a golden light, an entire court of them headed by a king and queen. A part of him was certain he had always seen them, since he was a child, on the edge of sleep, in the woods and the wild mountain tops. More dreams. More dreams?

Lucanus walked the spiral path.

A voice whispered, 'Only the Bear-King can save you.'

He jerked around, but no one was there.

*War is coming.* This voice was inside his own head. *Soon. Soon. Blood and death.*

A cry rang out. It sprang from lips to lips, growing in intensity. At first Lucanus thought this was inside his head too. But then the thrum of the toad's-stool ebbed and his wits returned. The torches were flashing back and forth.

He felt a pang of panic, though he was not sure why.

Catia raced through the trees, and, seeing him, ran over and grabbed his arms. Lucanus looked into her wide eyes.

'Marcus,' she began, her voice becoming a croak as if she couldn't bear to speak. 'Marcus is gone.'

'Where are we going?' the boy asked.

Amarina gripped his hand tighter so that he couldn't wriggle free. She was hurrying through the woods so fast his feet barely touched the ground, and feeling her heart pound she breathed in deeply to force herself to stay calm. She had the advantage. The others were lost to their Beltane games and even when they knew the two of them were gone, they wouldn't know in which direction.

'You would not see your mother die?' she said, more harshly than she intended.

'No!'

'Then together we have a chance to save her . . . and . . . and your father and grandfather and uncle. And Lucanus and all the others.' *Decima. Galantha.*

'But I don't understand.' His bewildered words rose to a cry and tears brimmed in his eyes.

Cursing under her breath, Amarina skidded to a halt. She crouched and rested both hands on his shoulders, staring into his eyes with well-practised adoration.

'You have the royal blood,' she murmured. 'You will bring forth a king, a great king, one who will never die and will save the lives of all . . . all who are suffering. You've seen what the barbarians have done, yes?'

Marcus nodded.

'You've seen the misery and the suffering and the death. You can stop that, Marcus. You can help save everyone.'

His eyes widened.

Amarina stifled a sigh. She was even convincing herself. 'But you can't act like a child any longer. Now you must be like the king you will become, and a king makes sacrifices . . . great sacrifices. To save lives. You can do this. It's in your power.'

'I want to go back to Mother.' His eyes welled up again.

'When you were a boy . . . younger . . . your father told you stories of the great heroes . . . of kings, yes? With swords, who fought giants?'

'Lucanus did.'

'Lucanus. Of course he did. Remember those stories, Marcus. What the heroes did, because now you are a hero.'

Amarina watched him soften a little. It was enough. She pulled him along again, listening for any sound of pursuit, but the forest was still and quiet.

At her hip banged the pouch she'd hidden under the holly earlier, filled with what few provisions she could steal without being discovered. It wasn't much, but it would suffice.

This wasn't treachery. This was for the sake of all of them, because no other there was brave enough to do it.

She would find that barbarian leader, Erca, and she would bargain for their lives with this boy. He would be kept safe – he was too valuable to be harmed. Erca would have no interest in the others once he had his prize, and they would be free to go their own way.

And if she was taken slave, or killed – her stomach twisted – then so be it. For once she would have done some good.

To keep running, and hiding, until doom caught up with them, as it always did – what kind of life was that? She'd spent too many of her own days running and hiding to see it inflicted on others.

Down a bank she scrambled, and along the muddy banks of a stream, the air thick with the tang of wild garlic. Her eyes had learned to see into the dark, a little, but she still wished she had a torch to guide them.

'I want to go back,' Marcus whined.

'It's too late for that,' she snapped. 'If you try to go alone, you will lose your way and the boars will eat you. They'll crunch up your bones and no one will even know you're dead.'

She sensed movement in front of her, but she was too slow to react. A figure loomed up. Hands grabbed her and threw her to the ground.

'The whore.' A voice laced with dark humour.

Amarina looked up into a familiar face. The centurion Falx hung over her, still wearing his armour. Behind him she saw a circle of the soldiers he had trusted most in Vercovicium, the hard men, the liars and the thieves. Her thoughts raced, trying to make sense of what she was seeing, here in the deep forest, so far from the wall. But all she could think of were the wood-priest's words, uttered so many times they had almost become a spell: nothing happens by chance.

'Aye,' Falx said as if he could read her mind. He leaned lower, a triumphant smile licking at his lips. 'We have followed you for many days, whore, biding our time until we could get what we wanted. Tonight was to be the night, but you have saved us a fight.'

'What do you want?' she spat.

'Why, the boy, of course. There's nothing more valuable in all the world. We'll take him now. Search her,' he commanded his men. 'These whores are a deadly breed. She'll have a knife on her somewhere.'

Amarina shuffled back, unsure if she should try to fight or run.

But the centurion only pulled out his sword and pressed its tip against her throat. 'Your life is worth nothing, though. Do not forget that.'

# CHAPTER THIRTY-EIGHT

# *The Crossroads*

'WHY WOULD AMARINA TAKE THE BOY?' GALANTHA PROTESTED. 'This makes no sense to me.'

'You know why.' Amatius glowered at her and Bellicus stiffened, ready to act if the coward raised a hand. 'Only gold moves you whores,' Catia's husband continued. 'She plans to sell the boy to get rich.'

'Amarina would never do such a thing,' Decima blazed. 'She has a good heart.'

Amatius advanced on the two women, one fist bunching. 'We should never have brought you treacherous sows along. Now my son has paid the price for that weakness.'

Before Bellicus could move, Lucanus lunged in front of the other man. 'Leave them. They're not at fault here.'

'They're all cut from the same cloth.'

'I say Amarina has a good heart too.'

'Aye. You like your women, do you not?' Amatius thrust his face towards Lucanus.

Bellicus saw his friend's eyes narrow, recognizing full well the meaning behind those words.

'At least I have the courage to defend *my* women,' the Wolf growled. 'And I'll do what it takes to save Marcus. I'm not afraid.'

Amatius bristled, but before he could lash out Catia pushed her way between the two rivals, her eyes flashing as she looked from one to the other. 'Enough. We must find Marcus. That's all that matters.'

'I don't believe Amarina would sell the boy for her own gain,' Bellicus rumbled, looking around the faces. 'I've watched her in recent days – she's not the woman she was. The horde's slaughter has taken its toll on her, as it has on us all. But she's as hard and cold as a frozen lake when she makes her calculations, and if she thinks giving up Marcus will save more lives, I am not surprised that she has acted.'

'She has no right to make that choice,' Aelius protested.

Myrrdin rammed his staff against the ground. 'This is not just about the boy,' he snapped. 'She is betraying all those who will die in days yet to come if there's no king to lead them out of darkness.'

Before the argument could start again, Mato loped into the circle of torchlight. 'I've found their trail,' he said, breathless. 'Amarina is heading back the way we came.'

'Towards the barbarians.' Amatius' voice was wintry.

Lucanus snatched up one of the torches. 'Marcus will slow her. If we're quick, we can catch her before she reaches danger.'

'Wait,' Catia called. She ran down the stone steps into the cleft and emerged a moment later with her bow and quiver.

None of the Grim Wolves protested at her decision to join them; she'd earned her place.

Amatius showed no feeling. As he turned away and began to walk towards Lud's temple, Bellicus caught his arm. 'My friend is a good man, and too gentle at times. But I'm a bastard. I've killed better men than you without thinking twice. Raise your hand against any woman here, and I'll snap you over my knee.'

Amatius wrenched his arm free, but Bellicus could see that behind his defiance he was unsettled. That was good.

Bellicus whistled and his dog scampered up. 'Come, Catulus. We're going hunting.'

And then he was thundering after the others, into the trees, watching the torch dance in the distance, one lone light in the dark.

Amarina crashed to the bottom of the hollow, her cheek burning where the fist had smacked against it. She looked up at the soldiers laughing at her and her fingers crooked into claws. If only she had her knife. They would not be laughing when blood was pouring down between their legs.

Falx marched down the slope and offered her a hand. 'I warned you,' he said. 'If you came along and slowed us down, you'd get the back of a hand to make your feet fly.' He yanked her up. 'I gave you the chance to run. You should have taken it.'

'The boy's safety is my responsibility.'

The soldiers laughed again. As if she could do anything to keep Marcus safe. She simmered, but pushed down her feelings; only a cold mind would enable her to recognize an opportunity to escape.

The centurion shrugged. 'Do as you will, for now. But know that you will not be spared because he needs a mother.'

She eyed Marcus, standing with a soldier's hand on each of his shoulders. His face was haunted, but he was not old enough to judge her for what she'd done. That trust would be knocked out of him soon enough, she thought with bitterness.

'Was it not enough to steal the wages of your men in Vercovicium? Now you have to fill your purse with the suffering of a boy.'

The centurion glowered. 'All I had was left behind when the fort fell.'

Amarina was pleased that she had touched a raw nerve, if only a monetary one.

Falx shoved her and they carried on along their way. Soon enough she saw a light flickering among the trees and immediately she frowned. Surely they were still far from where she'd last seen the horde?

Three wagons stood in a crescent in the clearing, five sullen men sitting by the wheels in hushed conversation. Beside them was a large amber tent, the light she had seen glowing within.

At the sound of their arrival, a vast silhouette loomed in the tent's entrance. Varro the merchant.

'You have served me well since Vercovicium, Falx, but this is where we part company.'

Amarina watched Varro hand over a fat leather pouch of coin. The centurion jingled it, his eyes lighting, and then he looked round at his men and nodded. 'Fair pay.'

'You earned it.' The merchant ruffled Marcus' hair.

Falx winked at her and she bit down on her desire to rake out his eyes. 'I'll be the first to say that you and your band of misfits led us a fine dance, whore, and there were times when we thought you'd slipped through our fingers. But those who saw you never forgot you, and tongues were easily loosened.'

'Where to for you now, Falx?' the merchant asked.

The centurion glanced at his men. They were a motley group, Amarina thought: heavy-featured, slow-eyed, hard men who would thrive in any situation. 'There's always someone who will pay for swords and good right arms.' He grinned. 'Those barbarians may have done us a favour. I've earned more since the fall than I ever did under the Eagle.' He jingled the coins again, and walked off to join his men. They all brayed with laughter at some muttered comment that Amarina couldn't hear.

As the centurion and his followers disappeared into the trees, Varro snapped his fingers and his men jumped to their feet. 'Get ready. We will be away soon.'

Amarina looked back the way they had come, praying that Lucanus and the others would have found her trail and be on their way by now. Of all the errors she'd made in her life, this had been by far the worst.

Bucco the fool danced out of the tent, leaned in and tweaked Marcus' nose.

'Don't torment him,' Amarina snapped, pulling the lad to her and crossing her hands over his chest.

Bucco raised an eyebrow. 'A new mother. Filled with fire. Just like the old mother.'

Amarina bared her teeth at him, but turned to Varro. 'Where are we going?' she asked.

'I've seen you before, have I not?' Varro furrowed his brow. 'In Vercovicium.'

'She is the whore,' the fool said. 'The queen of whores.'

'I'll be the queen of cutting off your balls.'

Bucco clasped both hands to his cheeks and tumbled back.

'Take the boy into the tent,' Varro commanded. 'Give him some bread. Some wine. Fill his belly. He must be hungry.' When they had gone, he looked at Amarina. 'I have no need of you. Leave.'

Amarina found her favourite smile and poured some honey on her words. 'You have no need of a woman?'

Her practised look had lost none of its potency. Varro moistened his lips. 'What do you offer?'

'Why, I'll care for Marcus. This boy needs a mother. Would you or the fool prefer that work?'

Varro nodded, considering. 'And you will be a good companion, of course. It is too long since I have been with a woman.'

Amarina flashed a smile. 'You will not be disappointed.'

While she thought of all the ways she could make this loathsome slug suffer, she watched the men hitch the horses to the wagons. Then, when his guard was down, she asked, 'But is anywhere safe for us?'

'Not here, no.' Varro rubbed his hands together, overcome with glee that he had finally got his heart's desire. 'Britannia is already lost. A land of the dead, I would say, from all I've seen. The age of light is gone and now there is only the dark. But beyond the sea?' He grinned at her.

'You can get us away from Britannia?'

'I have a ship waiting. On the south coast, which the barbarian horde has not yet reached. They've halted their advance for now, I am told, on a line between Viroconium and Durobrivae . . . the east is lost, of course. They came in their ships by the thousand.' He fluttered his fat fingers. 'They are not fools, these barbarians. They know they need to gather their forces, to rest, to build supplies. That gives us time . . . not much, but enough. Falx has told me the road to take so we can avoid any attacks. We will be gone soon enough, with no trace of our passing.'

Amarina slipped behind Varro as he walked into the tent, close enough for her breath to bloom on his neck. He was wheezing from even that mild exertion. She looked around, knowing it was futile to hope there would be a knife lying close by that she could palm to use later. Varro's guards stumbled past, laden with bales and cushions and ornately carved boxes, and Marcus squatted beside the fool, chuckling at Bucco's jokes as he gnawed on a strip of flatbread.

'What will you do with him?' she asked.

Varro studied the boy. He smiled in a way that left Amarina feeling uneasy. 'The Dragon will rise, sooner or later. The circle will be completed and renewed. But until then the boy must be kept from all harm. He will have no contact with any other until it is time for him to breed, and when he has provided a son his use is over. As a grown man, there would always be the danger that he would demand his independence, and there is no gain in risking his falling into the hands of another; rival claims to the bloodline, and all that.' Amarina felt his lizard eyes upon her. 'Does that trouble you?'

'That he will spend his childhood as a captive and then his life will be over?'

'Yes.'

'I'm a whore.' She smiled. 'I have no heart.'

He nodded, but she could tell he wasn't convinced. She would have to work hard to ensure she roused no suspicions that would hamper her attempts to escape. Seeing an amphora and two goblets on a small square table, she poured out some wine, pressing one of the cups into Varro's hand and keeping the other for herself.

'But if Marcus is not the king himself, what do you gain?' she said curiously. 'You'll be long dead by the time his offspring sits upon a throne.'

Varro sipped his wine. 'You are just a whore. I could not expect you to understand.'

'Tell me, then.' She smiled at him over the rim of her goblet.

'With the boy in my charge, I will be able to demand anything. For he is key to all that is to come. Thus, he is as valuable as the king himself.' He waved his cup, slopping wine. 'To wield power, one does not need to have it. Only to guide the hand of the one who does.'

Amarina thought of the miseries that were planned for Marcus and felt pity, but she showed none of it on her face. 'I know little,' she said with a shrug, 'but in my experience, when someone has something another wants they must spend their life defending it. Are you prepared for a lifetime of battle?'

'There are many looking for this boy now, that's true. Word of a saviour is spreading by the day, among those who are aware of these things. When people yearn for a god-given king to lead them out of earthly misery, it is only natural that such tales will spring from lips to lips.' He nodded. 'Many will wish to seize him, yes. But I will not stand alone.'

'You have allies?'

Varro grinned. 'In every town, in every village, from the northern reaches of the empire to the east, and beyond. You have heard of Mithras, even in that cold, benighted place you call home?'

She furrowed her brow, feigning ignorance. But she had, of course: the religion the soldiers followed, or some of them. But it was dying, so they all said. 'What does Marcus have to do with Mithras? This prophecy of a saviour . . . I have heard tell of it . . . it is not a saviour born of Mithras?'

Varro drained his wine and set his cup aside. His glee at finding what he had searched for for so long had loosened his tongue.

'With every god there comes a story of a king who will lead the followers to joy everlasting. And even if there were not, such followers would believe it none the less. Especially the followers of Mithras. Our emperor is a Christian now, though this was not always the case. Once a man could worship any god he saw fit. Soon we will be told that any deity but the emperor's own is false, and must be denied. The Christians already smell victory after long years of persecution, and like all those who have suffered they want victory, not equality. They destroy the temples. Punish the followers, drive them into hiding, as we drove the wood-priests once. But these things do not die. Not a belief in a god that has burned bright for an age. Sol Invictus. The Invincible Sun. They are angry, the worshippers of Mithras, bitter. Their heads are down and they see all they believed in slipping away. For now, they will continue their practices in secret. They cannot see any way to fight back, not when the emperor is against them. But if they had a king to lead them . . . if they had *belief* in a king . . .' His eyes gleamed.

Amarina looked at Marcus, laughing so innocently, and saw the hard road of the rest of his days laid out before him. This time it must have shown in her face, for she heard Varro say, 'The wood-priests want your boy. So do the worshippers of Mithras, and any man who seeks power. These prophecies have a habit of capturing hearts and minds, if a man is desperate enough. But that's not all. If the Christians find him, do you think they will suffer a rival Messiah to live? No, better he is kept alive with me, if only for a few more years, than to see his days ended now.'

Bucco hurried forward. 'Tell him,' he implored, his voice filled with glee. 'Tell him now.'

Amarina frowned, not sure who the dwarf meant.

'Yes.' Varro hammered one fist into the palm of his hand. 'He should know. Let it eat away at him. That bastard has made me work hard enough for this victory.'

The merchant lurched out of the tent, as fast as he had probably moved in an age, Amarina thought. She skipped after him as he made his way across the camp and hammered his fist on the side of the third wagon.

'I have him, do you hear? I have him, as I said I would.' His voice dripped with triumphalism.

Curious, Amarina leaned in. She heard a croaking voice reply, but she was not close enough to make out the words.

And then Varro wheeled away. 'Come,' he yelled to his guards. 'Faster. Faster. I would be on the road by first light.'

Amarina jerked from a dream of deep water. She had found herself far beneath the waves, in the cold dark, the sunlight shimmering above her head, always out of reach.

For a moment, she struggled to remember where she was, until she heard Varro's rumbling snores and saw the silhouette of his bulk at the far end of the wagon. The fool was curled up beside him, like a dog. Dawn had come, the thin light filtering in through the flaps at the rear.

Not long after they had packed up the camp and left, the rolling of the wagon had lulled her into sleep. She had been bone-tired and burdened by worries and she'd slipped away gratefully. But now she felt irritated by the lumbering rhythm. It was too slow and every bump rang through her. The track through the forest was rutted and uneven, not like the arrow-straight army roads. They rolled forward at barely any pace, for fear of breaking an axle or shattering one of the iron-clad wheels.

Marcus was slumped beside her. At first she thought he was asleep, but when she shifted he looked up at her. His cheeks gleamed in the half-light, wet with tears. She realized what an ordeal this must be for him, even though he had no idea of the fate that was planned for him. Stolen from the arms of his mother – stolen by her, and how guilty she felt now – and then transported by strangers to an unknown destination with no explanation.

Despite herself, she slipped an arm round his shoulder. 'You have what it takes to be a hero. I can see that now.'

The boy's eyes brightened.

'We are not going gently with this slug, but we must bide our time,' she whispered. 'When the moment comes, I will give you a sign. Do you understand?'

Marcus nodded, then surprised her with a hug.

'Oh,' she said, her arms hanging in the air, unsure what she should do. After a moment, she prised him off her.

Brighter now, he crawled across the rolling floor of the *rheda* and peered out of the flaps. Amarina caught a glimpse of dense woods, thick with shadow, and the muddy track silvered in the first light.

After a moment, Marcus turned back to her and whispered, 'Someone is following us.'

Her heart thumped and she felt a surge of relief. Lucanus, of course. She crawled beside Marcus and looked out, plans already forming in her head. They were trundling along at the rear of the line of wagons, and travelling slowly enough for her to drop the boy out of the back and jump after him when the time came.

She peered among the trees and sure enough she could see movement. A pale shape, fleet of foot, easily keeping pace with the lumbering wagon. *Mato.*

Squinting, she was certain she could see the other wolves following him. Biding their time for the right moment to strike.

Smiling, she turned to Marcus and pressed her finger to her lips. He nodded.

Varro and the fool still twitched and snored. The time was right. Easing behind Marcus, she slipped her hands under his armpits ready to ditch him over the side when the wolf-brothers made their move.

She followed the progress of the shadowy man in the woods, and when he seemed ready to rush out she lifted Marcus up.

The figure swept from the trees just behind the rear of the *rheda.*

Amarina recoiled and dropped the boy on to the boards. When he cried out, she heard the merchant and his fool wake with shock, but now that was the least of her worries.

The Attacotti warrior loped with the easy grace and power of a wolf at hunt. The ash-encrusted face and torso glowed white in the early light, charcoal-ringed eyes fixed on her.

There would be no mercy, she could see that.

With each step he drew closer. A short-bladed knife glinted in his right hand. The wagons rattled on, the drivers oblivious.

Amarina yelled a warning, but her voice was lost beneath the clatter of hooves and the rumble of wheels.

'Do something,' she heard Varro cry, his keening voice breaking.

Bucco scrambled beside her and she felt him shaking.

Turning, she grasped one of the chests in which the merchant stored his valuables and in one fluid movement heaved it out of the back. The casket smashed the warrior full in the chest, laying him flat.

A gruff command to stop rang out from somewhere along the road ahead and the three wagons slowed.

'Keep going!' the fool squealed.

Varro tried to claw his way to the rear, but the rolling of the boards threw his huge bulk off balance and he flailed around, howling.

When they lurched to a halt, the wagon slewed, and Amarina felt it half slide off the edge of the track into the undergrowth. The horses stamped and whinnied, sensing some kind of threat.

'We cannot stay here,' the fool whispered in her ear. 'Quickly. Under the *rheda*.'

*Futile,* she thought. But as Bucco dropped over the edge, she lowered Marcus to the ground and threw herself after them. All three crawled into the shadows beneath the wagon, while Varro continued to wail above their heads.

Peering under the wagons, she could see that the way ahead was blocked by horsemen. Then the floor of the cart above her began to shake, and a pair of trembling legs appeared over the edge as Varro lowered his bulk on to the muddy track. The fool grabbed her arm and whispered in her ear, 'We cannot stay here. Come.'

'Why should I trust you?' she hissed.

Bucco glanced at his master's legs, and she saw a shadow fall across his face. He scowled, a look filled with hate, she thought, and then a knife flashed into his hand from somewhere in his tunic and he lashed out.

The blade carved through the tendons at the back of Varro's ankles. No longer able to support his own weight, the merchant crashed face down on to the track, his screams tearing through the still morning.

Amarina was horrified by the speed and viciousness of the attack, but only for an instant. Bucco was already wriggling into the undergrowth at the side of the wagon and crawling away. Amarina pushed Marcus ahead of her and followed behind them.

In the dark of the woods, she glanced back. Ten or more barbarians were sitting their mounts in front of the wagons. These were not Attacotti, she could see. One of them looked like the leader of the Scoti with whom she had planned to bargain, the one Lucanus had called Erca. But what gripped her attention was the man standing beside him. Clearly, Falx had sold Marcus to Varro, and now he had sold Varro and Marcus to Erca.

As the merchant tried to heave himself up, still howling, the Attacotti flew out of the woods and fell upon him. His squeals rang out so loud and raw that Amarina couldn't bear to hear them.

She ran on. Her movement must have caught the eye of one of the raiders for a yell echoed, but she didn't look back.

Behind her, the sound of running feet crashed into the undergrowth.

## CHAPTER THIRTY-NINE

# *Short As Any Dream*

T HE MEWLING ROLLED THROUGH THE STILL MORNING. LUCANUS held up one hand to bring the others to a halt and listened.

'I've heard no beast or bird make a sound like that,' Bellicus said.

The Wolf looked along the sunlit track to where it curved to the left and disappeared among the trees. Nothing moved in the spring heat.

He felt his neck prickle, though his senses had been on fire since he'd led the Grim Wolves and Catia away from Lud's temple. The trail had been clear – Amarina had obviously been more concerned with speed than hiding her path. But then they had reached a spot where several feet had walked – heavy, men – and there had been a scuffle of some kind.

Whether Amarina had meant to bring the boy to these people, he couldn't know. Perhaps she'd been surprised by thieves or cut-throats. But he'd felt a wave of pity when he'd seen Catia's face drain of blood in the torchlight. To her credit, she'd given no voice to her worries, only lowering her head and keeping pace with them as they loped into the dawn.

Lucanus drew his sword. The others unsheathed their weapons too, and Catia pulled an arrow from her quiver and nocked it.

As they rounded the bend in the track, Lucanus dropped low, waiting. Three *rhedae* blocked the way ahead, whatever horses had pulled them long gone.

Mato pointed to where bodies littered the edge of the trail, five of them.

For a moment Lucanus watched the trees. Then, creeping past the puddles of blood drying in the sun, he crouched beside the remains. All of them hacked down with swords.

Solinus darted round the wagons. When he returned, he said, 'No sign of the boy, or of Amarina.'

Lucanus looked to Catia and was pleased to see the relief in her face, but it was fleeting.

'Where, then?' she asked. 'Are these the men that Amarina and Marcus met?'

The mewling rose up again, high-pitched, undulating, and ended with a drawn-out chattering.

The Grim Wolves looked at one another, and then Lucanus tracked the sound into the woods.

A corpulent man swung from the low branch of a spreading oak on an oiled rope tied around his chest and under his arms. Fat flies droned around him, landing in clouds upon his head, then swirling away when the mewling began. The sound was creeping from his lips, or where his lips had been.

His head and chest had been flayed, his ragged, dripping tunic hanging from his waist. Lucanus watched white eyes roll in that crimson mask with a madness born of agony.

'That . . . that is the merchant Varro,' Comitinus uttered.

Now Lucanus could see he was right. His thoughts raced, piecing together the information he had. 'Amarina and Marcus were brought here, by choice or against their will, I don't know. Varro was prepared to pay any price to get his hands on the boy.'

'And then he and his band were attacked,' Bellicus growled.

'There are many hungry people roaming the land,' Mato suggested.

Lucanus reached out a hand towards the hanging man. 'Would starving folk do this?' He turned to Bellicus and said, 'Put him out of his misery.'

Bellicus raised his blade and stepped forward. At his back Catulus let out a low growl.

An arrow thumped into the merchant's face and his quivering stopped. With graven features, Catia strode away from them towards the wagons.

'Follow the trail.' Her voice rang out, clear and strong and fearless.

303

At the wagons, she paused, thinking. Lucanus watched her walk along the line, hammering her palm on the side of each one. At the third, a muffled call rang out.

Lucanus ran forward and slashed the bonds fastening the rear door. Wrenching it open, he recoiled from a potent reek of shit and piss and sweat.

A figure lay on the boards on the far side. As when he had first seen Varro's flayed form, the Wolf found his thoughts struggling to comprehend what lay before him.

It was a man . . . but not. His arms and legs were gone, cut off close to the torso, the stumps bound with filthy cloth. It was a wonder he'd not already succumbed to death, from blood loss or the slow rot. He was thin, his cheeks hollowed out, and his skin had the look of someone who had not seen the sun in many a day. His grey hair was wild and matted. As Lucanus gazed at him in horror, the poor soul raised his head and stared back with rheumy eyes.

Tattoos darkened the man's neck, disappearing under his stained tunic. The Wolf heaved himself into the back of the wagon and asked, 'You're a wood-priest?'

'I am. My name is Vercingetorix.' His voice was like a knife scraping down wood, and Lucanus heard an accent he did not recognize.

'Where's your home?'

'Once? Gaul. I am of the Celtae and always will be, whoever claims to rule the land. Now this is the only home I will ever know.'

'Who did this to you?'

'The merchant Varro. He thought it the best way to stop me escaping.'

Lucanus felt sickened by the barbarity. It was as bad as anything that Erca and his men inflicted upon their victims.

Mato clambered in beside them, cupped the man's head and lifted a water-skin to his lips. When he was done, the druid croaked, 'My home . . .' His eyes rolled up so that Lucanus could only see the whites. 'I lived deep in the great forest, close to a wide river. Unseen, unknown, by the Romans, as all wood-priests live. But I served the folk of the woods . . . guided . . . healed. The wood-priests always serve. That is our work, given to us by the gods. Our wisdom will not be lost. It is alive . . . a serpent . . . a serpent that never ends . . . and we will pass it on to our sons.'

The Wolf thought that perhaps his wits were drifting, but then the man stared with piercing grey eyes. 'I was taken captive. A band of Roman bastards came looking for me. Twenty-five tortured . . . and dead . . . men and women . . . led them to my door. They were in the employ of others . . . who wanted all the secrets locked in my skull. I was taken to Rome and sealed in the dark with the rats. Beaten, every day, starved and beaten. But I did not give up all I knew . . . just enough to keep me alive.' His voice broke and he choked down a sob. 'And then Varro heard whispers about me, and one night he and his fool came and took me for themselves. And then he took my limbs, and this time I did speak . . . and I gave up all my secrets . . . I broke my vows . . .'

Tears brimmed in his eyes. Lucanus felt a rush of pity and he rested a hand on the wood-priest's shoulder. 'Anyone would have done the same. You are a brave man, Vercingetorix.'

'Don't worry,' Mato breathed. 'The master is dead. The fool is gone, but we will find him—'

The druid's eyes blazed. 'No, you are wrong. Varro is not the master, the fool is. And he is a blood-soaked monster who will stop at nothing to gain power.'

'I told the boy's mother I would help if I could,' Bucco said. 'And now Mithras has placed this opportunity in my hands.'

Amarina watched the dwarf splash along the stream with Marcus skipping in his wake. 'What do you have to gain?' she asked. 'Unless you sell us too.'

'I'm a poor excuse for a man, but I have a good heart. Varro beat me every day. He tormented me and made my life a misery. I did his bidding only to save myself more bruises. But now I have the chance to make amends.'

Amarina glanced back through the trees, relieved that the sounds of the barbarians pursuing them had long since vanished. The fool was cunning, she would give him that. He'd led them on a meandering path as fast as their feet would fly. They'd crawled under a net of bramble, tearing at their hair and necks, scrambled around rocks where the land had slipped away after heavy rains, and for a while rested in the high branches of an oak.

They had not escaped, she knew that. The barbarians would keep coming and coming until they had what they wanted. And they wanted Marcus.

How she regretted her plan to give the boy to the barbarians in return for the safety of her friends. She thought she was so wise, but she was more of a fool than the dwarf. Desperation had done that to her, aye, and fear too, and it had been a long time since she'd been afraid. She hated herself for that. Erca would never have bargained. He would have taken the boy and his men would have raped her and killed her. She wiped away a tear, born of self-loathing. Years and years of being strong and cautious and now she had thrown it all away in a moment of stupidity. And it could cost her and the boy everything.

'Where are you leading us?' she asked.

'There is no safety here, anywhere. Varro has his ship waiting, and a crew already well paid. We should not waste that. We must find some horses to steal, and food, and this will be over in no time.'

'No,' she replied. 'I must return the boy to his mother. *I* must make amends.'

Bucco flashed her a lopsided grin. 'You would fall into the hands of the barbarians?'

'They've halted their advance, for now. Varro said that himself. There's only this war-band. With some wit, we can slip by them and return to Lud's temple and the others.'

Bucco jumped out of the stream and began to claw his way up a steep bank topped with a ridge of hawthorn. He held out a hand to help Marcus up behind him.

'Easier said than done. Let us get away, to the coast, and then when we're safe we can think once more.'

Amarina grabbed the boy's other wrist. 'No,' she said. 'We must decide now.'

The fool held the boy for a moment as if he were about to wrench him free, and then he let him go. He slid back down the bank.

'You have a fire in you,' he said.

Amarina frowned. Something was troubling her. She thought for a moment and then she had it. 'Your words . . . the way you speak. It's changed.'

Bucco smiled. 'We all wear many faces, and a fool wears more than most.'

'Marcus, come here,' she commanded. 'My mind's made up, Fool. The boy and I will take our chance alone. You go your own way.'

Bucco clutched at his heart. 'You wound me. You would turn your back upon the hand of friendship?'

'This is for the best.'

He doffed his cap to her. 'Then this is where we part ways. One thing. A kiss upon the hand?'

He stepped forward and Amarina was surprised when he took her hand, but she could allow him this moment. The gods knew, she'd endured worse. He kissed the back of her hand, lingering for only a moment.

And then he drew himself up, and when she looked into his eyes she had a sudden vista into the abyss of his mind and the chasm of his heart. The knife was in his hand, as fast as when he'd struck down Varro.

And he was stabbing and stabbing, and in her shock she couldn't utter a cry. Her blood flew, her arms flailed and she was falling backwards.

Darkness flooded into the edges of her vision.

She slammed down on to the mud beside the stream, feeling fire flood through her veins. And she could hear Marcus screaming, and the dwarf shouting, and she could see Bucco dragging the boy up the bank to a narrow path through the hawthorn and she knew everything was lost.

# CHAPTER FORTY

# *Old Crows*

*Rome*

'WHAT'S WRONG?'

Corvus swept into the yard at the camp of the strangers. The summons from his friend had come less than an hour ago and it had sounded urgent. Under the hot midday sun by the barracks new faces greeted him, men sleeked with sweat and smeared with the dust of the road. As the boys led their exhausted horses to water, Theodosius walked among them, leaning in to conduct intense conversations.

When he saw Corvus, he came over. 'Messengers from the emperor in Reims,' he said, nodding to the new arrivals.

'Trouble along the front?'

'Some. The Alamanni are aware of our plans to attack. The tribal leaders have all sent envoys to Valentinian. They want a peace treaty. It's desperation, nothing more. They must know they won't be successful.' Theodosius shrugged. 'Except perhaps for Macrianus. He's offered to recruit a military unit for us from among his own people. A wise move.'

Corvus studied the drawn faces of the weary messengers. 'There's something more.'

His friend nodded. 'The emperor has lost touch with Britannia.'

'Lost touch? Has that whole godforsaken place sunk beneath the waves?'

'Messengers meant to arrive did not. Messengers sent did not return.'

'But what does that mean?'

'For now, none of the advisers who have the emperor's ear can reach any agreement, my father among them. Valentinian has sent a group of trusted men to learn the truth.' Theodosius glanced back at the messengers. 'But we need to make preparations to return to Gaul and wait for that news to arrive. If it's bad, we're all going to be needed.' Corvus realized his face must have fallen, for his friend clapped a hand on his shoulder. 'We've had a good stay in Rome, away from the miseries of the front, the cold and the damp. But we have our duty.'

'I know. And I'll thank your father for letting us stay here in comfort while you made arrangements for the supply routes.' Corvus paused, choosing his words. 'Besides, I think I'm ready to return to Gaul. It'll be safer for me there.'

Theodosius furrowed his brow. 'That doesn't sound like you. Something's wrong here?'

'I can't say. This is my burden.'

'Tell me,' Theodosius pressed. 'I'm worried for you, my friend.'

'I can trust you, of course I can. But you're the only one,' Corvus lied. 'It takes a lot to get me looking over my shoulder, you know that, but I'm worried too, I admit it.' He was trying to choose words which would work without giving too much away. 'It seems I've made some enemies. Hard to believe, I know.' He forced a smile which he knew would be unconvincing. 'I've found out too much, by chance mostly. About . . . plots. Secrets. And there are some who'd go to any lengths to make sure I didn't open my big mouth.'

'You think your life is in danger?' Corvus saw Theodosius' face darken. For all his many flaws, the other man was loyal.

'Rome was founded on blood, my friend,' he replied, knowing how cryptic it would sound. 'Romulus killed Remus in an argument over where the city should stand. Romulus learned the way of the wolf. Remus didn't, and paid the price.'

He walked away while Theodosius was still trying to make sense of what he had said.

The sun was setting and the Tiber was a river of blood as Corvus strode purposefully along the Via Flaminia. Pavo was waiting for him outside the house. His friend looked furtive, peering up and down the road as if he expected an attack to come at any second.

'You seem calm,' he said, almost irritated.

'I've reached an accommodation with myself.'

'Good work for a man with a mother who lavishes all her love and attention upon his brother, and a brother who would steal everything from him, including the woman who dazzles him.'

Corvus felt his chest tighten. 'We have had this conversation, old crow.'

'Just making sure your resolve is not weakening.'

'You'd never forgive me if it did.'

Pavo nodded, a flash of a grin. 'I only have your best interests at heart, old crow. You know that. We've been together for a lifetime near enough, two as one, side by side against adversity.'

Corvus thought he saw a gleam of sadness in the other man's face. 'Don't worry,' he reassured him. 'We might have enemies on every side, but we always come out ahead.'

'We do at that. No need to be scared.' Pavo shrugged. 'I'm a coward.'

'You're the strong one.'

Pavo laughed. 'Ever had the feeling that everyone is out to get you?' He glanced over his shoulder again, uneasy. 'But sometimes I see the shadows moving . . .'

'All will be well. Say it after me.'

'All will be well.'

Corvus nodded. 'Then it's time to catch our dragon.'

Ruga was pacing his room like a caged wolf. He glared when he saw Corvus at the door. So much hatred there. Could his brother really loathe him so much?

'Where is Hecate?'

'Somewhere you won't find her.'

Ruga came at him with fists bunched. Corvus stood his ground, pressing his arms to his sides, his hands open, showing he was no threat, but still he wasn't sure his brother wouldn't knock him to the floor.

'You will not ruin things,' Ruga hissed, 'as you always ruin them. Not this time.'

310

'I know you think there's much at stake, so much that you'd go to lengths that I can't begin to imagine—'

'There is.' Spittle flying from his mouth, his brother jabbed a finger at him.

'. . . but I won't see you harm her, or trick her, or break her heart. She deserves so much more than what you're threatening to do to her.'

Ruga snorted. 'Fetch her. And I'll forget this.'

'I know you were planning to marry her tomorrow. That's quite a way to go to get between her legs.'

'You don't know what you're talking about.'

'I know about the Dragon.'

Ruga stared.

'That he is supposed to be some kind of saviour. Mithras incarnated in a man. You, brother. That's the plot you and Mother have been burnishing for so long. This Dragon will lead all the poor and broken people of this world out of the darkness. But one thing I know above all else is that his protection shouldn't be left in your hands.'

'Who else, then?' Ruga sneered. 'You?'

'I have my faults, that's true. I like my wine. I find too much humour when everyone else has faces like the grave.' Corvus walked to the window and looked out at the thin line reddening the horizon. He heard his brother moving behind him, but he didn't look round. He hoped showing his back would put Ruga at ease. 'I have my values too, though I'm not one to shout about them. Too modest, Pavo says.'

Ruga snorted again, louder this time.

As the last of the light faded, Corvus took a flint and lit the oil-lamp. The dark rushed to the corners of the room. 'We've always been different, you and I. I don't say this to hurt you, but you think you care about Mother more than I do – you don't – and you care about yourself more than anyone.'

'And who do you care for? This witch who seems to have entranced you? And Pavo, your old, old friend?' Ruga laughed.

Corvus turned. 'At the risk of ruining my hard-fought-for reputation, I'd say I care above all about doing some good in this world. Does that sound . . .' he waved a hand, trying to summon the right word, 'childish? Weak?'

'You are not a complicated man, that is certain.'

'Why do you dislike me so much, brother?'

'You know why,' Ruga snapped.

'I wish I did. It's always been a mystery to me. And a hurtful one, I have to say. I've only ever thought well of you.'

'I don't just dislike you. I hate you. There, I've said it. I promised myself I'd hold my tongue, for Mother's sake. Despite everything, she's always looked on you fondly. But now it's done.' Simmering, Ruga advanced on him. 'There are so many reasons, too many to list, but one above all others. Do you not know what it is? Does it lie so light on your conscience that you never think about it? Can that be true?'

'Tell me, then.'

Shaking his head with disbelief, Ruga came to a halt a hand's width from Corvus' face. So much rage burned in those features. 'You killed our father. You pushed him overboard in the storm. That's why I hate you, Corvus. Even as a boy you were capable of murdering a good man.'

'No.'

'You can't remember your treachery? Or are you lying? Or lying to yourself? I saw.'

'He fell.'

Ruga hesitated.

'It was dark, the ship was heaving, and we all thought we were going down that night. Whatever you think you saw, he fell.'

'You are my brother and for that I always wanted to love you. But someone who could kill his own father is capable of anything. I've never been certain I can trust you, Corvus.'

'You are right there.'

Ruga flinched at this admission. He seemed unsure whether Corvus was joking.

'I'm going to save the Dragon, brother. Where you would do everything wrong, I'll do everything right.'

As quick as a serpent, he snatched out his sword and hacked off Ruga's right hand.

The shock only lasted a moment. Then his brother was flailing backwards, screaming. Blood sprayed everywhere. Corvus had seen much of it on the battlefield, but here there seemed a torrent. He watched as his brother crashed back on the floor. He trembled there, staring at the ceiling, looking through it, perhaps, to the heavens, and with each convulsion more blood spurted. A dark pool formed around him and his skin was like snow against it.

Corvus hurried to the window and leaned out. 'Come,' he yelled. 'Come now.'

He heard the sound of feet pounding up the stairs and a moment later six men burst in. He didn't recognize any of them. They took in the scene in an instant, showed not a jot of judgement, and without a word, or even an acknowledgement of his presence, they grabbed Ruga's tunic and dragged his twitching form across the floor and out of the chamber. A dark stain swept across the pale marble and out into the shadows.

Corvus was shaking. Taking deep breaths, he closed his eyes, but all he could see was Ruga staring into the dark. His brother would not survive that amount of blood loss, he knew. But he'd already accepted that the Christians would not make any attempt to save his life. His brother's body would be found beside one of the roads outside the city walls in the morning.

More footsteps echoed, a single pair this time. He watched as Theodosius walked into the wavering lamplight.

'He attacked me.' How hollow his words sounded, he thought.

'I warned you. These followers of Mithras cannot be trusted. They are the devil's own dogs.'

'My own brother . . .'

Theodosius gripped his shoulder. Corvus looked into his face and saw compassion, perhaps even pity. 'It's sad to lose a man like Ruga, but he had set his face against God. Be certain that you have done a good thing here. I know it will be hard for you. In the days to come. When your mother looks at you. That burden would crush lesser men. But you're strong, Corvus, you always have been. And I'll be there to help you through this time. Just know that you have served God well.'

Corvus swilled back the last of his wine. The tavern was foul and stank of vinegar and sweat, but that was how he liked it. He could lose himself in this place, where the shadows swaddled thieves and cut-throats and the scum that washed around the lower levels of

Rome. No questions were ever asked of him, no reflection was needed.

'No regrets?'

Except by Pavo. His friend sat opposite him, little more than a silhouette against the sole lamp that lit that place. Corvus couldn't read his features, but he hoped that if he could he'd see some reassurance there.

'I'd be lying if I said I had none.'

'It was the right thing to do. In the final reckoning, it was always going to be him or you.'

'I know.' He considered calling for more wine, but he knew he was only putting off the inevitable consequences of his actions.

'You're free now,' Pavo continued, his voice low and calming. 'For all your life you've been the second son. Your achievements unrecognized, your abilities ignored. All the love and care that should have flowed your way, denied you. I know you'd never see it that way, or if you did that you'd never resent it, or be consumed with bitterness. But as your friend, I can tell you that you deserved better. Ruga worked against you all your life. He whispered in your mother's ear, turning her from you. And now, with this business with the Dragon, he would have found some way to spin it to his advantage. And what then? Think of the harm that would have been inflicted on good men and women.'

Corvus stared into the bottom of his goblet. He didn't feel anything at all, and that puzzled him. It would come later, he was sure, when the shock had passed, but now he was empty. And he could no longer see the way forward.

'Everything's changed,' he muttered.

'Yes. For the better. Are you listening to me?'

Corvus set the goblet aside and steeled himself.

'The Christians have their story of a saviour. Theodosius has told you all about that,' Pavo continued.

'Many times, and at great length.'

'Jesus, the Christ, was sent by God his father to redeem the sins of all men. And now the faithful wait for his return, to fulfil his promises and all the prophecies made about him.'

He remembered Theodosius' long lectures during those cold nights on the Gaulish frontier. 'The Nicene Creed, agreed by all the wise men some forty years ago. "He will come again in glory to judge the living and the dead, and his kingdom will have no end."'

'At least you were listening.' Pavo leaned forward, and now gold glinted in his eyes from the lamplight. 'My point is, this world is hard enough, my friend, and all men need a saviour. In the temple of Mithras you hear words like the ones you quoted. Wherever people pray to gods, they talk of a saviour who will return one day to lead them out of the dark.'

'What are you saying?'

'I've already said it. All men need a saviour. Even you.'

'So . . . you're my saviour?'

'I would never lay claim to such a thing.' Though Pavo had slumped back into the shadows, Corvus could tell his friend was grinning. 'But if you ever take the time to reflect on my words, you'll understand that I'm talking about the *need* and not the saviour himself. Your brother would have denied the people this Dragon, would have denied them this thing that they desperately want. But you'll give it to them. You'll do a great good, and you'll be recognized for it, and all the rewards that have been denied you will finally come your way.'

'But I'm not doing this for myself,' Corvus replied. He felt unsettled, though he wasn't sure why.

'Of course not. You're the saviour of the saviour,' Pavo said, his tone wry. 'Now, are you ready?'

The juddering sobs echoed through the dark house. Corvus leaned on the threshold, listening to the reverberations rustling through that empty space, one that would always be a little emptier now.

Gaia hunched on a stool in the corner of Ruga's chamber. The lamp had been blown out, but the moonlight broke through the window, as bright as day. Gaia stared at the black smear on the floor where it carved through that silvery beam.

When he entered, she looked up at him with red-rimmed eyes. In that chiaroscuro world, her skin looked like a frosted field. 'It is over,' she croaked.

He found that odd. Not *he's gone*, or *my most beloved son has been snatched away from me.*

It is over.

'It's not over,' he said.

She looked away from him, that same dismissive turn of the head that he'd known since childhood, the one which said *you are a child, too naive, you don't know aught of these grown-up matters.*

'Don't worry about Hecate. She's staying in a tavern near here. I'll bring her back in the morning.'

Now she was staring at him again, and he could see all the calculations in her face. 'What happened, my love?' Barely a whisper. Then: 'What have you done?'

'Ruga is dead,' he replied, as if that were explanation enough.

'You killed your brother?' A choke.

'I cut off his hand. That was all . . .' The words tailed away. He walked into the room and lingered beside her, resting one hand on her shoulder. He was pleased to see that she didn't flinch. 'He would have ruined everything. All your plans. Your hopes.'

'Why did you do it?'

He wanted her to smile, to understand what a sacrifice he had made, and ultimately to forgive him. 'For you, Mother. I did it for you. If the Dragon was to live, Ruga had to die. There was no other choice. This wasn't a whim. I thought long and hard and realized what needed to be done. We talked it over, night after night—'

He felt her flinch. 'Talked it over? With whom?'

'Pavo. He agreed that it was the right thing to do. That I couldn't be blamed.'

'Oh, Corvus. Oh, my love.' She was clawing at his arm like an animal, her nails digging into his flesh, dragging him down. He fell to his knees, and she clutched at his face with those trembling hands, holding him there so she could look deep into his eyes. 'There is no Pavo. You know that. How many times have we talked about this?'

Corvus broke her stare and looked past her to the door. His friend stood there, leaning on the jamb. His arms were folded and he was grinning, somehow cocky and knowing and sad all at the same time.

'I remember you running through the fields with Pavo, all those long years ago, in Britannia, before we fled for the ship. You were as close as brothers, closer than you ever were with Ruga. But he died, from the sickness that took so many in those days. You remember? How often have we talked of this?'

He rested his head in her lap and let her stroke his hair, as she had done so many times. 'He's my friend,' he whispered.

'Oh, my love.' Her voice quavered on the edge of a keening cry. 'Now what is to become of us?'

## CHAPTER FORTY-ONE

# Lord of the Greenwood

AMARINA LAY ON HER BACK, STARING UP THROUGH THE EMERALD world to the patch of blue sky framed by the branches. Her back was wet from the mud along the stream's banks, her front sodden from blood leaking from the fool's stab wounds.

*I am dying.*

She closed her eyes. Her life had been so much of a struggle. How easy it would be to give up.

*No.*

She had never given up. Not when she was abandoned as a child, when she was beaten and left for dead, half drowned, burned, eating a dead bird in the forest to survive until she could see the dawn.

Amarina pushed herself up on her elbows. More blood trickled out. She dabbed her fingers against her dress and brought them up before her face, red and sticky.

Three wounds.

Three faces of the goddess.

Three, three, three.

But five was the magic number, always.

She shook her head, trying to clear her confused thoughts. Her heart was beating, she was still breathing. But soon her blood would have drained away and there was no one nearby who could save her.

Rolling on to her belly, she lifted herself up on to her hands and knees and began to crawl up the grassy bank. Halfway up, she watched the world turn to grey as her wits drained away and she began to fall back.

She swam up from the dark in the same place. As she turned her head, she felt disturbed when she saw that the puddles along the edge of the stream were now streaked with red.

*So weak.*

Once again she rolled over, and began her ascent. This time she almost made it to the top.

Her limbs were growing weaker by the moment, and when she levered herself up on her elbows she found herself shaking as if she had an ague.

She heaved one last time, but she could already feel darkness closing in around her vision. She crashed back, her thoughts fizzing away into the void. At the last instant before unconsciousness claimed her, she felt convinced she heard a voice – or perhaps it was a dream.

But it was saying, 'Lie still, sister. You are not alone.'

Amarina's eyes flickered open. The woodland canopy was drifting by above her, light flickering through the leaves. Birdsong swelled. She felt as if she were wrapped in a warm blanket, on the edge of a long, deep sleep in coldest winter.

Strong arms flexed across her back and under her knees. She looked up towards the face of whoever was carrying her, but the sun's rays blinded her and she slipped away again.

'You will live. The blade hit no vitals.'

The mist drifted from her eyes, and Amarina found she was lying in a clearing with shafts of sunlight punching through the trees on every side. She felt as weak as if she had not eaten in a week. Strange, bitter scents assailed her nose and she realized her dress had been torn and a brown paste applied to her wounds.

She squinted into the light. A man was standing about a spear's length from her feet. He shifted to one side to allow her to see him clearly.

He was tall, as tall as Bellicus. On his head was a helmet of a kind she had never seen before, but it looked very old indeed. It came down to the jawline, with only a narrow strip running from chin to nose and two eyeholes pooled with shadow, the metal a faint green, perhaps from verdigris, or from some stain so that he would blend into the forest setting.

His tunic, cloak and leggings were green too, filthy with the detritus of life in the forest, and he carried a round emerald shield made of painted wood on his left arm. A long sword hung in a leather scabbard from his waist.

'Who are you?' she croaked.

'The Lord of the Greenwood.' His voice was deep and rumbling.

'Your name?'

'That is the name I was given. It is a name as old as the ages. When I am gone, it will pass to another.'

Amarina tried to raise herself up, but she didn't have the strength.

'Rest,' he said. 'You have lost much blood.'

'You tended to my wounds?'

'No. Hecate did. She is wise in those ways.'

Amarina craned her neck and saw they were not alone. A woman crouched not far from her head, hunched like a crow. Her hair was a wild black mane, tangled with leaves and ivy. She was naked, her body and face smeared with mud. Her eyes were wide and white and staring.

'You have my thanks,' Amarina said.

The woman only stared.

Behind her, Amarina could now make out others waiting among the trees. Men, mostly. Some were crouching, some standing. Their clothes were earth-brown or leaf-green and they were all as filthy as the wise woman, hair and beards unkempt. She could see that some carried staffs, others bows.

'There are two worlds, sister, and always have been,' the Lord of the Greenwood said as if he could read her thoughts. 'The folk of the towns and the folk of the forest. Townsfolk think they know everything. Forest folk know all the secrets.'

'I have never seen them before.'

'They see you, sister. All of you.'

Amarina closed her eyes for a moment, trying to gather her thoughts. 'You were the one Myrrdin wished to meet at Lud's temple.'

'That is my temple. The Green Temple.'

'Then the wood-priest sent you to help.'

The Lord strode forward so he could more easily look down on her. 'He asked for aid. But I have been following you since the north. Watching over you all. As have many others.' He held out a hand towards the forest folk. 'The wood-priests, all of the hidden people, they have been waiting for the season to turn for too long. Now all must change, or be lost for ever. The Romans are fleeing. We will take back this land that was once ours.'

Amarina looked into the piercing eyes above her. Something about them seemed familiar, though she couldn't place what it was.

He leaned down and asked, 'Who are you?'

'Amarina.'

He sniffed the air above her. 'You smell like Hecate.'

She glared, even through the pain. 'Am. A. Rin. A.'

The Lord of the Greenwood shrugged.

Her head cleared, if only for a moment, and she remembered. 'The boy . . . Marcus . . .'

'The dwarf has taken him.'

'You know where he has gone?'

'I have seen the trail. He is being watched.'

'We must save him.' She felt her guilt rise again.

'We must. But your part in this is done. For now, at least.'

Amarina felt weak and pathetic, but she had no strength to do anything but hang in the arms of the Lord of the Greenwood.

Lucanus, Mato and Catia stood like sentinels on a track in the sun, weapons drawn. At that moment she didn't care how they would judge her. She deserved all their harsh words, and more, and she wouldn't shrink from any of them.

'Marcus is alive,' she croaked before anyone could speak. 'And I throw myself on your mercy. I was a fool to take him. I thought it would be for the best . . . for all of you. I was wrong.'

Catia's face was like stone. 'If he is not returned to me, you will pay.'

Amarina nodded.

She saw Lucanus frown. 'I saw you,' he said to the man who was carrying her. 'In the north, when I was close to death. I thought you were a dream.'

'Many think that,' the Lord growled.

'Did you bring the three women to save me?'

The green warrior said nothing. Amarina watched them hold each other's gaze for a moment. Lucanus' frown deepened, but before any more words could pass between them the Lord of the Greenwood laid her down in the long grass.

'She has lost much blood. She needs rest,' he said.

Mato ran forward and knelt beside her. 'Did he harm you?'

'No. He saved me. He's an ally.'

When they all looked up, the green warrior had gone.

'If you follow the trail in the woods, he and his friends will guide you to Marcus and the dwarf,' she continued. 'You must trust me on that.' Catia would not meet her eyes. 'The fool has him. He is not what we thought.'

'Bellicus has gone to fetch the others,' Lucanus said as he stood over her. 'Comitinus and Solinus wait with another victim of this war who's not long for this world. Mato, take her back to the wagons and wait there. His mother and I will go after Marcus.'

Amarina saw Mato look from his leader to Catia, unsure. 'Just the two of you?'

'You think between us we can't handle a dwarf?' Lucanus grinned, but Amarina saw no humour there.

'Go,' she urged. 'Let your feet fly and show that fool no mercy. I will pray to the goddess for you.'

## CHAPTER FORTY-TWO

# *In the Marshlands*

THE PIERCING WHISTLE RANG OUT. LUCANUS SEARCHED THE TREES for a long moment before he saw the figure stepping out from the shade of a holly bush. Seemingly more beast than man, his face was as filthy as his mane of brown hair and beard, and his clothes were rags. Though he'd been standing in plain sight, the Wolf hadn't noticed him.

The forest man waved a hand towards the south-east. Lucanus loped in that direction and Catia ran at his side. When he glanced back, the man was already lost to view.

'I wish these days had never come,' Catia said, her voice laced with bitterness. 'I thought times might be better, but now I've exchanged one life of misery for another.'

'We'll bring Marcus home. I vowed that when I set off into the north, and I vow it now.'

'What then? Endless days of running and hiding and fighting off enemies who see my son as the key to open their door to power?'

'Everything changes, by the day, by the hour. It may not always be this way. If Myrrdin's messengers can bring together an army, we can fight. If he can find us a sanctuary, we can build a new life.'

*Together*, he wanted to add, but he knew that was a faint hope. Catia was an honourable woman. She loved him, but she would never leave Amatius. But he would fight any battle to help her, and Marcus, for the rest of his days, as he'd always fought for her. He couldn't do other.

'It seems to me,' she said, 'that good people cannot prosper in this world. Only those whose hearts are as hard as ice thrive.'

'I don't believe that to be true.'

'Nevertheless, that's my view. And if I have to become one of them to see the people I love survive, so be it.'

Lucanus winced at her words.

Through the forest they ran, following the whistles of the forest folk. Soon Lucanus could see the trail himself: pairs of footprints in the soft ground, each as small as the other. Not long after that the high ground was at their backs and the forest gave way to gentle slopes leading to a green countryside of lush grassland and dark copses dotted with hamlets.

They slumped down beside a brook to cup handfuls of cool water to slake their thirst. As he rested, he watched Catia wash her face, perhaps trying to hide the tears of anger and frustration that had continually brimmed.

When she'd dried her cheeks on her cloak, she turned to him and forced a smile. 'I haven't thanked you enough for all that you've done for me. Since I was a girl, you've been a true friend and companion. Whatever is to come, know that I have much love in my heart for you.'

Her words should have given him some warmth, perhaps even hope, but at that moment he thought they sounded more like an epitaph.

Black clouds gathered on the western horizon. Lightning flickered and the air itself seemed to crackle around them.

Lucanus crouched and examined the ground. The trail had led to a vast area of marshland that reeked of rot. He looked out across stagnant pools reflecting the darkening sky, dotted by clumps of sedge. Flies droned above them. Islands of sickly trees floated everywhere, dense enough to hide anyone who did not wish to be seen.

'The fool is clever. If he's light on his feet, he'll be able to move through here quickly. He must know we'll be on his heels. This bog will slow us.'

'And if he's not light on his feet, he'll drag my son down to his death.' Catia pulled an arrow from her quiver and held it loosely against her bow.

'Any path through here will be treacherous,' Lucanus cautioned.

Much as he did not want to see her in danger, he knew better than to suggest she stay behind.

'Then I put my life in your hands. You must guide me. And if I get clear sight of the dwarf, I'll put this shaft through his heart.'

Lucanus sniffed the air. The fool had been clever indeed; he wouldn't be able to smell any sweat on the breeze. Steeling himself, he began to move out, testing for solid ground, leaping from one mound of sedge to the next, trusting Catia to follow him.

Bubbles surfaced on the still waters and popped. A toad leapt from his feet into a pool with a splash, and jewelled dragonflies whisked by his head. They were close now, he knew. His old senses, muffled since he'd left the Wilds behind, had returned.

'If I were the fool I would move through those copses,' he said, pointing. 'They'll keep him hidden from anyone watching from where the trail met the marsh.'

As if in answer to his words, a murder of crows took flight from the branches, shrieking as they soared up to the lowering clouds. Lucanus stiffened, instinctively dropping low.

'I don't care about any prophecy,' Catia muttered. 'I don't care about games of power and gods old or new.' She paused and then added, 'Swear to me that you will watch over Marcus if I die.'

'You won't die.'

'Swear it.' There was a crack in her voice.

'I swear.'

'I can't leave that to Amatius. He would put his own interest before that of his son.'

'Wolf-sister, you will be around to be a good wolf-mother long after I'm in the earth.'

Lucanus tugged down the snout of his wolf pelt and searched the nearest trees until he thought he caught a glimpse of movement. Instantly he was bounding across the clumps of sedge, hearing Catia's ragged breathing at his back.

The island neared.

He felt his foot skid on the vegetation and flailed to keep his balance. He'd heard too many stories of places like this, haunted sites that claimed lives to feed the daemons who lurked here, sucking them down into another world just beneath the surface.

He wanted to mutter a prayer, but he could no longer tell if he should be calling to Cernunnos or Lugh or Mithras or one of the Roman gods.

With a leap, he landed on the edge of the island and fell into a crouch. He could hear the crunch of feet on dry rushes. A muffled voice, insistent, harsh.

Catia landed behind him and he reached out a hand to steady her before she slipped back into the bog. He pressed a finger to his lips.

The fool was stumbling along the water's edge on the other side of the narrow strip of dry land. Lucanus eyed a path among the trees and threw himself along it, clawing his way among elder and willow, trying to be as silent as he could.

When he crashed out on the opposite side he saw the fool edging past an overhanging blackthorn, dragging Marcus behind him.

Lucanus drew his sword and crept forward in the shadow of the trees. He'd hoped to get close enough to grab the dwarf, but Bucco chose that moment to look up from his precarious footing.

The Wolf saw the murderous flash in those eyes. In an instant, the fool's left arm had curled around Marcus' neck and his knife had jumped into his other hand. The blade swept up to the terrified boy's throat.

'Stay back or I will bleed him,' Bucco snarled.

Lucanus looked into Marcus' imploring eyes and he felt a cold anger rise in him. 'Harm the boy and I will gut you and throw you into the bog.'

Rage flared in the fool's face. 'Stay away, I say. I will not lose him now, not when I'm so close.'

The Wolf stopped. He could see the dwarf was not going to back down. The knife in his hand trembled with his anger.

'Give up,' Lucanus said harshly. 'There's nowhere for you to go now.'

An arrow thumped into the trunk of a silver birch not far from the dwarf. Behind the Wolf, Catia was already nocking another shaft.

Shocked, Bucco recoiled, and Marcus seized the moment to wriggle free. Half dropping to his knees, he scrambled through the long grass and nettles to throw his arms around Lucanus' waist.

The fool's arms windmilled as he was thrown off balance by Marcus' sudden lunge. He shrieked, a keening sound that sent more crows crashing up from the branches, and wheeled backwards into the sucking bog. His flailing only made it worse and within an instant he had sunk to his chest.

'Help me,' he screamed. 'I beg you.'

Lucanus watched the fool's struggles for a moment, heard his shrieks become even shriller. A part of him thought Bucco deserved his fate for all the misery he had inflicted on Catia and Marcus and Amarina. But in the end he couldn't stand by and watch the fool die.

Easing Marcus aside, he sheathed his sword and strode along the edge of the bog.

'Lucanus!'

He whirled at Catia's scream.

'Take Marcus! Take him and run!'

Figures were emerging from the trees behind her. He glimpsed the crusted white skin of the Attacotti in the shadows, and at the front were Motius and the rest of the Carrion Crows. They had been stalking Marcus too. Of course they had. He'd been a fool to think they would ever turn their backs upon such a prize.

Snatching Marcus up, he ran, Bucco's screams ringing out at his back. The boy was heavy, slowing him down, and he knew how fleet of foot the Crows were.

He crashed through the undergrowth on the edge of the narrow island and leapt to the nearest mound of sedge. He threw himself on to the second one, just, his heart pounding as his skid almost carried him into the bog.

Behind him he could hear the whoops and shrieks of the hunters bearing down on them.

'Be still,' he whispered in the boy's ear. 'We will be away from this soon.'

At the third mound, his foot slipped into the brown stew. He looked back and saw Catia bounding behind him.

For a moment their eyes locked, a silent communication bonding them for all time.

'Save him,' she shouted.

Spinning round, Lucanus dredged up the last of his reserves and hurled himself from clump to clump, ignoring the rising war-cries at his back, all his thoughts drawn down upon the boy in his arms and the need to reach dry land.

Only when he crashed down on to the grassy edge of the marsh did he look back and see why Motius and his band hadn't caught him.

Catia was resting on one knee, loosing arrows that kept their pursuers at bay. One of the Attacotti was slowly sinking into the bog, a shaft protruding from his eye socket.

'Come now,' the Wolf bellowed. 'We're safe.'

Catia ignored him.

He understood then what he'd seen in her eyes. She had no intention of joining them; even when they were away from the treacherous bog, they would never be able to outrun the Crows.

'Catia,' he yelled again. 'Don't do this.'

'What's wrong?' Marcus said, trying to see round him.

'Nothing,' Lucanus replied. 'Run and hide in the long grass. I'll follow.'

He dropped Marcus and the boy scrambled away, throwing himself down as if he were diving into a green sea.

If he could reach Catia, he could at least hope to hold back the enemy with his sword. A thin hope, but it was all he had.

Yet even as he prepared to hurl himself on to the first clump of sedge, he saw Catia loose her last arrow. Beyond her, a grin leapt to Motius' face.

The Attacotti began leaping across the clumps of sedge, approaching from two flanks. Between them, the Crows advanced in a direct line towards Catia.

Lucanus willed her to turn and run, his chest tightening until he thought it would burst when he realized she was not going to make any such attempt. She stood, lifting her chin, proud to the last.

A desperate panic swelled within him. This was her sacrifice, for Marcus.

For him.

He reached for his sword, and then let his hand fall. Even if he dared to venture into the marsh again, it would be a futile gesture. Nothing he could do would save either of them.

With his nails biting into his palms, he watched Catia, defiant, almost beatific, arms outstretched as she looked up to the roiling clouds. The wind tore at her hair. Fat drops of rain lashed her.

And she waited.

The Attacotti and the Crows fell upon her.

Lucanus finally whirled away, unable to bear any more. Devastated, not even able to speak, he darted into the long grass and caught up with Marcus. Together they ran back the way he and Catia had come.

The flames roared in the howling wind and sparks spiralled in a wild dance towards the black clouds hanging overhead. Catia looked up at the men standing around the campfire. She felt only contempt for these warriors, a pack of beasts who would hunt down a boy. There were upwards of forty of them, the ranks reaching out into the gloom beyond the wavering circle of light, all of them wild-haired and bearded, swathed in leather and fur and stinking of sweat and piss. Hard men, forged in battle, with stares that hung on too long. She peered past them, trying to see the Attacotti. Those apparitions unnerved her. They were like the daemons that Lucanus spoke of, preferring the gloom, with ways that she could not begin to understand. But they had melted away the moment they had dragged her into the camp.

'I'm not afraid to die,' she said in a wintry voice.

'That is good.' Erca stepped in front of her.

Though she was sprawled at his feet she pushed up her chin so he wouldn't think her submissive.

'I saw you loose your arrows,' he continued. 'You're good with a bow. Better than most men.'

'I'm better than most men at all things.'

Laughter rumbled around the gathering, but Erca was untouched by it. Yes, his eyes brightened, but not from mockery. Catia knew that look – he was intrigued by her. She felt sickened by his attention.

'You would do well to kill me now. I'm no use to you. My band is on the move – I don't know where they are travelling.'

'The boy?'

'Lucanus will keep him safe.'

'Ah. The Wolf.' Erca pursed his lips. Thunder rumbled and he looked up at the darkening sky. 'They are calling him the Pendragon now. That's an ancient title, one that demands respect. The war leader. It has to be earned, but I've not seen much that shows he deserves it.'

'You will.'

'He is your man?'

Catia hesitated, surprised by the question, and surprised too that an answer did not come easily. 'No. I'm married to another.'

'He must be a fine man indeed to carry off a prize such as you.'

'I am no prize to be won. I make my own choices.'

More laughter.

'Be that as it may. But you did not choose to be here. I brought you to this camp. My will. My power.'

'And I say again, you have wasted it on someone who has no value.'

'Do you take me for a fool? The mother of the royal blood has no value?' He prowled around her. Catia stared into the orange heart of the fire, not deigning to give him her attention.

'You believe those old stories? Then you are a fool,' she said.

'I believe the wood-priests. The Romans may have driven them deep into the forests, but they still have knowledge and power. They hear the gods. I was first told this story of a king who will not die when I was a boy. From a man who had begged the druids to save the life of his dying child. They refused, for reasons no one knew, and when he returned to our village he looked as old as his father. White hair, eyes that had seen too much. He had learned other things, some that haunted him, which he would never speak of. But this tale of the king, he recounted it all, as it had been told to him.'

He came to a halt behind her. She didn't look round, but she could feel his presence like the heat from a smith's forge. His voice, low and resonant, hung over her head.

'One day the Romans will be gone.' Catia listened as his words took on the dreamy cadence of something remembered. 'And when their last ship has sailed and the last golden eagle has fallen, there will be a time of war and blood and madness as all in this island try to lay claim to the mantle of power. But only one will lead the people out of the darkness. Only one. A king. The Bear-King. And those who stand beside him will be showered with riches beyond imagining and their lives will reach far beyond the span of men. And those who stand against him will be drowned in a sea of their own blood.'

For a moment, only the crackle of the fire filled the silence.

'This story is an old one, and I have learned that old stories have truth in them.' His voice had hardened once more. 'Lies do not survive the test of years. The Bear-King is coming. And where would you stand? At his back? Or at the end of his sword?'

Catia let the words wash over her. She could see how this story meant something to men like Erca. But not to her. No, she was not afraid. She had resigned herself to her own death long ago. All that mattered was that Marcus lived. And Lucanus.

'You will not get your hands on my son.'

'They will come for him in waves, you know that. From all the four corners of the land. We are the only ones who can keep him safe.'

Erca paced around her and squatted so he could look her in the eyes. She saw a sharp intelligence there. No brute this, for all his appearance.

'We have long been planning this attack,' he continued. 'We have talked until our jaws ached and our throats were like dust. But in the end we reached agreement. All the tribes. Aye, even the Attacotti, who have never agreed with any and keep themselves to themselves in their dark land. Our plot was born in the heat of anger and the cold lust for vengeance. All we wanted was to crush those who had tormented us for so long.' He shrugged. 'Though a little gold would never have gone amiss. But then we saw how easily the Roman army fell apart, and we knew that so much more was ours for the taking. All this land, from sea to sea, under the rule of the tribes. And then, and then . . .' he moistened his lips as he warmed to his story, 'we heard tell of your son, and his great destiny, and the kings of all the tribes knew that here was our chance to hold on to all we had won, for all time. The Bear-King will be our king, answering to our call. He will be raised and guided by our teachers, and it will be our tongues whispering in his ear, telling him what to do. Who then will hold the power, eh?'

Erca reached out to take her jaw in his hand. She wrenched her head away, spitting at him like a wildcat. 'Do you value your women?' she spat.

'We value *our* women.'

'Are you a good man, who can hold his head up to the gods?'

Erca frowned at this unexpected question.

'Your men have raped women, and killed them,' she continued. 'I know this to be true. I saw what happened in Vercovicium with my own eyes. But are you so much of a beast that you would see harm come to a woman with child?'

'You?'

She pushed her hands behind her and leaned back, thrusting out her belly. For a moment he hesitated, then he cupped his hand against the curve, slowly, half expecting her to recoil, she could tell. Her belly was still small but it was possible to tell she was speaking the truth. Her blood had not come after she had lain with Lucanus on the slope by the lake. It was his child, there was no doubt of that. She hadn't yet told him, had not known *how* to tell him. She feared what Amatius would do if he found out, and what Lucanus would do too.

What fools they all were. Lost to their own loves and jealousies while the world was catching fire around them. The mother of the royal blood? She didn't deserve that accolade. She was as weak as any of them.

She looked deep into Erca's unwavering stare as he rested his hand upon her, and then he nodded. Turning, he barked an order to his men in his guttural tongue.

'No man here will try to take you, not while I am leader,' he said.

She nodded without showing any thanks. It was a small victory, but she knew there were still many bad things ahead.

'You are not done with Britannia?' she asked.

'Why would we be, when the victory has come so easily? To the north, our army rests. The men eat and drink and let the greatness of what they have achieved settle on them. And when they are done, they will know that only greater things lie ahead.'

'Then you will march on . . . before the snows come?'

'By the blood-month, all that you have known will be ours. From here to the southern sea, all will fall before us. The villages will be burned. Those who resist will be slaughtered. The rest will become slaves. The Romans will be driven from these shores, like the cowards we always knew they were. And then . . . who knows? Gaul? Rome itself?' He paused, a faraway look in his eyes. When he glanced back at her, he said, 'There is no hope for your kind now, you must know that? The Romans are deserting you. You have no other army.' He gave a throaty laugh. 'No army for your Head of the Dragon to lead. There is only blood and death ahead now. Make your peace with it.'

Listening to him, Catia could not disagree. Only misery and suffering lay before them. The barbarians had won. But there was hope, a thin one. That Marcus and Lucanus could escape.

Erca stood up, put his fingers in his mouth and whistled, three sharp bursts. Catia could hear movement at the back of the circle of warriors.

The barbarians parted as pale shapes pushed through them. Catia watched the Attacotti approach, trying to show defiance over the chill she was feeling. There were only five of them – the rest must have remained with the horde. Even so, they carried with them an otherworldly air that was as unsettling as their appearance.

'I do not know the minds of the Attacotti,' Erca said. 'They are not like us. They speak to strange gods. They bury their dead in spaces beneath the floors of their homes, stripped of flesh by their own knives, and bring them out for feasts. And they eat the meat of men because they believe it brings them closer to their gods, and they gain the powers of great enemies who have fallen. It is a mark of respect, they say.'

She heard the note of disgust in his voice.

'What they want, I cannot be certain. They have no interest in gold. We found only one man who could speak their tongue and he is not here. But they are the fiercest fighters I know. They seem to care not if they live or die. Their next world is as close and real as this one and they move from one to the next with barely a blink. Aye, and back, so they believe.'

The Attacotti came to a halt by the fire. Catia looked up into eyes as black as a moonless night. They stared at her, unblinking, unknowable.

'We needed their battle-fury. There are times I wish we did not,' Erca continued. 'One day, the Romans . . . if they survive . . . will bring these ghosts into their army, as they have done with all the conquered. For now, I would rather have them at my side.'

Catia felt her breath tighten in her chest as she looked into those faces. 'You said I would not be harmed.'

'No man will rape you. I have given my word.' Erca walked back into the ranks of his men. 'But there is still much that can and must be done.'

'Must?' she repeated, her voice strangled.

'First the Attacotti will have to taste you.'

Lucanus felt the first fat drops of rain splatter on his face. The storm would be a bad one. It had been building for days. Behind him, the others sheltered in Varro's wagons. Bellicus had returned with the rest of Catia's family and the wood-priest. But while he and Catia had been searching for Marcus, the merchant's long-suffering captive, the druid Vercingetorix, had finally given in to his wounds, almost as if he had been set free by Varro's monstrous death. Solinus and Comitinus had buried him in the woods. The two men now kept watch over Marcus a short way away, in case anyone had followed Lucanus and the boy back here. They would think, he hoped, that the boy had been spirited away to some sanctuary and their group would be left alone. A small hope, but if it bought them some time to breathe and think it would be worth it.

The rain came down harder.

The Wolf tilted his head back, letting it drench him, pleased by the coolness after the stifling warmth of the day. If only he could wash away his grief at the loss of Catia so easily. He could feel it cutting deep into his heart, as sharp as the obsidian knives that the priests of Mithras carried, and at that moment he was sure he would never again find peace.

A low roar of thunder rolled out across the trees.

When it ebbed, Lucanus realized he was not alone. Through the beat of the raindrops, he thought he heard movement in the forest ahead of him, dim, but senses honed in the Wilds were strong in him again. He drew Caledfwlch.

In a flash of lightning, the blade seemed to glow with an inner fire. In the past, he would have found wonder in that. Now there was no wonder anywhere.

As he half turned to call his brothers, a voice rang out. 'Peace. We are here to talk, not fight.'

Squinting against the worsening downpour, he made out five men emerging from the trees, barbarians all. Four of them were as big as bears, but they kept their blades sheathed. The fifth, smaller, he saw, was Logen of the Fire's Heart, a sly look on his ratty face.

Lucanus searched the dark woods on either side, but he sensed no further movement.

'There is no need to call your men.' Logen held out two empty hands.

'There is no need for talk,' the Wolf said.

'There is. If you would see the woman alive again.'

Lucanus stiffened.

'Aye, Wolf, she yet lives. There is no gain for us in killing her. Not yet, at least.'

He knew what would come next.

'We want the boy, that's all. Give us the boy and we will return the woman to you, alive. And we will leave you all to go your own way. You have Erca's word on this, and his word carries more weight than any gold.'

'Never.' Even as the word left his lips, Lucanus knew it did not sound as forthright as he intended.

Logen must have heard the hesitancy in it, for he smiled. 'The boy will be well cared for. He will be the father of a king. Would we not shower kindness upon him?'

'No.'

'Choose your words carefully, Wolf. The wrong one will end the days of the woman as if you had thrust your blade through her yourself. The right one will save not only her life, but those of your brothers, and all that now shelter under your banner.'

Lucanus felt hot sweat trickle down his back. He wanted to save Catia's life more than anything, but if he broke his vow to safeguard Marcus she would never forgive him. If he kept to it, she would die.

Logen must have seen his dilemma playing out on his face, for he said, 'This is no easy choice, Wolf, we know that. Take your time to reach the answer that is best for her, for all of you. Erca has offered you three days and three nights. Our camp is to the east and the south. A scout like you will smell the smoke a morning's march away. Come to us. Bring the boy. All will be well.'

Lucanus heard movement behind him. He looked back and saw that the others had emerged from the wagons at the sound of voices. Bellicus and Mato, Decima and Galantha, Amatius, Menius and Aelius. Only Amarina was missing, for she was still recovering from her wounds.

'You will not get your hands on Marcus,' he called, his resolve stiffening.

'Are you so sure?' Taking a step forward, Logen placed an object on the ground at his feet. 'The woman's death will not be easy, Wolf. That will lie on your soul too. She will be the plaything of the Attacotti and you know full well what games they like the most. Why, they have already begun.'

He turned on his heel and swept away into the woods, the four huge warriors beside him. The dark swallowed them up in an instant.

Lucanus raced forward and dropped to his haunches where he had seen Logen deposit his gift. His heart rose up into his throat and he wanted to roar into the night.

One slender finger lay there, like a pale slug in the grass. Catia's finger. And at one end, below the knuckle, were teethmarks where the flesh had been gnawed away.

## CHAPTER FORTY-THREE

# *The Song of the Lark*

THE NIGHT STAYED AND STAYED. LUCANUS HUNCHED INSIDE ONE of the wagons, listening to the rain drum on the roof. His brothers squatted around him, ready to offer what thoughts they had if they were called upon, but they knew this decision must be their leader's alone.

After a while, Bellicus asked, 'Do you see any way forward?'

'I can't leave Catia to suffer at the hands of those beasts.' Lucanus thought how hollow his voice sounded.

'And the boy?'

'I can't give the boy up to the barbarians.'

A long moment followed, filled only with the sound of the rolling storm.

'You know we stand with you, whatever you decide.' Bellicus scratched the fur on Catulus' head. 'No man should have to make a choice like this alone.'

'Your choice will be our choice,' Mato added. 'The burden will fall across all our shoulders, so it will be easier to carry into days yet to come.'

Lucanus looked around his men, their faces pale in the wavering light of a candle they'd found in the wagon that transported Varro's supplies. Every day he gave thanks that they were his brothers. He couldn't have asked for better.

'Unless your choice leads us into danger,' Solinus said. 'Then you're on your own.'

When first light came, the rain gave way to a fine mist that soaked through their breeches and plastered their hair to their heads. Comitinus managed to light a fire in the woods under the shelter of a broad oak, and once the flames flickered up Lucanus saw that the warmth gave their band some comfort.

They feasted on cheese and flatbread from the merchant's stores and he carried some of it to the wagon where Amarina was recuperating. She was propped up on sumptuous cushions and swathed in blankets as if it were the middle of winter. Galantha knelt beside her, wiping the sweat from her brow, while Decima changed the dressing on her wounds. The queen and her attendants.

Amarina raised one eyebrow at him, ready to deflect any criticism.

'You're much improved already,' he said.

'I'm hard to kill.'

'Or the witches worked their magic on you.'

'Or I am merely blessed by the gods for my beauty, wit and charm.'

He crouched beside her. 'I wanted to tell you . . . you're forgiven.'

'You think I care?'

'And you think I don't know you well?'

He watched her eyes narrow. 'Why tell me this now?' She paused, calculating. 'You're making peace. Why? What are you planning?'

She knew him well too. 'I've made no plans,' he lied.

Amarina would not be placated. She thrust Galantha's hand away from her forehead and shouted, 'Marcus. Marcus.'

Lucanus looked round as the boy popped up at the rear of the wagon.

'Fetch the Grim Wolves,' Amarina commanded. 'Now.'

When the Wolf climbed out of the wagon, he saw his brothers waiting for him on the edge of the trees, the others gathered behind them.

Grimacing from the pain, Amarina eased herself on to the ground with the help of Galantha and Decima. 'Your leader has plans,' she said. 'Ones, no doubt, only fit for a fool.'

'You wouldn't be thinking of risking only your own neck, would you?' Solinus asked.

'That would be fit for a fool,' Bellicus added, nodding.

'That gold crown must be too tight, squeezing all the blood from his brain,' Solinus continued.

'One man might be able to creep into their camp and free Catia.' Lucanus looked round at the faces of his friends. This was a moment he had tried to avoid.

Myrrdin stepped in front of the Grim Wolves and leaned on his staff. 'There's too much at stake here for a wild wager.'

'I won't sacrifice Catia *or* Marcus.'

The boy ran up to him. 'Let me go. I'll do it to save Mother.'

The Wolf ruffled his hair. 'You're a good and loyal lad. But we can't let you sacrifice yourself.'

'Quite right.' This time it was Amatius who spoke.

For much of their time on the road, Lucanus had kept one eye on him, worried by the jealousy that came in fiery bursts. But Catia's husband had only brooded, rarely joining in the others' conversation. He did his chores, fetched wood, tended the fire, and at night he slept beside Catia. But his face was always turned away from her.

Now Lucanus could see that his features were like flint.

'You talk as if you've not heard anything the wood-priest has been saying,' Amatius continued. 'The boy is everything. Worth more than any riches. It's clear we should protect him at all costs.'

'You would abandon your wife?' Lucanus couldn't hide the incredulity in his voice.

Amatius' eyes glowed with a fierce awareness and every muscle stiffened as if he was about to attack. 'At least I would be done with that whore lying with you behind my back.'

The words were frosted with the chill of deepest winter and for a moment only silence lay across the gathering. Then Lucanus said, 'Marcus, go to Amarina.' He watched the three women help the boy into the back of the wagon, and then he growled, 'You can say such things in front of your son?'

'He should hear the truth about the sow that bore him.'

'That is my daughter you speak of.' Menius' face was like thunder.

Amatius flushed. 'She has betrayed me. She is worthless.'

'She has stood by you, for all the fists you brought down on her,'

Lucanus said, no longer able to contain himself. 'She has honoured you at every turn.'

'You lie,' Amatius spat. 'Only as I expected. How long has she been betraying me with you? Always? Did you both laugh at poor Amatius? The fool who cannot see the treachery under his own nose.' Shame burned in his face. He had kept it all in for so long and now he could no longer control himself. 'She deserves to die.'

The Wolf lunged. He felt someone grab his arm and haul him back. 'You're a leader,' Bellicus breathed in his ear. 'Act like one.'

Lucanus dragged himself back, trying to swallow his fury.

But it was Aelius who snatched out his sword. 'I should gut you now, for all the misery you've caused Catia.'

Amatius sneered. 'A cripple? Try. I would enjoy knocking you on your arse.'

Though he had seemingly been at death's door for months, Menius pushed himself upright. Lucanus watched passion burn new life into the old man's face. 'I am the fool here. I sacrificed my daughter's joy, and for what? Gold and land and a power I once held too lightly. I sold her to you to try to heal the wound of my own betrayal. And now what have we? Nothing. All of it whisked away in the blink of an eye. All the pain my Catia suffered at your hands across the years, all for naught. And may the gods help me, I knew what you were like, what a vile and violent braggart. And still I thought it a price worth paying.'

The old man's eyes brimmed with tears. 'I am to blame for inflicting you upon her, aye. But to say that she deserves to die . . . my daughter, my lovely, innocent daughter . . . when she has been only dutiful while suffering at your hand . . . I will not hear it!' His voice cracked. 'You are the one who should beg for mercy. And if my daughter did betray you, it is because you are weak and worthless.'

Amatius trembled as if he had a fever. Lucanus thought he might strike the old man and he swung up Caledfwlch, ready to intervene. But Amatius realized how much of himself he had exposed. No longer could he carry his head high, damned as he was by all there. He hurried away into the trees.

Menius turned to Lucanus. 'Save my daughter,' he pleaded. 'You have always been like a son to me. Do this, Lucanus. Only you can.'

The Wolf felt the weight of responsibility settle on his shoulders.

Bellicus clapped a hand on his back. 'We'll fight at your side, never doubt it. But they outnumber us ten to one.'

'We are cunning, brother. That is why we are *arcani*. We will find a way to save her without sacrificing Marcus.'

Myrrdin thudded the base of his staff upon the ground three times. 'You are no longer Lucanus, leader of the Grim Wolves. You are Pendragon, latest in a long line of great men . . . kings of war. Raise Caledfwlch, the great sword of the gods, and you may shape this world by your will alone.'

Lightning laced the horizon beneath a canopy of slate-grey cloud. For now, the rain had held off, but in the open country beyond the forest it was hot and clammy. Summer was not far away now.

Mato lay on his belly in the yellow grass, swatting at the fat flies buzzing around his head. The stink of cattle dung hung in the air. He was looking down a gentle slope beyond a bank of nettles to where five houses stood in a circle.

'Life would have been easier if I'd become a priest,' he said. 'Some wine, some chanting, a little incense every now and then.'

'Aye, until you get your head cut off. Which in my experience happens to all priests sooner or later.' Solinus sucked on a straw of the coarse grass. 'Gods come and go. And new priests don't take kindly to old ones.'

Comitinus sighed. 'Speak louder. I don't think our enemies heard you.'

'Quiet,' Bellicus growled.

Mato looked along the line. Lucanus lay at the end, silent and serious. He seemed a changed man. A day had passed since the confrontation with Amatius, a day of planning and scouting until they had found what they needed.

Five pale figures emerged from one of the houses. Two of the Attacotti dragged a body out into the circle of baked mud at the centre of the hamlet, and then all five of them fell upon it with their knives.

Mato looked away, sickened. Myrrdin knew the ways of these barbarians – he knew more than he said of just about everything, Mato had started to believe. And he had suggested that the Eaters of the Dead would not sit easily with the other tribes. They had their rituals, and their own gods, and they would roam wide to follow their own path before returning to the war-band.

'I don't trust the wood-priest,' he murmured.

Solinus plucked the grass from his lips. 'Ah, he cares naught about you or me, only kings, and glory, and the mysterious ways of the gods. Don't trouble yourself about him.'

'The Attacotti don't eat men for food.' Comitinus furrowed his brow as he watched the fast movements of their blades. 'This makes no sense to me.'

'Their gods demand it.' Solinus wrinkled his nose. 'That is as close to sense as we are likely to get.'

Mato saw Lucanus raise his hand and they all fell silent, focusing, smelling the wind, hearing the rustle of the grass, becoming wolves.

A moment later they were loping down the slope, keeping low. The Attacotti crouched with their backs to the approach, caught in deep fascination with their bloody ritual.

As they neared, Mato could hear the rhythmic *whick* of blades upon bones, the work of skilled hands. His nostrils wrinkled at the earthy scent of death. He thought of his sister, as he often did; of her alive, and of her no more than clay. His attention drifted to the song of a lark, to the wonder of the crackling of the lightning, and he felt peace return. There was beauty, even here.

Lucanus slipped to the back of one of the houses and Mato slid beside him, the others close behind. In his head, Mato could still hear their leader's words before they left the camp.

*The wolf strikes when its prey is most vulnerable.*

When it is at feed.

For a long moment, they waited, listening to the sound of the knives and the smacking of lips. And then, as fast as his namesake, the Wolf drew his sword and darted round the edge of the hut. Mato threw himself behind his leader, and the rest followed.

Their feet barely whispered on the ground. Mato watched the figures hunched around the body, like white crows at feast upon the battlefield. Heads rose and fell, again and again.

Only at the last did the Attacotti look round, and then the Grim Wolves fell upon them.

Mato chose his opponent. The warrior's lips pulled back from red teeth as he lashed out with his weapon. But he was still upon his knees and Mato swerved round the attack with ease. Before the other could rise, he cracked the hilt of his sword across the man's forehead, dashing the wits from him. The Attacotti warrior slumped.

When he looked round, Mato saw that his brothers had made short work of the rest. Lucanus was a great and wise leader, he had never doubted it, but now he saw the plan unfolding in all its glory.

The Wolf stood over one of the Eaters, the tip of his blade nicking the fallen warrior's throat. A bubble of blood burst. The Attacotti's eyes were wide, but Mato could see no fear of death in them.

'Now,' Lucanus said, 'we shall have a reckoning.'

# CHAPTER FORTY-FOUR

## *Scale of Dragon, Tooth of Wolf*

IT WAS RAINING AS IF IT HAD BEEN RAINING FOR EVER.
The world had darkened and grown smaller in that ceaseless torrent. Bright hues leached away into a slurry of mud-brown and leaf-green. The earth drummed.

Lucanus stood on the edge of the forest and looked out into the greyness, barely able to see more than a spear's throw. He felt the cold breath of death upon his neck.

'The heavens have opened.' He sensed Myrrdin step beside him. The wood-priest had his hood pulled low over his brow, throwing his features into shadow. 'The gods know this is a time of import. When the storms crash, and the winds howl, that is a sign. Those who rule our days are here. They watch. They know.'

Lucanus looked back at his brothers. Swathed in the shadows of the woods, they waited for his order, sentinels, as much a part of the Wilds as the wolves whose pelts they wore. They would follow him anywhere, he knew. His pride, his burden.

'Five against fifty,' he murmured.

'Listen.' Myrrdin cupped his hand against the side of his hood. 'Can you hear it?'

Lucanus cocked his head, but all he caught was the rumble of the deluge.

'Listen harder. Deep in the forest. Cernunnos howls. The old world stands behind you, Wolf.'

This time Lucanus thought he could make out something, a deep yowl rolling through the trees, though it could just have been the wind in the branches.

'Look. See, the Morrigan is here.' Myrrdin pointed into the dark beneath the canopy. Lucanus thought he saw a mighty thrashing as if of many wings. 'The Phantom Queen smells blood upon the wind. Her heart thunders at the prospect of battle. She will be with you, now and always.'

Lucanus felt his lips prised open as the wood-priest pushed another of the dried toad's-stools into his mouth. He'd already consumed four. He chewed slowly, his mouth watering at the unpleasant iron taste upon his tongue.

'Be cunning like the fox,' Myrrdin continued. 'Be savage like the wolf. Be fleet like the crows. The five of you are not men. You are possessed by the souls of beasts, you are guided by the hands of gods. And you are the Head of the Dragon, Lucanus, and the fire of your righteous fury will smite all who dare stand before you.'

Already the Wolf could feel the effects of the spell licking at the back of his mind. Yet it was not the same as when he flew with the witches or when he undertook the ritual in Lud's temple. This time flames flickered in his belly and a cold focus settled on his mind. It was almost as if the power of the toad's-stool flesh responded to the words of the wood-priest. Was this the true magic the druids wielded?

'Cunning like the fox,' he repeated.

'It is the only way.'

His instincts were on fire, as they had always become when he had been about to venture into the Wilds beyond the wall, and he sensed others had joined them. He turned again and saw Amarina supporting herself on a forked elm branch. That familiar wry smile touched her lips, masking the pain she must still be in. Galantha and Decima were with her.

'You shouldn't be here,' he said.

'Because a battle is no place for women?' she taunted.

'Because I would see you live long and well. You need rest.'

'Are you such a great warrior now that you don't need allies?'

'I have allies.'

'Not enough.' Decima and Galantha were both smiling, and he wondered why.

'The storm will hide us.'

'You think you can sneak into the heart of that camp and free Catia without being seen? Then you are a jolt-head. There will be battle. There can only be battle.' Her eyes narrowed. 'But you know this, of course you do. You're prepared to die if there's a chance to save your woman. Brave and foolish and love-smitten Lucanus.' She glanced at Myrrdin. 'Is this what it takes to be the great Pendragon? How any war was won by a man I do not know.'

'Tell the Wolf what you can do.' The wood-priest's voice was laced with humour. Lucanus felt a beat of anger. Were they all playing a game with him?

'I've already done it. I'm here to see the fruits of my labour.' She flicked her hand, dismissing the druid.

Lucanus shook his head and turned away. Amarina had always been a mystery to him.

'The hour has come,' he said.

Night was falling. The rain came down.

The tent billowed in the gale. The ropes cracked and the downpour thumped. Catia sat by the entrance, looking out into the growing dark. The pain in her hand had settled into a constant dull ache that reached up the bone to her elbow. When the Attacotti had taken her little finger she had almost fainted from the agony, but she felt proud that she had shown her strength and remained conscious. They had sealed the wound with a red-hot blade, and one of the barbarians had smeared it with honey and herbs and bound it with a rag. Yet she hadn't spent time mourning her loss. Instead she'd found her peace. Her life had not been all that she'd wished, not by a long way, but there had been moments of joy and beauty, even under Amatius' iron rule. She gave thanks for Marcus, and Lucanus, and she was pleased that her childhood friend, the only one who really knew her, had been true to his vow. He was a good man, and if the gods smiled he would become the father Marcus needed.

Shapes swirled through the deluge and Erca strode into the tent, shaking the drops from his hair with a grimace. He grunted a greeting to the guard who had been waiting at the rear of the tent. Logen was with him, and the rat-faced man slipped by, seemingly untroubled by his sodden clothes. He struck up a low conversation with the guard in the Scoti's harsh tongue.

Erca pulled off his cloak, shook it and tossed it into the corner. When he looked round at Catia, she thought how ill-tempered he looked.

'There is still time for the Wolf to come crawling with his tail between his legs,' he growled.

'You know he will not give in to your demands.'

'Then you will not see the sun set on the morrow. Are you ready for that?'

'I am.'

Erca clenched one fist as if he might strike her, but he only cursed under his breath. 'It will do no good. You must know that. A waste of a life. We will still hunt down the boy. We will never let this prize slip through our fingers.'

'You see the sun even on a day like this, Erca,' she goaded him, her voice light. 'But *you* must know you have found no joy in your dealings with Lucanus the Wolf from the moment you first met him beyond the wall. He is too clever for you, too cunning. And I have watched him get wiser and stronger by the day. He was a good leader, and he will be a great one. He will outwit you. Chase him to the ends of the earth and he will always stay one step ahead of you.'

Erca grunted. 'The words of the lovelorn.' He fingered the hilt of his sword. 'I don't wish to end your days, but I will not shrink from the task.'

'I would not expect any less.'

Irritated by her calmness, he stalked to the entrance to the tent and looked out into the dark. She watched his brow furrow, and then he pushed his fingers into his mouth and whistled into the night. A moment later, Motius of the Carrion Crows bounded in, naked to the waist, his tattooed torso slick with rain. Catia didn't like him. He reminded her more of beast than man, in the way his shoulders hunched and in his restless searching gaze.

His eyes skittered around, lingering on her for a moment, and she felt her skin crawl.

'Your men have found nothing amiss?' Erca said.

'We watch the approaches. All is well.'

'Something's not right. I feel it.'

Motius strode to the tent entrance and sniffed the air. He shook his head.

'The Attacotti have not returned. Two days now. That's not like them,' the barbarian leader said.

Catia could hear the unease in her captor's voice. This upset of the natural order troubled him.

'They follow their own road, you know that,' Motius said. 'For now, it's the same road as ours, but—'

Erca cut him off with a wave of his hand. 'We need them. Take your men. Find them. Bring them back.'

Motius nodded. Ducking out of the tent entrance, he disappeared into the storm.

When Catia looked up, she found Erca staring at her. He was imagining killing her, she could see it in his eyes.

Lifting her chin, she smiled at him. She was a wolf-sister. She was not afraid. Soon there would be peace.

Bellicus crawled down the slope, away from the trees. The rain hammered on his back and his nose was filled with the reek of the clay he'd smeared on himself to mask his scent. He sensed his brothers beside him and he felt a warm glow that dispelled the chill. Like old times.

Ahead, in the ocean of dark, he could just make out a few guttering torches planted in the entrances to the tents. No campfire could have survived that deluge. He imagined the land as he had seen it when he scouted its fringes in the light of day. A broad floodplain around a meandering river, surrounded by grassland. A good defensive position. Near to the forest for hunting, close to fresh water. In fair weather, enemies could be seen approaching from a long distance.

Now, though, in the storm that Myrrdin had predicted, under the cover of a cloud-banked sky, they had clawed back some advantage.

It was still madness, of course. To think that they could steal Catia away from the heart of the camp without a fight. But he would follow Lucanus anywhere. Nothing could ever redress the debt he owed.

On he crawled, straining to hear any sounds ahead through the pounding of the rain. Mato would be moving off towards the river now, Lucanus, Solinus and Comitinus creeping around the camp's edge.

Madness.

Death was close, he could smell it. Who would it claim this night? All of them? A mercy, then. In the end, dying was easier than living.

Yet he heard Lucanus' words ringing in his head, the ones he had spoken just before they set off. They were scouts, *arcani*, not warriors living from battle to battle. But in the final account, that was what wolves did. They hunted and they killed. For the wolf, there was only prey.

Squinting through the downpour, he made out the faint silhouette of the shelter of branches and leaves and turf where the lookout hunched. Even through the rain, he could smell the man's sweat. He would be cold, bored, wishing he was gnawing on hot venison or drinking ale or between a woman's thighs. Anywhere but where he was.

It was time.

Crawling to the edge of the shelter, Bellicus rose up.

With one sweep of his left arm, he smashed the fragile structure aside. In the thick dark, he couldn't see the lookout's shocked face, but he had bludgeoned more than one man to death in his time. He knew how it looked.

His right arm clamped around the man's neck, he heaved him back and up so his feet were kicking, though no sound escaped his lips. Straining, Bellicus held him tight until the thrashing had ceased, and then he dumped the body among the ruins of the shelter. Turning, he loped towards the lights.

Erca's tent would be in the centre of the camp. Catia would be there, and an army between him and her.

Drawing his sword, he slowed when he could make out individual tents. Lucanus and the others would have made short work of the other lookouts by now, but it would only take one barbarian peering out from the camp and seeing movement to raise the alarm.

They would come from four directions, that was the plan. If one of them was discovered, that man would flee, drawing the rest of

Erca's army and leaving the others to do their best to get to Catia. He had heard worse plans, but not many.

And if they were all seen?

Best not to think about that.

And in that moment, he realized the truth in what one-eyed, one-handed Loca the Brave had told him when he was a boy: the gods liked to laugh and their jokes were cruel.

That rain, that terrible, relentless rain that had been crashing down for a day and a half, stopped. Gone in an instant. The storm that had been holding overhead to punish them moved away. In its place there was silence.

Bellicus heard a burst of laughter. A cheer. Voices calling. The camp coming to life.

And then the clouds swept away, and the full moon came out, and the whole landscape lit up as bright as day.

Lucanus watched the world become silver. It was as if the gods had turned the lamp of their gaze upon him and him alone. In his head, he could feel the tidal pull of the toad's-stool. The howl of Cernunnos, deep in the primal forest, echoed through his skull. The black wings of the Morrigan's crows crashed around the edges of his vision.

He was Pendragon, and his enemies would bow to his will.

A cry echoed from the camp, then another, and another. One of them had been seen, or all of them.

Lucanus pulled out Caledfwlch. Perhaps it was the effect of the fungus, but the blade fairly glowed in the moonlight, limned with a blue light, and the runes carved on to the bronze seemed as if they would rise out of the metal and speak to him, if only he could understand.

The sword of the gods, the power of the gods.

He felt no fear; he felt nothing except a fierce determination. He would not shrink from battle. The Dragon's fire would smite his enemies down.

With a roar, he ran across the grassland towards the camp. He heard his battle-cry picked up by Bellicus and Solinus and Comitinus.

Lucanus watched the barbarians begin to emerge from the circle of tents. Some were laughing. They drew their swords half-heartedly, swinging them from side to side as if they were preparing to spar with a child.

As he ran, he put his head back and howled his wolf's cry. Long and low and haunting, it rolled out across the grasslands, across the river, until it reached the edges of the great forest.

In answer to it, the white shapes emerged from the graves where they had been lying since dark fell, luminous in the light of the full moon. Pulling themselves up on two feet, they turned towards the camp.

Lucanus could see the hesitation in his enemies as they were gripped by the sight. The swords stopped their swinging. Feet ground to a halt. He imagined the thoughts rushing through their heads as they tried to make sense of what lay before their eyes.

And then the realization came, to every man at the same time, or so it sounded, as a gasp that seemed like the exhalation of a waking beast rustled across the still grasslands.

As one, the Attacotti drew their swords and swept towards their former allies.

Though there were only five of them, fear gripped the barbarians. Lucanus watched them lurch back towards their tents, lowering their shoulders and turning their heads in a desperate search for reassurance from their brothers that these terrible, terrifying warriors could not, would not, have turned upon them.

Lucanus smiled to himself as he ran. He remembered how they had dragged the captured Attacotti back to their own camp. Those white-crusted warriors did not fear death, but they still had their own strange needs and desires. Myrrdin had bargained with them in their own tongue deep into the night. What the wood-priest had promised them Lucanus did not know, but in the end they had agreed to change sides. Now they were ten against fifty.

A clamour erupted in the camp as the barbarians rushed to defend themselves. In an instant, a tall, broad-shouldered Scoti warrior with a broken nose loomed in front of Lucanus, slashing with his long sword.

Remembering everything his father had taught him, Lucanus ducked beneath the arc of the blade. He sensed it flash by just above the wolf pelt over his head, and then he was thrusting up, ramming his own sword into the man's gut and ripping it towards his chest.

Blood showered. The Wolf didn't slow his step, throwing the dying man to one side, but as he looked up he saw that one of the Attacotti had already fallen. The weight of numbers was beginning to tell, and the Scoti were growing more confident. They smelled victory.

Mato pushed himself up at the river's edge where he had been hiding and peered over the lip of the bank. The furious yells and screams told him everything he needed to know: their attempt to creep into the camp undetected had already failed.

When he had watched the full moon come out from behind the bank of clouds, he had known it was only a matter of time, but he was still surprised by the speed of discovery.

Now he had to play his part.

He clawed his way out on to the marshy ground edging the rushing grey waters and squelched towards the camp. He was no good with a sword, however much he tried, and Lucanus had spared him an early death. But sneaking through the shadows, that he could do.

As he neared the tents, he could smell the musky scent of the horses and hear their neighs and snorts and the stamping of their hooves. They were frightened by the din of battle. That was good.

At the pen, he tore down the fence of branches and untethered the lines of mounts. Shouting and clapping his hands, he whipped the animals into a fever and herded them towards the camp. They thundered among the tents, tearing them down, and screams echoed from warriors who had fallen under their hooves, just as he had hoped.

The confusion would help, but it was only the start. They needed more if they wanted to snatch anything from this night.

Turning, he looked deep into the night, waiting and praying. He need not have worried. Amarina had been true to her word.

The first flight of arrows whined through the air, punching into the barbarians as they fled the maddened horses. Mato smiled. What a strange and ramshackle army they were.

Now he could just make out the forest folk, nocking arrows to their hunting bows as they emerged from the dark. Lucanus had been right – they looked more like beasts than men with their wild hair and beards, hunched and restless, their ragged clothes flapping around them like ravens' wings.

Mato sensed movement. A figure rose up from the ground beside him and he cried out, spinning away. As he tumbled on to his arse, he looked up at a towering figure and felt his heart thunder. In the Wilds he had sensed the enemy from miles away, yet here he had not even known a man was practically close enough to touch.

In the moonlight, the figure all but glowed emerald. Mato felt a surge of relief when he took in the armour, and the shield, and the bronze sword.

Without any greeting, the Lord of the Greenwood bounded towards the tents, swinging his sword as he ran, carving into a barbarian's ribcage with such force that it almost lifted the man off the ground.

Mato looked around, unable to restrain a smile of disbelief. The forest people were close now, circling the camp. Shafts punched into flesh and bone. Like his brothers, he had had doubts about Amarina, but it was she who had begged for the aid of the Lord of the Greenwood, and his followers had answered. They knew the Pendragon title, understood what it meant, and now Mato was beginning to realize it too.

As he watched the barbarians fall, he felt some hope rising, however thin. The tide of battle was beginning to turn.

'What madness is this?'

Erca drew his sword and stood in the entrance to the tent. A riderless mount thundered by and he recoiled a step.

Catia crouched in the centre of the space, listening to the din whirling outside. Screams and battle-cries, the clash of blades and the whinnying of frightened horses. Every fibre of her was on fire.

She watched Erca and Logen trying to make sense of the confusion in the dark. When the first warning had rung out that the Grim Wolves had been seen, the Scoti leader had laughed. 'Five men,' he had said. 'What threat can they pose?'

She smiled to herself. Now his face was like thunder and he muttered feverishly to the rat-faced man who seemed to be his second in command.

The guard loomed over her, but he was distracted by the battle out in the night, she could tell. What need did he have to keep an eye on a mere woman?

Catia smiled again.

When a horse crashed against the side of the tent, almost bringing it down, she was ready. She rammed her fist into the guard's groin. He doubled up, falling back.

Thrusting upright, she raced past Erca and Logen, who had reeled away from the entrance of the tent. Their furious yells boomed at her back, but she kept on running as fast as she could, perhaps as fast as Mato, past the tents, dodging a careering horse, out to the edge of the camp.

The moonlight illuminated a scene of carnage. Blood puddled the ground and dead and dying barbarians sprawled everywhere.

An arrow whisked by her head a finger's length away, and after her heart had stopped pounding she muttered thanks to the gods for her good fortune. To die then, when she was so close to escape, would have been too unjust.

Hoping that whoever was loosing the arrows could see she was not an enemy, Catia dashed past the line of corpses. Two men waited ahead, and she felt a surge of relief when saw it was Lucanus and Bellicus. Their swords dripped blood as they stood over fallen foes. At first Lucanus seemed not to see her. He had a faraway look in eyes that seemed blacker than ever, but then the daze cleared, a grin crept to his lips and he called her name. She was surprised at how her heart leapt when she heard it.

'Witch.'

She whirled. The word had been laced with acid and given force with fury, and it could only have been directed at her.

Staggering across the grassland was Amatius. She thought how wild-eyed he looked, his hair flying up from his head, his cloak covered with dirt as if he had been sleeping in a ditch. But then she saw he was not alone and she felt a flood of fear.

Marcus was clasped to his chest. Catia could see her son thrashing, terrified, unable to comprehend what his father was doing to him. Amatius' face was filled with the terrible fury Catia had seen a thousand times, and she knew what it portended.

'No,' she screamed. 'Take him away.'

'Have the boy,' he roared, not to her, but, she knew, to the barbarians who were closing on her back. 'I did not sire him. He is a bastard. A sign of my wife's treachery. Take him.'

Catia struggled to comprehend what Amatius was saying. How could he believe that he was not Marcus' father? But then she saw him glare at Lucanus and she knew that he'd been consumed by the monstrous jealousy that had always hunched inside him, a jealousy she'd long recognized but had ignored, like a fool.

'No.' Her voice was a dying croak. She held out a hand to her husband, pleading. 'He is yours. I swear it.'

Feet thundered at her back. Erca, no doubt, and Logen, coming to end all hope. She could see from his granite face that her husband would not back down.

Spinning to Lucanus, she yelled, 'Save Marcus. I beg you. Save him.' When he hesitated, she shouted, 'Forget me. End this battle. Save him.'

Amatius seemed to jerk to his senses at the sound of her exhortation. 'No,' he bellowed. 'I will not be defeated.' He turned and ran into the night, hauling Marcus with him.

Three sharp whistles rang out – Lucanus' signal to his men – and then her love was racing after her husband with Bellicus close at his heels. From across the camp, the sound of battle ebbed away.

Catia felt hands grab her arms. She didn't care. Watching the disappearing wolves, she prayed harder than she ever had that all would be made right.

Logen began to pull her back to what remained of the camp, but Erca stood his ground, glowering as he stared into the dark. Somehow Motius was there too.

'Follow them,' Erca commanded the Crow. 'See where they take the boy. Bring him back to me, whatever it takes.'

'Is there any sign of him?' Amarina snapped.

Decima shook her head, her eyes flickering with fear that she might feel the lash of her mistress's tongue. And she should be afraid, Amarina thought, simmering. She had charged her and Galantha to watch over the boy. The old man and the cripple could not be trusted to protect so valuable a prize. But still Amatius had snatched him, rushing from the trees like a wild beast to beat both women to the ground with his fists.

'There.' Galantha was pointing to the edge of a copse on the bank of the river not far away.

In the moonlight, Amarina could just make out Amatius lurching into the trees, the boy grasped in his arms. Further along the grassland, two other figures were following. She squinted and thought they were Lucanus and Bellicus.

'Come,' she said, leaning on her makeshift crutch as she started towards them. 'You're too weak,' Decima objected, trying to hold her back.

Amarina glared. 'If that cockless cur has any wits, he will be able to escape along the riverbank before they can stop him. Now keep your tongue still and do as you are told. Run to Lucanus. Tell him Amatius is in the copse.' She turned to Galantha. 'Help me. We'll do what we can to slow his escape.'

As Decima ran off, Amarina hobbled as fast as she could towards the trees, holding on to Galantha with her free hand and ignoring the barbs of pain in her wounds. It was only a spear's throw to the copse, but it seemed like a day's march. Somehow she found herself on the edge of the trees. From the depths of the grove she could hear low juddering sobs.

Amarina let go of Galantha's arm and pressed her finger to her lips. She was weak, but she could still hold a pathetic coward like Amatius at bay. She pulled her knife from the folds of her dress, enjoying the feel of the deer-horn handle her father had carved.

She could hear the sound of running feet coming from the grassland. This bastard's day was done. She lurched forward into the heart of the thicket.

Amatius knelt in a shaft of moonlight. His head was tilted back, his eyes were shut, and tears streaked the grime on his cheeks. Marcus lay across his lap.

Amarina felt a sudden terrible fear. The boy's body was limp, his head lolling at an odd angle. A broken neck.

Fear turned into a rush of emotion: bewilderment that this man could take the life of his own son, fury at all that Amatius was, despair for all that had been lost, and finally an abiding grief for the boy, for Marcus.

Lucanus crashed into the copse. Amarina blinked away tears and watched the same trail of emotions cross his face. He slumped against a tree, his sword falling limply to his side, his lips moving soundlessly as he tried to give voice to all the confusion inside him.

The boy had been like a son to him, she knew that. But he would be feeling, too, for Catia, if she still lived. And laid upon that deep well of grief was another loss, one that affected every man and woman in the land. The prophecy was a lie. The king who would not die would now never be born. Who then could lead them out of the dark?

She sensed movement on the other side of the copse and saw Bellicus appear behind the sobbing husk of a man. Amarina saw him take in the tableau in an instant. Cold judgement clouded his face.

With a swing of his sword, he took Amatius' head.

Catia craned her neck round, desperately hoping to see some sign out in the night that would tell her Marcus was safe. All around her, the barbarians staggered through the ruins of their camp, trying to make sense of how they had lost so much to a band of beggars and thieves and farmers. She could smell the iron tang of blood on the wind.

Logen kept a grip on her wrist while Erca strode among his men, trying to bring order. Barely more than twenty had survived. Under other circumstances this would have been a great victory for Lucanus and the Lord of the Greenwood, but for Catia all that mattered was the fate of her son. Why had Lucanus fought to rescue her? Why had he not fled with Marcus, as she had hoped and prayed?

She watched Motius of the Carrion Crows dart back into the camp and her heart leapt. But he did not have Marcus with him.

He bowed his head to Erca and for a moment they whispered together, then both of them turned to look at her. In that stare, she read everything that she feared, and she felt the world fall away from her.

As if from a great distance, she heard Erca calling out to his men, 'Round up the horses. We are done with this place. We ride back to the army tonight.'

She felt as if hands were round her throat, choking the life from her. She watched the barbarian leader walk up to her without really seeing him.

She heard his words as if from the depths of a well, and she wanted anger or hatred in them, but she heard only sadness and that was the worst of all.

'You will come with us now,' he said.

Lucanus finished pounding the earth upon the shallow grave he, Bellicus and Mato had clawed out with their own hands. A circle of moonlight shone upon it. Marcus had been interred, with tears and muttered prayers to the gods, and what remained of Amatius had been dragged off to the edge of the copse and left for the wolves to consume.

He felt drained of all emotion, numb to the very bone.

At last, he looked up as Comitinus ran into the thicket. 'The barbarians are riding north, what's left of them,' he gasped, breathless.

'Whipped and frightened, tails between their legs,' Solinus said. Blood speckled his face and soaked one side of his cloak, though not his own by the looks of it.

Bellicus grunted. 'Heading back to their horde.'

Lucanus rested against a tree, feeling all eyes upon him. He could read their unspoken thoughts. Now that Marcus was dead, there was no need for the barbarians to remain here. They could get on with their business of conquering Britannia.

It would fall soon enough. And what then? The towns burned. The people slaves. And no hope for any of them, because he had failed.

'They have taken Catia with them,' Comitinus added. He let the words hang.

'We will fetch her back.' How hollow his voice sounded.

'No.' Bellicus stepped in front of him and laid a heavy hand on his shoulder. 'I'll go, with Solinus and Comitinus. You have work to do.'

'Catia needs me.'

'The people need you. You are the Pendragon now. You have a golden crown in case I forget.' Bellicus was trying to make light of it, he knew, but he recognized the hard look in the other's face that showed he would brook no resistance. Nevertheless, his voice softened a little when he added, 'You must trust us.'

Lucanus nodded. 'You're a good friend.'

Bellicus grunted. 'I'm a bastard.' He looked around at Solinus and Comitinus. 'You're with me?'

'I had hopes for some whoring and drinking, but this will do for now.' Solinus spat on his hand and started to wipe the blood from his face.

'We'll bring Catia home, however long it takes,' Comitinus vowed.

'You want me to join you?' Mato asked.

'What, and risk you sticking yourself with your own sword?' Bellicus said with a grin. 'The Wolf will need a good man at his side in the days to come. I'm not good. But you are. Good to the heart.'

Lucanus saw Mato's surprise at the compliment, but he felt troubled. It was almost as if Bellicus didn't expect to see either of them again.

'You will be his friend and wise counsellor,' the Bear continued. 'But more than anything, you must counter the deceit that trips so easily from the mouth of the wood-priest. Do you hear me?'

Mato nodded.

Lucanus felt weary. He dared not tell them that he was sick of running and of fighting. He had not asked for this, and he was certain he was not up to the responsibilities being heaped on his shoulders. But he had accepted them. 'You know I will do whatever is asked of me,' he said.

## CHAPTER FORTY-FIVE

# *Among the Stones*

S UMMER BLAZED IN AS THEY HEADED SOUTH. THE BAND TRUNDLED along sun-drenched tracks during the heat of the day, watching the dance of bees and butterflies and drinking in the perfume of the wild flowers that lined the way. At night, they rested in balmy warmth, looking up at star-sprinkled skies.

The Grim Wolves had rounded up four of the barbarians' horses to pull a brace of Varro's wagons along the path Myrrdin had set. Amarina grew steadily stronger as her wounds healed, and Menius seemed to find some purpose in each day's chores that gave him a strength greater than they had seen since they had left Vercovicium.

They filled their bellies with the abundant food they hunted and foraged along the road, but for all the peace of their journey they found little in their hearts. Grief suffocated them, as did the worry and the doubt and the fear. Soon the barbarian horde would sweep south, on a tide of blood and death that would wash away all they had known. And what did the future hold now that the hope epitomized by Marcus was gone?

To Lucanus' mounting frustration, the wood-priest offered no guidance, no answers. 'Be patient. All will be revealed,' he said, oddly untroubled by the passing of the one who was key to all that the druids had hoped for for so long.

After they emerged from the dense forests of the uplands, they rumbled into a lush green land rolling into the hazy distance, dotted with gleaming lakes and carved by rushing rivers. The farmers and merchants they met were hungry for news of the threat that waited to the north. All were afraid to leave their homes and businesses and flee south, yet incapable of defending themselves. The army was nowhere to be seen.

Lucanus' cheeks burned every time he heard Myrrdin talk of the great war leader who would fight for them, the Pendragon, and tell stories that rushed along the trade routes. Why give them false hope, the Wolf wondered? Once more the wood-priest had no answer for him.

Shared journeys forged bonds that lasted a lifetime. Lucanus had learned that during his forays into the Wilds with the Grim Wolves. Though he thought often of Bellicus and Solinus and Comitinus, and more of Catia, he fell into the lives of those who wandered with him. Mato spoke often of his dead sister Aula in ways that he had never done beyond the wall. Something consumed him, some desire for understanding perhaps, but what it was the Wolf decided he did not have the wits to understand. Aelius was keen to prove he was more than the man whose possibilities had been defined in Vercovicium. He sweated every day, dragging back firewood, heaving skins of fresh water, begging Lucanus to teach him how to use a sword more skilfully and learning how to balance himself in a duel with only one arm. Decima and Galantha spun tales of their past, of thieving and deception and high men brought low, both of them laughing as if all was right with the world. As they told Lucanus, though there had been slaughter and misery they had reached nightfall alive and with full bellies, and for that they gave thanks and always would, for in the past death and hunger had rarely left them alone. The Wolf found it hard to understand. Mato knew, though.

Amarina was an enigma. The woman was filled with secrets and he was convinced he would never learn any of them.

As they rolled across a great plain under a cloudless sky, Lucanus eyed Myrrdin beside him on the bench of the wagon and said, 'You still have hope?'

'Aye.'

'And how do we hold the barbarians at bay?'

'The old tribes have been summoned to the war-moot.'

Lucanus laughed, more bitterly than he intended. 'You have not been paying attention, wood-priest: there are no warriors out there any longer. This is not the time of the old stories when a queen of fury laid waste to an army from Rome. Folk have grown fat and idle on the profits of the empire. Merchants do not wield swords. Landowners do not fight. Farmers only have ploughs.'

Myrrdin shrugged. 'They will fight. Or they will die.'

Lucanus sighed. He was starting to believe the wood-priest's words meant little more than a handful of dust.

And then the wagons pulled through a line of trees and the Wolf yanked his horses to a halt. He leaned forward on the bench, unsure what he was seeing ahead of him.

In the centre of wind-blasted grassland that reached as far as the eye could see, a circle of standing stones rose up in the heat haze. They were capped in pairs, a temple by any other name.

'What is that?' he asked.

'Welcome to the Heartstones, Wolf,' Myrrdin said, allowing himself a faint smile. 'Here we will forge the days yet to come.'

In the furnace of the late afternoon, the travellers lounged in the shade of the wagons. Mato noticed that most of them could not tear their eyes away from the stones silhouetted against the blue sky. He felt awe in the presence of that temple to unknown gods too, without being able to say why.

To the south a winding river glimmered like silver. 'The serpent that gives life,' Myrrdin said as he followed its trail.

'Dragons and serpents,' Lucanus muttered. 'To hear you speak, they are everywhere.'

'They are.'

'A river is a dragon. A man is a dragon,' Mato mused. 'Now I am beginning to understand. Everything is the thing it is, but it can also be another thing.'

'And in the second thing, that is where the secrets lie,' the wood-priest said, 'and that is where the hidden bonds are.'

Mato chewed on a grass stalk. 'This is the wisdom you learn in your schools, wood-priest, and which you pass down the years? The knowledge of the hidden faces of all there is?'

'Once you know the hidden faces, you know the truth of the world.'

Lucanus lost patience. 'You make my head hurt. I'd rather know how a few may win a war against a barbarian horde. And why we even risk our necks in battle when there is nothing to fight for. No saviour. No way out of the long night that is drawing in.'

'Turn your face to the sun, Wolf. You have too much gloom in you.' The wood-priest hefted himself up and tapped the tip of his staff against Lucanus' chest before raising it to the sky. 'You have much yet to learn. Lugh looks down on you, brother; Lugh, who smiles upon priests and kings. Lugh, who has three faces, whom the Romans call Mercury. He brings all magic into this world, the wonder of words and the wisdom of stories, for that is where true power lies. The wood-priests have always known this, and it has shaped us, as we now shape you.'

Mato saw Lucanus narrow his eyes, trying to make sense of what the druid was saying. 'You lied to me. About the prophecy. About Marcus. It cannot be a prophecy if it does not come to pass.' The Wolf stood up, stabbing a wavering finger at the other man. 'Folk have died . . . the boy died . . . because we followed you. And now we have nothing, and we are . . .' he looked around, 'nowhere.'

'We are at the heart of all things. The world turns here.'

'We have nothing.'

'Nothing, you say? You have been turned from lead into gold, Wolf. You now have a destiny where you had none. The gods have looked upon you and they have breathed life into your breast. They have given you a sword of power, and a golden crown that makes you a leader of men. They have made you a king, of a kind, you, a wild wolf clothed in rags and smeared with the green of the tree and the turf. Is this not a wonder that could only come from the gods? Know this. The Dragon will still rise. The king who will not die is coming still.'

'How?'

Mato watched the druid's face, the light in his eyes, the power of persuasion that came off him in waves. There was something here, he was certain.

'The secrets we know are many-fold,' Myrrdin said, 'but there is one . . . there is one that will turn all men from lead into gold once they accept it. There is no need to fear death. It is not an ending. The Attacotti know this to be true. All men have a soul, and when the heart is stilled that soul moves into another vessel. No ending, Wolf. This is at the heart of our teachings. Marcus is dead, but he yet lives, and the king who will save us all lives too.'

Lucanus bowed his head, weighing the words, and then Mato watched him walk away among the stones.

'This is the Wolf's darkest moment,' Myrrdin murmured. 'He has suffered greatly, and if there is to be any chance of saving what we have we must guide him through this time and back into the light.'

'Stories have two faces too, eh?' Mato said. 'What you say and what lies beneath. I've been paying attention to your words.'

'At least one of you listens,' the druid grumbled.

'I hear more than you may wish to reveal.'

Myrrdin eyed him.

'You think your gods are wise above all others. Yet the Christians drive out all that you believe in, and they destroy the temples of the worshippers of Mithras.'

'The wars of men are the wars of gods. Or the wars of gods are the wars of men, one or the other.'

'That's not the only story I hear in your words.'

The wood-priest's smile slipped away. 'Speak.'

'You did indeed lie to Lucanus. This prophecy is not from the gods, is it? It's a plan made by men. By you wood-priests. Saying it is god-given . . .' Mato paused, looking down towards the river, and past it into the hazy distance where the army no doubt cowered. 'That is to convince weak-minded fools. Fools like me, and Lucanus, and all who hear your words.'

Myrrdin nodded, impressed. He was making no attempt at denial. 'You are a wise man, Mato. You see far more than your brothers. In a different world, you might have become one of us. Know this, then. I told Lucanus the truth, in a way. The king is an *idea* waiting to be born. He will come, and if enough men believe, he will do all that we say he will do. And he will lead the people of this isle out of darkness and into a better world. Would you deny them that by questioning what is truth and what is lie?'

'But Lucanus was right. Many have died to further this plan you have been shaping for I don't know how long.'

'Death is not the end. Did you not hear my words?'

'How easy it is then to send a man marching at your word into the Summerlands.'

The wood-priest stepped in front of him, no doubt hearing the unease in his words. 'What benefit to tell Lucanus your fears? Will it make right the ache in his stomach and help him grow strong? Will it help in the defeat of the barbarians? Or will it only wound him further, that all that he has lost has been for no reason? In the end, there is only one story. Who lays claim to it – that is the question. We will make the king who will not die. We, together. And men will fall in step behind him.' Myrrdin's voice was strong. 'Will you help me?'

'You wish me to lie to my brother?'

'I wish you to help build a better truth.'

Night had fallen on the plain; a deep stillness had settled across the stones. In the centre of the circle, Lucanus lay on his back and looked up at the full moon, the milky light edging the towering monoliths. Beside him, Myrrdin sat cross-legged, his staff across his lap.

In that peace, it was hard to believe a war was about to crash down upon them. But Lucanus knew the thoughts of the group rarely turned from death and blood. No one gave voice to their innermost fears, but he could see from their faces that they looked to him as their saviour. How had it come to this?

Myrrdin pointed to a bright emerald glow just beyond the circle. A firefly. 'A message,' he said, 'from the gods. This is an auspicious night.'

Lucanus grunted. 'It is a night, like any other.'

'There is magic around you at all times, if only you had eyes to see, and none more so than on this night, the eve of midsummer. Men look at the ground, or towards the next meal, or the next coin, and think the gods are not among them at all times. But they are.'

'Is this another of the secrets you have been taught, druid?'

'We see it in the flight of birds, or the call of beasts, or the stars in the sky. The gods watch, and they listen, and they speak, but you must know their tongue to hear.'

'And what do the gods tell you of me?'

'That there is no better man to lead the people towards the age of the Bear-King, Artorigios.'

'You truly believe that?'

'I do. But I am a mere man. The gods have chosen you, Lucanus. All that has been in your life, and in the life of your father, and your father's father, has led to this moment.'

The Wolf drew Caledfwlch and pointed it towards the sweep of stars. 'A sword from a lake, left behind by a warrior from another age.'

'A gift from the naiad who watches over that lake, a messenger who brought it to you from the gods themselves. That is the Sword of Light, and it once belonged to Lugh himself. In the west, they say it was given to him by Manannan Mac Lir who rules the oceans. With that sword, he saved the children of Dann from the great darkness, their enemy the Fomorians, led by the one-eyed god Balor.'

Lucanus watched the wood-priest close his eyes, remembering, and continue in a sing-song voice, '"The Sword of Light was bare in his hand. He fell on the Fomorians as a sea-eagle falls on her prey, as lightning flashes out of a clear sky. Before him and his companions, they were destroyed as stubble is destroyed by fire. He held his hand when only nine of them remained alive."'

'Nine,' Lucanus repeated, drifting in the soothing rhythm of the words. He looked past the great stone blocks and thought he saw movement there, away in the dark. A procession of the gods, perhaps, like the one he had seen when he had lain dying in the great forest beyond the wall. It felt as if they had come to see him, and to bear witness to the choice he was about to make.

'Numbers are important. This too is what we learned in our school. Three, five, nine. When you see those numbers, you must pay special attention, for the gods are speaking through them.'

The Wolf nodded, but he didn't really understand.

'Your destiny was decided at that cold lake in the far north,' Myrrdin said. 'There's no walking away from it.'

Lucanus slipped his blade back into its scabbard. 'Then my choice is decided. I'll lead, and I'll fight. For Marcus' sake. For Catia, for my friends, for all who need to be led out of the dark.'

He sensed a change in Myrrdin beside him, and he was certain he was smiling.

'Who set up these stones?' he said, looking around the circle. 'Is this a temple of the wood-priests?'

The druid paused, choosing his words. 'They are old, older than the tales we have, but it's our business to care for them now. Not just the Heartstones, but all these circles across these islands.' He looked up at the sky. 'Our stories tell us that long ago, long before there were any wood-priests, a star fell to earth. Fires blasted the forests and the heathland and the skies turned black. The ocean rose up and swept across all the land, and only the mountain tops were safe for men to cling on to. When the waters fell away, those who survived . . . the forefathers of the wood-priests . . . set up these stones.'

'As a monument, so the people would never forget those who had died?' Lucanus said.

Myrrdin pointed to a bright star, low in the evening sky. 'Do you see that, how it seems to hang above that stone lintel? In these circles we can watch and study so that we will be ready if another star falls to earth.' The druid looked around the circle of stones, black against the night sky. 'But there is more to this place than that.'

'More? How?'

'Until the Romans came and blighted this land, great moots were held here every midsummer and midwinter. Feasts the like of which you and I have never known. And, so we are told, there was a great drumming, a pounding upon hide stretched across wood. And when the drumming reached its pitch, the stones spoke back.'

'Spoke? How? They have no mouths.'

'They sang. And the people listened, and they danced, danced until they were in a frenzy, until they fell over in a dead faint. And when they woke at dawn, they were filled with the light of the gods. And they could go about their business for more seasons, safe in the knowledge that the gods were with them. Come.'

Myrrdin led him to one of the stones, and pressing his palms upon it he rested his cheek against it and closed his eyes. 'Sometimes, even without the drumming, you can hear them speak,' he murmured.

Lucanus pressed his own ear against the stone. It was cool next to his skin. After a moment, he thought he could hear a sound, but not a voice, a heart beating steadily, low and deep. Boom. Boom. Boom.

Myrrdin pulled back, but left one hand on the stone. He had a curious smile, Lucanus thought, almost gentle. 'The gods are in here,' the wood-priest whispered. He crouched and placed the same hand on the earth. 'And in here. In the land around this place, around all the circles, and joining them. On some nights, a blue light limns the stones. That is the light of the gods. If you ever see it, you will feel it in your heart, Lucanus, and you will be changed for all time.'

Lucanus turned to him, frowning. 'You are teaching me.'

'If you are to raise a king,' the wood-priest said, 'he must be wise in the ways of all that he is. I will be by your side for the rest of your days, guiding and teaching. And my son will walk with your son, and one day, when the Bear-King comes, Myrrdin will walk with him too.'

Four days passed, and on the morning of the fifth Amarina left the campfire and walked into the circle. The wood-priest had set up his staff there so that it cast a long shadow, but she had no idea what he was doing and was in no mood to ask.

'Would you have us wait here until the barbarians fall on us and chop us to pieces for the ravens?' she said.

He eyed her, his smile wry. 'With a tongue like that, you could cut them all dead.'

'Play no games with me, druid. I am not like the men who run around behind you.'

'No, that I can see. But I do not choose to wait. I am not the leader.'

'No games, I said. You sing a song in Lucanus' ear and he dances to it.' She narrowed her eyes at him.

'We wait until the war-moot can be held.'

'No one is coming. You must know that.'

Myrrdin shrugged and she felt a wave of irritation. 'If you had the wit you think you have, you would be taking us to a place where we could hide and grow strong.'

The wood-priest looked along the line of shadow, past the stones and into the distance. 'The only safety is to be found on the Isle of Apples, if you could find your way there,' he said, distracted.

'And you know where that is?'

'Aye. And sooner or later we will find our way to it and beyond it. For in the west, past that place, there is a land where the Bear-King can be born and where he can build his army, and his empire. In the west, where the old stories say the dead go on their way to the Summerlands. Where all good rewards wait. To the lands of the Dobunni, and the Durotriges and the Dumnonii. A land rich in lead and silver and tin, past the healing waters of Aquae Sulis. There are Wilds there too, like the ones the Grim Wolves knew in the north, beyond the fortress of Isca Dumnoniorum.'

'Then that is where we must go. You whisper over one of Lucanus' shoulders and I will have the other. We will see who wins.'

Amarina realized Myrrdin was no longer listening. She followed his gaze and in the hazy distance she saw a group of men with horses making their way towards the circle.

'Find Lucanus,' the wood-priest said, 'and bring him here. Now.'

Since first light Lucanus had been stalking the white stag among the trees that edged the grassland. How it had evaded all his attempts to get close to it he didn't know, and now the trail itself seemed to have disappeared. That too was baffling – he was no novice – but here he was, far from the stones and with nothing to show for it.

He bellowed a guttural howl of frustration, and a murder of crows took wing from the high branches, shrieking their disapproval. His band didn't need the venison, but the hunt had taken his mind off Catia and his guilt at Marcus' death for a little while.

As the echoes of his frustration died away, his nostrils flared at an odd scent, bitter and powerful, nothing he had ever encountered in the Wilds before. Motes of dust were floating in a sunbeam that broke through the canopy just in front of him and he realized he must have breathed them in.

He felt thick-headed for a moment, as if he had taken a blow to a temple. But it passed and then his thoughts swam with fascination at the complexity of branch and leaf and light and shade. He stared for a moment, drinking in the green world. After a while, his wits flickered and he realized he was seeing something that jarred.

Among the dense vegetation, a pair of eyes was staring back at him.

'Who goes?' he asked.

A face formed around the eyes, a familiar face, and a young woman stepped out from the edge of a hawthorn bush. She was naked, but smeared with clay and wrapped with ivy.

Hecate the Maiden stepped before him. Yet as he looked her up and down, he saw she was no longer the maiden he had seen beyond the wall. Her belly was swollen, her hands cupping it.

'You're with child.'

'Your child, Lucanus the Wolf.'

He laughed. Behind her, he saw movement. The two other women, the mother and the crone, waited half hidden among the trees.

Hecate the Young leaned forward until he found her face swimming before his eyes. 'That day, in our home, when we flew,' she murmured. 'It was not only the broomstick that I rode.'

Lucanus' mind whirled back to that first encounter. He had slipped into unconsciousness as the sisters' spell began to fade. 'You lie.'

She smiled. 'It will be a girl.'

'How can you know?'

'Any wise woman knows these things. Eat the right herbs, at the right time, and the choice is made.'

'This child is conceived through magic, then.'

Hecate only laughed.

He glanced down at her belly. 'My child?'

'Your blood, Wolf. The blood of kings, and now queens. Shall we see which is stronger?'

Hecate placed her hands on his shoulders and pushed him down until he was sitting at the foot of a tree. He didn't have the strength to resist.

'Rest,' she whispered. 'You will see me . . . and her . . . again.'

Despite himself, his eyelids drooped, and when he looked up again the three witches were gone.

The fire roared up higher than the tallest stone. It was what it was – a provider of warmth, a way to roast the venison that sizzled next to it – and it was something else too, a beacon, calling out across those flat, dark lands, reaching deep into men's hearts.

Mato hurried past the blaze, his limbs aching from an afternoon collecting the wood for the bonfire alongside Aelius, Menius, Galantha and Decima, and Amarina when she had returned from her futile search for Lucanus.

But now here was the Wolf, wandering into that quavering circle of orange light. Mato hailed him. 'Brother, we have been looking for you everywhere.'

Lucanus looked past him at the towering flames. 'What is this? A feast?'

Mato heard a dreamy quality in his friend's voice. Perhaps he'd taken a knock to the head. 'More than that. Where have you been?'

'Hunting . . .' The word trailed away as if he planned to say more then decided against it.

As Mato led him past the fire, Amarina marched up. 'I don't thank you for wasting my day trailing through wood and marsh trying to find you.'

Though she showed her frostiest expression, Mato knew her well enough to see through it.

'You're the leader. Now lead,' she went on, grabbing Lucanus' arm and pulling him into the centre of the Heartstones.

Caught in the flickering light breaking through the gaps among the stones, ten strangers were deep in conversation with Myrrdin. When Mato had left to collect the wood, there had only been eight.

'Who are they?' Lucanus asked.

'A chance for better days,' Mato said.

When he saw them, the wood-priest beckoned them over. 'Here,' he announced, 'is the Pendragon.'

As one, the strangers bowed their heads.

Lucanus looked shocked. Mato shoved him forward.

'Once the people of the land where I live were called the Trinovantes,' a man with flowing white hair said. 'Our teachers tell us the stories of days long gone. We do not forget. When word of the war-moot reached Camulodunum, we talked long and hard about what we should do.' He looked around at the other strangers, who were nodding along to his words. 'We do not have warriors as we did in days past, but we have men who can fight and we will send them to you. That is our vow.'

'Even now the call of the Pendragon means something,' another said. 'We do not forget. None of us will ever forget.'

'I come from Verulamium,' a third said. Mato saw that he kept his eyes down, as if he were afraid to look at Lucanus. 'My blood comes from the Catuvellauni. The army has deserted us, but we will do what we can. We do not forget.'

Mato heard in those repeated words something that sounded like an oath, one that was echoing across the years from days that everyone thought had vanished. He glanced past the gathering and saw two more men trudging into the circle on weary legs. 'And still they come,' he murmured.

'What do you say to those who have answered your call, Lucanus Pendragon?' Myrrdin asked.

The Wolf hesitated, and Mato could see the conflicted thoughts playing out on his face. But he was a good leader, and like all good leaders he understood his responsibilities.

'We are few,' Lucanus began. His voice was faltering, but Mato heard it grow stronger as he spoke, and his eyes caught the fire as he looked around the gathering. 'The barbarians are many, and they are strong, and savage. The land, our land, is burning. Good men and women made slave. Soon the bloody tide will wash up against our feet, here. Do not believe that it will flow away if we turn our backs or look to our own. Do not believe that we can wish like children and it will all vanish. We fight, or we die. We fight together.'

Mato saw Amarina watching his friend intently, as if seeing him through new eyes. She scowled when she saw him looking at her.

'We are few, but we are brave,' Lucanus continued, 'and I have seen that a few brave men can defeat the fiercest enemy.'

Could the tattered remnants gathering beneath Lucanus' banner truly defeat an overwhelming force of brutality the like of which they'd never seen before? Yet hearing Lucanus' words, Mato found himself believing that they could.

'We do not have the numbers, but we will fight with cunning,' the Wolf continued. 'We will strike when our enemy least expects it. We will be hungry like the wolves of winter. And we will chase the visions of days yet to come where there is not dark, but light, not war but peace. Where a new king can rise, who will lead us into a new age. Stand with me.'

His voice rose with the final three words, and Mato felt his blood thunder when he heard the cheers of the men around him.

'Pendragon,' they shouted as one. 'Pendragon. Pendragon.'

The fire had been lit, and from it the Dragon would rise anew.

★

'Are we in agreement?' The wood-priest walked with Mato to the far side of the circle where they could not be overheard.

Mato looked back to where Lucanus was surrounded by those who were prepared to invest so much in him. 'I've no stomach for your deception. But there's a greater good here. If lives can be saved, if hope can be found, I'll play my part. Know this, though, I'll do nothing that brings harm to Lucanus, or any of my friends, merely to further your plans.'

'There are dark days to come, of that I have no doubt. But you've not begun to see the extent of this plan. We will let nothing stand in the way of the Bear-King's being brought into this world.'

'Even if that sets me against you?'

'I answer to a higher power.' Myrrdin tried to soften his words with a smile.

'One thing still troubles me. Well, many things trouble me, but this one plays on my mind.'

'Go on.'

'What bargain did you make with the Attacotti to persuade them to fight at our side?'

Myrrdin looked towards the fire. In the dancing light, the shifting shadows twisted his features. 'I told them that, when the time was right, they could feast on the flesh of a king and thereby gain his powers. Powers beyond imagining.'

'What king?'

'Kings always die, wolf-brother. When they have outlived their usefulness they are sacrificed so that new blood can keep the land alive. This is the way of all things.' Mato winced at the regret he heard in those words.

Myrrdin walked off, his voice floating back. 'Your friend Lucanus the Wolf died a long time ago. Don't mourn for the man that has gone. Now he is the Pendragon, and all this will be in his hands.'

And as Mato watched the night swallow the wood-priest, he felt a rising fear at what was about to be unleashed.

# CHAPTER FORTY-SIX

# *Sol Invictus*

*Rome*

'NOW IS THE HOUR FOR TRUTH. OUR TIME TOGETHER IS SHORT AND there's much to be done,' Corvus said.

The light of the lamp limned Gaia, casting a halo around her ash-blonde hair. He thought how majestic she looked in that soft golden glow, the commanding woman he remembered from his childhood. At that moment he could believe that all the dark times had finally been expunged, like the blood that had once stained the floor of this chamber.

The midsummer's night was unbearably hot, made more so by the brazier glowing in the corner of the room. His nostrils flared at the caustic smoke suspended in the dead air.

The Hanged Man's features were ruddy in the light of the hot coals. 'You are sure of this? Your brother had doubts about your abilities.'

'Ruga's dead,' Corvus replied. 'That loss is painful, and I've never grieved so hard. But I'll carry on his work. He would want that, and he would trust me to do it well.'

Severus nodded, his twisted neck making it seem like a spasm. 'You are a Sun Runner now. Mithras has blessed you and raised you high. The Invincible Sun recognizes your worth.'

Corvus bowed his head. 'I'm honoured, Father. You know how much that means to me.' When his mother had given the cult enough gold to establish another temple to replace the one that had been lost, any barriers to his rising quickly through the degrees had swiftly vanished.

'Very well,' Severus replied. 'I'm told you are travelling to Gaul in the morning, to meet with the emperor. And then to Britannia?'

Corvus nodded. 'The barbarians have invaded, so my friend Theodosius tells me. His father, Theodosius the Elder, has been informed that the tribes are sweeping across the whole of the island. Valentinian won't let that stand. I know no more than that.'

'Despite the best efforts of the Christians, there are still a few of us who keep the light. You will find good friends in the army. Call on them in your hour of need. They will answer you, Heliodromus.'

'I'll live up to the faith that's been placed in me.'

The Hanged Man nodded to him, and then to his mother, and lurched out of the sweltering chamber.

Once he was gone, Gaia swayed over and rested her hands on his shoulders. She smiled, all the tears that had followed Ruga's death long since dried up.

'I'm placing all my faith in you, my love,' she murmured. 'Know this will be hard. Ruga was preparing all his life for what is to come. Now you must take up the mantle with no time to ready yourself. This fight is going to be harder than anything you have ever had to do.'

'I won't let you down. This is what I've always wanted.'

'We cannot afford to lose, Corvus.'

'If things get hard, Pavo will help me.'

'Of course he will,' she said with a firm nod. 'You must do whatever it takes to claim victory.' She drifted to the window and looked out into the suffocating night. He could see the sweat glistening in the V of naked skin from her nape to the small of her back. 'Sometimes I wonder if the gods . . . if Mithras . . . is truly watching over us.' She sounded distracted, as if she were talking to herself. 'You are being sent to Britannia, which is exactly where you need to be. I was told once, nothing happens by chance. Perhaps that is true.'

'And when I get to Britannia I will kill my half-sister Catia.'

'And anyone she has gathered around herself?'

He nodded.

'When you took Ruga's life, I knew I should have chosen you from the start. Your brother would always have let me down.'

That pleased him more than she knew.

'I underestimated you in so many ways. You knew, didn't you?'

'About the Dragon?'

'You've known for a long time.'

He smiled. Ruga and his mother had thought they were being so clever. But he'd heard the tales of the Dragon long ago, the one who would become the incarnation of Mithras upon the earth. And when he'd spent long hours torturing the druid that his mother had once kept captive in the cellar where Hecate now lived, he'd learned that this vision of a saviour was a shared one. An old, old story, he had been told. The Christians. The wood-priests. They all believed their saviour would one day come to lead them out of the dark. What power that chosen one would hold. Ruga was never deserving of those heights.

Gaia brushed a strand of hair from his forehead. 'Catia is a selfish, spiteful girl,' she continued. 'An evil girl. All she will want is for the saviour to fall under her influence, so she alone will have power over him and all that he stands for. That cannot be. You would be doing a great good if you rid the world of her.'

'I'll do whatever is necessary.'

She nodded, pleased.

'And Hecate?'

Gaia ran her fingers through his hair, as if she were acting out what was to come for him with the witch. 'When you marry her, my love, and when she bears you a child, she will help secure our claim. A new bloodline established, and it will be tied to me . . . to us.' She smiled. 'Here is a truth I learned long ago, my darling. The Dragon is elusive, with all the substance of the mist. He is whoever the people say he is. And our voice will always speak louder.'

'At the start, I was searching for a wood-priest, that was your command. But they all seemed to have disappeared into the forests like the morning mists. And then you bade me find a witch . . .' His thoughts flew back to that icy forest in Gaul when he had bribed the Alamanni warrior to lead him away from the battle to that dismal hut where the sisters lived.

'I had a wood-priest in my grasp once.' Gaia's voice hardened and her face became ugly with anger. Corvus looked away. 'And that fat slug Varro stole him from me so he could follow the trail to the Dragon. *My* wood-priest was to have argued my claim with his forest brethren. After all my coercion, how could he have refused? I hope Varro the grotesque dies a painful death.' When she paused, he looked back and saw her face light up once more. 'But this is better. Oh, so much better! Nothing happens by chance. Why did I compel you to bring me a witch? Because, my love, when she joins with you that union will be seen to be great. The wood-priests and the wyrd sisters will not be able to ignore it. Your child will have greater power than anything my worthless daughter can produce.'

Gaia whirled around the room as if possessed, her eyes bright with fire, her arms outstretched. Ecstatic, now. 'All these years of plotting . . . forcing you and your brother to follow the path of Mithras so we would have allies . . .' She dropped to her knees, bowing her head so that her hair fell over her face. 'Mithras,' she breathed, 'a dying god with a fading band of worshippers. One day soon, they will join with the pagans to preserve the sacred knowledge, mark my words. Sun Runners and Fathers and druids, side by side, keeping the secret of the saviour for generations to come. And you will be there among them, praised by all. So many times I thought this plot would fail, but now . . . now you are unbeatable.'

Corvus grinned. 'I am invincible now. I, your son.'

'Sol invictus,' she breathed, understanding. Then: 'Are you ready?'

He nodded, and watched his mother draw herself up, composing herself, becoming regal. 'I was chosen first, did you know that?' she breathed. Turning, she slipped that beautiful white silk dress off her left shoulder. On the bare flesh, he saw something that had never been revealed to him before: a brand, dark against the pale skin – a serpent eating its own tail.

'The Ouroboros,' she whispered. 'The mark of the bloodline. I was chosen by the wood-priests when I was a girl, and, oh, it was glorious. I was special.' She closed her eyes, beatific for a moment. But when she spoke again, he heard her voice become wintry. 'And then I had a daughter with that weak husband of mine. How could I let her become special? I wanted a son, a strong, powerful son, to continue the line, but that feeble Menius could not give me one. Three girls I killed at birth, stifled them with my own hands, but this fourth time he came in before I could finish the deed, and swept her away, overjoyed that we finally had a child.'

Corvus heard such contempt in her voice that he winced.

'A girl. A pathetic, mewling girl. I ordered Strabo to take her out into the forest so I could be done with her. But the wood-priests, or the sisters, or the forest folk knew . . . they see all that happens in their world. And they saved her.' She turned to him, eyes wide. 'They could not forgive me, Corvus. Me! I had wanted only the best, but they hated me then for my selfless act. I had no choice but to flee. They were coming for me. Now they had Catia, they had no use for me, you see. Can you imagine how that feels? But I was chosen first, not her. I have a greater claim upon this bloodline. And between us, we will take it, Corvus. You and I, mother and son, united.'

Corvus felt her passion inflame him too. He rushed over to her and hugged her tightly. She folded into him. 'Tell me one thing,' he breathed into her ear. 'I'm not a man who easily believes in these stories, these prophecies that the devout tell each other. They're for people like Theodosius, not me. Is it true? That this saviour will come, this king who will not die?'

'It doesn't matter if he is a saviour, or if men believe him to be a saviour. The result will be the same. He will wield power by the words he proclaims. Followers will come, disciples, and they will heed his every utterance. It may be a hundred years until this saviour is born, but until then, whosoever controls the bloodline controls the power invested in him. And that will be our family, Corvus. Our blood.'

Corvus stiffened, a flame flickering into life deep in his head. 'Our blood,' he repeated.

Gaia pulled back, frowning. 'What is wrong?'

He looked into her face. Still the beauty that had ensnared two men, still youthful. 'I will give you the son that Menius never could,' he breathed. 'I will be the father, you the mother, and then all will be well.'

He had expected some resistance, but there she was, smiling, the glow from the brazier twinkling in her eyes. 'Yes. Yes.' She shivered. 'Why weaken the blood by mingling it with that of the witch? The wood-priests declared me worthy to bear the bloodline when they branded me.' The light in her eyes took on a different tone, but he could not tell why.

'And Hecate?'

'She loves you, you know. She will do whatever you ask of her. She will guide us. She will be our intermediary with the wood-priests, and argue our claim. This . . . this is perfect.' She hugged him tight to her and kissed him on the forehead.

What a trail of blood had led to this moment. Hecate's sisters, killed by the Alamanni warrior at his behest, so she would have nothing to keep her in that frozen forest, and then the barbarian himself slaughtered so he could never speak. Strabo, drowned in the Tiber, to prevent him from revealing what he knew about their family's secrets. And finally his own brother. But it had all been worth it.

Now only his half-sister stood in their way, a bloodline that must be brought to a sudden end so there would be no rivals to the claim.

Striding over to the brazier, he stooped to pick up a cloth from the floor and wrapped it around his right hand. Grasping the handle of the iron brand in the hot coals, he raised it. The circle glowed red in the gloom of the room. The serpent eating its own tail.

'Here,' he announced. 'So all will know who I am. A king who will beget kings. A Dragon who will beget Dragons.'

Shucking off his tunic, Corvus stood naked before her.

For a moment, he felt barbs of agony drive his wits from him, and he breathed in the stench of his own searing flesh. But then he shook his head, clearing it, and closed his eyes in ecstasy. Though he couldn't fully see the brand upon his side, he could imagine it.

The endless circle of death and rebirth, the serpent coiled, consuming itself.

Now he was the Dragon, and he would lay waste to all who dared stand before him.

*The strong voice ceas'd; for a terrible blast swept over the heaving sea:*
*The eastern cloud rent: on his cliffs stood Albion's wrathful Prince,*
*A dragon form, clashing his scales: at midnight he arose,*
*And flam'd red meteors around the land of Albion beneath.*

William Blake

# *Author's Notes*

Five steps away from the click of the gate and the past swallowed me. It was Midsummer's Eve, and the day had been bathed in gold and lazy with the drone of honeybees. Now everywhere was silver and black, bright fields and hedgerow shadows as stark as under the afternoon sun. The rumble of traffic had stilled and there was only the beat of my footsteps.

I left the few bats still swooping around the eaves and walked along an old track made new by boards smelling of cooling creosote. My father had walked this way, as had his father before him, and generation upon generation of feet before that, drawing a line upon the earth and on time that connected now and then.

The track opened out on to woods clustered around a winding stream. A barn owl screeched, an omen perhaps, as the Greeks and Romans once thought. When I was a child I was told not to come to these woods on Midsummer Night for fear of meeting the spirits of the newly dead who had been released for the journey into the next world by the sun's turning south.

This was an old story and you can hear it all over the country. The Midsummer festival has been celebrated since Neolithic times. It's a time when the barriers between worlds thin – the living and the dead, the present and the past – like Halloween. Christians claimed it as St John's Eve and started new stories of witches abroad cursing any innocent traveller who dared venture out after dark.

Beyond this old woodland was a new forest, planted in recent memory to cover one of the mine workings that once scarred this corner of the old Kingdom of Mercia in the English Midlands. The shaft has been capped and ash trees tower above it, but the tunnels still run underground. The locals tell of encountering tree-climbing rabbits here, feral, bloodthirsty things, the offspring of bunnies trapped underground, forced to become predators to survive.

My grandfather was a miner. As a boy I was fascinated by his missing fingers and his blue skin, the result of impacted coal dust after a tunnel collapse when he was trapped beneath ground for a night and a day, up to his chin in freezing water. He used to tell me tales of the Tommyknockers, the spirits of dead miners who would tap on the tunnel walls to lure the living into their world. This is an old story too, and you can hear it around Cornish tin mines and Scottish collieries. My grandfather's friends used to entertain me with a wealth of stories. They lived every day close to death, there, hundreds of feet beneath the earth, and they'd created their own mythology to explain the vicissitudes of life and to give them hope down in the dark.

There's no sign of the mine now and the tangle of oak and birch and ash and rowan looks as though it's always been in this place. Old stories are buried, new ones will grow.

On the edge of the trees, I walked along the towpath of the canal that once carried barges laden with coal to the ironworks in Birmingham, and on to an old drovers' path that pre-dated it by hundreds of years. I'd walked this way time and again since I was a boy, at all hours of the night and day, in all weathers, and every one offered something that lodged in the memory. This time I was rewarded with a badger lumbering across the road, its eyes glowing like headlamps in the light of a passing car, a rare sighting that made me jump as if I'd witnessed the appearance of a mythical beast, emotions that you usually don't access in the world of men, pulled from their deep sleep in the unconscious: a shiver of fear, a glimmer of wonder.

I wandered on to a playing field, wide and silent, and then under a bridge that once allowed access beneath a long-gone railway, and on into more forestland. No track here, the eye told me, no ancient path, except there was. Under these trees lies Via Devana, the old Roman road that bisected England from the north-west to the south-east, long since buried and barely excavated.

As I crept through the woods, I remembered a story told me by an old man in the local pub, a beer-memory, of hearing the tramp of a Roman legion as he walked here one Boxing Day. I'd told a few people. They had told others.

And then I saw a light glowing in the dark, an unearthly light with an odd, greenish tinge, and I heard the whisper of all those old stories and felt a prickling down my back. Time and occasion makes superstitious fools of all of us. Chest tight, knowing this was something I'd never encountered before, I plunged on through the trees to investigate, determined to put a knife to that lizard-brain fear. And on the edge of a sweep of grassland, I found the cause: a firefly.

I was honestly astounded, by the brightness, and the, to me, unnatural colour, and more, its effect upon me. If you open yourself up to it, the world still has the power to amaze you, and change you.

Nothing happens by chance, they say.

This book arose from that walk and many like it. When you're a writer, you like to think that you consciously shape things. But the truth is, all the heavy lifting comes from the unconscious, far beyond your control, and it surfaces when your mind is doing something else. Most of my creative moments have come far away from my desk, drifting into daydreams that merge with the world around me. If you're an eastern mystic, of course, you would say those dreams and the hard world are one and the same.

I love history, and I studied history, and I'm impressed by the vast body of work sweated into existence by archaeologists and other historians, discoveries that have shaped our understanding of our heritage, the long tramp of experience that has made us who we are.

But sometimes I wonder if we're shaped as much by the intangibles, the abstracts, the folklore, the myths, the legends, the stories we tell ourselves, that arise out of history but are not part of them, and add a deeper layer to explain what events truly mean to us.

The power of a story, well told, is sometimes more affecting than the real experience. And sometimes the two merge to be something new entirely. History and stories blur, each one affecting the other, and rippling out into the world. Something that doesn't exist, in any tangible terms, can have just as much of an effect as something that does.

This fascinates me.

When I was writing my last series of books, about the English rebel Hereward who led the resistance against William the Conqueror after the Norman invasion in 1066, I began to think about how legends were formed out of the world around us. Within a hundred years of Hereward's death, stories were circulating about how he carried a magical sword and slayed giants. Not true, yet true, because it explained what he and his endeavours meant to the people of England in living memory of his struggle. History and symbolism bound together.

This book is about the creation of the legend of King Arthur, and about the very simple belief that it doesn't matter whether he existed or not. That thought might be anathema to evidence-based historians, and I fully understand that. But if the belief in something that isn't there still affects the world, is it any less important?

I've looked at elements of the Arthurian mythos and how they might have arisen out of the history we know. But the more important question is: why did the legend of King Arthur come about in the first place? Why did we need it? Why do we still need it?

There are elements of this tale that you might want to explore further. The survival of the druids beyond the slaughter at Ynys Môn has long been debated. There's a long-standing belief that the druids were snuffed out that day, but I would ask you to consider the likelihood of a belief system's being destroyed in one night, especially one that reached across continental Europe. The historian Peter Beresford Ellis has written extensively about the survival of the druids, and there are several books which pick up this work.

If you are interested in the story Myrrdin told Lucanus at the Heartstones, read *Uriel's Machine* by historians Christopher Knight and Robert Lomas, which expounds upon the theory that the stone circles are a response to an apocalyptic meteor strike. And there is some excellent work out there about how the stones may have been designed to respond to shamanic drumming, to create a hallucinatory experience at a mass gathering within the circle.

One key aspect of this book is the importance of the magic mushroom, or psilocybin, to world history. One aspect of historical research that I find interesting is how it's responsive to cultural mores – the Victorians, for instance, saw the past, and 'discovered' the past, in a very different way from how we do it now. It's indisputable that psychedelic drugs have been key to human development – depictions of these mushrooms have been found in art from three thousand years ago. There is a large body of work that propounds the theory that our most breathtaking cave paintings were conducted under the influence of these hallucinogens, and that they may well have been responsible for the emergence of both art and religion in human evolution. There is certainly evidence that they were used in the rituals of all early religions, a way of contacting the 'gods', including early Christianity. If you want to dive deep into controversy, take a look at *The Sacred Mushroom and the Cross: A Study of the Nature and Origins of Christianity Within the Fertility Cults of the Ancient Near East* by the English archaeologist John Marco Allegro. The spiral imagery prevalent in a lot of Celtic artwork may also have been influenced by hallucinogens and you can find studies of their use in the Mithraic mysteries.

The Dark Age is a fascinating time. It's a gulf in our knowledge, waiting to be filled, but no less rich in history than the times before and after. We don't have much in terms of historical record from that era, but what we do have is the emergence of myth and legend, which in its own way tells us just as much about the people of that time, their hopes and their fears.

The legend of King Arthur which rose out of those benighted centuries shapes our perception of who we are even to this day. This, then, is a historical novel about the invisible hand of history, the things that can't be found in the substrata, or in the few surviving fragmentary writings. Legends, faith, religion and the need for gods and heroes in a harsh world.

It's about the dream of King Arthur, and of Camelot, and how it might have formed from the mists by the will of men in an age of destruction and war.

# ACKNOWLEDGEMENTS

Thanks to Elizabeth Cooper, of the University of Newcastle, for advice and guidance.

# ABOUT THE AUTHOR

**James Wilde** is proud to be a Man of Mercia. He was brought up in a home full of books and studied economic history at university before travelling the world in search of adventure.

He has been a journalist, writing for the national press, and is now a scriptwriter and novelist, author of the bestselling series about England's near-forgotten hero, Hereward the Wake. James Wilde divides his time between London and the family home in Derbyshire.

To find out more, visit: www.manofmercia.co.uk